Waiting FOR A GIRL Like You

KA TIE DELAHANTY

Make it Come True

For Jason.

It's awfully nice out.

Chapter Playlist

Chapter 1

Year of the Cat

Fun fact: Cat tongues are like sandpaper, and if male cats lick their nether regions enough, "things" can scab over, making it impossible for them to pee. And if cats don't pee, their bladders can explode.

Apparently, the universe felt *this* information was imperative that I learn this weekend.

Between last night's rehearsal dinner and today's wedding, I learned via frantic text that my roommate discovered my cat is a *champion* licker. Fortunately, the vet was able to operate before the bladder exploding part happened.

I would do *anything* for Toto—named after the band, not the dog from *The Wizard of Oz*. He's worth any cost. The good news is that Toto and I are now the proud owners of a $2,980 refurbished cat penis.

The bad news is that I had to max out my credit card to pay for said penis. I have, like, $100 to my name. I work as an undercover bridesmaid, a plant in a wedding party paid to prevent drama. The paycheck from tonight's wedding is already designated for rent and law school loans. Which leads me to where I am now: hiding in an art-deco style bathroom at the Penthouse Hyde Park.

After being up all night at the pet hospital, I'm about to drop. I dizzily grip the porcelain counter with one hand and catch my foot behind me with the other to take some pressure off my toes. The strappy gold high-*hells* that Ginger, the bride, insisted we wear with our peach chiffon gowns, are killing me. I close my eyes, fighting back hot tears, not daring to disturb the "vixen" eyelashes the makeup artist painstakingly glued to my eyelids this morning.

Pull it together. It's cocktails, a.k.a. the witching hour—when the demons drink their fuel.

There are 160 guests at this wedding. One hundred and sixty ticking time bombs that could disrupt the bride and groom's fairytale at any moment. I need to get back out there.

Normally, I take my job very seriously. In seven years of bridesmaiding, I have *never* taken a bathroom break during cocktail hour. I've almost never left a reception to use the restroom.

Right now, I should be out there babysitting a drunk uncle or watering down the groomsmen's shots. *Style Me Pretty* has named my boss, Max, *the* premier wedding planner in Chicago for the last ten years running. He has a reputation to uphold and demands perfection.

But tonight, after facing down the cost of a near bladder combustion *cat*-astrophe, I can't help wondering what happens to bridesmaids who don't pee.

The door behind me creaks open. I jump at the intrusion and get busy checking the complimentary toiletry tray to make sure there are enough breath mints.

Ginger's grandmother enters the restroom. Our eyes meet in the mirror, and she smiles. "Oh, Rosie, maybe you can help me."

At the sound of her name, my bridesmaid alter-ego, Rosie, clicks into place. I'm instantly alert. My real name is Gwen. *Gwen* may be drowning in cat-penis debt and law school loans, but *Rosie* . . . Rosie is always in control. *She* always knows the right thing to say. I spin around. "Of course. Anything. What do you need?"

She tugs her mauve gown off her shoulder and shows me her severed bra strap. "Would you believe my strap broke? What luck."

"Were you the first one out on the dance floor, Grandma E?" I peer at the strap and wrinkle my nose. It shredded at the top, which will make it difficult to repair. "You're supposed to wait for the bride and groom to make their entrance, you know."

"Oh, no." She chuckles. "It broke before I made it into the ballroom."

"Let me see what I can do." I examine the safety pins on the tray, but they're too flimsy and small to hold the thick elastic without digging into her shoulder. "What size bra do you wear? 34 C?"

"Maybe in the old days." She grimaces. "Try 36 Long."

I laugh. "Well, I'm a 34 D. How about I trade bras with you? It's not the perfect size, but it should work for one night."

"Oh, no. I couldn't let you do that." She waves me off.

"This is your night, Grandma E. Your first granddaughter's wedding. You can't miss a minute. Please. Take mine. I just bought it to go with this dress, and I've barely been wearing it for two hours—I wore a sports bra and robe most of the day. I promise I didn't sweat an ounce on the rooftop during the ceremony. Besides, I only need one strap." I unhook my convertible bra from beneath my one-shoulder dress. I've got to give Ginger credit; it's not the worst bridesmaid dress I've ever worn.

She holds up both hands to stop me. "There has to be another way."

Chewing my lip, I nod. "You know what? I have a needle and thread." I open my clutch and push aside the necklace I always wear in real life—the one that is *never* bridesmaid-approved. The oblong gold pendant, painted deep blue and dotted with tiny diamond chips, was a gift from my brother Tyler for my seventeenth birthday. A lump rises in my throat as the diamonds glint in the yellow light from the vanity mirror.

I swallow and force my focus to the contents of my bag. My fingers connect with my sewing kit just as the bathroom door swings open again. The woman who enters is incapable of smiling, her unmoving features reminiscent of a post-Botox Vladimir Putin.

Lex is the assistant event designer. She's managing this wedding alone for the first time while Max is in Italy preparing for "the wedding of the year." Over six feet tall in spike heels and wearing a black dress that accentuates the sharp angles of her body, Lex is all edges. Even Grandma E flinches when Lex enters the ladies room.

"Rosie. I've been looking everywhere for you. We are late," Lex says in her thick Slovakian accent. She holds a finger to her earpiece, pausing as she listens to whoever is talking on the other end. "It is time for the bride and groom's entrance, and the salad course is ready to go out. You know how Max feels about soggy salad."

"Oh. Sorry." I widen my eyes, pretending I'm an innocent friend of the bride and not about to get sent back to Bridesmaid Bootcamp for salad interference. "I was just helping Grandma Esposito with—"

"Actually, honey?" Grandma E interjects. Standing stiffly like a soldier ready to do her general's bidding, she casts a furtive glance at Lex. "We can trade if that's still okay with you. It's quicker, and I don't want to be the one to hold things up."

"You aren't holding things up. That's what my bra is for." Winking at Grandma E, I unhook the band, pull the bra out of my dress, and hand it to her.

She laughs at my joke, takes the bra, and disappears into a stall.

"Just let me make sure Grandma Esposito gets back to the reception, and I'll be right there," I whisper to Lex.

"Thank you." With a curt nod, Lex narrows her steel gray eyes to suggest I hurry. Dark, stick-straight hair that hangs halfway down her back swishes behind her as she whips out the door.

As soon as she's gone, I exhale.

When Grandma Esposito emerges with her bra in an outstretched hand, I duck into a stall and strap it on. The band is a little loose, but at least it has underwires. I can make this work for a few more hours. After tucking the broken strap into a floppy cup, I rejoin Grandma E.

"Thank you, dear," she says as we exit the bathroom into the hall and head toward the ballroom. "How should I get this back to you?"

"Give it to Ginger. She'll get it to me the next time I see her." I internally wince at my lie. Cat-drama aside, I've enjoyed being part of the Esposito family over the last couple of days. Unfortunately, I'm forbidden from seeing any of them again.

Max makes his employees sign NDAs that prohibit us from having future contact with anyone we meet at a wedding, and not just because the weddings are often high profile. The hard truth is that most of the brides who hire a bridesmaid do it because they don't have many close friends. Sometimes even the groom doesn't know I'm an undercover employee. It's of utmost importance to Max that this potentially embarrassing lie end with the wedding to protect the bride's integrity.

"You're a true friend." Grandma E squeezes my hand. "Ginger is lucky to have you."

I bite my lip. "No, she's lucky to have *you*."

We come to a stop outside the double doors that lead into the reception. My stomach tightens as the soft strains of The Wedding Bandits covering "What a Wonderful World" drift out of the ballroom.

This makes it twenty-eight.

Twenty-eight weddings I've worked with Duncan Avila, wedding singer extraordinaire and God's gift to bridesmaids everywhere.

The music amplifies as I crack open the doors. "I'll see you on the dance floor." I nudge Grandma E into the ballroom.

With a wave, she disappears inside, and I glimpse Duncan on the stage, clutching the microphone with his eyes closed as he sings. A hint of scruff accentuates his sharp jawline, giving him an edge that keeps him from looking too classically chiseled. His white dinner jacket sets off his bronze skin and is perfectly tailored to accentuate his broad shoulders. To me, there's something about a guy in a tuxedo, and Duncan probably has a closet full of them.

The Wedding Bandits are Max's go-to band and, tuxedos aside, they look like they belong on the indie stage of a summer music festival. Music has been my passion since I was a teenager, and even though I just turned thirty, there's still nothing I love more than discovering new bands. I have standards higher than these heels. To say they're talented is an understatement, which says a lot coming from me.

I've written several posts on my music website Shut Up & Sway debating whether cover bands are mere performers or true artists since they don't write their own music. The Bandits do put their own spin on songs—and Duncan's after-hours DJ sets are next-level—which is enough to tip them in favor of artists for me. More than once I've wished I could record them covering "Africa" by Toto, so I could include it on a list of "sway-worthy" covers.

But the thing that keeps my platform Wedding Bandit-free, aside from Max frowning upon the interaction, is Duncan's misuse of music, a medium that speaks truly and authentically to my soul. As my roommate, Corina, would say, music has such a high-vibrational frequency, it's the perfect conduit for transmitting energy. Knowing that the intention behind a performance is pure—meant to complement, *not persuade*—is of utmost importance to me.

And of course, Duncan uses his minor fame to woo ladies from the microphone. On multiple occasions I've seen him escort a bridesmaid to her room after his afterparty DJ set. And all my coworkers are in love with him.

Even though it's against Max's rules to reveal we're acquainted with the band at a wedding, he can't control what happens off duty. The other bridesmaids in his To the Max fleet seem more comfortable bending the rules than I am. They often mention hanging out with the band on their days off.

I've never spoken to Duncan beyond passing along a song request, but I swear he's hooked up with every single one of my coworkers, countless maids of honor, and probably a hot, single mother-of-the-groom or two.

Everyone except me.

Which is fine. Being the last bridesmaid standing is a freaking badge of honor at this point. #Strangers4life.

Still, even from the other side of the doors, Duncan's soulful voice sucks me in. I'm tempted to burst into the ballroom so I can sway at his feet.

Fortunately, Lex and the rest of the wedding party arrive behind me before I act on the impulse. I quickly take my place in line with the rest of the peach dress brigade.

"Remember to strike a pose when you reach the dance floor," Lex directs. "Then move to the side for the first dance."

She opens the ballroom doors wide, and I loop arms with the groomsman I'm walking in with.

Inside, Max has outdone himself as usual. He prides himself on never creating the same scene twice and plans his design from scratch for every couple. Flickering white pillar candles cover every available surface. The warm light softens the geometric lines of the black and white tile floors. Dangling from the coffered ceiling, hundreds of burgundy and pink flower chains combine with twinkling fairy lights to create a moody, magical scene. The Chicago skyline glitters outside the floor-to-ceiling windows that line two of the walls.

"What a Wonderful World" ends, and Duncan puts the microphone on a stand with practiced swagger, a lock of his dark, messy hair falling across his forehead. "Ladies and gentlemen, please stand and welcome our wedding party!"

He announces the bridesmaid/groomsman pair in front of me, his smooth voice reverberating from the stage over the guests' applause, and the couple walks toward the dance floor with their arms linked. My groomsman and I take their place in the doorway as next in line. My legs are so tired my calves are cramping, so I lean into my groomsman for extra support while trying to appear poised.

"Next up, let's put our hands together for the groom's cousin and the bride's best friend, Rosie!" Duncan announces.

As I stiffen like I do every time he says my cover name—I'm pretty sure he has no clue my real name is Gwen—The Wedding Bandits shift the music and play the opening drumbeats to "Rosanna" by Toto. Swishing into the ballroom with my groomsman, I bite back a smirk.

If only Duncan knew my affinity for Toto.

With each step, Grandma E's bra inches lower on my boob, but I plaster my best bridesmaid's smile across my face like everything in my life is in place and well supported. We hit our mark, strike a *Charlie's Angels* pose, then move to the side.

"Please welcome our best man, escorting the *lovely* Katherine, the bride's sister and maid of honor." Duncan's green eyes practically smolder when he mentions Kat, and it's all I can do to keep from rolling mine.

I see the bridesmaid of the night has been chosen.

Kat's face lights up as she reaches the center of the dance floor. Her gaze locked on Duncan, she bats her eyelashes at him as she shimmies around the best man, and then they join us on the sidelines.

Duncan is too professional to react. I'll give him that.

"And finally, the moment you've all been waiting for. Please stand and join me in celebrating our bride and groom!"

The ballroom erupts in cheers. Holding hands, Ginger and Tim make their entrance. He twirls her around as The Bandits launch into the first dance, a cover of "All of Me" by John Legend.

My job right now is to keep my expression pleasant and watch Tim spin Ginger beneath the dangling flower chains, but I can't help peeking at Duncan as he sings.

His sparkling eyes narrow to slits and his face feels out each note like the music is alive inside him. He's a magnet, drawing me in and taking me on a journey. I believe him when he sings about a girl being his undoing but still his inspiration. The candles and twinkle lights blur around me, and I zone out in a haze. The song takes me away to a place where perfect love exists. It's like I'm floating in a fairytale, a dream reserved for everyone else.

To me, "the one" is an impossible ideal. In my thirty years, I've only met one person who made me feel cherished enough to let my guard down. But that was almost half a lifetime ago, and the way it ended still mortifies me.

But I love the *idea* of love. For other people, anyway.

Minutes that feel like seconds pass and too soon Duncan's eyelashes flutter open. The song draws to a close and his gaze connects with mine.

In my cloudy exhaustion, maybe I imagine the laser beam rocketing across space and time, morphing into a lightning bolt, and piercing my chest.

Definitely.

My face gets so hot at the possibility I was caught staring, the tips of my ears burn. Jumping like I've been zapped, I take up immediate fascination with the bride and groom.

They hold each other close, their foreheads pressed together.

Duncan wasn't looking at me. He simply possesses a superpower that makes everyone feel like he's singing directly to them. It's a huge part of his appeal, and you know this. Being awake for twenty-four hours is no excuse for letting him distract you.

As the thoughts swirl in my brain, The Bandits seamlessly transition into a cover of "Wobble" by V.I.C.

That's my cue.

Forcing my aching legs into action, I take my place with the rest of the wedding party around the newlyweds. Choreographed wedding party dances are one of Max's favorite ways to wow guests at receptions. The steps to The Wobble were drilled into me at Bridesmaid Bootcamp. I, in turn, made sure everyone knew the line dance by heart at rehearsal last night.

Facing the stage, we jump forward as one and wiggle our hips for four counts. We jump back and wiggle again to shouts and whistles from the guests. With each jump, Grandma E's bra droops lower, revealing more of my boob. Leaning right, I roll my arms. Again, it seems like Duncan is watching me.

Surely, I'm imagining things . . .

But, if I'm not mistaken, his mouth twitches like he's holding back a smile.

My skin erupts in goosebumps.

Is he *testing* me?

It's almost like he knows my bra situation. That more of me is wobbling tonight than usual. I grit my teeth. Even if I'm so tired my quads are twitching and half my bra is now hanging somewhere around my ribs, I will make sure this wedding concludes with dignity and grace, as is Max's motto.

Duncan would know that if he knew anything about me.

I slide forward and march out the coaster step, having practiced it so many times I don't have to think. Realizing I'm kind of dancing *at* Duncan, I lift my chin as I turn to the side. I "wobble" to the right, severing whatever connection I've fabricated between us. But this time, when I jump forward, my boob makes a leap of its own and pops out of the shoulder-less side of my dress.

Yelping, I stuff it back beneath the peach chiffon and keep dancing. I "wobble" like nothing happened, even though I'm so flushed I could disintegrate.

With fourteen of us, including the bride and groom, wobbling on the dance floor, hopefully nobody was paying attention to me. Still, it takes everything I've got not to peek back to see if Duncan noticed the wardrobe malfunction.

Blessedly, the song ends, and the band takes a break. Duncan hits start on a prearranged playlist while waiters stream toward the dinner tables, (hopefully not soggy) salads in hand. The music fades into the background beneath the din of clanking silverware and conversation.

Lex directs the wedding party to take our seats, and I weave through the tables to my seat left of the stage. As I approach, Duncan starts down the stage steps. He walks straight toward me and my heart stalls.

Is he coming to talk to me?

My throat closes up. But just as I'm finding my voice enough to ask if I can get him and the band some water, Kat brushes past me.

"Hi." Breathless, she comes to a stop in front of him and touches his sleeve. "Do you take requests?"

Of course he does.

Cringing, I curl into myself and keep walking.

Across the room at the bar, the best man is lining up tequila shots.

Code Red: best man about to get hammered before his speech.

Even sober, the best man has trouble remembering to *not* mention the long-term ex-girlfriend the groom, Tim, was dating when he met his now-wife, Ginger.

My adrenaline spikes. Coming between a best man and tequila is exactly what I need to get me through the rest of the night. I make a beeline for him.

Chapter 2
I Can't Go for That (No Can Do)

Clutching my shoes in one hand and my phone in the other, I anxiously watch my Lyft driver's progress on the app.

Please hurry. I want my bed. And Toto.

I'm standing barefoot under the streetlights on the sidewalk outside the final wedding destination of the night—the afterparty. The night is still, the skyscrapers mostly dark. Even though it's well past midnight, the cement beneath my toes holds the last warmth of the August afternoon. After the reception, I grabbed the duffel bag with my regular clothes and walked two blocks from the wedding venue to the restaurant where a small group of friends of the bride and groom will continue to party.

Everything is in order. I saved the best man speech, and when the bouquet flew straight to me, I spiked it into Kat's arms. The bartender has instructions to hand out water with every drink. A hotdog cart serves late-night Chicago dogs on the patio. Ginger and Tim have room service and wedding cake waiting in their suite because they probably didn't eat much.

I am *done*. I'm so tired I can't even muster the energy to dig my flip-flops out of the duffel I dumped on the sidewalk.

The streets are quiet at this hour except for the muffled strains of Duncan mixing "One on One" by Hall & Oates with a funky dance beat inside the restaurant. I turn toward the sound, unable to resist swaying to the intoxicating remix. Beyond the patio, where fire pits blaze, the restaurant windows glow with the afterparty's golden light. On the other side of the glass, Kat sidles up to Duncan.

His bow tie is long gone, and his tuxedo shirt is untucked with the top two buttons unbuttoned, exposing his defined chest. Standing behind his turntable, he holds his headphones to one ear while leaning over to listen to whatever Kat whispers to him. She's practically falling out of her dress.

Not that I'm one to talk.

I tug on the shoulder-less side of my dress to make sure everything is covered just as Duncan looks up from the bridesmaid buffet. Our eyes meet.

He arches an eyebrow, and his gaze sparks lightning in my veins.

Sucking in my breath, I turn my back on him.

The bridesmaid of the night has been chosen and she's never me. Any connection I'm feeling is imagined.

I wrinkle my nose as my chariot, a silver Prius, whooshes to a stop in front of me. The driver rolls down the passenger window. "Are you Gwen? Headed to West Ridge?"

"That's me." I hurl myself into the backseat.

Inhaling the woodsy scent of the tree-shaped air freshener laying on the dashboard, I buckle my seatbelt, then sink into the gray cloth, letting the tension leave my shoulders. The car rolls forward, and the fire pits in the rearview mirror shrink to tiny dots.

The driver turns up the radio, which happens to be tuned to SiriusXM's *Yacht Rock Radio* and is playing Hall & Oates' "One on One," the same song Duncan was mixing at the afterparty. The synchronicity is dizzying.

My phone buzzes in my purse and my neck re-knots. I know it's Max. Ginger only reserved me until midnight, but I stayed later to make sure everything was perfect. I always do. Max probably sensed it was time for me to be on the move.

I don't want to answer, but I don't have a choice. With a groan, I pull the device out to a lit-up picture of his chiseled, grinning face. His teeth are bright white against his rich, brown skin, and he's wearing a navy sweater with a pink heart on the front that always reminds me how many times I've had to lint roll him over the years.

I grimace but swipe across the screen. Holding the phone to my ear, I plug my other ear to blot out a blaring car alarm as we pass it and brace myself for our debrief.

"Hi, Max. I just left the Esposito wedding. Lex did a great job coordinating and everything was perfect—"

He cuts me off. "I need your help, Gwen. I'm in the middle of a crisis." His voice is deep and soothing, honed over years of settling the jittery nervous systems of clients who pay him top dollar to create unforgettable event experiences. He may say he's in the middle of a crisis, but the voice on the other end of the phone does not betray a trace of panic.

Still, my heartrate spikes. Did he somehow hear about my bra mishap? Even though it was beyond my control, he'd still hold me responsible for it. *Everything* is a crisis to him. A wedding cake sitting out for thirty-*one* minutes is a crisis. A bride sitting—*gasp*—to the right of a groom, even if he's left-handed? Crisis. A groomsman ordering a round of chocolate cake shots is a (valid) crisis.

"Gwennnndoliiiine." His voice goes up a full octave at the end, and that's how I know he's legitimately freaking. I reach for my necklace, but it's not at my throat. While cradling the phone against my shoulder, I dig it out of my purse.

"Terra broke her foot. She might need surgery and is forbidden to walk down the aisle. I need you to fill in for her."

Exhaling that it's Terra who is the crisis, not me, I put him on speaker and clasp the thin gold chain around my neck.

"You two are almost the same size, so you'll fit her dresses. Normally I'd have scheduled a back-up bridesmaid, but it's our busiest wedding weekend of the year. Everyone else with Elite Status is booked." Max only has a few bridesmaids he trusts with high-profile weddings. It takes *years* under his tutelage to be deemed worthy of working them.

"When?" I close my eyes, pretty sure I already know Max's answer.

"The wedding is next weekend, but I need you on a flight tomorrow. Now, before you say no, consider this—"

"Max, I already said no. I've worked *every* weekend this summer and you *know* I'm going to the Outside Lands music festival." Pressing my necklace's starry night charm between my fingers, I try to connect to my calm even though it's useless. "I've been saving for this trip all year. It's my thirtieth birthday gift to myself and a reunion with my college roommates. Via is *so* excited to show us around San Francisco. I've had these tickets for *months*. They cost over $400—"

"I'll pay you time and a half for the last-minute coverage—"

We talk over each other.

"My bags are packed with adorable crochet minidresses," I wail, putting the phone back to my ear. My head spins like I'm standing too close to the edge of a cliff. I missed Lollapalooza because of the Simpson-Mitchell wedding, and this is my last chance at a summer music festival, my last chance to get content to make Shut Up & Sway a success. "And I haven't seen Jude and Via in forever. I miss them."

Max doesn't seem to hear me. "If everything goes flawlessly and everyone rides off into happily-ever-after without any hiccups, I'll give you a $3,000 bonus."

That shuts me up.

"Gwen. Please. I'm on my knees. I'm begging you."

I picture the day he asked me to join To the Max. He *did* get down on one knee, engulfing my hand in both of his and promising that if I worked for him, I'd gain negotiation skills no summer law internship could give me. Plus, I'd have personal, intimate access to one of the partners at Kirkland & Ellis whose daughter was getting married that summer. Max had been planning the wedding and he promised he'd make a one-time exception and allow me to use my real identity—Gwendoline Watson, aspiring intellectual property lawyer—to network. Unfortunately, I failed the bar. I haven't been able to bring myself to retake it, so that connection went down the drain.

At any rate, Max can be very convincing, as evidenced by me sitting here in this peach confection seven years later with my temples throbbing at the thought of putting on one more bridesmaid dress. "Wait. You said dress-*es*?" I squint.

"It's the Conner-Costanzo wedding. We have events scheduled for five days and a stylist designed the wardrobe for each one. You can wear all of Terra's clothes." He's come up off his knees now. I can tell because his words are crisp and concise, lacking the breathy quality of his pleading.

"It's in Positano. Italy! And Toto just had surgery. I can't leave him yet." I deliver the kill shot to Max's proposition. He knows how important Toto is to me, that my cat was the last gift my brother Tyler gave me before he passed away in a car accident thirteen years ago.

My roommate offered to watch Toto while I go to Outside Lands. She's his second mom, but tomorrow is too soon after surgery for me to leave him even with her.

The decision is out of my hands.

Collapsing in my seat, I watch the streetlights stream past my window. I bask in the warm relief that I don't have to turn down money I could desperately use to follow an irrational dream of swaying to festival music and sipping wine on a blanket while filming bands for my thirteen YouTube subscribers.

"I'm sorry to hear about Toto. What if I hire you a cat sitter? Someone who can watch him 24-7?" Max is undeterred. I picture him straightening one of his Gucci ties with the interlocking G print. "My sister will know who to call. You know how much she loves animals. Trust me, finding elite cat care on short notice is easier than finding an elite status bridesmaid."

I could really use that money to pay for that law degree I'm not using. Or that cat penis.

Unable to prevent the tiny voice in the back of my mind from inserting her opinion, I hike up Grandma E's bra that is sagging toward my waist, in search of support. Max is making too much sense. Even though, outside of wedding dinners, I've been living on a ramen and rice diet to save for this concert, I feel guilty about spending money when I still have so much debt to pay off—let alone how bad I'll feel leaving Toto. But, like my roommate, Corina, says, "Sometimes a leap of faith shows the universe you're willing to risk it all to follow your heart."

Outside Lands was supposed to be my last attempt at making Shut Up & Sway work. I'd promised myself that if I didn't come home with a clear sign that music is my path, I would do something else that scares me: take the bar again. Now that I'm thirty, I can't keep going into debt to make an impossible dream manifest. If I don't find a way to monetize my miniscule platform, it's time to get a real job.

"Come on, Gwen. Remember the lemon grove we created for the Romano-Scrafano wedding? The *scialatielli* pasta? You raved for weeks after that. This is your chance to experience the real thing. We're touring a lemon farm in Amalfi on day two."

I hear his smile spread into a grin, and I know he thinks he's got me.

My mouth waters. I can almost smell the lemon blossoms and taste the luscious handmade basil noodles tossed with charred tomatoes, creamy mozzarella, and sharp pecorino. It was one of my favorite weddings. One that—I admitted to Max after too many proseccos during our post-wedding recap—I would dream of for myself. *If* I dreamed of weddings where I'm the bride. The concept is so far from my reality, it never occurs to me.

I fold my arms over my chest. "Yes, but I'd rather go to Italy on vacation. Not to work the whole time."

"I won't take no for an answer," Max says, like he didn't hear me. "At least tell me you'll think about it. I can get you on a flight that leaves tomorrow at 3:50 p.m. I need to know by 6 a.m. if you'll be on it."

"No, I will *not* think about it." I grit my teeth, determined not to cave. "You know how important Outside Lands is to me."

"All I heard is *I will think about it*," he sings. "Thank you, love."

"Max. You can't manifest me going by pretending to hear what you want to hear. I'm choosing me for once." I rush to get in the last word. But it's too late. He hangs up.

Ugh.

Tossing the phone aside, I glare at the car's gray cloth ceiling.

The Lyft turns down a sleepy street lined with brick apartment buildings and stops in front of mine. "Wow. Italy. Lucky you." The driver puts the car in park, then turns to face me. "The closest I get to Italy is driving people to Taylor Street."

I moan and bury my face in my hands. "Why is nothing obvious and easy?"

Chapter 3

Smoke from a Distant Fire

"How was the wedding?" Corina asks.

Wearing skimpy summer pjs, she kneels at our coffee table. With her black hair piled on top of her head in a messy bun and her creamy olive skin void of makeup, she's surrounded by flickering white prayer candles. The twinkle lights that outline our doorways cast the cluttered living room in a soft glow. She's pushed aside the stack of metaphysics books that usually graces the glass table in favor of a stone essential oil diffuser that is puffing out spicy, orange-scented vapor.

"Your makeup looks pretty," she says, glancing up from the white stone she's polishing.

"That's a miracle. I'm amazed it hasn't melted off my face yet." I shut the door behind me and add my shoes, handbag, and duffel to the pile of accessories on the bench next to the front door.

Corina is an esthetician who just completed her level one Reiki certification. She specializes in skin care with a side of energy work. We met four years ago when my mom treated me to a spa day for my birthday. Corina performed my facial, and we hit it off over microdermabrasion. It turned out we both needed roommates, and we moved in together shortly after that. At this point in our relationship, I'm unfazed by her rituals and wander through the wafting orange vapor straight for Toto.

"The wedding was beautiful, but I'm glad it's over. I'm about to drop." I crouch next to the makeshift cat bed we made for Toto out of an Amazon box. He's fast asleep, curled up the best he can with the cone around his neck. I gently stroke his warm marmalade side, his fur so soft he's practically a chinchilla. He doesn't budge. He must be as exhausted as I am. As much as I want to cuddle with him, I let him be.

"Max wants me to fly to Italy tomorrow because Terra broke her foot. But I told him no." Too tired to do anything else, I sink into the pillows on the cushy beige couch across from Corina and pull out the hairpins that are digging into my scalp.

"Italy?" Corina cocks her head and pauses before gently dipping a cloth into a pearlescent bowl of water. "Does Italy not resonate with you? You have a passport, right?"

Unwinding my French twist, I let my brown hair tumble to my shoulders. "I do. Max makes us keep them current in case there's a destination wedding, but I haven't used one since I went fishing in Canada with my dad and brother fourteen years ago. I'd love to finally get a stamp in my new one, but I'd have to miss Outside Lands, and I can't leave Toto so soon." With a groan, I rake my fingers through my wavy mass of hair, loosening my aching roots.

Corina polishes an orange stone with the damp cloth before setting it down and concentrating on me. "If you want to go to Italy, I'm happy to watch Toto for you. You should see the adorable recovery onesie I just ordered for him. I thought it would be more comfortable than the cone. He's going to look so cute in it."

I straighten my spine. "Do you feel like I *should* go to Italy?"

"Maybe." She shrugs and sweeps a selenite wand over the orange stone.

"Maybe?" I clutch my hands to my chest. "But I thought we decided I needed to risk everything to go to Outside Lands."

"That was before Italy was an option. What are your instincts telling you?"

My jaw drops. "I don't know. I'm confused. Rationally, Italy makes sense. I need money. I have no idea how I'm going to make the minimum payments on my credit card now, and the wedding bonus alone is almost exactly the same amount as Toto's vet bill. That feels like a sign . . . But what if this is the universe testing my dedication to music? I need to prove I'm willing to take a risk and go to Outside Lands. Confront my fears and trust, right? And I don't want to miss the reunion."

She picks up a green stone. "I don't think it's a test. What would you choose if you knew you couldn't miss what's meant for you? Focus on how you want to feel. Let that guide you."

I stare at my palms wishing I could read them and find a line that ends at Italy or Outside Lands. "I want to feel supported—like I can support myself. To do what I love and not have to think about money all the time. I don't want to work a job I hate just for a paycheck." Groaning, I sink into the couch. "But I've been doing what I love, and the money isn't showing up."

Bridesmaiding may not be my ultimate goal, but I'm good at it and, theoretically, it leaves me time to create content.

"Maybe Italy is a sign that Shut Up & Sway is supposed to be a hobby." I sigh. "That it's not a realistic career. I could use the money to pay for Toto *and* have room on my credit card to register for the bar. Plus, my parents would be *so* relieved. I wouldn't be so broke that I'm in danger of having to move back in with them."

They'd never say it out loud, but I know my parents wonder when I'm going to quit bridesmaiding and get a "real" job. The reason I went to law school in the first place is because it's important to them that I have a solid education and a high-paying career. After the way they lit up back when my brother Tyler got accepted into law school, I knew I had to follow in his footsteps.

Since Ty died, I've gone out of my way to keep them from worrying about me. I'm their everything, now—not that I could ever be enough—and I text my mom every day, so she knows I'm okay. They *cannot* find out how bad my credit card debt is or that my true calling is being a music influencer. Even I cringe at calling myself that. The last thing I want is them thinking I can't take care of myself.

"You *are* supported." Corina sets down her stones to concentrate her attention on me. "Even if the money and the dream job haven't shown up in your physical reality yet, you have to be open to letting them in. Don't buy into old programming. Believe, and it will be. Raise your vibration."

"I'm trying. It's just not so easy to make believe I'm loaded when there are tumbleweeds rolling through my bank account. I wish there was a clear sign telling me what to do."

"Ask your guides for one."

I have never heard my guides, but Corina seems to hear hers. Apparently, all of my chakras are blocked. She's been practicing Reiki on me to clear them, but I don't think it's working yet.

"Or let's pull an oracle card." She stands.

"Yes." I point at her. "Let's do that."

She disappears down the short hallway that leads to our bedrooms and returns a minute later with her deck. Back at the table, she kneels on the rug we thrifted at Randolph Street Market, shuffles, then fans the cards out face down over the glass tabletop. With her eyes closed, she hovers a hand over the spread until a card speaks to her. After plucking it out, she turns it over and shows it to me.

"Surrender?" I squint in the flickering candlelight at the picture of a broken chain on the card. "That is not helpful. Surrender to Italy and money? Or to Outside Lands and what my soul wants? I have to choose my heart over money, right?"

"Not necessarily." Her eyebrows pinch together. "The universe doesn't judge, and money isn't evil. It's energy. Maybe it's a sign that money wants to flow toward you." Cocking her head, she zones out and nods like she's listening to a secret being whispered in her ear. "I think it means surrender to life. Say yes to whatever comes your way, even if it feels uncomfortable.

Don't judge situations as good or bad. Just be open to experiences and follow the breadcrumbs the universe lays out for you." Seeming to come back into this space-time reality, she refocuses on me.

I wrinkle my nose. "So, you think I should go to Italy?"

Before she can answer, Toto stirs in his box. He rolls onto his back, exposing his fluffy, white tummy. I hurry over to see if he wants a belly rub, but when I reach him, the hairs raise on the back of my neck.

"Corina, come here. Does it look like his stitches are oozing to you?"

She joins me and peers into the box. "Maybe?"

I stroke Toto's chest, hoping he'll peek up at me with his paws curled like he's begging to play our favorite game where I tickle him, and he pretends to attack my hand. But his eyes remain closed.

"It doesn't look like he's eaten much, either." I frown at his still full food dish.

My throat constricts and I cross the room to the bench by the front door. After digging my phone out of my purse, I start googling.

"He seems kind of lethargic, right?" My heart pounds as I read a list of warning signs of post-op complications. "Not eating or drinking normally. Redness. Swelling . . . He could still have crystals in his urine from the blockage." Heat floods through me and I press a damp palm to my cheek. "I think I need to take him in again." Even though I was ready to pass out fifteen minutes ago, there's no way I can sleep unless I know Toto's okay.

Corina startles. "Are you sure? Maybe my crystals can help. It's a full moon and they should be fully charged."

I shake my head. "I don't know if your crystals can combat *those* kind of blocks." With jittery fingers, I use my debit card to order a Lyft to the pet hospital with the little cash in my checking account, then yank on a pair of battered orange Chucks that clash with my peach bridesmaid gown. I don't care what I'm wearing. The only thing that matters is Toto. When my phone indicates my Lyft is one minute away, I grab my purse.

"Keep me posted on how he is," Corina calls after me as I rush out the door with the Amazon box full of Toto tucked under my arm. "And remember, the universe is always conspiring *for* you. Even if it feels like everything is falling apart." She follows me into the hall. "Trust your instincts. Don't overthink anything or let your ego hold you back."

The last thing I hear before I enter the stairwell is, "Surrender to the flow."

***

It turns out my instincts are not to be trusted. Toto is fine. The vet gives him a thorough examination and declares he's healing nicely. The Google freak-out costs me another $250, and I hold my breath as the receptionist runs my credit card, doing mental math to calculate *how* maxed out it is. The charge miraculously goes through, but I'm sick to my stomach. This is enough of a sign. I can't live without a safety net. Life is clearly telling me it's time to hang up the music dreams and study for the bar.

Toto and I take the bus home. As soon as we're settled in a seat, I cancel my ticket to San Francisco in exchange for a flight credit. Then I message Via and Jude that I'm a horrible friend who won't be able to make it to Outside Lands while asking if they know anyone who wants to buy my festival ticket.

With forty-five minutes to spare on my 6 a.m. deadline, I text Max:

> I'm in. And I'll take you up on the cat sitter.

Chapter 4

Waiting For a Girl Like You

I'm the last person to board the plane.

Still in my bridesmaid dress, I crashed the minute I got home. And I apparently turned off my alarm in my sleep because I woke to the cat sitter ringing my doorbell. I let her in—she seemed really sweet—and with only an hour and a half before my 3:50 p.m. flight, I grabbed the suitcase I had already packed for Outside Lands. After dumping the contents of my makeup drawer inside, I yanked on my Chucks, kissed Toto goodbye, and raced out the door.

I used the last of my cash to order a Lyft, and somewhere between the car and the airport departure desk, my phone died. It's super old and barely holds a charge these days. I need to replace it but haven't wanted to spend the money. Without my phone I have no connection to my parents or Toto.

Filling my lungs with jet fuel-laced air in an attempt to breathe myself calm, I limp down the aisle through first class, the dirty hem of my peach dress dragging on the floor. I was so close to missing the flight, a customer service agent printed me a paper ticket before escorting me through security and walking me to the gate. The airplane door closed behind me the moment I crossed the threshold. Even if my suitcase hadn't been rushed away to be stowed with the checked baggage, I still wouldn't have had time to change. Wishing I'd remembered to apply deodorant, I press my arms to my sides.

As I walk past first class, thankfully the passengers in their sleep pods are too busy kicking their feet up on their footrests and sipping champagne to notice me. They're clean, comfy, and enviably perfumed in their loungey travel clothes. Grinning and chatting, they seem excited for their trip to Europe. I can't imagine what they'd think of me if they were paying attention. My hair is so matted with hairspray it will take a rake to untangle it, and having rubbed my false eyelashes off hours ago, I probably look like I should be riding in on a Día De Los Muertos parade float.

I wish I was home. I want food. I want a bath. I want clean pjs and to snuggle with Toto and watch Hallmark romcoms in bed. To get an entire night's sleep dreaming of my Outside Lands trip and reuniting with my college roommates.

But it's not to be.

A flight attendant swishes the curtain shut behind me as I pass into the stuffy economy section. The seats are cramped back here, and I squeeze past a man shoving his luggage into an overhead compartment. Further up to my right, I spot the next best thing to bed: an empty window seat in a two-seat row. Undoubtedly, *my* empty window seat . . .

The man snaps the overhead bin shut, and I come to a halt. So does my heart.

Oh please, no.

Recognizing the unruly dark hair, bronze skin, and scruffy hint of a beard that accentuates the razor-sharp jawline of the passenger occupying the aisle seat in that two-seat row, a bubble of fear expands in my chest. I clutch my ticket and double-check my seat assignment, praying 26A doesn't coincide with the available chair next to the dashing Duncan Avila, one-night-stand choice of bridesmaids everywhere.

After everything I've been through, the universe wouldn't make me sit next to the lead singer of The Wedding Bandits who can cover "Africa" like no one else (Weezer included) with deodorant-less armpits. Would it?

If I wasn't sweating already, I am now.

"Hey, we know you." Duncan stands as I approach.

Do you, though?

Emitting a tiny whimper, I triple-check my seat assignment.

Duncan moves aside so I don't have to climb over his lap to get to my seat, which is, in fact, 26A.

His bandmates sit in the four-seat row across from ours.

Ours.

Ugh.

Leo, the bass player, sits in the aisle seat with his fedora lowered over his eyes and his arms folded across his chest. Only the cool umber of his chin and the sides of his shaved head are exposed. Next to Leo, Hayden, who plays *everything*, fails to acknowledge me. He's riveted by whatever is on his phone. Only B.J., the drummer, looks up, glances back and forth between Duncan and me, and absently strokes his full, black beard. Next to him, Duncan's partner in crime, emo guitar player Jonah, peers at me from under dark hair slicked down to cover one pierced eyebrow. He raises his black-painted fingernails in greeting.

Duncan and Jonah were roommates at UT Austin. They met the rest of the guys when they were working as techs at South by Southwest. I know this from the one time (only once, I swear) I googled them. It is due solely to my obsession with band origin stories that I committed their bio to memory.

"Hey." I manage a half-hearted wave at the band before checking the seat number on my ticket against the numbers above our row one last time. They still match. My insides constrict and I reach for my necklace, but it fails to work its magic, to undo the knots in my neck.

With a heavy sigh, I turn my back to Duncan and slide past him. Unfortunately, the woman in the row behind us chooses this exact moment to get something out of the overhead compartment. Duncan ducks to avoid getting hit, pinning me between him and the seat in front of us. His heat envelops me, sending—much to my chagrin—a delighted shiver down my spine. I've never stood this close to him.

He's a nice height.

A little over six feet tall, I'd guess. Not too tall, not too short for my five-foot-seven self.

Not that it matters.

I'm the last bridesmaid standing, and I intend to keep it that way.

As my rear end slips past his crotch, with sinking horror it occurs to me that beneath all the layers of peach chiffon, I'm not wearing any underwear, let alone a bra. A hot flush that starts low in my abdomen sweeps through me all the way to the tips of my ears. I picture Grandma E's bra and my Spanx crumpled on the floor next to my bed—*and not in my suitcase*—which also doesn't bode well for whatever dresses the stylist tailored to fit my co-worker, Terra. We wear *almost* the same size, but she's a good three inches shorter than me.

Grimacing, I move past Duncan, then collapse in my seat. I scoot as close to the window as possible.

He's wearing a thin green T-shirt and worn jeans. I've never seen him in anything except a tuxedo. Glimpsing him in street clothes is like meeting a movie star at the grocery store. I get all fluttery, inexplicably fangirling at this private Duncan I get all to myself for the next however many hours. Then I remember Kat fawning over him last night. For all I know he just came from her hotel room. The taste in my mouth turns sour.

Scouring my purse for earbuds and a phone charger so I can escape into music, I turn the bag nearly inside out before I'm forced to admit I left them both at home. My temples throb as I shove my purse under the chair in front of me.

"Is there a wedding on this flight? Or did you dress up just for us?" Duncan buckles his seatbelt. The corner of his mouth lifts in a crooked smile as he surveys my ragged dress.

Resting his elbow on the armrest, he leans toward me, awaiting my answer.

The full impact of his gray-green gaze bursts the carefully preserved bubble in my chest, sending an effervescent stream of giggles straight to my throat. I'm like a shaken soda, full of fizz. I try to retort, but the words won't come.

Is it hot in here?

I'd love to reach up and twist on my fan, but I don't dare raise my arm.

"I'm guessing you're working the Conner-Costanzo wedding, too. You know the ceremony isn't for another five days, right?" He prompts me, quirking an eyebrow. His eyes sparkle with mischief until he blinks. I can almost feel the breeze wafting off his dark fringed eyelashes. It tickles me to my core.

Pathetic. Man up, Gwen.

"You're very funny. I know it's in five days," I manage to say.

The safety video illuminates on the screens built into the seats in front of us, and I become fascinated with the emergency exit locations so I don't have to elaborate on why I'm still wearing last night's dress. Besides, hurling myself out an emergency exit might be preferable to bumping elbows with Duncan all flight.

Lurching into motion, the plane sways as it reverses out of the gate. Blessedly, the air conditioning kicks on. Duncan stretches out his legs as best he can and pushes back into his seat. The plane bounces toward the runway and we sit in awkward silence, both watching how to strap on a flotation device. I'm hyper-aware of his presence next to me. He's radiating warmth like the sun, demanding I bask in his rays. And no matter how dangerous it is to look directly at the sun, there's no way I can ignore him for the entire flight.

If he just came from Kat's room, he might assume my night took a similar trajectory with one of the groomsmen since I'm still wearing this dress . . .

Rolling my eyes toward the fasten seatbelt sign, I lean over to set him straight. "I'm a last-minute substitution. It was a late night, and I didn't have time to change."

"Who was supposed to be working?" He gives me his full, glittering focus, and little sparks shiver through me.

"Terra." I tamp down my reaction to him.

"Ah, Terra." Settling back into his seat, he studies the ceiling, and I can hear memory in his voice. "I know her."

Of course, he does. This week would probably have been more "fun" for him with a broken-in bridesmaid . . . But then, maybe he likes the chase?

My breath hitches at the possibility, and I clear my throat.

Last. Bridesmaid. Standing.

"I'm Gwen, by the way." Making sure to keep my arms glued to my sides lest my lack of deodorant pump any pheromones his way, I offer him a limp hand.

He cocks his head. "I know."

All the muscles in my body turn to mush and I stare at him, my lips parted.

Searching my face like he's trying to figure out if I'm high, he slowly takes my fingers in his. "I'm Duncan. And these are my friends—Jonah—"

A flight attendant passes by. "Seatbelts, please." She points at my lap before continuing toward the front of the plane, instructing passengers to push their bags farther under the chairs in front of them.

Grateful for a moment to gather my wits, I snatch my hand back and buckle my seatbelt with trembling fingers.

"Jonah on guitar, B.J. on drums, Leo on bass, Hayden on keyboards," I recite, giving myself time to recover my faculties. "I know the drill."

"And sax and marimba," Hayden announces from across the narrow aisle, leaning forward like Dracula sitting up in his coffin.

He locks eyes with me. His are bluer than they look onstage, seeming to glow against his pale beige skin and shocking red hair.

"Never forget the marimba." Not waiting for a response, he lowers himself back against his seat.

Okay.

Awaiting explanation, I slowly nod and shift my focus to Duncan.

The pilot's voice sounds over the intercom. "Flight attendants prepare for takeoff."

"We don't travel with a marimba." Duncan ducks his head toward mine like we're conspirators. "There's no way we could move one of those things." Smirking, he squints in a James Dean sort of way, and I again see why bridesmaids find it impossible to resist him.

Fortunately, I'm very disciplined. If I can live on ramen and rice to afford a ticket to Outside Lands, I can sit next to Duncan Avila for a few hours without hyperventilating at his feet.

At least I think so.

"But you've been paying attention." He juts out his chin like he's impressed.

My heart flutters at his approval. But I refuse to find him cute. "You pretty much play the same set every wedding, and we've worked a few weddings together." I shrug.

"Twenty-eight of them." He punctuates the statement with an emphatic nod.

My stomach drops, and I jerk back in surprise.

"And *you* usually go by Rosie," he adds.

"Well, we all go by Rosie." I lift my palm, unwilling to give him credit for that bit of name trivia. "It's easier than trying to remember a bunch of cover names, and Max thinks we're more attentive if we put our personal preferences aside and stay in character. Rosie the "riveted" as he likes to say. Plus, if there ever has to be a last-minute substitution, like in this case, it saves face for the client who has 'Rosie' on the guest list."

The plane's engines fire up with a roar.

"It's such a strange job." Duncan shakes his head. "I've always wondered, how does someone become a professional bridesmaid in the first place?"

I rub my arms against the suddenly chilly air, contemplating how to abbreviate the story without having to mention failing the bar. But at the same time, for some reason I want him to know I'm more than just a bridesmaid.

"I used to wait tables when I was in law school, and I waited on Max once."

He startles. "You're a lawyer?"

"No. But I will be. Soon." I sound out the declaration, trying it on, but it doesn't ring true. Yet.

The plane picks up speed and barrels down the runway. Clutching the armrests, I peer out the window at the airport rushing by in the late afternoon sun.

"We had a super early dinner rush that day and I was the only server on," I continue, so I don't have to elaborate on what I've *really* been trying to do with my life. I never tell people I'm a wannabe music influencer. The Shut Up & Sway newsletter has exactly one subscriber who is a stranger—ScaggsDupree222—and my social media accounts average less than one hundred followers each, with YouTube bringing up the rear at thirteen subscribers. I don't make money from any of it, so it doesn't feel like a valid profession.

"Max left me a huge tip and a note that said he was impressed with how I handled all those tables with dignity and grace. Then he came in every week for a month and sat in my section before he offered me a bridesmaid job."

The overhead compartments rattle as the plane soars into the sky and Chicago becomes a miniature grid below us.

Duncan nods. "I know how convincing Max can be. He came to every one of our shows for two months straight to convince us to give up clubs and come work the wedding circuit."

"That's a huge compliment. He only works with the best of the best, and he's a control freak about music, as I'm sure you know. The only thing he's more anal about is lighting."

"*The essential elements that can make or break the mood,*" we say at the same time, both mimicking Max's smooth, firm voice before we burst into laughter.

His bright eyes hold mine for a moment and my ears pop—either from the air pressure or the pressure of his gaze—I can't be sure which.

As our laughter subsides, he takes a deep breath. "Max might be uptight, but I'm grateful he keeps us so busy. I'd rather be playing music than doing just about anything. I mean, free drinks, free food, and getting paid to play." His shoulders meet his ears. "It could be a lot worse."

Not to mention having your pick of the bridesmaids.

I picture him clinking glasses with a different bridesmaid every night, like I've seen him do twenty-eight times, and my shoulders sag. Reminded I have no intention of being another notch in his guitar strap, I erect a wall between us. "It does seem like a pretty fun job." I nod, keeping my voice diplomatic.

We fall silent and a flight attendant's voice sounds over the intercom. "You may now use approved devices, but please remain seated until the captain turns off the fasten seatbelt sign. We'll be coming through the cabin with our beverage service shortly."

To my surprise, Duncan doesn't pull out a laptop or iPad. He keeps his attention on me.

"You still haven't told me why you're wearing the dress from last night's wedding." He arches an eyebrow. "I know you didn't stay for the afterparty. Where were you running off to that you haven't changed yet?"

"Oof." I cringe. "It's a long story."

"We've got nine hours." He grins.

The plane levels out and the engines quiet to a dull hum. Overhead, the fasten seatbelt sign goes dark with a ding. Buckles unclick all around us.

I shake my head. "I should sleep so I can hit the ground running when we get to Italy. I have so much to learn. I don't know any of the players in this wedding. The groom, the bride, the mother of the bride, the—"

"Drunk uncle." He finishes my sentence with bulging eyes.

Surprised he knew the direction of my thoughts, I suppress a giggle.

He watches me and goosebumps tingle up my arms. On some level it feels like he gets me. If I'm not careful, that could be my undoing. But luckily, I'm wound really tight—or so my spirit guides have told Corina.

I busy myself smoothing the chiffon draped over my thighs. "Normally I would have memorized the guest list by now. I'd be able to recite everyone's bio on command and recognize them from their headshots. I'm used to keeping the peace for one night, two in a row tops, if the rehearsal dinner is big. I don't know how I'm going to handle multiple days and events. I'd be cramming right now if my phone wasn't dead. I'm sure Max sent me a homework packet."

He wrinkles his nose. "You never have any fun at these things, do you?"

"I'm not there to have fun. I'm there to make sure everyone else has fun, that everything goes smoothly. No excessive drinking. No flirting. Dancing only when necessary. It's all about the bride. Those are Max's rules, as you must know." I flatten my lips into a thin, serious line.

"And you never break them." His eyes flash.

"Never." I solemnly fold my hands in my lap. Max allows us a cocktail or two at weddings because it would look strange if we weren't toasting, but I always limit myself to one drink. The best bridesmaid is a sober bridesmaid.

The beverage cart trembles to a stop next to our row. "Would you like something to drink?" the flight attendant asks Duncan.

He orders a bourbon, then turns to me. "Are you getting something? You're not on the clock now. You can have a drink, right?"

"It's complimentary," the flight attendant adds, handing Duncan a cup full of ice and a napkin before setting two miniature whiskey bottles on his tray.

My stomach growls. As much as I would love a cocktail, I need to eat, or it will go straight to my head. "What I could really use is food. Is that free?" I wince up at her.

"We'll be serving a complimentary meal, but not for another six hours." Frowning, she checks her tablet. "Unfortunately, the snack packs are all spoken for. They had to be preordered through our app, but I can bring you some pretzels. And we do have a hot meal left over from an earlier flight that's available for purchase."

"Oh." A lump forms in my throat that I'm so broke I can't afford dinner. Hopefully Max will give me some petty cash when we get to Italy, but until then, I'm officially tapped out. Deflated, I bonk my head against the window, leaving it to rest there. "I guess I'll take the pretzels."

"You know what, it's on me." Duncan hands her his credit card. "She'll have whatever hot meal you've got. And a . . . " He waits for me to fill in the blank.

I straighten and place my hand over my chest. "It's okay. Really."

He squares his jaw. "I'm going to order for you if you don't decide. A Midori sour?"

"A gin and tonic," I say quickly, not wanting to risk the headache that usually accompanies sweet drinks.

"You got it." Smiling, she punches the order into her tablet then runs Duncan's card. "And could you please lower your window shade for anyone who is trying to sleep or watch a movie?" She hands me two little bottles of Tanqueray, a can of tonic, and a plastic cup containing ice and a plastic sword speared through two limes. "The salmon curry will be right out."

I lower the shade against the golden sunlight streaming through the window then pour one of the gin bottles into my cup as she turns to take drink orders from the rest of the band.

"To airplane salmon." Duncan taps his cup against mine once I've topped my drink with tonic and squeezed in one of the limes. "What could go wrong?"

With a glance down at my tattered dress, I flinch. "So much." Laughter bubbles in my chest and meeting his big-eyed stare with my own, I swallow a gulp of my cocktail to silence it. The liquid is heaven on my throat, but the alcohol instantly dizzies me.

"Thank you for this. I'll pay you back when we get to Italy. Hopefully Max will give me some cash when we get there. I just spent all my money on a new cat penis, so things are a little tight right now."

He almost spits out his whiskey. "A what, now?"

"Oh, you heard me. Literally, a cat penis." I do my best Rob Lowe "Literally" impersonation.

Throwing his head back, he laughs a booming guffaw that lights up his face.

Butterflies flap to life in my belly. I can't help but crack up with him and all tension officially leaves my body. Now that I know Toto is going to be okay, I see the humor in my predicament. After swallowing another big sip of my cocktail, I launch into the story.

"I mean, whose cat licks their penis enough that it scabs over? Mine, apparently. Can you imagine his little orange leg sticking up in the air while he goes to town?" I drop my face into my palm.

Duncan presses his lips together, his eyes twinkling. "Maybe he was lonely. Had too much time on his paws?"

"I don't know." I take another sip of my drink. "Seriously, of all things to spend your nonexistent life savings on. Why, universe? Why?"

The salmon curry arrives, and I dive in, but not before the dim plane lighting takes on a hazy glow.

"He must mean a lot to you."

"Oh, he's my best friend." I finish a mouthful of creamy curry. "It's been just him and me since I was seventeen."

"You don't have a boyfriend?" He tilts his head.

I flush. "Oh, no. Toto is Prince Charming enough for me." The plane spins around me and I don't even know what I'm saying.

I didn't mean that, universe!

Corina always tells me not to make present tense declarations unless I'm trying to manifest something.

"Are you sure about that?" Duncan scans my bridesmaid dress, reminding me of my nakedness beneath the thin fabric.

My heart shoots straight to my toes.

Well, when you look at me that way, no.

I take another bite of stew to combat my reaction to him, hoping the food will help sober me up. If I'm not careful and I get too tipsy, I'll start talking music. Once that happens, there's no going back.

Clearing my throat, I change the subject. "So, what about you?"

"I've never purchased a penis." He crosses his heart. "I swear."

I laugh.

"And I don't have a girlfriend," he adds, peeking at me sideways.

Just a different girl every night.

Heaviness dips in my chest and my laughter stills. I rub the back of my neck. "No. I was going to ask, what did you do before you got into the wedding biz? Weren't you guys a real band before?"

"A real band?" His smile drops. "I'm pretty sure we're a real band."

The plane hits a patch of rough air, jostling the tray tables. I steady my drink.

"You know what I mean. Like, a band that writes their own music." I finish the last of my cocktail so the turbulence doesn't spill it. "Isn't it easier to play songs that are already hits than to sing your own stuff? Covers are like glorified karaoke. You used to play original music, right?"

With a ding, the fasten seatbelt sign blinks on.

Uh oh.

Part of me knows I'm on the brink of disaster, but it's impossible to pull myself back from the ledge. The gin is talking now.

He stiffens. "It's been a while, but yeah... We used to play our own stuff." A moment passes, and he turns toward his bandmates who are all watching movies, reading, or sleeping in the row across from us before fully facing me and narrowing his gaze. "So, you're saying being a wedding singer is for hacks?"

"No." I shake my head. Aware I've offended him, I press my lips together.

"Music is a tough industry. It's hard to make a living at it." His jaw twitches and I get the impression I've struck a chord. "But we do pretty well. The Bandits aren't a joke band."

"I didn't say that. You guys are *really* good as far as cover bands go." I attempt a peace offering, but then, for some reason, I continue. "And hey, the groupie bridesmaids are a perk, right? I mean, you get to hook up with a new girl every weekend."

His face hardens.

And this is why I shouldn't drink when I'm sleep deprived and starving. Can you spell d-i-a-r-r-h-e-a o-f t-h-e m-o-u-t-h. But I can't take it back now. I've already stepped in it.

"You know me so well." His eyes are splinters. "And you know, some might say you're a cover band, yourself, *Rosie*." Ignoring the illuminated fasten seatbelt sign, he unbuckles his seatbelt and stands. "I'm going to get some air. Something stinks around here."

I fold my arms over my chest and clamp my armpits shut, hoping he's talking about the salmon.

He disappears down the aisle and I slump in my seat.

Why don't you tell him what you really think, Gwen? I didn't mean to criticize cover bands . . . But I could have just shamed the next U2 for all I know. They're certainly talented enough. Ugh.

The air smooths out and the fasten seatbelt sign turns off. After meekly handing off what's left of my dinner to a passing flight attendant, I flip through the in-flight magazine.

When Duncan hasn't returned in ten minutes, I poke my head into the aisle. He's at the back of the plane flirting with the flight attendant—*of course*—and I'm mollified my impression of him isn't completely wrong.

Without headphones, I can't watch a movie to pass the time and I *should* sleep. I consider the second bottle of gin. The booze would make sure I pass out, but I also might start purring on Duncan, Toto-style.

Too risky.

Instead, I tuck it into the seat pocket in front of me, then curl into a ball against the window.

In the distance someone coughs and a baby cries, but all grows quiet as passengers settle in. I squeeze my eyes shut.

When Duncan returns a few minutes later, I pretend to be asleep.

His seatbelt clicks into place and our row grows darker when he switches off his overhead light. Relief that I won't have to talk to him lets my body relax. I'm starting to believe I'm actually going to fall asleep, until he sighs and places a blanket over my shoulder.

The simple gesture ignites a flame deep in my gut that spreads through me like wildfire, warming me in ways no blanket ever could.

"And my abuela says I've been waiting for a girl like you," he mutters under his breath.

My lungs seize and it takes everything I've got to keep my eyes from flying open.

Chapter 5
Right Down the Line

The next morning, Duncan and I land in Frankfurt tolerant strangers. Any camaraderie from the previous night has been erased, and I can't be sure I didn't dream him muttering about waiting for me. He ignores me for all of our layover and slight flight delay, and we don't sit near each other on the next plane. Without access to the wedding "Who's Who" Max surely sent to distract me, I can't stop berating myself for offending Duncan. By the time we land in Naples, I'm quivering with the need to make things right and I catch up to him as we exit customs.

"Hey. Duncan." I clear my throat. "About last night . . . " Breathless, I fall into step beside him. Our suitcase wheels rattle over the white tile floor and I keep talking before I lose my nerve. "I was really tired. Delirious. I owe you an apology."

He waves me off without looking at me. "It's cool."

My stomach churns. "No. It's not. But I don't know how to fix it." I lower my chin to my chest and peer at him from under my crusty eyelashes. "Is it possible you believe in second chances?"

He finally glances at me. Sucking in his cheeks, he considers as we slow down behind Hayden who is pushing a pile of instruments on a luggage cart. "Yeah. I guess I do. Last chances, at least."

My shoulders relax. "Good enough for me." I plaster my best bridesmaid smile across my face and grin at him.

His mouth twists into a crooked half-smile that doesn't travel to his eyes. Stepping aside, he lets me go first through the turnstiles that lead into a stark, white arrivals lobby where a deep male voice is announcing flights over the loudspeakers. Even though I have no idea what the voice is saying, I sigh. The Italian language makes everything sound romantic.

Max is waiting for us in a line of drivers holding signs with passengers' names on them. Wearing pale blue shorts, a fitted T-shirt with tiny flamingos printed on it, and boat shoes, he's the picture of #resortlife. But I know he's not relaxed. He never is.

"The bridesmaid and the band. Thank you, Lord, they're all here." He folds his hands in prayer and raises them to the ceiling as we roll our luggage to a stop in front of him. "I wouldn't normally fly you in hours before you play a party, but what could I do? Two clients *had* to have you, and I *always* deliver. I'm so relieved everything is coming together." He hugs Duncan, but when he spies me over Duncan's shoulder, he gasps. "Almost."

Releasing Duncan, Max looks me up and down. "Gwendoline. *What* are you wearing? You look like Mother's Day died. We *cannot* let Zoey see you like this."

"Who's Zoey?" I blurt before I think to stop myself.

His jaw drops. "The bride. Your *best friend*. Didn't you review the packet Lex sent you? The one with all the pictures and bios?"

I shrink into myself.

Grumbling at my blank stare, he nudges me toward the restroom. "Never mind. Tell me you have something else to wear."

"Believe me, I will gladly change." Dragging my suitcase behind me, I disappear through the swinging bathroom door, grateful for a chance to discard the peach dress of doom.

Once I'm inside a stall, I put on the first dress I pull out of my bag. The gauzy white maxi with crochet trim feels beachy enough to work on the Amalfi Coast and it sort of holds my boobs in place, but it's a little low cut. A bra sure would be *lovely*.

Chewing my lip, I dig through my bag, praying some aspect of my past self had the foresight to squirrel away even one pair of clean underwear and a bra. I push aside lace and eyelet dresses I haven't worn all summer so they'd feel new for my trip. Deep down, I know my search is useless. I didn't own enough undergarments to prepack for Outside Lands, so everything I have is either on my body or in my hamper. Cursing myself for oversleeping and not thinking to at least grab dirty underwear, I'm forced to admit I'm out of luck.

Hopefully, there's a boutique in the hotel where I can buy some once I get some cash. I swallow, hard.

I'll have to ask Corina who I screwed over in a previous life.

I planned to wear the gauze maxi at Outside Lands with face jewels and the combat boots I've had since I was a teenager. They're the only other shoes I brought, but picturing the death stare Max will give them, I stick with my orange Chucks and exit the stall.

At the sink, I brush my teeth and apply (I wish I could say re-apply) deodorant. It will take an hour to detangle the briar patch that is my hair, and I don't want to keep everyone waiting, so I tie it in a bun on the top of my head. Satisfied I look my best given the circumstances, I stuff the peach bridesmaid dress in the trash and exit out the door.

"What are you wearing?" Max screeches when I emerge from the restroom. "White? You can't wear white!"

Duncan's gaze flickers over me and I almost believe I glimpse approval in his eyes—that does *not* cause little fireworks to explode through me, I swear—before his expression hardens. But there's no time to contemplate his reaction. Max has a vein bulging in his neck.

Scrunching my forehead, I picture the contents of my suitcase, certain I mostly packed white. "I think this is all I have . . . Maybe there's some black crochet."

Max groans and rubs his temples. "No. No crochet. Oh, never mind. Let's get you to the hotel and pray nobody sees you until you've changed into your assigned wardrobe. This way. The cars are waiting." He turns toward the exit but not before adding, "I brought you all *il caffe nocciola*. You're going to *die* when you taste it."

I smile to myself as I follow Max out of the airport. Despite his outward annoyance with me, I know deep down he's a teddy bear.

When the automated doors slide open, we exit the airport into the humid Italian afternoon. I expect the air to smell different, like pizza or bread, but it mostly smells like exhaust and cigarettes. Max leads us around garden beds planted with olive trees to a curb where two white vans are waiting.

"*Buona sera!*" A jolly round man wearing crisp white pants and a button-down shirt that gleams against his olive skin jumps out of the driver's seat of the first van. He comes around and meets us on the sidewalk. "Welcome to Napoli. My name is Luigi—no like Mario—I take you anywhere you want."

"Thank you, Luigi. You can put the luggage and instruments in the back of the first van," Max says, ever the gentleman to everyone who is *not* his employee. "Gwen and Duncan, I need to talk to you both. You two ride with me. Everyone else, you take van two." He climbs inside the first van and pats the seat next to him while Luigi opens the back doors and slides equipment over the seats that are laid flat.

"Thanks, Luigi," I echo, leaving him with my suitcase before joining Max inside the air- conditioned vehicle.

I'm sure I'm the last person Duncan wants to sit next to, but I am obedient and take the middle seat on the black leather bench, leaving him the seat next to the door.

"*Muchas grazie, señor.* You just reminded me of one of my favorite songs—*Questi sono algunas de miei canción favoritas,*" Duncan says to Luigi as he helps load the van. "'*Bailar Con Me*' by the band Orleans."

"*Sì, sì! Bellissima.*" Luigi grins and his round cheeks bunch. "'Dance With Me.' I love it, too. But please. Go sit. This is my work."

Duncan obliges and climbs into the van.

"You speak Italian?" I ask as he settles next to me, leaving as much space as possible between us.

"Not really." He shakes his head. "My grandparents are from Mexico and they lived next door to us when I was growing up in Texas. My abuela only spoke to us in Spanish, so I'm fluent. Italian is pretty similar. I guess you could say I speak Spa-talian."

Whatever language it is, it's spa-dorable.

Max hands us coffees that are still warm. He watches me take a small sip from the paper cup. My eyes roll back into my head at the taste of the nutty, bittersweet brew. Leave it to Max to find the *best* coffee in probably all of Italy.

He presses his lips together, *told you so* written all over his face. "Drink up. We have a *long* night ahead of us." Max grins, exposing a dimple in his left cheek that endears him to everyone.

Luigi shuts the van doors and gets behind the wheel. "*Allora.* Sit back. Relax," he says over his shoulder. "We will arrive in one hour, twenty minutes."

I balance my drink in one hand and hunt for a seatbelt but come up empty.

Hoping I don't brush against Duncan's leg—or accidentally flash him in my low-cut dress—I squeeze my thighs together.

Relax? Ha.

Luigi pulls into traffic.

With his coffee in one hand, Duncan slides his other arm over the back of the seat and rests it above my shoulders.

Practically feeling the heat wafting off his defined forearm, honed, no doubt, from years playing guitar, I swallow a ludicrous urge to squeal. At the same time, I kick myself for my fan-girly reaction to him. I *need* to focus on the wedding.

Leaning forward, lest I give in to the urge to nestle into the alluring crook of his arm, I clench my abs and pray for gravity to hold me in place during my one hour and twenty-minute workout in resistance.

Chapter 6
Get Closer

I turn my full attention to Max. "So, Zoey is the bride. What else do I need to know?"

"I've hired a local events team fluent in Italian to assist in making sure the festivities go off without a hitch. And the hotel has given us Luigi here. He'll be available 24-7. All you need to worry about is the emotional well-being of the wedding party and guests." Max pulls up a Google doc on his iPad.

No pressure.

"Zoey's mother, Maria, was born in Rome. She met Zoey's father, Giorgio, when he was studying abroad in college. He's *the* Giorgio of the restaurant chain and cooking shows." He turns the iPad toward me so I can see a picture of Zoey's parents standing in front of one of their restaurants. I recognize her dad from his countless cooking competition shows.

"Zoey grew up in Italy until she was four, then the family moved back to Chicago where Giorgio is from. She's a foodie who is about to get her own Food Network show. This is the calm before she becomes a star." He shows me Zoey's headshot. She's pretty with long dark hair. Her sparkling brown eyes draw me in, giving me the impression she's friendly and approachable. I thought maybe I'd recognize her, but her smooth, flawless skin and full lips are unfamiliar.

"Will I get to meet Zoey before tonight?" Sipping my coffee, I peer out the window past Max, getting my first glimpse of Italy. So far, it's all highway.

Max frowns at his iPad, tapping the frozen screen. "Most of the guests are arriving today so she's very busy. I'll try to arrange a meeting, but if it doesn't happen before the yacht party tonight, just know, *she'll* be the one wearing white." He narrows his eyes at my dress. "You won't be able to miss her. This picture doesn't do her justice. She's even more gorgeous in person."

I cringe as the van jolts over a bump. The bounce catches me off guard and I don't have time to brace myself before my coffee sloshes through the opening in the lid and splashes onto *my* white dress.

Yelping, I clap my hand over my cup.

Max sighs and produces a handkerchief from his pocket and hands it to me.

Karma. This is what I get for competing with the bride.

I blot at the stain, determined to get everything right from here on out. "What's our backstory? How did I meet her?"

"Zumba class."

"Zumba?" My spine collapses. "Seriously?"

"Mt. Vesuvius," Luigi says.

"Exactly," I mutter, abandoning my dabbing attempt. "One hundred percent guaranteed to blow up."

Max glares at me.

Luigi laughs. "No. Outside."

Out Max's window, a massive gray mountain rises from behind the hills, its tip eclipsed by clouds. Or smoke. I fall silent, in awe of its size and power.

"*Cuándo fue la última vez è esploso?*" Duncan asks, leaning toward Luigi so he can be heard over the rush of the highway.

"*Nel quarantaquattro,*" Luigi replies over his shoulder. "*È strettamente monitorato. Avremo un buon preavviso in caso di esplosione.*"

I turn to Duncan, awaiting explanation.

"The last time it erupted was 1944," he translates, settling back into his seat. "It's closely monitored. Everything will be fine."

"It's an intimate wedding." Max clears his throat like we aren't here to sightsee. Which, of course, we aren't. He continues like he was never interrupted. "Ethan, the groom, is poised to become CFO of the entire Giorgio empire, so most of the guests are top-level execs and family. There are a few Food Network people coming, so you can't be a work friend. Zoey is an only child and was so sheltered growing up, she didn't have the opportunity to make close friends. She doesn't have cousins or family members her age. They're all older. Like many of our clients, she'd like to hide this hole in her life, even from the groom. She wants to control the narrative, so she's been mentioning her new Zumba friend to him for months."

This has bridezilla written all over it.

"That's why her parents agreed to hire you. For the sake of appearances," he continues. "Her father rented the entire hotel and is treating forty guests to five days of vacation. Some VIPs have chosen to stay at their own villas for privacy reasons. Berkeley Dalton and Olivia Bloom, for instance. Their twins are the flower girls, but they won't be attending any events except the rehearsal and wedding. As you can imagine with celebrity guests like this, the Costanzos want everything to be perfect. No surprises. No awkward moments."

My head spins. The first concert my brother ever took me to was at Ravinia with Berkeley & the Brightside headlining. I've worked some high-profile weddings, but never with guests who regularly grace the covers of gossip magazines. This is next-level for both Max and me.

Luigi exits the highway and makes a hard left onto a tiny two-lane road, sending me and my never-seen-a-Zumba-class-in-my-life rear end careening across the seat toward Duncan. Without anything to hang onto, I'm unable to stop the slide, and my hip bumps against his before I can scoot back to center.

Sparkling beneath the clear blue sky at the base of the craggy cliff we're perched on, the sea appears beyond a guard rail outside Duncan's window.

A breeze ripples the surface of the turquoise water, gently rocking the boats that dot the bay.

"The Bay of Sorrento," Luigi announces, driving around a bend that hugs the drop-off and makes my stomach meet my toes. I clench my burning thighs, determined to stay glued to my seat as Luigi navigates the winding cliffside road.

"Where have I been that I haven't attended any showers or bachelorette parties?" I ask, sweating from the effort to keep what's left of my coffee steady.

Normally I would have met Zoey for lunch so we could get to know each other. I'd have learned all the details of how she met her fiancé and what makes them special, the ins and outs of her family dynamic, her wants, her dreams. Depending on the package she bought, I would have attended the bridal shower and probably the bachelorette weekend in character to make sure everyone stayed safe and was fed and hydrated. We would have bonded by now.

"There was no wedding shower," Max says, seemingly oblivious to the vast stretch of sea and sky outside. "The Costanzos are so wealthy it seemed tacky. In lieu of wedding gifts, they're asking for donations to the Loving Way Foundation."

"Would you like to stop for some *limoncello* or *granita di limone*?" Luigi asks, nearly sideswiping an adorable blue pickup truck painted with lemons and oranges parked on the side of the road. The open bed of the truck is crammed with crates of fresh lemons and rows of glass bottles filled with syrupy yellow liquid. Nearby, a man is scooping sorbet into clear plastic cups.

"That's very kind, Luigi," Max says. "Unfortunately, we're in a hurry."

"Hurry, it is." Luigi grins and steps on the gas.

I frown, watching the charming truck disappear over Duncan's shoulder, wishing, for what I'm sure won't be the only time this trip, I could take a moment to admire the view. To stop by a roadside fruit stand and sip sweet limoncello while taking in the colorful villas built into the cliffs. To marvel at the ferns and palms growing out of the sides of the rocky walls that give way to slips of beach far below us.

But that isn't to be. Max keeps talking, and I force myself to focus on the wedding as we swerve around a curve.

"There was an engagement party that took place before Zoey hired us. The story is that you had to miss it because you travel so much for work. You oversee the managers at several Marriotts in the Midwest and you're always visiting them on weekends, so you haven't been able to attend any events. Nobody beyond Zoey has met Terra, so we can easily slip you into her place. And due to Zoey's intense shooting schedule, instead of a bachelorette party, there was only a last minute, low-key spa day with Zoey, Aubrey, and their moms. Aubrey is the groom's younger sister, but she and Zoey aren't that close." Max swipes at his iPad and holds up a picture of a gorgeous blonde girl grinning on a beach in a huge floppy hat. "She's the other bridesmaid and a mid-level lifestyle influencer with around 300,000 followers. You're the maid of honor."

"What?" My jaw drops. "I have to give a speech? In front of celebrities?"

Luigi speeds around a hairpin turn and in my momentary fluster, I slide into Duncan's armpit. Horrified to discover he smells like some alluring combination of cedar, citrus, and spice that could only have been divined by angels, I scramble away from him.

"Don't worry. Zoey will write it with you. And you're fantastic at delivering speeches. You'll be fine. She's lovely. This will be easy. You'll see."

We wind around another bend and a van appears, coming straight at us, seemingly in our same lane.

We all screech—even Max—and the hairs raise on the back of my neck, either because I'm pretty sure we're about to fly off the cliff to our deaths or because this time Duncan drops his arm around my waist and hugs me into his side. I tense even as my insides clench against the shiver that runs through me—a shiver of fear, not delight, thank you very much. I'll swear it until my dying day. Which might be today.

"The Tyrrhenian Sea greets you!" Luigi gestures at the brilliant blue water twinkling like it's crusted with engagement rings below the ancient guard rail.

"Just so long as we don't end up at the bottom of it," I whisper, my heart in my throat as I try to wiggle out from under the weight of Duncan's arm.

"Just stay here." He holds me tighter.

I'd find the suggestion endearing if it wasn't so automatic, probably an instinct long honed to lure unsuspecting bridesmaids into the security of his arms. Not that he seems to be enjoying our proximity based on the square set of his jaw.

But then we merge into the oncoming lane to pass a person on a moped. My heart pounds as Duncan tightens his hold on me, and I quit wrestling away from him in favor of pumping invisible brakes.

"Do you have the set list finalized for tonight, Duncan?" Max swipes at his iPad, his voice calm, but I don't miss his gaze nervously flickering to the road.

Duncan's face lights up. "Totally. Tonight is all about the smooth, slow sounds of the seventies and eighties. It's going to be non-stop yacht rock. We're going to kick it off with 'Sailing' by Christopher Cross, a song that has the cartoon finger effect."

"Cartoon finger effect?" Max cocks his head.

"Yeah, like a scent wafting across the screen in a cartoon that smells so good, the character imagines it taking the shape of a finger that beckons them forward. It's so intoxicating the character has no choice but to follow their nose and float toward the source. 'Sailing' is instantly transportive like that. The song will waft toward the guests, enticing them to float aboard the yacht."

Knowing Duncan's allure, I have no doubt the guests will be swept away. Even now, the gravelly reverberation of his voice lulls me into a state of peace. Until we bounce over a hill into a town. The street is lined with quaint pastel buildings and seaside terraces hanging over the cliffs. There are no sidewalks. Cars and mopeds are parked bumper to bumper on either side of the narrow road making the passage even tighter.

"*Allora*," Luigi says with a wave at a police officer as he veers around the traffic and drives down the wrong side of the road. "Welcome to Positano." He zooms past people carrying beach bags and towels, laying on the horn whenever someone ventures too far into the tiny street.

"Lots of tourists in August. One less, no big deal," he explains with a laugh.

Duncan and I look at each other, our eyes wide, momentarily united in our terror.

"Life? Is that what *'allora'* means?" Duncan asks like he wants to remind Luigi we'd all like to arrive at the hotel alive.

Luigi grins. "No. *Allora* is a filler. It buys you time to think, so it means whatever you want it to mean. Your job in Positano is to find out what it means to you. What is revealed for you when you take the time to pause, to experience the in-between." He turns down a tiny cobblestone road lined with colorful shops, their arched doorways framed by fuchsia bougainvillea.

Wherever the in-between is. The ether?

I can't wrap my mind around it and I don't have time to because—

"Stop!" Max screams.

Luigi slams on the brakes and we all fly forward. Duncan throws his arm across my chest, catching me in a full embrace to keep me from catapulting through the windshield.

A guy leaps out of the van's way as we screech to a stop in front of him.

And he's not just any guy. He's a *really* attractive guy.

A really attractive guy, I slowly realize as I suck in a deep breath and my sinuses clear, that I *know*.

I haven't seen his tanned, golden skin, chiseled jaw, or mussed light brown hair outside of my dreams in over a decade.

It's a face I haven't stopped thinking about since the last time I laid eyes on it. It is the face of my first—and only—love.

My muscles go weak and a gasp catches in my throat. I'm glad Duncan is holding me up when Max announces, "We need *that* tourist. He's the groom."

Chapter 7

Never Gonna Fall in Love Again

"**M**ax?" The *groom* walks toward us in full Hemsworthian glory. Wearing a pale blue button-down shirt with the sleeves rolled to expose his defined forearms and teal shorts, he practically steps out of a J. Crew catalog. Luigi has parked in front of the arched entrance to a melon-colored hotel covered with ivy. While I stumble out of the backseat, I watch the groom take Max's hand in one of his while simultaneously embracing him with his free arm.

I can do nothing but stare. Perched on the edge of the cobblestone road with the balmy ocean breeze fluttering my coffee-stained white dress around my ankles, I gape at him.

In the distance, church bells bong in deep, resonant tones. Beyond the hotel, the vertical town is a maze of tiny streets and stairs tucked into cliffs that descend to the sea. The tile rooftops, iron balconies, and clay pots teaming with colorful flowers are a postcard, but they blur into a watercolor painting with only Fish in focus.

I mean Ethan. His nickname was Fish when I knew him.

Clutching the necklace at my throat, I count the seconds until those blue eyes land on me. Until they maybe recognize me.

Or maybe not.

I'm dying to know if he will. It's been *so* long. So much has changed. I've imagined this moment for over a dozen years. Agonized over it. Dreamed of it. And now that it's happening, I don't know if I want it to.

"Here we measure in steps." Luigi pauses unloading our luggage and faces Duncan. "We are 400 steps above the sea. The beach is at zero steps and the bar is at 365 steps." He grins and nods toward me. "She looks like she could use a drink."

"He's right. She could," I say, my gaze never leaving Fish.

"Too bad she's on the clock." Duncan tsks so only I can hear.

The reminder jolts through me.

OMG, OMG, OMG. Fish is the groom . . . I'm supposed to be his bride's best friend. Her maid of honor. And he doesn't know she hired me.

The moment is *now*.

It's happening . . .

"I just got back from an airport run to pick up the band." Max turns Fish/Ethan my way. "And found Rosie. She's Zoey's maid of honor we've all been dying to meet." Max raises his eyebrows at me, and I get his telepathic message to get to work. But I can't move. All I can do is curse myself for not asking Max more questions about the groom on the way here. The few facts I've been given rattle around in my brain.

He's poised to become CFO of Giorgio's conglomerate. Which makes sense.

He was an economics major at Northwestern when I knew him. And my brother Tyler's best friend. I haven't seen or heard from him since the funeral.

"Rosie, this is Ethan. The *groom*." Max enunciates the introduction like I'm a kindergartner learning to read.

Ethan/Fish finally looks at me, and my throat goes dry. Time stands still as he takes my right hand between both of his, a huge grin spreading across his glorious golden face. He's a gift from the heavens and light rays practically radiate out of him.

"Rosie. I've heard so much about you."

I say nothing. My jaw slack, I absorb his beauty, noting the tiny changes, the fine smile lines forming around his eyes that somehow give him character and make him prettier than I remember.

Duncan shoves an elbow into my side, and I snap out of my daze. "You have?" I manage to say.

"Zoey says you two have been Zumba-ing nonstop to get ready for the wedding. It shows." His gaze dips below my face, and my lungs seize.

Does it, though?

I'm a healthy weight, but I do have boobs and hips. I could be thinner if I tried, but I don't really have time to work out. Brides don't want a bridesmaid who's prettier or skinnier than them anyway, so I tell myself indulging in wedding cake every week is good for business.

Holding my breath, I wait for stunned recognition to light his eyes.

When he knew me, I was going through a goth phase. My hair was dyed black, my face powdered white, and I probably kept Mac in business thanks to my obsession with their black-purple "Cyber" lipstick. I wore all black everything, opting for ripped tights under oversized concert T-shirts that hid my curvy frame.

After the way our relationship ended, I've dreamed of seeing him again. He was a driving force in my reinvention. Everywhere I go, I wonder if Fish will be there. Will he be at this bar? This restaurant? What will he think when he sees the new me? When he realizes who I am?

Now, wearing a flowy white dress that nips in at my waist, accentuating what I consider my best feature, with my hair its natural brown shade and pulled into an (extremely) messy bun, I'm not sure I'm recognizable as the girl Fish knew thirteen years ago.

His attention returns to my face, his smile friendly. For a split second he cocks his head, like he's asking if he knows me. A jolt spikes my core, but the moment passes so quickly, I'm probably imagining it.

With his expression otherwise blank, he doesn't seem to peg me as Gwendoline Watson of Mackinac Island. I exhale with a whoosh, unsure if

I'm glad he doesn't recognize the weird goth girl he once knew or disappointed he isn't instantly stunned by my miraculous transformation. I've certainly worked hard to erase the old me, to become someone worthy of someone like him.

Duncan pinches the back of my arm, and, realizing I've been mute so long it's getting awkward, I come to life. "Zumba life is the best life," I say, having no idea what words are spewing from my mouth. "She looks ah-mazing. But that's Zoey. Unstoppable. Me, I've got some baggage to handle." I pat my round hip.

Max looks at me cross-eyed, like he's going to send kidnappers to duct tape my mouth shut and throw me in a steamer trunk bound for Timbuktu. "You must be exhausted after such a long flight, Rosie. Why don't we get you checked in so you can freshen up before the party tonight?"

"Good idea." I nod, knowing I've been gawking at Fish too long. But I'm unable to stop ogling his broad shoulders, his perfectly bowed lips . . . His thick neck . . . I swallow.

Oh gawd, he's pretty.

"Ethan, you must have so much to do," Max says.

Ethan.

Ethan Fisher Conner, but my brother always called him "Fish." Of course, he's "Fish" no more. It wouldn't be fair for me to emerge from my teenage chrysalis a butterfly while he remained a caterpillar.

A sexy, sexy caterpillar.

And who am I kidding? *He's* clearly morphed into the butterfly. Rich. Handsome. About to marry a gorgeous foodie TV star. After everything I've been through in the last forty-eight hours, I'm a moth at best. Coffee-stained, broke, and jet-lagged is not how I imagined myself in this moment, and I press my hand to my abdomen against a wave of nausea.

"Let me get Rosie and the band settled and then I'll go check on the terrace to make sure it's ready for cocktails." I register that Max is still talking. He links arms with me and leans toward Fish—I mean *Ethan*. "If you'll excuse us."

"Of course. We'll get to know each other later, Rosie," Fish/Ethan says with a wink before turning to greet another guest who has just arrived.

Mental note not to eff up and call him Fish!

I can*not* let Max know I know Fish—*Ethan*. It is one hundred percent against Max's rules to have a bridesmaid know a member of the wedding party. He will *freak* and probably stage some sort of accident that puts me on the next plane back to Chicago. Yes, legally, my contract requires that I recuse myself from the wedding in this situation, but the second I consider leaving, tears well in my eyes at the thought of my poor, cone-headed Toto. I *need* to pull off a perfect, drama-free wedding to get my bonus and pass the bar so I can land a job so I can be a good, debt-free cat mom.

Not to mention I've been waiting to see Fish again for thirteen years.

"You two, this way." Yanking my arm, Max drags me up a short flight of stone steps while gesturing for Duncan to follow. "What was that?" Max growls under his breath once Ethan is out of earshot. We enter the hotel through a set of wrought iron doors flanked by lanterns.

"He's, ummm, really cute." Blinking away my tears, I screw up my face, at a loss for how to explain why I'm so overly emotional. "I wasn't expecting that."

In the hotel lobby, a languid breeze wafts off the sea. The lounge beyond the check-in desk opens to a terrace that overlooks spectacular turquoise water and pastel houses built into the cliffs. Soft, jazzy music plays, and the air is scented with a mix of sweet lemon blossoms, peppery wild herbs, and sea salt. The *allora* beckons.

"Young, rich, CFOs-to-be are often attractive, but he's the *groom*. You're *not allowed* to notice." Max's voice is stern but then his lips twitch, like he's holding back a rare smile, and I know I've got him.

"Neither are you," I say out of the corner of my mouth.

He snorts, swallowing a giggle, and for a second, we're friends.

My stomach knots. I'm sickened that I'm lying to him, but then his smile falls. "Enough about that," he says. "We're professionals. Remember. No flirting—"

"It's all about the bride." I finish his sentence, punctuating the rules that have been drilled into me for years. The rules I have never broken and never have any trouble following. But this time, I need the reminder. My mind is back to racing a million miles a minute.

Fish is Ethan. Ethan is the groom. And I'm a professional. Fish is Ethan. Ethan is the groom and I'm a professional.

Ethan's name refuses to penetrate.

An older woman wearing a blue-and-white print dress swishes past us in a cloud of perfume. Her coral lipstick looks freshly applied; she's probably on her way to some swanky happy hour. As her gold heels clack away from us, I glower at the orange, blue, and yellow mosaic tiles beneath my feet and lighten my step. This floor is probably a hand-painted work of art that belongs in a museum. It deserves to have a shoe far more elegant than my tired orange Chucks treading on it.

"Mrs. Conner." Max spins around, leaving my side to chase after the woman. "We were able to secure the hats for the yacht tonight."

Mrs. Conner, as in, the mother of the groom.

I wince that I didn't recognize her.

"*Buona sera.*" A man who might as well be Luigi's twin joyfully leaps out from behind the front desk and comes to a stop in front of Duncan and me. "I am Roberto, and I welcome you to Il Desiderio. *Bellissima.*" He gestures down the length of my white dress, then looks back and forth between the two of us. "It is your honeymoon?"

Duncan and I look at each other. My horror is reflected in his eyes.

"Oh, no." I gasp, praying Max is out of ear shot lest his head explode at my wearing white faux pas.

"Definitely not." Duncan waves Roberto off.

"No? *Ciao, bella.* You are available?" Roberto gets down on one knee and takes my hand in his. "You will marry me, then?"

My jaw drops. "No." At a loss for more words, I snatch my hand away and gesture him to his feet. If Max sees him, he will end me.

Roberto laughs and stands. "You break my heart." He presses his hand to his chest then leans toward Duncan. "She is very beautiful, though, no?"

Duncan nods. "Yes. *Very* beautiful."

Goosebumps race up my arm, and I change the subject. "We're here for another wedding."

"*Allora, the* wedding. *Sì.* Come. This way. Let me bring your welcome drinks. You must sit and have *aperitivo.*" He leads us toward a lemon-yellow couch nestled in a sunny corner next to palms potted in white ceramic pots. The scene is positioned at the best vantage point to take in the glorious view.

I would like nothing more than to sink into the couch and process my Ethan debacle over an Aperol spritz, but Max chooses this moment to reappear.

"No. No time for *aperitivo.* They're with me." He finds the reservation on his iPad and shows it to Roberto. "We have four rooms reserved. Three for the band and one for Rosie, Zoey's maid of honor."

"Mr. Max. Of course. Let me get your keys." Roberto smiles and hops back behind the desk before punching something into a computer.

I hang back with Duncan, half-listening, dizzily letting the heady sea air wash over me, hoping it will settle my nerves.

"So, you're into the groom, huh?" Duncan leans close enough that his breath tickles my ear.

I flinch. "No. I'm … Uh. I don't know what got into me." For some reason I don't want Duncan to think that I think Ethan is cute. "I must be exhausted."

"You slept at least six hours on the plane. Trust me. You were out. I had to push you back against the window at least four times." Narrowing his glittering eyes, he rubs his shoulder like he can still feel the imprint of my head resting on it. "Something else is going on."

My cheeks heat at my apparent snuggling attempts, but I squint at him. "Nothing is going on. Not that it's any of your business."

Max returns with our keys and leads us toward the elevator. "You two are in 326 and 328."

We come to a stop next to an empty iron cage that runs parallel to the staircase. Max punches the gold-plated button and the elevator cables creak to life, lowering a small wooden car with glass doors.

"Duncan, the band is expected on the yacht for sound check at 8:00. And Rosie, I'll see you at Franco's Bar at Le Sirenuse for sunset drinks at 7:30. That gives you an hour to freshen up. Maybe you can use some of it to read the itinerary Lex sent you."

"That was my plan," I reply. "I'll have everyone's backstory on lock, promise."

Especially Ethan's.

Luigi arrives pushing our luggage on a cart, and I move to retrieve my suitcase.

His head jerks back like I've committed some cardinal sin, and he waves his hands. "Oh, no. I'll carry it for you."

My blood pressure spikes. The real reason I want my bag is because I don't have money to tip him and I cringe, wracking my brain for a way to avoid the inevitable awkward moment. I need to ask Max for cash, but based on the borderline crisis-clench of his jaw, it's definitely not the right time.

The elevator comes to a stop. Max pulls open one of the glass doors and moves aside so Duncan and I can enter. We squeeze into the tight wooden box and stand wedged side by side against the back wall, trying to make room for Max. Seeming to read the situation, Duncan stealthily pulls a few euros out of his pocket and shoves them into my palm. My spine goes slack, and I lightly squeeze his forearm in thanks.

Max ducks inside and the sapphire-carpeted floor groans beneath the extra weight. The cables shake and it feels like the ancient elevator will never heave all three of us off the ground. Grumbling, he retreats into the lobby. "I guess you don't need me. You know where to be. Don't be late. And no white. Or crochet. As in leave the booty shorts behind."

"I would *never*." I gasp, waggling a finger at him. "And you know it."

Max laughs as Duncan presses the button for the third floor.

His mirth gives me hope. "Oh, Max. I forgot my phone charger. It's the old iPhone kind. Do you have one I can borrow so I can find Lex's email with the itinerary?" I also want to ask him for cash, but Luigi shuts the glass doors before I get a chance.

The tiny elevator ascends, its walls trembling. Max gives me a thumbs-up before disappearing from view.

"You can borrow my charger," Duncan says.

I sigh at how unprepared I am. "Hopefully Max will send one, but thank you for this." I wave the money he gave me. "As soon as I get some cash, I'll repay you."

"No worries. You can repay me by telling me what's going on with you and the groom." He presses his lips together, like he's holding back a laugh.

I glare at him. "You're a gossip."

He shrugs. "Nah. Just curious. It was almost like you both saw a ghost."

"What do you mean *both*?" I grip his arm.

The elevator shudders to a stop on the third floor and Duncan holds the doors open so I can exit first. "I mean you and Ethan. I thought he was going to pass out when he first saw you."

My pulse thuds in my ears and I dig my nails into Duncan's flesh, desperate for details. "Tell me everything. Tell me exactly what he looked like."

We enter a whitewashed hallway barely wide enough for us to walk side by side. As we head down the tiled corridor, the floor this time painted with yellow lemons and twisted green vines, we can't help bumping each other.

At the far end of the passage, sheer white curtains bluster in front of open glass doors, wafting in briny sea air, but I'm too anxious for the breeze to calm me. "He almost got hit by a van. Do you think he was in shock? Or did it look like he recognized me."

"Why would he recognize you?" He arches an eyebrow, playing innocent, but his question is loaded.

The truth is, I'm dying to tell someone. Dying to get the play-by-play of Ethan's exact expressions when he saw me.

Could he have recognized me?

I've already taken comfort in having Duncan on my side, so without overthinking it, I lower my voice and reveal, "I know him."

He sucks in his breath in mock disgrace. "But that's against Max's rules. Doesn't he have a list of every person you've ever been acquainted with that he cross-checks against the guest list?" He grins. "This week just got interesting."

"You *are* a gossip."

"Maybe just a little." He winks, and I feel it in my belly. A tiny squeeze that endears me to him. *Just a little.* I tamp it down.

"Max can't know." I make my eyes round. "Promise me you won't tell him."

"Hmmm." He searches my face. "What's in it for me?"

An image of him pushing me against the wall and pressing his lips against mine flashes through my mind, making my skin burn. I use the flames to sear the thought to ashes. He knows exactly what he's doing, and I refuse to be charmed.

"My undying gratitude." I place my hands on my hips. "Duncan, I'm being serious."

He startles when I say his name and instantly sobers. Something guarded enters his gaze. "Okay. But maybe you should fill me in on the details so I can help keep your secret."

I remain silent, unsure of where to start.

"So . . . you know Ethan," he prompts as we arrive at our doors: two white wooden arches next to each other with 326 and 328 hand painted in navy on them—326 for him, 328 for me.

The navy numbers blur as memories of the magical week I spent under the stars with Ethan overwhelm me. "I used to look different," I finally say, concentrating on inserting the old brass key in the ancient lock. "I was seventeen when I knew him. He was my first everything."

"You mean . . . " His head bobs from side to side.

"No." Snapping back into reality, I punch his bicep. "Not that—never that with him. I mean kiss." I face him, my jaw clenched. "Love. It only lasted four days. But it was perfect. *Nothing* will ever live up to it." I don't mean it to, but it comes out sounding like a challenge.

"You fell in love that fast?" His eyes flash with an intensity that has my nerve endings standing at attention. "You fall easily." Also, a challenge.

I recoil, afraid he's somehow accepted his role in the gauntlet I just threw. "Oh no. That was then. I know better now." Opening my door, I square my jaw. "I will *never* fall."

With that, I shut myself inside.

Chapter 8
Cool Night

My head is spinning, and I lean against the door. I need to think. Figure out what to do about Fish—Ethan. Duncan. Across my room, the tile floor painted with blue filigree and orange marigolds, puffy white curtains frame French doors. The turquoise sea glints in the sun under a cloudless blue sky, beckoning me toward the terrace. I walk to the center of the creamy, white space scented with the same lemon and wild herb sea salt essence as the lobby. A straw beach bag embroidered with *La Dolce Vita* in navy script sits on the crisp white bedspread. I drop my purse on a cushy yellow chair and pounce on it.

There's no way Max didn't put a bottle of limoncello in this thing.

I toss aside a hand-painted ceramic olive oil bottle, crackers, chocolates, and a lemon-printed paper fan, practically turning the bag upside down before admitting Max (*of course*) confiscated my booze. Groaning, I collapse on the bed and stare at the domed ceiling, wishing I'd thought to put the mini bottle of airplane gin in my purse. The room strangely doesn't seem to have closets, let alone a minibar.

Not that I could afford those drinks anyway.

A knock sounds outside my door. On the other side, a cheerful Luigi waits. He deposits my suitcase on a luggage stand then hands me a phone charger with an international adapter in exchange for the tip money Duncan loaned me. The euros remind me that I need to get to work. In less than an hour.

If I hurry, maybe I can steal a moment on the balcony . . .

Luigi leaves and I plug my phone in to charge on the antique desk near the bed before racing to the marble bathroom for a hot shower.

After scrubbing myself clean with zesty bergamot body wash, I slip on the decadently soft white bathrobe I find hanging on the back of the door and wrap my hair in a fluffy white towel so plush it makes Toto feel like sandpaper.

Refreshed, I press the button to turn on my phone so I can text my mom and the cat sitter, but the screen remains dark.

Ugh. Hopefully it just needs to charge more and hasn't chosen this moment to die for good.

On the other hand, maybe it's for the best. I don't have an international plan and can't risk extra charges. I can barely pay my bill as it is. I probably need to get on Wi-Fi, but even then, this being my first time abroad, I'm uncertain if I need to have activated international roaming to connect.

Leaving my phone to charge more, I get dressed in the only thing I packed that's not white: a vintage black Hall & Oates T-shirt with cut-off sleeves (sans bra) and a black miniskirt with a fringed crochet overlay (sans under-wear).

My combat boots are *definitely* not wedding party approved so I again opt for my orange Chucks to complete the look. My stomach twists that I have to go to cocktails in this getup. I'm certain it's not the vibe Zoey is going for, but what choice do I have? The assigned wardrobe Max mentioned is nowhere in sight. I was half-expecting Luigi to bring it with my luggage, but Max's 'no booty shorts' warning leads me to believe it will arrive later. This will have to do. Maybe a festivally bridesmaid is better than no bridesmaid.

After sweeping on light makeup and painting my lips a deep berry, I head for the terrace to let my hair dry in beachy waves.

I step through the French doors into the balmy evening and am greeted by twittering birds and the roll of waves crashing over rocks along the shore. To my right, sun-bleached pastel villas tucked among vertical gardens are stacked into the cliffs all the way to the sea. My lips part as I move to the edge of the terrace in slow motion, like I'm walking in a dream. I lightly rest my hands on the white iron railing that surrounds my balcony. Below my feet, yachts bob and dip on water that undulates from turquoise to cobalt.

Somehow the air is different here. It has weight. The salty sea breeze settles into my skin and soothes my jittery nerves. I can't help believing there's magic in the wind.

Before I can crumple into one of the terrace's white canvas chairs to rationally process everything that has happened today—to figure out if I should tell Ethan who I am or confess my predicament to Max—a throat clears beside me.

Apparently, Duncan has chosen this same moment to indulge on his deck. Our balconies are so close we could hold hands, and he comes to a stop at my side, leaning against his railing.

I observe him out of the corner of my eye and goosebumps race up my arms at the sight of his perfect profile silhouetted by the sea.

Swallowing a sip of the Peroni beer he was lucky enough to score, he takes in my black Outside Lands attire. "Nice outfit."

My entire body puckers under his scrutiny. Assuming he's suggesting my outfit may not be white, but it's *still* zero percent wedding party approved—and to combat my puckery reaction to him—I narrow my eyes.

"You should talk. What exactly are *you* wearing?" I tug the sleeve of . . . the thing . . . he's wearing.

"This?" Raising his eyebrows, he tugs on the . . . *lapels* . . . if you can call them that, of the blue and green floral print towels that must have come straight from the JCPenney catalog circa 1970 that he's wearing. The vintage towels are sewn together to form a robe-like jacket with elbow-length sleeves. Washcloths form pockets at his hips. "*This* is Towaya. *This* says party."

I screw up my face. "Toe-why-ah?" I sound out the word. "I have never seen anything like that. Where did you get such a thing?"

He's wearing it over worn jeans and a white T-shirt fitted enough to showcase the defined outline of his chest. The whole effect *does* make the corners of my mouth twitch. But I refuse to give him the satisfaction of a smile, to be just another bridesmaid in his belt.

"At a thrift store in Duluth. Somebody's grandma probably made it in 1975, but if we recreated these things, I bet they would sell for $500 a pop. People are obsessed with Towaya."

And by people, surely you mean "bridesmaids."

But I keep my thoughts to myself for once. "Seriously?"

"It comes with cup holders. What's not to love?" He slips his beer bottle into one of the washcloth pockets at his hip.

"Oh my gosh." I smack my hand against my forehead. "And Towaya is your name for it? You nickname your clothes?"

"Yeah. You don't?" He says with mock seriousness before he laughs. "But honestly, I wasn't insulting your outfit. I like it. Hall & Oates. They're firmly planted in my top five yacht rock bands of all time based on album covers alone. They're the H2O that the yachts are floating on. H20—that's an actual album title."

"Oh, I know." I square my jaw. "God bless the album that gave us 'Man eater.'"

He tears his attention from the view and turns to me, his full lips agape. "That shirt isn't ironic? You like Hall & Oates?"

I look at him sideways, letting him talk to my profile. "'Maneater' is great, but personally, I'm partial to 'One on One' and I like to pretend my bridesmaid name Rosie is actually short for Rosanna."

His jaw drops and he clutches his chest like he's having a heart attack. "Like the Toto song?"

"My cat—the one who just had surgery—his name is Toto." I nod. "Named after the band, not the dog." I face him full on. "I was packed to go to Outside Lands this weekend, but I came here instead. That's why I'm wearing this." I run my fingers through the fringe on my skirt. "It's all I have.

I know it doesn't exactly say 'wedding,' but at least it's not white, so I'm not totally disobeying Max I-told-you-no-crochet." I grimace at the talking-to I'm doomed to receive.

He closes his gaping mouth and gives his head a little shake as he takes his buzzing phone out of Towaya's pocket and checks a text.

"Hey, were you able to get on Wi-Fi?" I ask. "Is there any chance I could borrow your phone to check on Toto and text my mom so she knows I made it here safely? My phone is dead, and I don't have an international plan."

"Sure. I have unlimited international messaging." He hands the phone to me. "Text as many people as you want. We can share my phone if you need to."

"Oh, I'm sure that won't be necessary. That would be so annoying for you always loaning me your phone. I'm sure I can figure out my Wi-Fi situation once my phone turns on, but maybe I can use yours just this once."

"Sure." He hands the phone over the railing to me. "It's yours any time you want it."

"Thank you. That's really generous." I take the device and disappear inside to retrieve the cat-sitter's phone number. My phone blessedly turns on long enough to get the numbers, but in the essence of time, and not wanting to risk international charges, I leave it on airplane mode and quickly check in with her, my mom, and Corina using Duncan's phone.

"Did you see that?" Duncan points toward the horizon where the sky fades from periwinkle to peach when I return to the balcony. The houses on the cliffs lining the indigo bay are cast in a blaze of pink from the evening sun. Golden lights flicker in their windows, winking like fireflies.

"What?" Steeling myself against the sight of his dark messy hair and Towaya-clad frame waiting for me at this magical hour in his terrace chair with his feet resting on the iron rail, I follow his gaze.

"A shooting star." He aims his beer at the sky, tracing its trajectory. "You should make a wish. This hotel is called *Il Desiderio,* after all. That means *the wish.*"

Snorting, I hand him back his phone. "No, thank you. The last time I made a wish it came true. The last time I wished, I wished for Ethan. I used up my fairytale. *This* is what happily-ever-after looks like." Pulling two pieces of my skirt's fringe out on either side of my hips, I curtsy.

"Seriously?" He jerks his chin toward me.

I shake my head at his silent request, not wanting to get into it. "It's a long story."

Duncan checks the time before slipping his phone into Towaya's pocket. "We've got a few minutes before you need to be at Franco's."

Twisting my necklace, I consider it.

It would *be nice to have someone understand my predicament . . .*

With a glance at the gentle smile on Duncan's lips, I sigh and sink into my chair. "Okay. Fine. Fish—Ethan was my brother Tyler's best friend from college. Ty brought Ethan along on our family vacation to Mackinac Island when I was seventeen. It was love at first sight. For me, anyway. I was super awkward and in a goth phase." My cheeks tingle and I press my hands to my face, still embarrassed at how hard I tried—and failed—to be cool. At how naïve I was. "And he—well, you saw him. That, but nineteen."

Duncan fans himself.

I giggle, liking that he's secure enough to admit another guy is attractive. "The week started out with me tagging along with Ty and Fish, I mean Ethan." I pinch the bridge of my nose, vowing to make a concerted effort to call him Ethan from now on lest I ruin this (his) wedding. "The three of us spent the first few days biking and swimming and eating fudge on the beach. The more time I spent with Ethan, the harder I fell. I knew I didn't stand a chance with him, but it turned out we had a lot in common. We really connected over music—we both loved Phoenix and the Yeah Yeah's, The XX."

"All great bands." Duncan tips his beer toward me in agreement.

"They really are." I clasp my hands around my knees and turn my attention to the waves before he derails me with music talk. "That week was the

Perseid meteor shower, and one night I was lying on the beach in front of the cottage we'd rented when I saw a shooting star. I was holding this necklace that Ty had just given me for my seventeenth birthday, and I wished that Ethan would kiss me." I show Duncan the oblong "starry night" charm I wear at my throat.

"And somehow my wish came true." Chilled, I absently rub my arms, still in awe. "The next day my brother suddenly felt like reading all the time, so Ethan and I spent the day together and he asked me to dinner that night. He took me to the Pink Pony. It was so beautiful there on the patio under the pink umbrellas overlooking the water. Everything had this rosy glow. We talked the whole dinner—were totally focused on each other—until out of nowhere a waiter popped up behind Fish like a creepy elf and asked in this high-pitched voice, 'Would you like sssoome sssticky toffee cheesecake?' It struck us as so funny it became our thing. We kept offering each other sssooomme ssssticky toffee cheesecake for the rest of the trip."

"And did you order sssome sticky toffee cheesecake?"

I smile at his impression. "We did. Later it became our code for making out."

Duncan covers his mouth with his palm, pretending to be shocked.

Shrinking in my seat, I continue the story before he gets a mental picture of me and Ethan making out. "But before that, we sang 'The Less I Know the Better' by Tame Impala at karaoke."

"That song has total yacht-rock potential." Duncan nods, knitting his brow like he's impressed. "I mean, even though there's no mention of the sea, it has the cartoon finger effect. It would entice me onto a boat."

"I get the feeling it doesn't take much to lure you onto a boat." I laugh.

He leans back in his chair, laughing with me. "Fair enough."

His unexpected yacht quirk sends a rush of warmth through me. From his tousled hair to the stubble along his strong jawline to the unconventional cool that is Towaya, there's something intriguing about him. I get the feeling he'd be welcome—would fit in—on *any* yacht.

Is it his secret yacht-sauce that makes bridesmaids fall at his feet?

A breeze kicks up, molding my shirt to my body. My skin tingling, I fluff the shirt out to keep my bralessness from becoming too apparent. "Anyway, when we got back to the cottage that night, before we went inside, he kissed me."

The giddy flutters I had then awaken in me now. I've relived that date a thousand times. It exists like a scene in a snow globe in my mind. It is the happy place that I escape to often, the memory awash in a swirl of sparkles. Maybe the reason I've never googled Ethan or let myself believe he could be married with kids—despite suspecting his life may have taken that trajectory—is because I'll do anything to keep that glitter from settling. I don't know what I'd do without it.

The ocean blurs into the sky as memory clouds my vision. I continue in a faraway voice. "We were inseparable that week. We really connected. It was like we got each other on a soul level." I sigh. "But it fizzled after we left the island. We only saw each other in person one more time even though we texted for a while."

And by "texted" I mean, sexted. At least, I tried to. He never reciprocated.

But I keep that bit of mortification to myself. "Then my brother died a few months later, and things got weird. Ethan stopped talking to me after the funeral."

And after I overheard some of Ty and Ethan's fraternity brothers laughing behind my back about my sexts.

There wasn't any nudity at least. Just me, a clueless teenager, trying desperately to look gothically provocative. But it still makes me sick that I was the butt of their joke.

I lower my brow. "The funeral was the last time I saw him."

Ethan was the driving force in my reinvention after that. Of course, he could never be seen with Goth Girl in real life. Dating me on an island where he didn't know anyone was one thing, but if we were to ever meet again, I wanted him to be blown away by me. I imagined a pretty lawyer type would fit into his world, so that's who I became.

But I don't tell Duncan that.

"Maybe I was too much of a reminder of my brother. I don't know. Nobody knew what to say to me back then, and I didn't know what I wanted to hear."

Duncan's bottom lip juts out and the pity I know so well crosses his face. "I'm sorry."

"It's okay." I stand and lean against the balcony railing. "It's been thirteen years. I still miss Ty every day, but life goes on. He always looked out for me, and I believe he still does, just in a different way."

"That's a great way to look at it."

"Thanks." Avoiding his gaze, I adjust my shirt again.

We fall silent. Hating that I'm such a buzzkill, I stare at the cliffside villas where a couple drinks wine on their terrace in the golden evening light, their heads bowed close.

If only that's all I had to do tonight.

They are a sobering reminder I should be on my way to Franco's Bar if I want to arrive a little early to hopefully meet Zoey. But having no desire to leave Duncan's side, I don't budge.

"I didn't think I'd ever *actually* see Ethan again," I say, attempting to lighten the mood. "And definitely not at a wedding where he's the groom and I'm his fiancée's hired bridesmaid who isn't even wearing underwear."

Duncan flinches, and if I didn't know better, I'd swear he blushes. "You're not wearing any underwear? That skirt is really short."

"I know." I survey the micro-mini and frown. "I knooooow. But I somehow managed to not pack any."

"I hope those people are enjoying the show." He gestures over the railing toward the pool.

Below us, dozens of people are lying on lounge chairs, staring at the sky.

With a gulp, I scoot away from the terrace edge.

He smirks as he takes his buzzing phone out of Towaya's pocket.

Pursing his lips, he nods as he reads whatever is on the screen before handing me the phone with a text from the cat sitter.

> Toto is great. He's healing nicely and eating well. He's the sweetest.

The text includes a picture of a cozy Toto curled up on a pillow. Even with the cone around his head, his eyes are happy little slits and he seems totally blissed out. I can almost hear him purring. My heart swells to bursting and I text her back a thank you. Whatever the cost, seeing Toto so content is worth it.

Church bells ring out, their enchanting song rising from the green-tiled cathedral beyond our balconies. I hand Duncan his phone back. "I should go." I need to leave now if I'm going to be on time for cocktails.

Before I disappear inside, Duncan catches my wrist and thrusts his credit card toward me. "Do you want to go downstairs and buy some underwear first?"

Pausing, I mull his offer over, my instinct to refuse. "I can't let you buy me underwear. Besides, there's no time. I don't want to be late."

"Gwen. Please. *I'd* be more comfortable if you were wearing underwear, and I think you would be too." He forces the card into my hand and closes my fingers around it. "It's okay to put your needs first once in a while. Let me help."

A jolt strikes my core when he says my name. I forgot he knows the real me, and I hesitate.

He holds my hand, his piercing gaze never leaving mine as he waits for my answer, though I imagine his eyes want to dip lower. The possibility sends my pulse off to the races. An image of him lowering me onto the taut, white bed ignites a burst of heat that expands low in my abdomen, and I am powerless to resist him.

"I owe you so much already," I say, disentangling my fingers from his, but taking the card. "And I don't know when I'll be able to pay you back."

"Don't stress about it." He shrugs before arching a mischievous eyebrow at me. "And you don't have to pay me back in cash. Maybe you could be The Wedding Bandits backup dancer or something. Can you keep a beat? You could play cow bell."

I grit my teeth. "Oh, I'm more of a 'cheering from the crowd' sort of girl. I don't even clap along, I sway. But don't worry. I'll find you cash. And thank you for this." I flap his credit card at him and back into my room to make a mad dash to the boutique before I let on what I was really thinking.

Chapter 9

Escape (aka The Piña Colada Song)

I'm beyond late for the party.

Once I was in the boutique, I realized I couldn't show up to cocktails looking all festivally. The prices on the dresses were astronomical, but I splurged by ditching my Chucks and adding strappy black heels to my extravagant undergarment purchase on Duncan's credit card. Having turned my Hall & Oates T-shirt inside out, I'm a bit more presentable as I slink around the green hedge that hides Franco's Bar from the street.

The party is in full swing under darkening skies as the last blaze of sun disappears into the water. Two dozen pretty people mingle on the rooftop patio that boasts 360 degree views of the twinkling hillside town and sea.

The guests all hold shallow, gold-rimmed martini glasses fizzing with orange bubbles and garnished with curly citrus peels. In the background, soft loungey music thumps with a slow hip-hop beat. Everyone is tastefully dressed in simple, classic silhouettes, instantly confirming that my outfit is still all wrong.

My stomach is in knots. Despite my best efforts, I'm letting everyone down. I duck behind a potted plant that is subtly up lit with some of the only lighting on the terrace. The moody dimness is a classic Max technique to make everyone look more attractive. I'm counting on it to make my ensemble morph into a play on a little black dress.

A warm breeze ruffles my black fringed skirt as I search the party for Ethan.

He's standing under a blue-and-white striped awning next to a bar lit with colorful glass lamps shaped like jellyfish. Dressed in a crisp white button-down with khaki pants rolled at the ankles, he's holding hands with a breathtaking girl who can only be Zoey. Her photo on Max's iPad didn't do her justice.

Her long, silky dark hair is tied in a low ponytail and secured with a white scarf printed with lipstick-red kisses. She's wearing a midriff-baring floral-print tank over a matching full skirt that shows off her petite frame. She is at once classic and new. Demure but sexy. The epitome of *Roman Holiday* for the millennium. She exudes sweetness, and it's clear I was right that Ethan would never end up with a goth future wannabe music influencer.

A lump rises in my throat.

Here I am in all my Outside Lands glory, still an eyesore in his world.

Ethan leans down and kisses Zoey's nose as one of the many photographers documenting tonight's event snaps their picture.

They're so beautiful, tears prick my eyes.

"Some couple, huh?" An older man, with dark, thinning hair and a round belly who looks like he could star in the next Scorsese mafia film joins me, gesturing with his bright orange cocktail.

"They are." Remembering I'm on duty, I smooth over my features. "You must be Uncle . . . " I know a drunk uncle when I see one, but at a loss for his name, I silently curse myself for still having not read the Who's Who packet.

"Al," he supplies.

"Nice to meet you, Uncle Al. I'm Rosie." I put on my best bridesmaid smile even though in this outfit I can't fully summon Rosie to take over.

"Rosie, eh?" His eyes freely rove over my T-shirt. "Are you the bride's friend or the groom's?"

Groom's.

"Bride's," I say, glad I've been asked that question so many times my words don't betray my thoughts. "I'm the maid of honor."

"Well, well, well. Lucky me." He chuckles. "Zoey has told us so much about you. Let's get you a drink. Aperol spritz?" He raises his glass.

"Oh, no, I shouldn't." My stomach growls as if reminding me the alcohol will go straight to my head.

He silences me, engulfing my hand in his.

"But you should. We're in Italy. Look at this place. It's meant to be enjoyed. *Life* is meant to be lived." He squeezes my fingers.

Mashing my lips together, I relent. "If you insist . . . Okay."

I can nurse it.

Uncle Al grabs a cocktail from a waiter carrying a tray full of them, and I watch as Zoey and Ethan are joined by his sister, Aubrey. I immediately recognize the tiny blonde girl channeling '90s Kate Moss. She wears a red-and-white striped bodycon dress with puffed sleeves and her hair is tied back with a kiss-print scarf that matches Zoey's.

"Look at all these yuppies." Uncle Al hands me my drink.

"Thank you." After accepting the shallow glass, I take a micro-sip. "Are yuppies still a thing?"

"We *are* about to get on a yacht." He guzzles a big swig of his spritz and smacks his tongue. "But what would you call them? Hipsters?"

"No." I cock my head, observing the refined crowd. "They're quiet luxury, for sure."

He laughs a big guffaw. "I don't know what that is, but they're not like us, that much I know." Elbowing my arm, he leans in close enough that I can smell the bittersweet Aperol on his breath. "You're a breath of fresh air. You don't play by the rules, do you? I know a fellow outcast when I see one."

Beyond Zoey, Ethan, and Aubrey, I spot Max spotting me and my outfit. His jaw clenches and he fixes me with a death stare I know well. *I* am the crisis. I'm surprised steam isn't shooting out of his ears. He starts toward me and my stomach drops.

"Actually . . . " I bite my cheek scanning the party for an escape route. "I don't want to burst your bubble, Uncle Al, but I'm usually a total rule follower." Based on Max's expression, if I mess up anything else this week, I'll be digging myself out of cat-penis debt for the rest of my life. If I live that long. I silently gulp.

Maybe I can hide behind Uncle Al.

Max would never lay a hand on a guest.

Uncle Al grins, clearly not buying it. "Have a few more of those—" He points at my drink— "and we'll see about that."

I give him the we're-friends-but-don't-fuck-with-me smile I've crafted for drunk uncles. "You are trouble, Uncle Al."

"You know it." He peers at my fringed skirt approvingly.

"I know I'll find out," I say, catapulting him to the top of my babysitting list for the week as Max closes in. "Now, if you'll excuse me, I just got here and I'm dying to say hi to Zoey. I'm sure we'll have time to talk, later." I pat his shoulder.

"I'm going to hold you to that." Uncle Al waggles a finger at me.

Don't I know that, too.

I duck behind Uncle Al and shrink down, making myself as small as possible as I tiptoe toward the safety of another group of guests, having every intention of slinking back to my hotel room to hide, but Zoey squeals before I can make a clean getaway.

"Rosie!" She rushes over and wraps her arms around me in a huge hug. "I'm so happy to see you." Her joy is palpable—so genuine that my lips part at her acting ability. I know for a fact this is her first time meeting me and even *I* feel like we're old friends.

After releasing me, she turns me to face Ethan and Aubrey, keeping her hand clasped in mine. "Rosie, this is my fiancé, Ethan, and his sister, Aubrey." She nods toward the Kate Moss blonde. "And this is Rosie. My maid of honor." Exhaling, she tilts her face up toward Fish. "Ethan. I'm so excited for you to meet her."

Ethan. It sounds foreign, and I remember he used to hate being called Ethan.

"We've met." Ethan eyes my questionable attire, lingering on my legs for a little too long, causing a dip in my abdomen. "It's good to see you again, *Rosie.*" His emphasis on my name sends a hot shiver down my spine.

Suddenly seventeen again, I freeze, searching his expression for signs of recognition, for something that signifies he knows we met *years*, not hours, ago. Hoping he's not remembering the pathetic girl from Mackinac Island, my chest tightens. This is *not* how I imagined our meeting again playing out, and I wish I could run.

Before I can take flight, Zoey squeezes my hand.

I startle to life and Rosie snaps into place. "It's good to see you again, too, Ethan. And Zoey! You look gorgeous as always." Swinging Zoey's hand out to arm's length to showcase her skirt, I try to remain professional and hold my trembling fingers steady.

"I'm so sorry I didn't get the memo about the dress code tonight." I grip my necklace with my free hand, my chest caving in apology.

Nearby, Max watches with his arms folded over his chest. His expression is a mask of calm, though I know inside he's a dragon trying to douse a fire.

Maid of honor shows up to Roman Holiday-esque yacht party in black fringe. Code Red.

Blood red. As in my blood is going to spill.

"Did you look in your closet?" Aubrey asks over the top of her orange cocktail. "I put all of your outfits in there this afternoon."

"Really?" I swallow, hard. "It was a long flight. Maybe I'm a little disoriented. I didn't see a closet." I widen my eyes at Aubrey, trying to gauge how much of an ally she might be.

"Traveling is *totally* exhausting. I always schedule two extra days whenever I go anywhere so I can adjust to the time." A slight southern accent softens Aubrey's supermodel sexiness. The salty-sweet combination is confusing, and I can't get a read on her.

Though it must be nice to be able to afford two extra days to acclimate to *anything*.

"The closets are a little tricky." Zoey moves closer to me, drawing us into a tighter circle. "They're on either side of the balcony."

I picture my room. "There's . . . framed paintings on either side of the balcony."

Zoey nods. "Those are the closet doors."

I plant a hand on my forehead. "I'm so sorry. I had no idea."

Max pretends to be passing by. He pauses as if he wasn't eavesdropping and just *happened* to overhear our conversation. "If you want to run up and change, you have time," he interjects. "We aren't walking down to the boat for another . . . " He consults his iPad. "Thirty minutes."

"You don't have to change, Rosie." Zoey lightly touches my arm. "You look great. I like you just the way you are. Besides. Have you tried any of the *antipasti*?" She points to a buffet near the bar. "I handpicked everything and the buffalo mozzarella ravioli with truffles and prawns . . . You *have* to taste them."

I bite my lip. On one hand, I'm starving. But on the other, Max will have my head if I compromise Zoey's vision for tonight by refusing to change.

And don't get me started on what will happen if I let on that I know the groom.

In this moment, I decide to spare myself the wrath of everyone at this party and make sure Ethan doesn't figure out who I am. The last thing I want is anyone mad at me. "But you spent so much time planning this, Zoey. I don't want to ruin the pictures," I say.

I don't want to ruin anything!

"I'll go change and be back before you know it. Then we can catch up."

Without waiting for an answer, I put my untouched drink on a passing tray, then slink past Max. He subtly narrows his eyes at me as I pass, and I wince. Now there's no way I can ask him for cash to pay Duncan back. He clearly thinks I'm a disaster.

And he's not wrong.

Chapter 10

Swayin' to the Music (Slow Dancin')

Back in my room, I press the corner of the wood-framed Renaissance painting on the wall to the left of the terrace. The three-painting panel pops open to reveal a safe and (*at last*) the minibar. Behind the picture panel to the right of the balcony, a closet is filled with outfits, each labeled with an event.

First in line is a red-and-white striped romper with a halter neckline. A white scarf printed with red kiss-lips is tied around the hanger's neck along with a tag that reads, "Welcome/Stargazing Yacht Party." I lay the outfit on my bed and wiggle out of my skirt and T-shirt. After tossing them aside, I squeeze into the romper tailored for Terra and do a little happy dance when I get the zipper up. The hem is shorter on me than it would have been on her, but at least it's not hugging my crotch.

I attempt to shove my D-cups into the halter built for a B until I'm forced to surrender to the fact the convertible balconette bra I bought downstairs does *not* work with this cut, so I'll still be going braless. A glance in the full-length bathroom mirror confirms I can't avoid side-boob, but I give up and tie my hair back with the scarf. This situation is what it is.

The closet offers me a variety of shoe options—espadrilles, flip-flops, strappy kitten heels—but I mash my feet into the white tennis shoes that seem the most boat friendly. I know better than to choose fashion over function. When my toes rebel at the one-size-too-small shoes, I opt for the flip-flops instead. My costume complete, I head out the door, starting to feel more like Rosie, more like the type of girl who fits into Ethan's world, despite the side-boobage.

I arrive back at the bar in time to dip below street level and join the parade of guests descending hundreds of ancient stairs that zigzag through the town toward sea level. Warm from my rush, I catch up to the girls in a narrow passage wedged between villa walls that rise far above my head. The sky is dark enough that stars are appearing, and the only other light comes from the occasional iron lantern providing a pool of yellow that spills over the path.

Zoey walks single file in front of Aubrey, their shoes shuffling against the stone steps. Ethan is nowhere to be seen.

"You finally made it." Aubrey squints back at me.

"Sorry about the mix-up." I finger the hem of my romper and fall into line. "It won't happen again. I figured out the closet."

Zoey turns. "You look beautiful. And I love that necklace." She grins.

"Oh." I clutch the charm at my throat as we descend. Every few feet a mysterious arched door or window appears in the stucco walls, leading, from the smell of it, to someone cooking a delicious, buttery, garlicky dinner. "I changed so fast I forgot I was wearing it. I can take it off."

"Don't worry about it." Zoey waves me off. "It's pretty and perfect for tonight. Feel free to wear it anytime."

I raise my eyebrows. She's so easygoing. Most brides would have bitten my head off for styling myself. She's definitely not the bridezilla I was expecting.

We round a corner and are rewarded with a slim glimpse between the walls of midnight blue sea speckled with the golden lights from yachts bobbing and dipping on the gentle waves. A few feet below us, Ethan leads a line of guys around another corner.

"Why don't you fill me in on who's who?" I ask. "Which ones are the groomsmen? I was super bummed I had to work and missed the engagement party. I've never met any of them."

"I can't believe you've never even met the *groom*," Aubrey says over her shoulder.

Ha.

Around the next bend, the path widens. We walk through a well-lit arched corridor lined with potted flowers and I make my way to Zoey's side.

"It just never worked out that they could meet." Zoey links arms with me without missing a beat. "Rosie is my Zumba buddy. We literally only get to hang out in class. And sometimes we grab smoothies or a salad afterwards. But we see each other twice a week, which is more than I see almost anybody. You *know* how busy I am. I never see anyone."

"Including my brother." Aubrey laughs, keeping pace just behind us.

The arch gives way to another narrow set of stairs with alcoves and tiny passageways jutting off in all directions. We choose one of the ivy-covered walkways that rounds a bend and opens to a full view of the sparkling hillside villas overlooking the dark water.

"We do our best. Our schedules are impossible." Zoey shrugs, leading us down a winding staircase with an iron railing covered in bougainvillea that guards us on one side. Again, we catch up to Ethan. "So, the best man is Ethan's twin brother, Payton." She points to the guy walking behind Ethan on the stairs below us.

Ethan has a twin?

My scalp prickles. I knew he had a sister and a brother, though I never knew what they looked like. He never mentioned his brother was his *twin*, and I'm having trouble reconciling this giant omission.

Payton is tall and broad-shouldered with a strong jaw like Ethan's, but that's where the similarities end. He's equally hot, but with unruly brown hair and olive skin, he's dark where Ethan is light. Despite wearing the khaki/button-down uniform dictated for the party by his brother, his pants are looser, slightly rumpled, his shirt unbuttoned one more button. He appears more relaxed than the perfectly pressed Ethan. His crooked smile and laid-back vibe make Ethan seem like a strait-laced suit by comparison.

"Fraternal twin, obviously." Aubrey bends to pat a fluffy gray cat that slinks past us and I'm reminded of Toto. My throat constricts and I reach for my necklace. Recalling the picture the cat sitter sent of him blissed out on a pillow, I swallow my anxiety and strengthen my resolve. I am here for Toto, not Ethan.

"The two guys in front of Ethan and Payton are the other groomsmen," Aubrey continues, as the cat jumps into the bushes growing into the side of the terraced stone wall to our right. "The four of them have been inseparable since middle school."

"And all three are single," Zoey says.

"Extremely." Aubrey grimaces as the path flattens out. "Not that it does me any good. They might as well be my brothers."

"Brothers" strikes a nerve, and with a pang, it occurs to me that *my* brother might have been at this wedding. Sometimes the grief still catches me off guard, and the knowledge that I'll never see Ty in this world again hits me like a tidal wave. For a moment, the sheer unfairness that I'm here and he isn't levels me.

As we descend the final stair and arrive amid brightly lit shops with flowy resort dresses hanging outside their arched doors, I'm overcome with the sense that he *is* here, that he's never left me. On either side of us, sidewalk cafés are packed with diners eating luscious ribbons of pasta and fresh seafood under ivy-covered trellises by flickering candlelight. The night is laden with an intoxicating mix of seaweed, wine, and basil. Ty would *never* miss this party.

Sidestepping vendors selling art on the walkway that runs the length of the rocky stand, we turn onto a boardwalk. I check in with each of my senses to calm myself.

Taste: salt. Smell: ocean. Hear: our feet thumping on the wood boards. Feel: the gentle breeze. See: I'm about to see Duncan.

The crushing emotion eases its stronghold on my chest, cracking open the armor shielding my heart and revealing pinpricks of light that glow through me, lifting my spirits. It's comforting that Duncan knows who I am in all this madness.

He's something of a life preserver.

Buoyed by the knowledge I'm not alone, I slip back into being Rosie.

Above us, crisscrossed hanging lights illuminate the boards that lead to a glowing white yacht in the distance. Tears prick my eyes, blurring the lights into a blob.

Zoey drapes an arm over my shoulders and gives me a quick squeeze, seeming to intuit that I need a hug. "I only mention their singleness because we're hoping nobody tries to hook up with any of the locals or staff. We have a lot of high-profile guests who like their privacy, and we don't want anyone trying to gain access to them. We're hoping to keep the wedding drama-free."

Assignment noted.

"I'm sure they'll be on their best behavior," I reply, and Zoey briefly drops her head to my shoulder.

We arrive at the massive, four-story white boat and are greeted by a steward. He takes each of our hands, guiding us individually across a small gangplank and aboard the ship where we're handed captain's hats. The bottom level of the boat has been transformed into a moody lounge with circular white couches. Candles inside glass globes flicker among white flowers on a white wooden bar. Toward the front of the ship, a buffet is piled with fried seafood and skewers piercing creamy mozzarella and the reddest tomatoes I've ever seen. My empty stomach growls.

But before I consider food, the soft strains of The Wedding Bandits covering "Sailing" by Christopher Cross drift down from an upper deck. Duncan is singing about finding faraway lands and I can't help but smile. He's right.

His voice is like a cartoon scent crooking a finger and beckoning me toward him. Some part of me likes being on the inside of his soundtrack, and a hot rush of goosebumps erupts on my arms.

I put on my captain's hat and practically float up the stairs. On the next open-air deck, a checkered dance floor is the centerpiece. Crisscrossed string lights form an "X" overhead and gas hurricane lamps provide the only other light so as not to distract from the star-swept sky. The band stands on a small stage near another bar where Duncan, in his captain's hat and full Towaya glory, is singing.

A glow expands in my chest at the sight of him. Coming to a stop, I tilt my face toward the stage, weirdly happy to see him.

His eyes are closed, and he's lost in the song, moving with it like it's part of him. He sings about getting lost in dreams and I'm instantly swept away. The party disappears into the shadows and he is the only light. He sucks me in.

"Oh, hello, wedding singer." Breathless, Aubrey arrives at my side, snapping me out of my trance. With her hand pressed to her chest, *she* seems weirdly happy to see him, too. Taking no notice of me, she saunters toward the stage.

Duncan taps out a beat on a wooden box with a mallet while Hayden plays a keyboard solo. Finding me in the crowd, Duncan holds back a smile and nods at my wardrobe change.

I smile back and he cocks his head, arching an eyebrow as if to say, "This could be you playing up here."

A little thrill shoots through me, and I bite back a laugh.

Aubrey stops in front of him, and it's my turn to raise a brow. He glances down at her.

My breath hitches, but I inhale, willing my lungs to expand as he takes her in. When he said people love Towaya, clearly, I was right in thinking he meant *chicks* dig Towaya.

And his bridesmaid of the week has been chosen.

I slowly shake my head, burying a twinge of disappointment.

Zoey appears next to me, her face tipped toward the sky. The moon casts her in a silvery glow, highlighting an innocence about her. I tear my attention from Duncan as he returns to the microphone. Forcing my focus to my job, I scan the deck for Ethan. He and Zoey should be making a grand entrance, but he's nowhere to be found.

It's all about the bride and here she is looking so pretty and hopeful on the first night of her wedding festivities and her groom is MIA.

WTF. My insides shrink, mirroring what Zoey must be feeling, and I slip into full Rosie-mode.

Ethan should be doting on her.

I use my annoyance with the groom to further suppress any guilt I have about not telling Max that Ethan is my long-lost love. I will *not* ruin this wedding. In fact, I will prove how much I've blossomed out of my gothic teenage years by making it perfect and getting my bonus. If Ethan ever figures out who I am, he can be blown away by *that*. Win-win for all.

"Do you want me to help you find Fis—ha—I mean Ethan?" Praying she didn't notice my blunder, I loop my arm through Zoey's and quickly keep talking. "Do you two want to make a grand entrance or anything?"

Her perfect lips part. "No. That's okay. We're not like that." She waves me off. "The less people are looking at us, the better. We just want everyone to have fun."

Quiet luxury. Right.

"But you *need* pictures of you two dancing together." I finally spot Ethan at a bar, drinking cocktails with his groomsmen. Max hovers nearby, no doubt analyzing when to tell the bartender to slip them a watered-down drink. "Come on. We need to make sure we get the shot before everyone has *shots*."

Zoey considers, her long dark ponytail swishing as her head bobs. "I guess you're right." She sighs and allows me to lead her to the groom.

"Ethan." I wedge myself in the center of the groomsmen while silently reminding myself that Ethan is a stranger. "Could we get a quick picture of you and Zoey dancing?"

His eyebrows pinch and he looks at Zoey, scratching his temple. "Is that what you want?"

Her shoulders meet her ears in a prolonged shrug. "I, um, think it would be nice."

A strange tension courses between the two of them and my focus darts back and forth as I attempt to figure out their dynamic. "It'll be super quick, I promise."

"Okay." He relents with a nod and takes Zoey's hand. "I'd love to. Be right back, guys."

I lead them to the center of the checkered dance floor. Flapping a hand at Duncan to suggest he play something special, I grab one of the photographers.

Duncan picks up an acoustic guitar and the band seamlessly transitions to "Dance with Me" by Orleans.

Any trepidation Ethan had seems to evaporate. As the yacht leaves the dock, cutting through small, sloshing waves, he takes Zoey's hand and spins her around with rehearsed precision. The chattering guests fall to a hush and form a circle around the pretty pair. I join their ranks.

Ethan pulls Zoey close. With gooey smiles, they stare into each other's eyes and rock back and forth, while Duncan sings about being surrounded by music and love. His voice wraps around me like a blanket, warming me against the crisp breeze that ruffles the scarf in my hair.

Across the dance floor Max nods his satisfaction, and I exhale. I may not have earned my bonus yet, but maybe I've erased one of my recent sins.

Duncan strums his guitar, commanding my attention. His eyes are closed and he's in his element, living out every note of the song. Feeling like everything is under control with Ethan and Zoey, I surrender and let the music carry me away. The yacht party fades into my periphery, a blur of faces beneath the midnight sky.

When Duncan opens his eyes, it feels like they find me, and my pulse quickens. I know it's his gift to make everyone feel like he's singing directly to them. But, deep down, I can't deny I want him to be singing only to me. As Duncan crosses the stage to stand next to Leo, the bass player, he remains the only star I care to see tonight. I couldn't look away if I wanted to.

The two bandmates share a microphone, harmonizing, and the rasp in Duncan's tones gets under my skin and into my bloodstream. My heart thumps like he's alive in my veins. And as he sings about his promise to take me anywhere I want, the hairs at the nape of my neck rise.

The yacht accelerates and, in this moment, with the wind tickling my cheeks and the Positano hills sparkling in the distance, I'd follow him anywhere if it meant feeling like this. Like I'm infinite potential that is still fully present in the moment.

I stand in a daze, swaying to the song until, too soon, Hayden switches from piano to harmonica, playing a solo that brings the tune to a close while Duncan plucks the final notes.

Duncan whispers, "Congratulations Zoey and Ethan," into the microphone. The deck erupts in applause, breaking the spell. Ethan kisses Zoey's forehead as I drift back to earth.

Zoey curtsies, then leads Ethan off the checkered floor. The band jams a funky beat while Duncan urges the rest of the guests dance.

"That was fun. Thank you for making us do that." Zoey grins, bringing Ethan to a stop in front of me.

"Yeah, it was great." Ethan drops Zoey's hand, and I can't help but notice the physical distance between them. I've worked a lot of weddings and usually the bride and groom are way more touchy-feely than this. In fact, Ethan's attention is already back at the bar with his dudes.

But Zoey doesn't seem to notice. She grabs both of our arms and tugs us forward. "Come on you two. We need to liven up this party, and you need to get to know each other."

I stiffen and dig in my heels. "Oh, um, I'm not a great dancer."

"Yes, you are. I've seen you Zumba." She winks.

"Right." I force a smile.

Ethan keeps his expression neutral and politely offers me his hand. "I'd love to dance if you're up for it."

I clench my jaw, but with no choice other than to accept, I place my fingers in his palm. A flash of heat surges through me as his hand closes around mine, and with a gulp, I allow myself to be pulled onto the dance floor.

Chapter 11
Give Me the Night

As soon as we're in the center of the floor, Zoey rushes off to grab the groomsmen and Aubrey, leaving me alone with Ethan.

Before I can run away, Ethan turns me to face him, blinking rapidly. For the briefest moment, I swear he's silently asking if we know each other. My heart seizes. But right then, the band—or I should say *Duncan*—chooses to launch into "Give Me the Night" by George Benson. This song *grooves* with a Pharrel-esque grind not easy to dance to for someone with questionable rhythm like me. Especially with a boat rocking beneath my feet and my long-lost first love searching my eyes.

After seven years of weddings, I can Cha-Cha Slide. I can Old Town Road. And I can clearly do The Wobble with the best of them. But when it comes to my own choreography, I'm a lost cause. There's a reason my website is called Shut Up & Sway. Swaying is my go-to move. Placing my hands on my hips, I tear my gaze from Ethan and glare at Duncan to see if he's serious.

He is. He looks straight at me, his eyes sparking.

I squint at him, and his lips stretch across his face, pressing into a knowing smile before he starts singing. He doesn't miss a beat. In fact, he punctuates that beat with a dance move of his own. Crossing his feet at the ankles, he spins around, Towaya swinging out behind him.

There is no doubt in my mind this song was chosen to make me as uncomfortable as possible. But zero percent of me is willing to let Duncan think he can get to me that easily.

Max is on the bridge deck above us, speaking with the boat captain. I weigh my options between ignoring Zoey's request that I liven up the party, suffering Max's "dancing only when necessary" wrath—especially with the groom—and accepting Duncan's challenge.

The bride demanded I dance . . . That sounds "necessary" to me.

Plus, if Ethan *does* find me familiar, giving this song my all should erase any correlation between current me and my former goth self. Seventeen-year-old me did not dance. Not even ironically.

And for some reason, Corina's voice is in my ears, telling me to surrender to the flow no matter how uncomfortable it seems. My gut insists the universe wants me to dance. So, I go for it. With a scowl at Duncan, I silently convey:

I am a professional. If you want me to dance, I. Will. Dance.

Zoey has been successful in her plight to bring guests onto the dance floor and is swaying with a man I would know was her grandfather if I'd read my packet. Aubrey darts behind them with Uncle Al hot on her tail calling, "Come on Pop-Tart, just one dance," and my path to victory becomes clear.

Placing my hand over my chest, I raise my gaze to Ethan. "I should save your sister." Before he can answer, I step between Aubrey and Uncle Al and offer him my hand. "I'll dance with you."

His face lights up. "Sure. If you think you can handle me."

I take a deep breath and glance one last time at Duncan. "Try me." Pretending I have a remote clue what I'm doing, I square my shoulders and dig deep into my nonexistent arsenal of dance moves. I bob my head to get the tempo then sidle up to Uncle Al like a stripper on a mission.

Ethan steps back to give us some space, nodding as he watches us with narrow eyes, his lips clamped shut against a bemused smile.

Uncle Al bursts into laughter and waves his arms in the air as I dance around him, rubbing my rear end against his and singing along incorrectly to the lyrics.

The guests form a grinning, cheering circle around us and with a peek at Duncan to make sure he's clocking *all* the "Vogue" hands I've got going on, I face Uncle Al. Gripping his shoulders, I swing my hair so it whips around and my captain's hat goes flying. I shimmy down into a squat and gyrate my hips back to standing. Uncle Al, for his part, makes a pretty good pole at this point; one that now stands rigid, watching with his mouth hanging open like he's afraid I'm going to pull back, get a running start, and launch myself into a *Dirty Dancing* lift over his head.

Ethan most certainly thinks I'm ridiculous as he claps along with the rest of the spectators. But it doesn't matter. The only thing I know is I will not back down. I will not give Duncan the pleasure of seeing me sweat, even though my cheeks are for sure flushed, and my forehead is glistening.

The song eventually—blessedly—ends and Duncan tips his captain's hat toward me in a silent touché as the music winds down behind him. Breathless, I respond with a minute shrug, like I dance like that all the time.

"Wow. Those were some moves." Uncle Al's cackle turns into a cough, and I lead him off the dance floor to a circular white couch so he can get some air. On our way, Zoey, who is being pulled somewhere by Ethan's twin, Payton, passes by. She briefly puts her hand on my arm. "You really know how to kick off a party. Thank you."

"Of course." I smile at her as she's dragged away, then return my attention to Uncle Al. "Let me get you some water." After making sure he sits, I hurry to the bar.

Max falls into step with me.

"What. Was. That?" he asks through gritted teeth.

I flinch. "Zoey asked me to liven up the party," I reply, keeping my expression neutral. "It's all about the bride."

"Yes. But also, dignity and grace for the person paying the bills. Zoey's father would prefer Uncle Al *not* be a spectacle." His voice is smooth and pleasant, but I don't miss the undertone that I won't be able to pay *my* bills if I don't reign it in.

"Got it. I'm sorry." I wrinkle my nose as we reach the bar. "I'm jet-lagged and a little punchy. I promise everything will be perfect tomorrow."

"It better be." With a curt nod, Max leaves me.

I order two Pellegrinos, glad for a minute alone to gather my thoughts. But before my mind clears, Ethan arrives at my side.

"Were those Zumba moves?" he asks me. Pointing to a bottle of bourbon, he signals the bartender.

"Um. Something like that," I mumble, heat seeping up my neck.

"Can Zoey dance like that?"

"Of course, she can." I inhale to slow my pulse, trying to picture poised Zoey gyrating at him. "She's never shown you her moves?"

"No. It would make her feel silly."

The bartender arrives with my waters and his bourbon. We're out at sea now, away from the light pollution of the coast. Beyond the bar, on the side of the stage, Max hands Duncan a piece of paper.

"Can I get you something else to drink?" Ethan asks me before sampling his bourbon.

"I'm good with this." I twist the cap off one of the green bottles and swallow a sip of bubbly water as Luigi passes by. Grabbing him, I ask him to take the other water to Uncle Al. Ethan is still at my side, and I know I shouldn't commandeer the groom, but curiosity gets the best of me.

"So, are you from Chicago originally?" Ethan leans against the bar, resting his elbow on the wood top once Luigi leaves.

Surprised he cares to know something about me—or maybe is trying to place where he knows me from—I shuffle back a step. "Born and raised."

"Cool. I'm from Charleston originally but grew up mostly in Chicago." Ethan raises his glass, toasting our Chicago-ness. "Where'd you go to college?"

Northwestern and University of Chicago for law school.

But I don't say that out loud. I keep my Rosie cover in place. "Davidson in North Carolina." Max chose a small college for the "Rosie" cover story because we're less likely to run into anyone else who's graduated from there. "How about you?" I cock my head, like I don't already know the answer, my nerves vibrating in anticipation. I've imagined this conversation hundreds of times, the moment he figures out who I am and his lips part in awe ... It's practically going exactly like I dreamed.

"Northwestern for undergrad. U of C for my MBA."

I had no idea he went to Booth, University of Chicago's business school. He'd already graduated by the time I attended Northwestern. The realization that he was getting his MBA at the same time as I was getting my JD ripples through me. We could have run into each other at any moment.

"I have some friends who went to Booth, too. How long ago did you graduate?" I'm desperate to know how close our paths were to crossing.

He squints skyward like he's mentally doing math. "Seven years ago. I worked for a while before going back to school." A single square ice cube clinks against his glass as he raises it to his lips.

I started law school seven years ago. If he graduated in summer and I started in fall, we just missed each other.

"And then I went to work for Giorgio as a business operations manager," he continues. "That's where I met Zoey."

"Right. I knew that." My stomach contracts. Never in my fantasies did he mention his fiancée. I can't help wondering what might have happened if he'd re-met me first, if we'd had a chance run-in on campus. Maybe I'd be a successful lawyer now. But I don't get to fully fall down that rabbit hole. Duncan interrupts.

"Welcome, everyone," Duncan says into the microphone. "What a night, don't you think?"

The crowd falls silent as everyone turns their attention to the stage.

"I've been asked to read a little bit about why we're out here." He consults the page Max gave him. "August tenth, here in Italy, we celebrate the Tears of Saint Lorenzo. It's known as the Night of Wishing on Falling Stars." He pauses, his forehead creasing as he silently reads ahead, and his gaze snaps to mine.

The night of what now? Wishing . . .

My breath stalls and we stare at each other for what feels like a full minute, his words slowly penetrating, taking effect like a drug.

I can't move, can't look at Ethan to see if he feels the impact of this night. He shouldn't. He doesn't know that once upon a time I wished on a star for him—and I can only focus on Duncan.

Duncan scans the page in his hand. "Okay. This is a lot of Italian. Luigi—come read this. You'll make it sound a lot prettier than I will."

Grinning, jolly ol' Luigi steps up to the microphone and takes the paper. "Tonight is *la festa di San Lorenzo.*" He pinches his fingers together, gesticulating as he speaks. "The feast of Saint Laurence. It is tradition that as the Earth passes through the Perseid meteor shower, the shooting stars that rain across the heavens are known as *le lacrime.*" He cups the air like it has mass. "The tears of the weeping saint."

The Perseid meteor shower?

Dizzy, I grip the bar to steady myself.

"We look to the heavens and say, '*Stella, mia bella stella, desidero che.*' Star, my beautiful star, I desire." Luigi peers out at the crowd, his eyes shining like starlight. "Tonight is the night all your wishes come true. Join us in wishing for all the happiness for the couple that has brought us together."

Everyone raises their glasses, and—as if on cue—the sky erupts in a cascade of shooting stars.

With a collective gasp, everyone applauds.

I almost pass out. The boat rocks beneath only me and it's a miracle I stay on my feet.

Luigi steps away from the microphone and Duncan returns with an acoustic guitar. He drapes the strap over his shoulder while widening his eyes at me like he's trying to jolt me out of the shock that has me rooted in place and staring blankly into the magical heavens.

Slowly, I shake my head, as if that could rattle some sense into my brain.

This can't be happening.

A star falls from the sky in a blaze of glitter.

What does it all mean?

The only thing I know for certain is, the universe makes zero sense.

Chapter 12

Moonlight Feels Right

Ethan is replaced by an intoxicated Uncle Al who insists we dance, albeit slowly this time.

"You've changed. I liked you the way you were," Uncle Al slurs. Eyeing my wedding-party approved romper, he spins me around while Duncan sings "Cool Change" by Little River Band.

Oh, why can't Uncle Al be my biggest problem this week?

Eventually, I manage to lead Al to the white-cushioned lounge chairs at the front of the boat. We wrap ourselves in fluffy fur blankets and eat spicy garlic-parmesan-basil popcorn while the stars perform their show in the sky. He regales me with tales of his childhood growing up in Chicago, making sure I know his brother followed in *his* footsteps. Giorgio learned the ropes of the restaurant biz while working at *Uncle Al's* pizza place, and not the other way around.

For the most part I'm grateful I don't have to talk and am happy for the distraction from my own history repeating itself. I can't begin to understand what has reunited me with Ethan on this night of wishing on the Perseid meteor shower. Letting my eyelids grow heavy, I shut out the patchwork sky.

When the boat docks, I stay back to find Zoey's grandmother's purse that she left somewhere on the yacht while the guests file back onto land for the steep return to the hotel. By the time I find the bag in one of the restrooms and hand it to Luigi to deliver, there's nobody left aboard but the band and me. Before I walk across the gangplank to begin my trek to bed, Duncan catches my wrist.

"Payback." He hands me a guitar case.

I do a double take but accept the instrument. "You want me to carry this up all those stairs?"

"Gotta start somewhere." With a shrug, he holds out his hand. "I'm guessing you got what you needed?"

Hyper-aware of the miniscule bits of Italian lace beneath my romper, I flush and quickly fish his credit card out of my pocket. Fortunately, he keeps his gaze trained on my face. If his eyes were to dip toward the region we're talking about, I'd lose it.

"Yes. Thank you." I plop the card onto his open palm.

His lips twitching into a smile, he steps backwards as he shoves the card into his jeans pocket, creating much needed space between us.

Max and the guests have long since disappeared and even though I'm on thin ice, I decide it's unlikely anyone will see me walking back with the band. Even if they did, it would make sense for them to escort me to the hotel after I was delayed by a purse hunt.

"Okay." I lift the strap on the guitar case over my head and drape it across my body. "What else can I help with?"

"You can open this." He hands me a bottle of prosecco.

"You don't have to tell me twice." I triple-check the boat and beach to make sure Max is nowhere in sight, then twist the cork until it pops open. "I mean, what is happening?" I raise the prosecco to the heavens. "The night of wishing on falling stars? The Perseid meteor shower? The stars have aligned to fuck with me." I take a giant swig of the crisp bubbly liquid straight out of the bottle.

"Well, yeah. There's that." He laughs, sliding his arms through a guitar case so he can wear it like a backpack before picking up another instrument case. "Ready?" He motions with the case toward the distant cliff stairs. "The rest of the band won't be far behind us."

"As ready as I'll ever be." I picture the hundreds of steps between me and my bed and take another sip of prosecco before offering him a drink. "Want some?"

"Yeah." He swallows a mouthful and carries the bottle.

We cross the gangplank. Glimpsing him in the soft glow of overhead string lights with the guitar slung on his back and the ocean lapping at the shore behind him makes my inner fangirl flap to giddy life. She fizzes up inside me. Starstruck after his performance that totally transported me, I can't believe I get to be alone with him and it hits me *he's* a star. Every song in the set tonight could top my blog's list of sway-worthy covers. Having sway is the highest compliment I can give something.

But I don't tell him that. "That was a great performance." Keeping pace next to him on the boardwalk, I keep my music blogging aspirations to myself. "It was so romantic. Transportive. Cartoon fingers. You were right."

"You can't say I didn't warn you." He laughs. "That was like my dream set. I can't believe we actually got to yacht rock a yacht."

It's nearing two o'clock in the morning. The white lights zigzagging above our heads extinguish, plunging us into darkness. The moon is low in the sky and with only the yellow pools of light from the other boats bobbing in the bay for competition, the stage is set for the lustrous grand finale in the sky.

"So, that's your thing. Yacht rock." We step onto the beach, our feet crunching over the rocky sand.

Most of the restaurants lining the shore have turned off their lights. It's so dark, I can't fully make out his expression, but he walks close enough to my side that he nudges my arm with his elbow. My skin tingles at his touch.

"Yeah. I might even start a Yacht Rock podcast someday . . . *We're Yacht-Worthy*. I'd discuss in depth what makes a song yacht rock."

"Or not."

"Exactly."

Reaching the stone path leading up the hill, we begin our ascent around a stucco restaurant. My thighs immediately revolt, burning under the guitar's extra weight.

"If I could get Davis Collings to be my co-host . . . He's my idol, the messiah of yacht rock, in my opinion." He lets out a low whistle. "Look out, world. I'd be sailing on *my* yacht, the *Saint Christopher Cross*, in no time." Spinning around, he faces me, walking backwards and gesturing with his instrument case at the dozen boats scattered across the sea behind us. "Saint Christopher is the patron saint of boating."

"And Christopher Cross is the patron saint of yacht rock. It's brilliant." Already winded from the climb, my breath comes out in little puffs as it dawns on me that Duncan and Christopher Cross have a lot in common. "Did you know Christopher Cross got his start in a San Antonio cover band called—"

"Flash." He finishes my sentence. "Yes, I do know that. The question is why do *you* know that?"

"I have a weird obsession with how musicians got their start." I shrug. "I just turned thirty and I always feel like I should have more of my life figured out by now. I guess it gives me hope to know that lightning can strike and life can come together in an instant. And see? Christopher Cross's dream came true, so why can't yours? What's stopping you from starting your podcast?"

"I don't know. Who would listen?" He turns back around and side by side, we climb a narrow set of time-worn stairs. "There are other yacht rock podcasts out there. I'd *need* Davis Collings to do it with me for anyone to pay attention."

"You don't know that nobody would listen unless you *try*. I'm sure you have a unique perspective." I bump my shoulder against his. "Start your podcast."

"Easy for you to say, Miss I Used Up My Fairytale." He taps my hip with the prosecco bottle. "Tell me, did you make a wish for Ethan to recognize you on this night of wishing on falling stars?"

We turn up a steep corridor with steps embedded between high stone walls.

"No way." I pant. "I'm never wishing again."

By the time we reach the top of the staircase, we're both breathing hard. Duncan tugs me into a stone outcropping that offers sweeping views of the sky and sea. Far below us, the sea laps against the rocky sand in sloshing little waves.

Leaning into a private alcove that hides us from view of the stairs, we take a breather. "How can you ignore all this synchronicity, though?" he asks, handing me the prosecco. "Has history ever repeated itself like this?" He moves his hand in an arc across the starry blanket above us. A warm breeze carrying his spicy-citrus scent ripples off the water as if he conjured it. "Don't you think this feels meant to be? What if the first fairytale isn't over and it just needs one more wish to nudge you toward happily ever after?"

"You're a romantic." I tug on Towaya's sleeve and lower his arm. "You probably believe in magic, too."

"Maybe I do." He shrugs.

"'You Can Do Magic.'" Desperately wanting to change the subject, I ask in a mock-serious radio announcer voice, "Yacht or not?"

He thinks for a second. "Yacht. And stop trying to distract me. I don't think it hurts to make a wish."

"But Ethan is getting married." I groan and swallow a sip of prosecco. "I can't break up his wedding. Besides, Max would fire me, and I need the money."

"You're *not* going to break up the wedding." His shoulders collapse under the weight of the obvious. "Or lose your job. But you should tell him who you are. Get some closure. Maybe to open the door to your future, you need to resolve your feelings about the past."

Picturing myself confessing, I hang my head. "I don't want to make anyone uncomfortable." I exhale, concentrating on adjusting my halter top so it covers more side-boob. "And my job is to *prevent* drama, not *be* the drama."

"But maybe you need to choose yourself for once." He takes the prosecco back from me and swallows a mouthful. "What do *you* want?"

Pausing, I consider.

It's not that I want to win Ethan back . . . I just want him to realize what he missed out on.

But that need for validation sounds so pathetic, there's no way I'm admitting it to Duncan.

I wrinkle my nose. "You sound like my roommate. She's been trying to unblock my chakras to help me figure out what to do with my life. She says I need to surrender to the now so I can attract what's meant for me—whatever that means."

"Why don't you try it?" Shrugging, he returns the bottle to me. "Trust the moment. See where it takes you. Make a wish on the next shooting star. It's easy."

Burning overhead in a fiery ball, a star punctuates his statement.

"I'll show you." He tips his chin toward the sky, and I can't help but trace the outline of his profile, his smooth, bronze skin in the night.

But then I realize what he's doing, and I clamp my hand over his mouth. "Don't you dare," I say through gritted teeth.

"Too late," he mumbles against my palm.

I drop my arm to my side, my chest caving. "You wished? For me?"

"Yep." He nods and wavers, seeming unsteady, but quickly regains his composure.

My eyes bulge. "What did you wish?"

He shrugs. "Can't tell you. Then it won't come true."

I could strangle him. "Don't tell me you wished for Ethan to find out who I am."

Smirking, he shakes his head and zips his lips. "I still think you should tell him."

"Not happening." My shoulders slump. "Did you wish for me to hate you? Because it's working," I mutter.

Laughing, he raises his palms skyward.

"Ugh." I grunt and shove the prosecco bottle into his chest. Folding my arms over my waist, I stalk onto the path.

Duncan falls into step next to me and we continue the climb in silence. The only sound other than our shuffling footsteps is the waves lazily rolling on the beach far below. My feet ache with just thin flip-flops separating them from the stone staircase.

Duncan nudges my arm. "Hey. If you want, next shooting star, you can make a wish for me."

"No, thank you."

"Come on. Maybe if you make a wish for someone else it creates goodwill in the universe. It could activate that future your roommate is helping you to be open to. Besides. It's a wish for me, not you, and I'm willing to risk the karma."

Rolling my eyes, I come to a stop, hating to admit he might be right. Corina probably would side with him.

"My roommate also says I'm going through a Saturn return, so I'm pretty much screwed. Are you sure you want to risk being part of that?"

"What's a Saturn return?"

"It's when Saturn returns to where it was in your astrological chart when you were born. It's a life test, apparently. Everything is supposed to fall apart. It happens every thirty years. Fun, right?"

"Hey, I'm thirty, too . . . " He clenches his teeth.

"Buckle up. You too could be the proud owner of a new cat penis."

"Don't wish *that* for me."

I can't help laughing.

He laughs with me, then sobers. "But why don't you try surrendering. See where life takes you. Where does it feel like it wants you to go now?"

Closing my eyes, I let the salty breeze wash over me and listen to my gut. "It feels like it wants me to make a wish for you," I admit.

"Then do it."

"Fine." I mock-glare at him. "It probably won't come true, but if this activates some sort of curse, remember you asked for it."

His teeth flash pearly white as he smiles. "I accept all responsibility."

Another star bursts across the heavens. I take a deep breath. Tilting my face to the sky, I close my eyes and grip my necklace, concentrating like I did on a night like this all those years ago. My mind clears and, my temples buzzing with energy, I wish the first wish that comes into my mind.

I wish Davis Collings would make Duncan's Yacht Rock dreams come true.

The wish rushes through me. Letting my lungs deflate, I open my eyes. Duncan's pretty face comes into focus. "It's done."

"Don't tell me what it is." He crosses his arms over his chest. "Then it won't come true."

The tension goes out of my neck, and my mood unexpectedly lightens. "I'll never tell. Not unless it *does* come true."

"Deal." Taking my hand, he shakes on it. "We should write our wishes down so we can prove it when they do."

Balancing the instrument case against a stone guard rail painted with a mural of the Madonna, he hands me the prosecco bottle, then digs around in the case's side pocket until he produces a notepad, pen, and plastic bag full of picks. He flips through notebook pages scrawled with what looks like lyrics. I strain to glimpse if they're original lyrics, but the pages turn too quickly, and I can't make out the words. Once he finds a blank page, he rips one out and hands it to me with the pen. "Ladies first."

"Really?" I lower my brow.

"Really." After setting the case down, he leans casually against the mural, then shoves his hands into Towaya's pockets.

"Okay." With a slight shake of my head, I stoop and set the prosecco bottle aside. Using the side of the case as a desk, I cover the page with my hand so he won't see me write out my wish. When I finish, I fold the paper into a square and hand him the pen.

He turns his back to me, props the notebook against the wall, and writes his wish inside before ripping the page out and folding it up. After dumping the picks into the pocket of the instrument case, he places his paper inside the empty plastic bag. "Put your wish in here too. We can put them in the prosecco bottle for safe keeping. We'll have to break the bottle to get them out so there's no peeking."

"Is there much prosecco left?" I drop my wish inside the bag on top of his.

"A little. Bottoms up." He takes a drink before handing the bottle to me.

We pass the prosecco back and forth until it's empty and I'm feeling fuzzy. Then he rolls up the plastic bag and shoves the whole thing down the bottle's neck. The wishes slide to the bulbous bottom.

"You can hang onto it." He offers me the bottle. "I trust you."

Accepting the bottle, I peer through the green glass at the wishes. For a moment, I'm floating in a sea of possibility. Then I remember who I'm wishing with. Refusing to be another doting member of his flock, I put a cork in my optimism. "Do you do this with all the bridesmaids?"

"What?" He startles and his eyes widen like I've slapped him. But the expression quickly passes, and his features soften. He tips his head to the side. "Make wishes?"

Cursing my rash tongue, I lower the bottle, letting it hang at my side. "Yeah," I concede, my throat thick.

His eyelashes flutter rapidly. To my surprise, he grips my shoulders. My heart seizes as he brings me in close and bumps his forehead against mine. "Gwen, I've never wished for any bridesmaid but you," he whispers.

His breath is hot on my cheek and chills erupt all over my body. Overcome, I stiffen. "Good."

I duck out of his grasp. Starting up the stairs again, I inhale the sweet blossom-scented vines that curve overhead to slow my pulse. The passage narrows so we're only able to fit single file, so I walk ahead of him.

"You know what we need?" His voice drifts up from behind me. "Stakes. Whoever's wish comes true first wins."

"Wins what?" I ask, my legs wobbly from climbing—at least that's what I tell myself.

"Bragging rights. The winner earns the title of Wishmaster and can lord their superiority over the Wishminion for the rest of our lives."

"You are *so* weird," I say, over my shoulder, sobering a bit now that there is some distance between us.

"Or, even better, how about this: If your wish for me comes true first, I'll pay Toto's vet bills. And if my wish for you comes true first, you owe me that amount of legal services."

I screw up my face. "I can't give you $2,980 worth of legal services. I'm not a lawyer."

Yet. He could be my first client . . .

"But you went to law school. You could still negotiate a contract."

"I guess."

But there's no way. I can't make Davis Collings come true! And I'd never let him pay for Toto.

"How do I know I *want* your wish for me to come true?" I glance at him over my shoulder.

"That's true." His lips curve into a wicked grin. "You should have thought about that before you let me wish a career as a personal injury attorney for you. I can see your face plastered on a billboard over the inbound Stevenson now . . . " He sweeps his palm overhead.

My jaw sags. "Exactly. What if I don't like your wish *and* I then owe you legal services. I feel like we need a deactivation clause." Reaching the top of the stairs, I pause to catch my breath.

"Good point. You should be a lawyer." His eyes twinkle.

I roll mine.

"How about this?" He reaches me. "The person who wished the first wish to come true—the Wishmaster—also gets to keep the prosecco bottle. Then it's up to that person to decide if—and when—they read the Wishminion's wish for them. They can wait for it to come true or read it if they want to deactivate it."

I think for a second and decide it sounds like a good offer. "Well, in the event you wished for my face to be plastered across a billboard, I would love to read—and deactivate—your wish, so I like it." I hold out my hand. "Deal."

We shake on it. With his fingers still gripping mine, we continue around a corner and come face to face with Ethan.

I gasp. Coming to a halt, I drop Duncan's hand and step sideways to create as much space as possible between us while hiding the prosecco bottle behind my back.

Ethan is leaning against a stone alcove in a circle of yellow light from a hanging lantern. Like a spotlight from the heavens, it illuminates his Grecian godliness.

"Rosie. I know it's late." He steps forward, blocking my path to the hotel. "I was waiting to see if you have a minute to chat. It won't take long."

"Sure. Of course." My limbs are shaking, and if I wasn't sweating from the climb, I am now. But somehow, I manage to keep my voice steady.

With my heart in my throat, I peek at Duncan to see whether he wished for Ethan for me.

He remains silent, his expression frustratingly neutral as he takes his guitar from me. "I think it's time for me to *surrender*." His eyebrows flash up. "Have a good night, you two. I'll see you at the limoncello tasting tomorrow." With a nod, he continues past Ethan toward the hotel, leaving me to stare after him, terrified his wish might already be coming true.

Chapter 13

I'm Not in Love

Once Duncan is out of earshot, Ethan leads me to a stone bench tucked under a grape arbor in the alcove.

"I know it's late and you must be exhausted." He sits and pats the spot next to him. "But something is bothering me, and I don't want to be up all night trying to figure it out."

My stomach drops, but I take a tentative seat, keeping a respectable distance between us. I can't hide the prosecco bottle any longer and the glass dings on the stone bench as I set it next to me. "I was just bringing this to the hotel to recycle it," I say by way of lame explanation. "But how can I help you?" I try to keep my voice light, innocent, but I'm quaking on the inside, certain this is it. This is the moment I've been dreading/dreaming of, and I can't run.

He drums his fingers on the bench, studying me. "You're really familiar. Do I know you? Have we met before?"

Chilled that he didn't instantly recognize me, my instinct is to lie. To play dumb. To say I have a familiar face. But I've reverted to my seventeen-year-old self and am having trouble forming sentences. I tug on the romper's hem, concentrating on shielding my thighs against the rough stone bench.

It turns out I don't need to say anything. I must be giving off seventeen-year-old vibes because his blue eyes suddenly brighten (if it's even possible for them to get brighter) as he observes my necklace. He snaps his fingers. "I've got it. I know who it is." He points at me. "Are you Tyler Watson's little sister?"

A wave of dizziness washes over me and my chest collapses.

He doesn't remember my name?

It never occurred to me that the week we spent together didn't mean as much to him as it did to me. That his knowing who I am isn't enough to sabotage the wedding. That he hasn't been carrying around a deep-seated desire to make things right after he ignored me at the funeral. After his friends made fun of my sexts.

OMG.

My cheeks burn and, grasping tightly to Rosie, I throw myself into character.

"Oh, wow." I clasp the charm at my throat and my face lights up like a deranged jack-o-lantern. "I don't remember the last time someone called me Ty's little sister."

A shadow darkens his features, and he clears his throat. "Right. Probably not. I'm sorry. I actually think about Ty all the time . . . " He doesn't meet my gaze, and I sense the pity I know so well.

"It's okay to mention Ty, Ethan. It was a long time ago." I gingerly pat his muscular shoulder, keeping Rosie plastered across my features.

Focusing on his hands that are folded in his lap, he nods. "I miss that guy. He was like a brother to me. We were so similar."

We fall silent and after a moment, he peers up at me and cocks his head. "But your name isn't Rosie."

My lungs deflate and, dipping my chin, I whisper the words I've imagined saying to him for a dozen-plus years. "No. It's Gwen."

He closes his eyes and when he reopens them, recognition lights them. "That's right. It's all coming back to me. Tame Impala." He laughs, shaking his head. "I haven't thought of that night in forever. I think that's the last time I sang karaoke. And you! You look so different. You've really grown up."

Different? Grown up?

These are not the reactions I've long imagined. A lump forms in my throat, but I force myself to swallow it.

"What a coincidence that you'd meet Zoey at Zumba. The universe amazes me sometimes. I think seeing you in that fringe outfit at the cocktail party is what made me remember. It's more like the you I used to know." Pausing, he furrows his brow. "But if your name is Gwen, why are we calling you Rosie?"

The energy shifts between us. Suddenly, I'm on trial, like maybe he thinks I'm a stalker who infiltrated his life to embezzle money or blackmail him or something.

My mouth goes dry. "Well . . . " Wringing my hands, I search for a way to keep my cover, keep my paycheck and bonus. I want to keep Zoey's secret, I really do. But I don't see a way around telling him without making things more complicated. Maybe the jig is up.

Biting my lip, I confess. "The truth is, I'm a professional bridesmaid. Zoey hired me to be her maid of honor. Actually, she hired my coworker Terra, but Terra broke her foot and I'm the last-minute replacement."

"A professional bridesmaid." He raises his eyebrows. "That's a thing?"

"Yep." I press my lips together, waiting for him to send me home. "I'm here to keep the wedding drama free."

He taps his foot. "That sounds like Zoey. Appearances are *everything*. She has trouble being vulnerable, even in front of me. Do her parents know about this? Are you *sure* the original bridesmaid broke her foot? Because I wouldn't put it past Giorgio to find a beautiful girl from my past to test my dedication to his empire."

I flush that he called me beautiful, and my seventeen-year-old heart is off to the races, but I do my best to set him straight. "I think they know, but truly, there's no conspiracy. Us knowing each other is a total coincidence, I promise." Clasping my hands over my chest, I will him to believe me. "I'm sure they just want someone totally focused on Zoey to help the week go smoothly." And even though I don't want to, on an inhale, I drive the final nail into my own coffin. "But I understand if you want me to leave. Technically, I *should* excuse myself because it's against my employment contract to work a wedding where I know any member of the guest list, let alone the wedding party—"

Ethan raises a hand to stop me. "No, no. I believe you. Stay. Please. I won't tell anyone we know each other if you don't. Zoey is under enough pressure this week. It would look worse for her to have to explain that you left because you knew me or because she hired you. I don't want to get in the way of what Giorgio wants for his daughter. If you don't mind, can you just be her maid of honor? It will be easier for all of us." His expression softens, and he half smiles, exposing the dimple in his cheek I used to love to trace with my finger. Not that he remembers that.

The tension releases out of my spine. "Of course. Whatever you want. But, if you could also make sure Max doesn't find out we know each other, I'd appreciate it. He'd fire me for sure if he found out I knew you and didn't say anything."

"I won't tell anybody. I promise. Not even Zoey. It'll be our secret. Just between you and me. And even if Zoey somehow finds out, we can pretend we don't remember each other, right?"

Except Duncan knows I have a past with Ethan . . . but he can keep thinking Ethan doesn't remember me. If I keep my agreement with Ethan secret from Duncan, Ethan can at least play dumb if anyone finds out we know each other. Not that we have to worry about that because neither of us are going to tell anyone . . .

"Totally." I nod.

"So, we have a deal?" He offers me his hand.

"Deal," I agree, placing my fingers in his palm. "I won't tell anyone you know me," I clarify to cover my having already told Duncan I know Ethan.

He clasps both hands around mine and we shake on it.

"This is great, actually," he says, standing. "Ty would have totally been in the wedding and having you here is the next best thing."

My insides crumble ever so slightly, but I pull myself together and stretch my bridesmaid smile across my face. "I'm so happy for you. And I know my brother would be too."

"He was the best, wasn't he?" Grinning, he wraps me in a hug, and I do my best not to collapse against the heat of his firm chest.

"Now, why don't you head to the hotel first. I'll hang back here." He gives me a squeeze, then releases me. "Wouldn't want it to look like we're coming back together."

Gripping the prosecco bottle, I take an unsteady step toward the stairs. "Good thinking. Goodnight, Ethan."

"Goodnight, Rosie."

With a fake smile and a wave, I turn my back on him. The second I start up the stairs my face falls.

OMG. What just happened?

In a daze, I hurry back to my room, desperate to get inside and scream into my pillow.

Chapter 14

You Can Do Magic

When I arrived at my room last night, two envelopes were waiting for me. Inside the first envelope was the itinerary and "Who's Who" with a note scrawled across the top in Max's handwriting that said *Please read.* The second envelope contained a note from Zoey asking me to meet her for breakfast.

And so it is that I arrive at La Sponda, a restaurant at nearby Le Sirenuse hotel, at 8:15 a.m., my stomach flip-flopping that Zoey somehow knows about my interlude with Ethan last night. Squinting past the green ivy climbing the walls framing the restaurant's arched floor-to-ceiling windows, I scan the crowded outdoor patio for her.

She stands next to a sundrenched table overlooking the bay and cliffs. Removing her cat-eye sunglasses, she waves me over. I cross the green tiled floor, heading out French doors toward her. My full coral skirt ripples around my calves and I catch bits of Italian conversation I don't understand as I weave through tables on the terracotta terrace.

Today the bridesmaids are channeling Sandy from *Grease* and I'm rocking a white tee tucked into a high-waisted skirt paired with too-small espadrilles. My toes are crunched inside the shoes, but I'm happy I can actually wear a bra for once.

"Hi." Reaching the table, I grin and hug Zoey like we just got through an intense Zumba session.

While I am embodying "sweet" Sandy, Zoey's vibe hints at Sandy post cool-girl makeover. Her navy striped off-the-shoulder tee shows off her delicate collar bones and a full orange skirt accentuates her miniature waist before flaring out just above her knees. With her high ponytail and espadrilles, she again is at once classic and new.

She hugs me back. "Thank you for coming."

"Thank you for inviting me." We part, and I slip into the iron chair across the table from her. "I was hoping we'd get a chance to chat. Normally I'd know everything there is to know about you by now, but given the circumstances, I'm flying blind. I'd love to review your expectations of me."

A waiter hurries over and moves an umbrella closer to our table to shade me.

Zoey nods. "I picked this place so we could be alone. Less chance of wedding guest interruptions at this hotel. And I ordered for us. I hope you don't mind." Wiggling her fingers, she gestures at the waiter who promptly brings me a cappuccino with a foam heart swirled on top. "We have the pizza-making excursion this afternoon, but you have to try the lemon-basil olive oil cake. Made with Le Sirenuse's home-grown lemons." She pushes a platter piled with a variety of flaky pastries toward me.

I choose a tiny butter-yellow cake dusted in powdered sugar and dotted with white basil blossoms.

"It's springy, yet dense, lightly sweet, and *so* moist." Zoey narrates as I sample the cake. My eyes roll back into my head at the decadent morsel.

She watches my reaction. "They found the perfect balance of lemon and basil, don't you think?"

"All I can say is this is incredible." I exhale and devour another cake. "But you described it perfectly."

"I hope so." She smiles. "Finding perfect bites is kind of my job."

"Congratulations." I cradle my coffee cup to keep from grabbing a third cake. "I heard you're getting your own Food Network show. That's so exciting."

She sips her cappuccino, a slight breeze blowing a wisp of hair across her cheek. Brushing the strand away, she nods. "It's something I've wanted since I was a little girl. I grew up on the food scene and my dad has, what, ten Food Network shows he either stars in or produces? I've always seen myself filling his shoes." She delivers the lines with rehearsed precision.

Normally, I would have binged her social channels before meeting her. I fidget with my necklace, flinching that I'm so unprepared. "I'd love to watch your show. I've never seen any of your work," I admit.

She could probably teach me a thing or two about monetization, about what content works.

"It's okay." She waves me off. "Not many people have. My social accounts are mostly a formality."

Or not.

I force a smile until my jaw aches from clenching my teeth. Everything seems so easy for her. She is the epitome of what Ethan wants in a wife *and* she gets an instantly viable brand without having to prove her concept first.

To stop comparing her perfect life to my disaster, I picture Toto, concentrating on the reason I'm here. "You're probably not even thirty yet and your dream is coming true. *And* you're getting married. You must have done something right in a past life. Tell me, how did you meet Fi—" I shake my head. "—Ethan."

She concentrates on swirling her spoon around in her coffee. "My dad introduced us on set at a taping of *Giorgio's Kitchen*. Ethan's father is an investor in one of my dad's restaurants, so they go way back. That's why Ethan is getting promoted to CFO." Her eyelashes flutter as she peers up at me. "The Conners are a great family. I'm really lucky to be gaining Payton as a brother and Aubrey as a sister since I'm an only child. They're kind of what I always wished for."

She sounds like she's trying to convince herself as much as she's trying to convince me. My heart pounds at the possibility she's making a mistake with Ethan, that they aren't meant to be. Terrified of what that information could mean for me—that maybe Duncan is right, that my fairytale is still possible, and worse, out of my hands—my shoulders knot.

But then she continues. "Ethan is amazing. Stable. Kind. He's really thoughtful. Like the other night he stopped at my place on his way home and brought me cashmere socks and gave them to me after a foot massage because he knew I'd been on my feet all day. And he makes *the* best hot chocolate."

With a little bit of cayenne.

A memory of a night spent sipping hot chocolate on Mackinac arrives with a pang at the same time as she says, "With a little bit of heat. I'd marry him for the recipe alone. He refuses to share it with me by the way, because he always wants to have something only he can give me."

Clearly, they're perfect for each other, and I am inventing the possibility that someone like me *could interfere with that.*

"And I'm twenty-nine." Her mouth lifts at the corner. "So, there's still plenty of time to screw things up before I turn thirty."

I laugh, warming to her, and some of the tension goes out of my neck. "I just turned thirty, and trust me, plenty can get screwed up *afterwards,* too." I catch myself being too real and scramble to reassure her. "But I promise I won't screw up your wedding. Is there anyone you want me to watch out for?" I tuck a beachy wave behind my ear. My hair is loving the salt air. "I'm here to help you avoid awkward moments and scenes. I'll babysit Uncle Al, obviously."

Zoey grimaces. "Please do. Uncle Al doesn't think before he talks and that drives my dad nuts. But we couldn't not invite him." She stares at her hands that are absently twisting her green cloth napkin. "I'm sure you're wondering why I hired you. Why I don't have a best friend to be my maid of honor? Why I need to pay someone, so we don't look completely lopsided during our vows with only Aubrey standing on my side and three guys standing on Ethan's?"

I cock my head and keep my expression neutral, having had this conversation with brides many times before. I'm not going to lie; I'm slightly mollified that not *everything* in her life is picture perfect.

But when she looks up at me again, her eyes are brimming with tears. My heart constricts and all feelings of satisfaction that she has a challenge in her life go out the window.

"It's pretty embarrassing that I don't have close girlfriends. I guess I've been so busy working toward getting perfect grades and going to great schools and getting my own show, I never had time for stuff like slumber parties." She dabs away tears with her napkin. "Sorry. I don't mean to unload on you. I've never actually said any of that out loud before and it's been an emotional week. Somehow it's easier to tell a stranger."

"Hey." I place my hand over hers. "You're not alone. I hear stories like yours all the time. A lot of successful women get caught up in being perfect. There's so much pressure, especially when you're in the public eye, to be flawless. We can't show our truth to anyone." I squeeze her hand. "Thank you for confiding in me. We don't have to be strangers. My real name is Gwen. I'm here to be your friend."

I should tell her I know Ethan.

The thought rams into me, shaking me to the core, but I steady myself.

I promised I'd keep it secret. He wants her to have this secret. It would be embarrassing for her if he knew she hired me.

And the truth is, deep down, I can't deny part of me is curious to see what having a secret with Ethan will be like. Which makes me an awful person.

The cappuccino revolts, rising in my throat, but I swallow it, pushing my disgust with myself so deep that I lose my appetite—even for those lemon basil thingies.

"I want you to know this isn't just a job to me," I say, forcing the obscene secret motive out of my mind. And I mean it. I like Zoey. Studying the walking fifties throwback *Vogue* editorial sitting across from me, I can't imagine anyone else by Ethan's side.

Zoey wipes away an escaped tear with the back of her hand and her glistening face erupts in pink blotches that somehow makes her skin appear dewy and sun kissed. "Thank you, Gwen. That means a lot to me." Her eyes shine. "And even though you weren't originally supposed to be in the wedding, maybe the stars aligned to bring you here."

"It sure seems like it." I sigh, picking at a croissant that probably isn't called a croissant because I'm in Italy.

I can't let my feelings get in the way of the wedding. Ethan and I will keep my identity secret, we'll get them married, and I'll be out of cat-penis debt in no time. There is nothing between Ethan and me, no residual relationship from our past. I am only in his life to facilitate the wedding. I must move on and close the chapter on him and me.

Determined to do my job, I straighten. "We should get down to business, though. And of course, keep calling me Rosie in public." I rummage in my bag for a notebook and pen. "What do you want me to say in my speech? Do you want to tell me what to say or do you want me to write something, and you approve it? I can do a Zumba metaphor and say how inspiring you are and how you keep me showing up and how I know you'll always show up for Ethan? He's so lucky, but so is Zoey." I jot the lines in my notebook. "The way he looked at her when they were dancing on the night of wishing on falling stars, I think all the single girls were wishing for someone to look at them like that blah, blah, blah . . . "

She laughs, a sweet, tinkling sound. "Did you just think of all of that?"

"Yeah." I put down my pen. "I've worked a few of these."

"It's perfect."

"Great. I'll keep going then and show it to you in a day or two."

She gazes past me, over my shoulder, and groans. "Oh. My mother's coming. I swear she put a tracker in me at birth," she mutters. Grabbing her navy wicker bag that has the kiss scarf tied around it, she stands. "I'll spare you having to talk with her, but I'll see you at the boat in a little bit. And help yourself to anything you want. This is all paid for." She gestures at the pastry mountain.

"Thank you." I turn to see where her mother is and gasp.

She's stopped at a rectangular table, talking to a white man with floppy gray hair and a close-cropped silver beard who appears to be having breakfast with his family.

Against all odds, it's Davis Collings.

Duncan's yacht-rock messiah in the flesh.

My jaw drops as *"it's Davis Collings"* reverberates through my brain.

The earth tips on its axis and I almost fall out of my chair.

The universe is definitely fucking with me.

Chapter 15

This is It

Before Zoey can leave, I grip her arm. "Zoey. Who is that man your mom is talking to?"

She shields her eyes against the sun. "Hmmm. I don't know. Hopefully she's not bothering them. She talks to *everybody*. She probably thinks their breakfast looks good and wants to know what they ordered. I better go save them. See you on the boat." Waving goodbye, she heads for her mom.

I absently wave back, already formulating a plan to capitalize on this, to find a way to get Davis to meet Duncan. My skin is jumping with the need to see Duncan's reaction when I make his (my) wish come true.

But how? I can't just go talk to Davis, can I? It's going to be beyond awkward and incredibly rude.

A waiter passes by, and I ask him to pack the rest of the pastries up for The Bandits. While I wait for his return with my to-go box, I rack my brain for every kernel of information I have on Davis Collings. And, thanks to my lifelong obsession with all things music, it's really more than anyone should know. Maybe if I come across as an adoring fan, he'll forgive the intrusion?

The waiter returns with my pastries and setting my sights on Davis, I take a deep breath.

Just go talk to him. He's probably used to it. The worst that could happen is he'll tell you to go away.

I know I have to do it. My head is throbbing with Corina's reminder to forget my ego. This is obviously a chance to surrender. If anything could make me believe it's possible for the stars to align, Davis Collings is it.

No time like the present to make a fool of yourself.

But I can't make my legs move, can't get over my fear of Davis rejecting me, of making a scene. I sit frozen in place, my chest tight, and watch Davis and his family stand and walk out of the restaurant.

I will myself to chase after them, but I can't overcome my inertia.

They disappear out the door and, sick to my stomach, I bury my face in my hands.

What is wrong with me? Why couldn't I go talk to him? That might have been my only chance to make Duncan's wish come true.

A glance at my watch tells me I need to hurry to meet the boat that is soon departing for the limoncello tour, and I groan. I let Duncan down. Let myself down. But there's no way to fix it now. I've got to get to the boat.

Next time, I can't let opportunity pass me by.

I'll just have to make sure there *is* a next time. Before I dash outside, I stop at the hotel's front desk.

"Excuse me," I ask the girl behind the counter. "I've just come from breakfast and the buffet looked wonderful. Can you tell me if it's included if you're a guest at the hotel?"

"*Sì.* Breakfast is served from six to ten-thirty every morning."

"Thank you." I exit through the lobby doors.

Outside, the bustling, narrow streets smell like coffee, freshly baked bread, and saltwater. Church bells clang in the distance, and the cramped sidewalks are packed with tourists in summer dresses and sun hats shopping for colorful lemon-themed souvenirs. Wisteria-cloaked doorways whir by in a blur as I think of a way to make the Duncan-Davis connection happen.

Maybe if he sees The Wedding Bandits play, he'll believe.

All I know is, if I see Davis again, I'm not chickening out. I am facing the fear and finding a way to make this wish come true no matter what.

***

By the time I cross the rocky sand and reach the colorful beachside dock where the *Il Desiderio II* waits, I've hatched a plan. I can't wait to put it into action tomorrow morning.

"*Buongiorno, bella.*" Luigi stands on the back deck of the sleek wood motorboat with navy inlays. He offers me his hand and helps me aboard.

"*Buongiorno, Luigi.*" The boat rocks beneath my feet, water splooshing its sides, and I wobble in my espadrilles.

"Take your shoes off." Zoey walks barefoot towards a bench. Lifting the lid, she shows me the compartment inside where her shoes are sitting. "It's easier."

"Good idea." She doesn't have to tell me twice. I'm *grateful* to ditch the too-small espadrilles. After untying the bands at my ankles, I place the shoes in the box and flatten my aching feet. The warm deck is heaven on my toes.

After leaving La Sponda, I stopped by my room to drop off the pastries and grab my phone. I'm keeping it on airplane mode, so it doesn't make any random international calls, but I need it to get video of The Wedding Bandits performing later as part of my Davis Collings plan.

Despite the detour, I'm right on time. Yet I'm somehow the last person to board.

Everyone is sitting on a creamy U-shaped couch at the center of the boat beneath a sunshade except for Ethan's twin, Payton. He's flung across the cushions on the bow with his chin tipped to the sky. Wearing only board shorts and sunglasses, he's tanning his shirtless—and ripped—torso. He has a curious little tattoo that looks like tally marks on his ribs under his left arm, but I avert my gaze before it seems like I'm ogling him.

Zoey gestures for me to sit next to the groomsmen and I make my way toward them, the boat tipping beneath the weight of my steps.

I slide past the dining table onto the couch. Luigi gets into the driver's seat directly behind me, so our backs are to each other. To my surprise, Duncan is directly across from me next to Aubrey.

Fireworks explode in my belly. He's wearing white jeans that are cuffed at the ankles, black wayfarer sunglasses, and a green and white wide-striped T-shirt paired with low gray Chucks that are more boat-friendly than my espadrilles. With one ankle balanced on his opposite thigh, he's relaxed and cool.

And about to be my Wishminion.

Loggins & Messina. Hall & Oates. Seals & Crofts. Duncan & Davis. That's a yacht-rock band name if I've ever heard one.

I cannot wait.

"We are ready, no? To Amalfi, yes?" Luigi asks over his shoulder.

"Yes, we're ready, Luigi." Zoey offers me a glass of prosecco from a bottle that is chilling in an ice trough built into the side of the boat, but I decline and opt for a mini bottled water.

Luigi turns the key and the engine rumbles to life. Payton jumps up and unties the boat from the dock as Zoey takes the seat next to me, which is diagonal—and as far away as possible—from Ethan.

Ethan sits in the corner of the U between Duncan and one of the groomsmen. Zoey sits on my other side. I find the distance between the bride and groom strange at best.

"*Allora.* Amalfi," Luigi announces. "We will be there in twenty minutes." The boat slowly moves forward, cutting through the sloshing water.

I ride backwards as Luigi navigates away from the dock, a gentle breeze tickling my neck.

Across the table, Ethan, in his winsome peach polo shirt and khaki shorts, chats with Duncan. Combined with the towering white cliffs, terracotta villas, and orange umbrella beach club behind them, it's a whole lotta beautiful in one place.

The backdrop gets smaller as we head out to sea.

Duncan is midway through a story. I have no idea what he's talking about, but I'm instantly on guard for any wish-maneuvering he might be implementing.

Aubrey, who has her knees angled toward Duncan, is leaning as close as she can without actually touching him while sipping prosecco and hanging on his every word. She's dressed similarly to me in varying shades of pastel poodle skirts, though her top is skintight and dangerously low cut. Her vibe is more Rizzo than Sandy.

Ethan laughs at whatever Duncan said. "You know, we don't get out much. We're both so busy with work, when we do get to see each other, we pretty much order takeout and watch movies."

The engine gets louder as Luigi shifts gears and the boat picks up speed. We bounce over waves and the rushing wind sends my hair flying. I gather it into a low ponytail at the nape of my neck, holding it with one hand.

"The one activity we've managed to stick to is dance lessons, so I hope that 'Wonderful World' cover is coming along." I strain to hear what Ethan is saying over the snapping Italian flag streaming behind us from the top of the boat. "We learned a routine and everything."

Even though I can't see his eyes behind his sunglasses, I feel Duncan's gaze briefly connect with mine. The flash of his eyebrows reverberates through me, and I immediately know he has an opinion on this. I bite my bottom lip. Part of me can't wait to be regaled by his first dance song insights.

"There's so much pressure to choose a song," Zoey chimes in. "I mean, people will be asking us for the rest of our lives what song we first danced to. Sam Cooke feels safe."

"It's a great song," I assure her as the boat turns and a fine sea salt mist sprays us. We're away from the town now and we hug the coastline, passing caves and forts built into the cliffs on the impossibly blue water. "Classic. It will never go out of style."

"We've got it down, so don't worry about the band." Duncan adds. "You guys are going to be great."

"Aren't you playing in the lemon grove today?" I call to Duncan, straining to make my voice heard over the wind but hoping to get some intel as to why he's here. "Loved your set last night, by the way."

"Oh, sorry, I forgot to introduce you two." Zoey leans forward, seeming to remember we're supposed to be strangers.

"We've met." I hold my hand up to stop her. "We were on the same shuttle from the airport."

The one that almost flattened the groom.

"Oh. Right." She settles back into her seat. "The band is playing after everyone else does their tour. We thought it would be fun bonding for the wedding party if we did the early lemon tour and then took a pizza-making class. While we're cooking, our parents and their friends will take the tour, and then we'll all eat together. That's when The Bandits will play, but Aubrey asked if she could bring Duncan along since they seemed to . . . " She pauses, seemingly at a loss.

"Get along so well last night," Aubrey interjects, patting Duncan's thigh.

I don't know what I missed while I was babysitting Uncle Al, but with a twinge, I wonder if I'm *actually* the only bridesmaid Duncan wished for last night. Not that it matters. I already know *she's* the bridesmaid of the week. And *I* am destined to remain the last bridesmaid standing. *I* am the champion. Not that it's a competition.

"We didn't get to talk much since I was busy playing." Duncan takes off his sunglasses and uses the hem of his shirt to polish them, looking up at me from under his thick eyelashes.

I try to convey with my eyes that I'm fine with this.

Totally fine.

"And I didn't have any plans today," he continues. "So, I thought it would be fun to tour the lemon farm and get to know everyone better. It always makes a performance more intimate when I've had a chance to connect with the wedding party." His lips twitch like they do when he teases me, and my lungs contract. I get the feeling that by "everyone" he means Ethan, that he's plotting something, and I attempt to glare at him while keeping a pleasant expression on my face.

The sun dips behind a puffy white cloud, casting a shadow over the boat. Feeling the heat from her stare, I glance at Aubrey.

She's watching me with her head cocked, and I check to see if I have a lemon basil cake stain on my shirt or something.

"You're so familiar to me." She squints, even though the sun is still hiding. "But we haven't met before last night, have we? I know you weren't at the engagement party."

My heart stalls but I keep my voice calm. "I don't think we've met. Unless you came to a Zumba class with Zoey?"

I've definitely never met her. Ethan never introduced me to anyone, let alone his family. He never even showed me a picture of them . . .

With a shiver, I again realize how little he shared with me.

"Nope, never." Aubrey wrinkles her nose and shakes her head. "Hmph. Payton." She calls to where he's returned to tanning on the front of the boat. "Does Rosie look familiar to *you* at all? Who does she remind me of?"

Payton sits up and I peer over my shoulder at him.

He studies me. "Don't know. I see what you mean though." Standing, he pulls on his polo shirt then walks along the side of the boat, clinging to the rails as he makes his way toward us. "What about you Ethan? Maybe she looks like some babysitter we had as kids?"

I am a glorified babysitter.

But I also know I've *never* seen Payton before, seeing as I didn't even know Ethan *had* a twin until this trip.

Payton faces us, sitting on the bench that contains the shoes. Another colorful town appears stacked into the cliffs behind him.

Duncan jumps in. "Rosie kind of looks like an actress. Or . . . " He pauses, squinting at me before clapping his hands. "I've got it. One of the Bachelorettes."

I raise my eyebrows at him. "You watch 'The Bachelorette?'"

His lips twitch with the hint of a smile. "Sometimes. But I can't remember which season you were on."

My shoulders slump. "I was *definitely* never a bachelorette," I clarify for the benefit of everyone.

Ethan shakes his head. "I don't see it. She just looks like a pretty girl to me." He catches my eye knowingly.

My insides crunch like fall leaves. "I do have a familiar face." I manage to say. Being on the inside of a secret with Ethan—and Duncan—reverts me to my seventeen-year-old self, but I put on my best Rosie face. "People think they know me all the time."

I peek at Zoey to see if she's bothered that Ethan complimented me. She's sitting with her feet crossed at the ankles, watching the scene play out with a serene smile. I marvel that she's so confident. She doesn't seem to have a care in the world. But maybe when you look like her and are about to be the star of your own show, you're used to everyone else paling in comparison. It probably doesn't hurt to throw others a bone once in a while.

The boat slows and the engines quiet to a low hum as Luigi guides us toward Amalfi.

"You're no help, Ethan. You're always surrounded by pretty girls." Payton teases his brother with a grin, and I'm grateful to him for taking the spotlight off me. "And you never pay attention to any of them. They probably all blur together. I mean, you're marrying the prettiest of them all." He stands then crosses the boat to where Zoey and I are sitting and playfully tugs her ponytail in a way that's borderline affectionate.

I lower my brow.

Weird.

Luigi cuts the engine, and we drift into a marina. "Welcome to Amalfi."

Payton tosses bumpers over the side at the front of the boat.

Reminded of *my* brother Ty, who would have helped dock the boat were he here, I jump up and toss the bumpers over the back side. I sort of remember my way around a boat from when I used to fish with my dad and brother, though I haven't been since Ty passed, and our boat is now rusting behind a shed in my parents' backyard.

When we're close enough to the dock, Payton leaps ashore and loops rope around a metal cleat securing the boat to a dock. He tosses a rope to me, and I tie up the back.

Everyone else stands.

As I'm putting my shoes back on, Duncan catches my eye and gives me an approving nod.

A burst of heat seeps through me, but it cools when Aubrey loops her arm through his.

"You definitely remind me of someone. It'll come to me," she says, snuggling close to Duncan. "Probably in the middle of the night, when I least expect it."

I can't fathom her recognizing me. She would have been, what, twelve when I knew Ethan? But my throat still constricts.

And hopefully she's not sleeping over next door when it comes to her in the middle of the night.

Duncan leads her to the deck on the back of the boat where Payton waits to help us ashore.

Zoey and I fall in line behind them with Ethan and the other groomsmen behind us. I eye the back of Aubrey's blonde head.

Flinching, I push the sleepover thought out of my mind. It's not like it's any of my business what they do after hours.

Remembering the blissed out image of Toto curled up on the pillow that the cat sitter sent, I remind myself that if I'm going to get my bonus, my focus should be on *the bride*. I'm here to keep Zoey happy. I link arms with her as we exit to shore.

Chapter 16

Just When I Needed You Most

We walk from the coast into *Piazza Duomo* through an arched corridor lined with shops selling everything from postcards to leather handbags. At the center of the square, a green and white checkered cathedral looms at the top of hundreds of stone stairs. Church bells clang, and the heady scent of incense from a recent mass mixes with diesel from the mopeds that navigate through the tourist-filled streets.

A photographer takes candid pictures of us as we stop to browse at shops awash in yellow: lemon-printed dishes, bottles of limoncello, and olive oil decanters. Ethan and Zoey aren't anywhere near each other. Up ahead, Zoey and *Payton* pause at a colorful fruit stand selling lemons bigger than my head. Meanwhile, Ethan hovers near *my* elbow. I frown, seeking out Duncan to see if he finds this weird, too.

He's busy taking pictures of Aubrey posing on the back of a mint green moped while holding a double scoop gelato cone. Any doubt I had that she's the bridesmaid of the week are erased.

"Have you been to Italy before?" Ethan leans down so I can hear him over a gurgling stone fountain depicting Saint Andrew surrounded by nymphs and cherubs. He towers over me, his hulking frame blocking out the sun—and the Duncan/Aubrey scene.

I squint at him. "No. I've never been anywhere like this." We walk together, passing coffee shops and quaint cafés with bistro tables under market umbrellas nestled among flower boxes packed with marigolds. "I imagine you've been here before?"

"A few times." He ducks his head almost like he's embarrassed by his abundance. "You've got to try the *spaghetti al limone*." He points to a menu that pictures a buttery pasta nest with parmesan ribbons and lemon zest. "It's the local specialty. Maybe I can sneak you away from Zoey one night and show you. You know, for old times' sake. Didn't we eat at a place with umbrellas once?"

I flush as my inner seventeen-year-old's wildest fantasies fan to life, causing my insides to do unfortunate somersaults. All around us stone staircases and cramped whitewashed corridors jut off, offering glimpses of tucked away terraces. Hidden wine shops with bundled chili peppers hanging in their doorways beg to be explored. Seventeen-year-old me would have loved nothing more than to discover this place with Ethan.

"The Pink Pony?" I pretend I could possibly have forgotten the most wonderful night of my teenage life.

He snaps his fingers. "That's it. You have a good memory. I never would have remembered that. I'm serious, though. I've got to take you out some night."

My mouth goes dry. "That sounds fun," I manage to say, not knowing how else to respond.

Rounding a corner, we reach *De Cape 'e Ciucci Fountain Presepe*. The bubbling stone Nativity Fountain is covered in moss and dotted with hundreds of tiny figurines that include everyone from shepherds to sheep to dudes putting pizza into pizza ovens. Feigning interest in meeting the guides wearing yellow hats who are waiting for us, I separate from Ethan. But really, I just need space. Rationally, I know it would be wildly inappropriate for me to have dinner with Ethan, but the fact he suggested it has me spinning.

The guides tell us the history of the fountain, explaining that the figures depict town life and are a tradition that dates back to St. Francis of Assisi.

I try to concentrate on what they're saying, but I can't focus. Can't help wondering if Ethan was truly serious.

He said he was . . . But he was probably just being nice.

Digging deep, I will Rosie to take over, forcing the wistful teenage fantasies out of my mind. Somehow, by the time green and yellow golf carts deliver us to the long pink building covered in ivy that marks the start of our tour, I've managed to regain Rosie's composure.

Franco, the stooped Italian grandfather with a shock of white hair who owns the farm, comes outside to greet us. The weathered lines in his brown cheeks deepen with a smile that peeks from beneath his bushy white mustache as we exit the golf carts. He seems genuinely happy to see us, his knowing blue eyes twinkling as he hands us each a pink depression glass flute filled with limoncello.

"To sip among the vines." He raises his glass to the sky. "Follow me."

Using a gnarled walking stick that must have once been a thick vine, he leads us down a narrow path. The trail winds back and forth down the hillside beneath crisscrossed branches that create a trellis to support the hundreds of lemons dangling over our heads. Despite his years, Franco's steps are sure and his brown hands strong, earned from life on the farm. He brings us to a stop in the dappled shade of trees blooming with sweet-tart scented flowers that buzz with bees.

"Dunc. I need a picture of this. Will you?" Aubrey calls from lower on the hill as we sample the bittersweet lemons.

She thrusts her phone toward Duncan as he joins her.

He takes the device. "Just tell me where you want me."

"We'll just be a second." Aubrey motions us away. "You guys go ahead."

Franco stops and leans on his stick. "We'll wait," he calls down to them.

I use the pause to tear Zoey away from where she and Payton are chatting with Franco, so the photographer can take pictures of her and *Ethan* among the vines.

Meanwhile, Aubrey sorts out the perfect backdrop, ultimately choosing a place that showcases the sparkling turquoise sea in the distance. She reapplies her coral lipstick before striking a pose. Duncan dutifully snaps pictures as she moves in front of the camera phone with the ease of a supermodel. After picking a lemon from a vine, she holds it in front of one eye, grinning.

I frown that Duncan has adopted the role of influencer-boyfriend/photog. But when I see the passion on her face as she confidently stares directly into the camera, seemingly unfazed by the fact we're all watching, my ribs squeeze.

I'm so trained to never be the drama, to never inconvenience anyone . . . I could never hold up a tour so I could create content. If this is what it would take to be an authority on music—a tastemaker, an influencer, as much as I hate to call it that—then this is a clear sign Shut Up & Sway is not meant to be. Even though I wanted my platform to be about music and *musicians*, not *me* looking adorbs at a music festival, I can't deny that to be taken seriously, I may need to put myself in front of the camera. Me as a brand might matter.

Aubrey seems to have unlocked the secret code that made 300,000 people pay attention. She's so self-assured, she doesn't care we're all waiting on her and potentially judging her. I clutch my necklace, wincing as I admit I could probably learn something from her.

But my To the Max contract requires me to limit my internet exposure.

Personal pictures have to be kept private and accessible to friends only for bridesmaid secrecy sake. The reminder soothes me.

Aubrey takes her phone from Duncan and tucks it into her wicker bag before they start back up the hill. "Thanks for waiting, everyone," she says when she reaches us. Her chin dips, a light flush staining her cheeks that betrays her seemingly over-the-top confidence and surprises me. But maybe she's just warm from the climb.

"Now, you have to try the lemon wine." Franco smiles.

"Isn't that what this is?" Payton raises his now empty limoncello flute.

"No, no." Franco shakes his head. "The wine is born in the fruit. Come. We'll stop by the magic fountain." Turning, he beckons us to follow him.

Franco leads us back toward the pink, ivy-covered main building and brings us to a stop outside a tiny green storefront with a yellow-and-white striped awning. "This is our factory and gift shop. And this is the magic fountain." He gestures to a stone fountain with a naked goddess carved into the center. Her hair flows in waves over her shoulders, and her hands hold her breasts where water trickles out of nipple spouts. "This is a replica of the Fountain of the Breasts. A lactating fountain." He cups the air like he's lifting one of the fountain's ample bosoms.

Ethan chooses this exact moment to stand next to me. "Having fun, Rosie?" he whispers, thrusting his hands into his pockets.

He's so beautiful he could be carved from stone himself. His heat sweeps over me.

How is Ethan Fisher Conner standing next to me at the Fountain of the Breasts? What is this life?

My inner seventeen-year-old rises up, and I shift back on my heels, caught between a lactating rock and Ethan's hard body.

Duncan, who is standing with Aubrey, catches my eye over her head.

The fear that me being put in an uncomfortable situation with Ethan might be what Duncan *wants* is all it takes for me to find my shaky voice.

"I am. What a beautiful day. What an incredible experience. I'm so happy to be a part of it. Thank you." I keep my voice low, still focusing my attention on Franco so as not to appear rude.

"The original statue is at the base of the fountain Sant 'Andrea—she is the protector of seamen—near the steps to the Cathedral," Franco continues giving the fountain's history. "You probably walked by it earlier."

As soon as he says "seamen," Duncan startles, and I'm done for. A hysterical giggle rises in my throat, and I fight to swallow it.

"These sorts of statues were popular in the 16th century. The breast milk was seen as a symbol of protection and regeneration. Fertility. Today, when we combine it with the lemons, we make the wine of life." Franco takes a lemon from a nearby basket and holds it to the sky like an offering.

I squint, sweating, trying to keep it together, my sides aching. This is the equivalent of laughing in church, and I am the worst.

I am way too immature for this.

And I don't want Franco to think I'm laughing at *him*. It's the absurdity of the situation—Duncan quietly pretending to stagger backwards—that has me losing my grip.

Franco cuts the lemon in half with the knife from his pocket before showing us how to dig our fingers into the center to loosen the pulp. Placing the lemon cup under the flow from the fountain's breast, he directs us to catch the water, then hands out lemon halves to each of us while I inhale to restore my equilibrium.

When Franco gets to me, I force my face expressionless and accept the offered lemon, with a small "thank you." Following his instructions, I plunge my fingers into the pulp and all I know is I can't look at Duncan or it's over.

We take turns placing our lemons into the water streaming from the nipple spouts, capturing the "milk" and somehow, I manage to maintain a straight face. Once all our cups are full, Franco raises his lemon in cheers. "Come. Drink. To your health and a long, happy life. *Salute.*"

"*Salute!*" We all repeat the toast. Before I drink, I dare a final peek at Duncan and find him watching me over his rind. His glittering gaze connects with mine and my lungs seize.

Did he wish a long, happy life for me?

Over my dead body is his wish coming true when mine is so close.

I try to convey this with the briefest of death stares as I throw the lemon milk over my shoulder. I don't know if drinking after the toast would count as me receiving a long, happy life and his wish coming true, but still. No way I'm risking it.

Duncan shakes his head at me.

"I need video of this too." Tugging on his sleeve, Aubrey drags him toward the fountain, her phone in hand, and breaks our connection.

He turns his attention to her and, somehow, the charming Amalfi farm turns lackluster and drab without Duncan's buzzy energy coloring it.

Franco dismisses us to explore the family museum and limoncello gift shop while he goes to meet Max who is accompanying the rest of the guests on their tour.

Before I move to ogle all the pretty glass bottles of sweet liqueur I can't afford—that are just begging to be poured over ice cream—Ethan picks up our earlier conversation.

"I can't take credit for any of this." He gestures toward Duncan filming Aubrey drinking from the boob. "This was all Zoey's idea. This sort of thing makes her really happy." He shrugs his massive shoulders.

I knit my eyebrows, sobered at the resignation in his voice. "But what makes *you* happy?"

"Me?" He scratches his chiseled jaw like he's never considered himself before.

"What would you rather be doing today?" I tilt my face upwards toward his pretty profile silhouetted against the blue sky.

He thrusts his jaw forward, thinking. "Maybe playing golf. Or it might be fun to watch pre-season football at a pub with some of the guys? I don't know. This is good, too."

Over Ethan's shoulder Zoey and Payton are exploring the limoncello factory and my insides twist. I'm pretty sure I've never met a more disconnected bride and groom. It's almost like this is an arranged marriage. Zoey and Ethan are *both* A-list spouse material. Beautiful. Rich. Benevolent. There's no reason they'd need to be set up, but I suppose continuing the lineage is normal for wealthy families. I've never witnessed a situation like this from the inside, but it's possible that's what is going on here. Maybe the arrangement is understood but not explicitly stated?

My pulse quickens at the possibility Ethan has interest in me beyond friendly chatting, but I immediately tell myself to chill out.

"Ethan. You're never going to believe this." Aubrey approaches us, Duncan in tow. "Do you know who Duncan just told me his brothers are?"

I blink at Duncan. For his part, he smiles weakly, like this is not his favorite topic of conversation.

"Who?" Ethan raises his palms in question.

"The Avila brothers." Placing a hand on her hip, Aubrey drops her bombshell.

Ethan's eyebrows shoot up. "*The* Avila brothers? Like, the most badass tight ends in football, ever?"

"The two and only." Duncan nods. "I'm their lesser-known middle brother. Also known as the 'other' brother. Or, on good days, 'the wedding singer.'"

I do a double take. I was raised a Bears fan, and since I can't afford to play Fantasy Football anymore, I don't really know who anyone is, but even I know the Avila brothers. One plays for the Chiefs and the other plays for the Steelers. They star in commercials for soup. For pizza. For shoes. They're everywhere. It never occurred to me—or came up in my (one) internet search—that Duncan could be related to them.

"I didn't know they had another brother." Ethan's mouth hangs open.

Dunc wrinkles his nose. "Most people don't. My brothers are pretty good at keeping me out of their spotlight."

"Did you play football, too?" Ethan studies Duncan like he's trying to equate his slim-but-defined build with his massive brothers.

"I tried," Duncan says with a half-hearted shrug. "We grew up in Austin where the three tenets are football, barbeque, and music. I'm too scrawny for football so I made music my thing."

Aubrey punches him in the arm and pretends to hurt her hand. "You are *not* scrawny."

Duncan laughs. "That's because of the barbeque. And speaking of barbeque . . . What's next? Pizza making?" He rubs his hands together as we make our way uphill toward the terrace. "You know what I've been craving lately? This might sound weird, but toffee sounds delicious. Like sticky toffee pudding."

Coughing to cover a gasp, I glance at Ethan to see if the reference to sticky toffee triggers any reaction.

Did Duncan wish for Ethan to figure out who I am?

Ethan keeps walking without so much as a flinch.

I glare at Duncan. "That *is* a weird craving. I don't know about pudding, but I'm sure we could find you some toffee gelato." I bat my eyelashes at him. "It would be such a shame if you choked on in it, though," I add under my breath so only he can hear.

Duncan smirks but doesn't look at me.

"Definitely. I bet you Zoey knows the best place for it too." Ethan gestures to where Zoey, Payton, and the other groomsmen are standing on the patio up ahead. "I'll put her on the case."

"That'd be great." Duncan smiles and claps Ethan on the back. "Man, you're lucky to have a girl like Zoey. She's the type who makes wishes come true." He arches an eyebrow at me as Aubrey takes his side and entwines her arm with his, leaving me to scowl at their backs.

Chapter 17

Biggest Part of Me

We arrive on a terracotta-tiled patio perched above lemon groves that disappear over the surrounding cliffs to the sparkling cobalt sea. Puffy clouds dot the bright blue sky, and the air is thick with the scent of burning wood from the brick ovens.

Max appears at the top of the stone stairs that connect the terrace to the lemon grove, and I stiffen. Hanging back, I distance myself from Ethan. Zoey is behind a weathered wooden counter examining ceramic bowls filled with fresh basil, mozzarella, and olives. She's as far from Ethan as she could possibly be.

Despite the warmth of the sun and ovens, I shiver.

Max isn't going to like this.

"Who's ready for pizza?" A guy wearing an unbuttoned black silk shirt that showcases a thick gold necklace tangled in a mass of chest hair claps his hands to get our attention.

"I'm Franco's grandson Brando," he explains in an accent lighter than Franco's as he hands out yellow aprons. "And I'm going to teach you to make the pizza. Please take a place." He gestures to the long wooden bar in front of the ovens where balls of dough wait on pizza paddles.

"I'm starving, but unfortunately I have soundcheck." Duncan refuses his apron and detangles his arm from Aubrey who is curled around him.

"Play one for me," she purrs.

She reminds me of Toto winding himself in and out of my legs, begging to be stroked.

"Absolutely," Duncan promises with a wink. After successfully separating himself from her, he heads to the stairs. "See you guys later." He hurries to join the band setting up at the far end of the clearing in the grove below.

Aubrey watches him disappear below the terrace and the flutter in her heart must be contagious because I feel it in mine. Taking a slow breath, I force myself to relax.

"Just wait until you try the lemon-ricotta pizza." Zoey chef-kisses her fingers. "*Bellisima!* Let's get started."

We file behind the counter. Knowing Max will be taking inventory of who is standing where, I take Ethan's arm. "You two, get next to each other. Photo op." I drag him closer to Zoey before choosing a place near the end of the bar next to Aubrey.

"Oh, right. I keep forgetting." Ethan laughs. "I'm used to Zoey being the one on camera."

He picks the spot next to Zoey and she freezes, standing stiffly next to him.

The photographer raises her camera. "Come on, you two. Show me some pizza love."

Zoey relaxes, her movements fluid and camera-ready the moment the lens focuses on her. "Like this, Ethan." She kneads the dough, and Ethan dutifully plunges his hands into the springy ball next to hers. He forces a smile that makes his dimple appear as the photographer snaps pictures.

But as soon as the shutter stops clicking, Ethan steps sideways.

"Stay together!" Max orders, his voice booming across the patio. "Let's get some candids. Those are always the best." He softens his tone as he approaches the bar.

"Nah. We don't want *those* candids." Ethan lifts an eyebrow at Max. "Trust me. I've cooked with her before. She's a perfectionist when it comes to food, and I'll totally screw it up. I'll be over here where it's safe." He moves away from her, taking the open place next to me.

Zoey playfully sticks her tongue out at him. "You know food is my life."

"Yeah, well, I love eating what you make, but I don't need you judging my technique, thank you very much. We both know we get along better if you cook, and I eat. The *only* thing I make is hot chocolate."

"It's great you know your boundaries." Max comes to a stop across from Ethan and rests his fingertips lightly on the counter. "But this is your wedding week. Don't you want to make this memory with your soon-to-be wife?"

"Nope. I know better than to cook with her." Ethan crosses his arms over his chest and winks at Max.

Shaking her head, Zoey laughs, and I concede that maybe this is a running gag for them. I try to tell Max as much with a brief glance.

"Payton. You cook with her." Ethan nods toward Zoey. "You could probably stand to learn some kitchen skills. Do you even have a kitchen?"

Payton's shoulders tense. "Just because I prefer to go where the wind takes me and spend my days in nature rather than behind a computer screen doesn't mean I don't know my way around a kitchen." He forces a smile, his white teeth flashing against his olive skin as he takes Zoey's side. "But I'm always up to learn something new. I'm happy to cook with you, Z. Teach me. I'm dough in your hands." He nudges her arm with his elbow.

Zoey's flushes and swallows a nervous giggle.

Max stares at them for a beat before cocking his head at me. His expression remains neutral, but his silent message blares in my mind.

Code Red: twin brother/ best man has a thing with the bride.

He confirms it. It's not just me. There's undeniable chemistry between them.

With an imperceptible nod, I let him know I'm on it. I can get rid of Payton and reconnect Zoey and Ethan.

No problem.

Max raps his fist on the bar, one knock for each syllable of his motto "dignity and grace," before striding toward the stairs.

With a gulp, I slip my apron over my head. Franco has reappeared and offers everyone glasses of crisp white wine. I'm oblivious to the task before me while everyone else smashes the dough with the heels of their hands.

Where is Duncan when I need him?

I take a deep breath, then release it through puffed cheeks.

"So, you and the wedding singer, huh?" Ethan asks, and I jump.

"He's adorable." Aubrey reaches over me to pinch her brother's arm.

Chiding myself for thinking he could have been talking about Duncan and *me* when clearly Aubrey is the bridesmaid of the week, I shake my head.

"Plus, I need something fun to do this week, here on the island of my brothers." She leans closer to me and lowers her voice like she's telling me a secret. "My brother is *so* boring. This brother, I mean." She points her thumb at Ethan. "Not that one." She nods toward where Payton is whispering something to Zoey.

My mouth goes dry and I tell myself it's Zoey and Payton's relationship making me uneasy, not Aubrey and Duncan's. Or mine and Ethan's. Because it's not.

None of this bothers me at all.

"Payton has always been the fun one." Ethan presses his dough into a perfect circle. "I don't try to keep up anymore. We have different talents. I will never surf or dive or ski as well as him, but he'll never balance a budget as well as me." He shrugs.

"There's something to be said for knowing which path you want to take." I smile diplomatically but it quickly turns to a frown as my misshapen dough shrinks back to its tiny original size.

"Payton must have some sort of budget." Aubrey rolls her pizza flat with a wooden cylinder. "Somehow he manages to live off our puny trust fund."

"I don't know how he does it. He can't make that much extra taking people on trips." Ethan tips his head toward me. "We get a small monthly stipend from our parents' trust as a way to avoid taxes later, but it's nowhere near enough for even the most frugal person to live on." He claps his hands together to brush off the flour. "But he's the free spirit of the family. And Aubrey is the baby." He rolls a tiny dough ball and flicks it at her.

Aubrey rolls her eyes and bats the dough away. "You can stop calling me 'the baby,' Ethan. I'm twenty-five. Old enough to rent a car or an entire Airbnb. I've met all my milestones." She places the dough on her knuckles and tries to spin it around like it was demonstrated.

"But have you started a Roth IRA or solo 401k like I told you to?" Ethan asks. "You should be saving for retirement. You don't always have to stay at Aman or the Four Seasons."

Aubrey purses her lips. "I'm a luxury brand, Ethan. My fans come to me because of my fashion and trend prowess. To experience the lifestyle they can't afford *through me*. I'm *not* a budget influencer." She wrinkles her nose. "But I wish you'd talk to Pay more, Ethan. I hate that you aren't close like you used to be."

Shifting my stance, I scan the other end of the bar to see if Payton is listening, but he's busy laughing with Zoey as he tries to toss a pizza in the air and it lands on her shoulder.

"Like when we were five?" Ethan clenches his teeth. "There's always been a weird competition between us. I don't like it either, but I don't know how to fix it. It is what it is."

Hating for anything to go unsaid—because you never know when your last chance to say it will be—I can't help but speak up. "You could tell him how you feel?"

Ethan looks at me and smiles. "Nah. Too easy." He dips a spoon into a ball jar containing homemade tomato sauce and spreads it on his pizza and then adds grated parmesan, olives, and basil. "The truth is we drifted apart a long time ago. Not all brothers, not all twins, need to be best friends."

I frown, wishing more than anything that my brother Ty was still around, that we never *ever* let something as silly as sibling rivalry come between us. If he were here, he'd be my best friend for sure. I'd tell him everything, confide in him all the time. And again, I can't keep quiet.

"But you share so much history, such a similar upbringing, wouldn't it be nice if you could commiserate? Could get past your differences and really support each other? Wouldn't it be better that way since you're going to see each other for the rest of your lives . . . "

"In a perfect world? I guess so. It's not that easy, unfortunately." Ethan sighs and peers at me sideways. "You know, Rosie, I've never told anyone this stuff. For just having met you, I feel really comfortable with you." He smirks. "Like we're old friends. I can't say that about most people. I kind of feel like I can tell you anything."

"He can't say that about *anyone*." Aubrey sets rounds of fresh mozzarella on her pizza. "Even Zoey," she adds under her breath.

"Well, you can," I say, my smile overly bright to compensate for the warmth of his words seeping through me. "Tell me anything. I'm a great listener."

"Maybe I will." Ethan's lips twitch and for a moment his gaze holds mine. His familiarity wraps around me, holding me in an embrace, and my heart opens.

"*Allora.* Time to get these pizzas into the oven." Brando breaks the spell. "Why don't all of you head down to the tables. We'll bring them out as soon as they're ready. They're the first course in a *bellissima* dining experience we've got planned for you."

The soft strains of The Wedding Bandits covering "Rosanna" by Toto float up to the terrace, and it's almost like Duncan is calling to me. Max's itinerary says the limoncello party is supposed to have a classic rock soundtrack. I guess "Rosanna" sort of qualifies, but I can't help smiling, because it feels like Duncan's playing one for *me*, not Aubrey.

I leave my station and walk to the stairs. In the clearing below, at the far end of two long tables set with mismatched china, their centers piled with lemons spilling out around hand-painted jars of flowers and carafes of decanted wine, the band is in full reenactment mode.

Behind Duncan, the guys sing backup, whipping their heads around like they could twirl their ponytails à la the girl in the original "Rosanna" music video.

I close my eyes, overcome with pure joy until I feel Ethan's presence at my side.

He offers me his arm and I start to take it, but Duncan covering Toto reminds me why I'm here and I think better of it.

"Let me get Zoey. This is your party. You two need to make an entrance." I escape quickly to find the person who I must remind myself is *the bride*.

Chapter 18

Summer Breeze

The pizza is crisp and light and salty and warm. And it is followed by pasta. Lucious, simple, cheesy *cacio e pepe* ribbons that are so delicious I want to twirl myself in them. Here, under the fluttering handkerchiefs crisscrossed overhead, reminiscent of the laundry strung between the balconies in town, with the scent of sweet lemon blossoms swirling in the sea breeze, my appetite is voracious. I indulge myself with Duncan's soothing voice in my ears. The band is covering "More Than a Feeling" by Boston—which is *not* yacht—but still beckons me to slow down, to chill, and I float in a delightful haze.

Thanks to my prodding, and pleading the need for pictures, Ethan and Zoey are *actually* sitting together for once, leaving me wedged between a groomsman and Aubrey.

Clearly, I'm not the only one distracted by Duncan. It's not fair to the bride; many of the guests can't take their eyes off him. I'm again struck with the notion that he's a *star*.

"Can you believe he's one of the Avila brothers?" Aubrey's voice is a record scratch that brings me back to reality.

"No, I can't," I say, realizing how little I know about Duncan. He's been a good listener as I rattle on about cat penises and fractured fairytales while my tongue decides to assault him at every turn. Though, to be fair, it seems like he'd rather talk about yacht rock than his feelings. And honestly, who can blame him? I'm in that camp, too. Besides, it's technically both of our jobs to not talk about ourselves.

"He's *so* hot." Her pasta untouched, Aubrey's elbow is on the table, and she rests her cheek in her hand. "I've got to get him to take some pictures with me. My followers would *love* him."

I frown, making a mental note to borrow Duncan's phone and look up her socials later. As much as her wanting to flaunt him on her feeds irks me, I must admit that it would probably be good for the band—if they ever wanted to move beyond being a cover band, that is. And, based on our conversation on the plane, I'm not sure they do. My stomach twists that the world could be deprived of experiencing Duncan living his fullest potential and suddenly I lose my appetite, even for pasta. It's a crime for him to keep his talents reserved for weddings.

"And he's *so* funny." Aubrey's voice is dreamy.

"Is he?" My blood pressure spikes, and I swallow hard. Aware I have no right to feel territorial, I keep my tone even. "I hadn't noticed."

"Oh my gosh. He's the *most* charming and down to earth. And those lips." She exhales. "I made a promise to myself this year to always go after what I want, and I'm not letting him get away."

I observe her expertly applied eyelashes, her flawless complexion, the nose she might have paid for. Everything down to the shimmery peach blush highlighting her high cheekbones is perfection, exudes money. She can buy anything. "I imagine you usually get what you want."

For an instant her face falls, but she quickly composes herself. "Mostly."

The song ends. Duncan leans into the microphone, drawing everyone's attention. "What a beautiful experience we're having, right?"

The guests clap their agreement.

"It's so out of the everyday, it reminds me how important it is to break with routine." Duncan accepts a new guitar from Luigi as he talks, handing Luigi the old one before slipping the new guitar strap over his head.

Concentrating on his guitar, Duncan strums a few notes. "I give you, 'Escape (The Piña Colada Song).'"

Laughter ripples through the crowd.

I giggle at first, too, but when he starts singing about a guy who is so tired of his girlfriend that he places a personal ad to find someone to cheat on her with, I sit upright. Considering the potential Zoey-Payton situation, I don't need infidelity running as a theme in anyone's subconscious, and I shoot to my feet.

Aubrey startles and looks up at me.

"I have an idea for a song request." I scramble to cover my sudden movement. "Does Duncan take requests?"

Aubrey's mouth curves into a slow, secretive expression. "He's been super obliging of all mine."

I'm sure he has.

I don't want to think about it.

Ugh.

But when I do, I'm not so sure he has.

When would he have time? He's almost always with me.

Bolstered, I shrug her off and stalk toward the band.

Standing on the side of the stage, I watch Duncan sing with my arms crossed over my chest. And even though I want to keep glaring at him, I can't help swaying a little. If my situation was different, I would thoroughly enjoy his performance.

Duncan's lips—Aubrey is *not* wrong about them—smile at me as the song ends, and my nerve endings prickle. Steadying myself, I harden my features.

"We're going to take a little break. We'll be back in five," he says into the mic before joining me.

"What are you singing?" I whisper through clenched teeth when he's close enough to hear me. "I get it, sex on the beach is super yacht—"

"Nope." Cutting me off, he takes a sip of bottled water before sitting on the edge of the stage so he's level with me. "Too much sand. I don't mean to poo-poo it, but ouch." He winces.

I blink a few times. "That's not where I expected you to go with that."

"I'll always keep you on your toes." His eyebrows flash up. "Besides, it's a song about two people trying to have an affair through personal ads. A couple so tickled by irony they ignore attempted infidelity?" His eyes bulge. "Above all, yacht is *loyal.* And there's all that stuff about being not so smart. It's a song about mediocrity, of all things. That doesn't belong on a yacht." With a mock-frown, he shakes his head.

I stifle the urge to giggle, refusing to let him derail me. "I see your point. But do we *need* to hear about infidelity? And sticky toffee pudding? What was that about? Did you wish for Fish to guess who I am?" I don't think anyone is listening, but I use Ethan's nickname just in case.

"No." He wrinkles his nose and drinks more water. "I expected you to tell him last night. What did he want?"

Tucking a strand of hair behind an ear, I think fast. "Um. For me to help him with a surprise for Zoey." My chest tightens and I suck in my breath, hating that I have to lie to him. But I don't have a choice. It's in everyone's best interest that I keep my promise to Ethan and keep his knowledge of my identity secret. This way, if Max finds out I'm conspiring with the groom, I can take the fall and Duncan can deny any part in helping me.

I lower my voice. "This is top secret, but he wants me to help him choreograph a song and dance so he can surprise serenade her at the reception. It's really sweet, actually."

Duncan cocks his head, as if searching his memory. "Like the groom did at the very first wedding we ever worked together? Do you remember that wedding?"

I remember every wedding I've worked with him.

I flush that he knows *exactly* where I got my lie but keep talking. "Yeah, I do. That's right. That groom did have a surprise serenade."

"That groom was my cousin."

"Oh, really?" I start to sweat. "Why weren't your brothers there?"

"They were at training camp. But we played that wedding as our gift. I helped my cousin with his song."

"Wow." I force a smile. "Maybe you can help us with this song then. Thanks to your 'Give me the Night' rendition, Ethan thinks I'm some sort of dance sensation. We could use all the help we can get."

"Hey. I can't help if that song gives everyone instant rhythm. That's *all* George Benson. Those moves were *all* you. Maybe you could help him work on a Tame Impala cover, though."

"Definitely not. Too close to home." My skin heats that he knows about that too, and it's almost a relief Max is stalking toward us so I won't have to lie anymore.

From the set of Max's jaw, he's in crisis mode.

"Shit. I gotta go." Straightening my spine, I back away from Duncan. "I wanted to make a request," I say loudly, in case Max can hear. "Zoey loves Davis Collings. Do you have a favorite song of his you can play?"

"You want me to pick just *one*?" His jaw drops.

"I'm trying to create a moment that Zoey and Ethan will always remember."

He thinks for a minute. "Okay. I've got one."

"Thank you." I start to go but, biting my lip, I turn back. "Oh, and Dunc, wait to start until I'm back in my seat. Then give it your all."

Seeming unfazed by the request, he salutes me. "You got it, Rosie."

He picks up a guitar, and I move toward my seat, but run into Max.

He grips my arm and walks with me. "Where is your phone? I've been texting you."

"Oh." I gulp. "It's on airplane mode. I don't have an international plan."

"Ah. I'll have to remedy that." He nods at Zoey's grandma as we pass her. "We've got trouble."

"Right here in Positano?" I quip while thinking to myself, *no shit.*

"We're currently in Amalfi." He frowns and there is not so much as a hint of humor in his expression. But then, though his jaw remains taut, he adds, "Which starts with 'A' and that follows the 'P' in 'pain' . . . which stands for Payton." He imperceptibly slides a picture into my hand. "The photographer just handed me this."

I glance down at the photo of Zoey and Payton tucked into a corner of the limoncello shop only hours ago. Their heads are bowed close, and she's smiling knowingly while he stares down at her with a gaze so intense it can only be described as love. The picture practically vibrates with their energy. My knees go weak, but in one smooth motion, I slip the picture into my poodle skirt's pocket.

"You have to fix it, Rosie," Max says through clenched teeth, while grinning at a guest. "Her dad will kill me if anything goes wrong. This whole experience cost seven figures, and nothing is refundable at this point. This needs to be handled with dignity and grace. We need to save face for everyone."

Nothing is refundable for Giorgio, so if this wedding week gets cut short, Max will pay me only for the days I've worked. That won't make a dent in Toto's vet bill. I've been meaning to renegotiate my contract with Max for years to include a "payment in full in the event a wedding is called off" clause rather than the "payment only for time worked" line that's currently in there. But it has never seemed like the right time. Until now.

"We don't know that anything is going on. It might be nothing. I'll talk to her, and I'll find a way to fix this," I whisper, patting the photo in my pocket. "I promise."

Zoey's parents are waving Max over and he deposits me at my seat. Looking me directly in the eye, he mouths, *Thank you. I'm counting on you,*" before marching toward them.

The second I sit, Duncan leans into the microphone. "This one goes out to the bride and groom."

He launches into "Nobody's Perfect, But You Are for Me" by Davis Collings, and Zoey and Ethan are momentarily forgotten while I scramble to find my phone and hit record.

Chapter 19

Even the Nights Are Better

By the time I finally plop onto my balcony, the sun is an orange ball that sinks behind the cliffs and casts the pastel villas in gold. Streaky pink clouds edged with silver glow in the sky like a magic storm sweeping in. Down at the pool, some of the wedding guests are having an impromptu gathering, and a mini cocktail party is in full swing. The sounds of happy chatter and clinking glasses drift toward me. Wishing, as usual, this was my destination for the evening, I cringe that my work is not done.

When we returned to the hotel, crisis-Max secured a cell phone for me to borrow for the week. He made it clear the phone is for local use only. International text and data rates will apply to me personally, except for checking in with my mom—he recommended getting her to download WhatsApp—because he knows how important that is.

I immediately texted my mom, Corina, and the cat sitter to invite them to the app.

I also managed to wrangle petty cash out of Max, but not enough to pay Dunc back for the shoes or lacy undies I'm wearing with my Hall & Oates T-shirt beneath my white waffle robe. Hopefully Jude and Via will be able to sell my Outside Lands ticket and will Venmo me a refund that will cover the loan. I messaged them, too. Most of Max's money paid for the aperitivo and wine, along with a copy of "the picture" Luigi is currently delivering to

Zoey's room. He included a note with the room service telling her to call my room, so I'm expecting my room phone to ring any minute.

Duncan's terrace doors open, and he appears carrying two little glasses and a bottle that looks like wine but turns out to be Collessi, an Italian beer.

"*Birra*?" He holds up the glasses.

With his scruffy jaw and messy hair getting messier still in the evening breeze, I involuntarily thrill to him. He's wearing Towaya, and I have to admit, this chick digs it.

"*Sì*." I smile.

"Are you in for the night?" He pours the amber liquid into a glass before handing it over the balcony railing to me.

"I wish." I wrinkle my nose. "I'm on Zoey duty. Have you noticed something weird going on with her and Payton? The photographer took this insinuating picture of the two of them and . . . " I swallow a mouthful of cold, bitter beer and exhale heavily. "Max is in an uproar. We're beyond Code Red. He's afraid the wedding is going to get canceled—which it won't. I'm sure this Payton thing is nothing. Just pre-wedding jitters."

"You never know. Ethan and Zoey are going the rehearsed Motown route for their first dance. That says a lot." He shrugs. "If 'Wonderful World' was *actually* their song it would be great. Sam Cooke influenced Robbie Dupree after all, so we have him to thank for 'Steal Away.' But in this case, it feels like Ethan and Zoey are trying to make us buy into their fairytale. Honestly, I'm not feeling it. If she's marrying the wrong guy, then it's a good thing if the wedding gets canceled, right?"

"Not for her dad. Lots of non-refundable contracts." I grimace.

"Right." He makes a face like he just scalded his fingers on a hot stove before his expression morphs and his eyes light up. "But if she did break it off with Ethan, that would open the door for you to tell him who you are, right?"

I shake my head at him. "I don't think post bride-leaving-him-at-the-altar-for-his-twin-brother is exactly the best time to spring my identity on him." Shuddering—and desperately wanting to change the subject so I don't have to lie to Duncan more than I already have—I turn my attention to the sea. "What about you? Are you in for the night? You and Aubrey seemed pretty chummy today."

"Hate to break it to you, but this is my only plan." He raises his glass in a toast to the waves that are ablaze with pink, reflecting the sky. "The sea is my lady tonight. Maybe I'll work on some lyrics."

An unexpected weight lifts off my shoulders and my mood lightens. I cock my head. "Lyrics? Like for an original song? So, you do write them."

Balancing a foot on the terrace's iron rail, he briefly considers me. "Sometimes." He sips his beer before setting it on the small table next to him.

"Do you ever play them out? I'd love to hear one." I talk to his profile.

His chin dips to his chest and he sinks lower in his seat, shoving his hands into Towaya's pockets and wrapping the jacket around him like he's guarding himself against a sudden chill.

"We don't usually do originals. I might be into it, but the rest of the band is happy playing covers. It's working for us. We're doing a college tour when we get back from this trip and then we're booked solid with weddings through next summer."

Remembering from the airplane that this is a touchy subject, I tread lightly. "Do you ever get tired of playing the same songs over and over, though?"

"Not really. It's always fun. Maybe I wouldn't mind adding more variety, though." He picks a piece of lint off Towaya. "That's probably why I write lyrics." His gaze briefly flickers to mine. "But there's no point to them, really. Our customers want to hear songs they know."

Annoyed he's selling his talents short, I lean toward him. "It sounds to me like you're playing it safe."

His jaw twitches. "Listen. I get what you're saying. But the wedding biz is super lucrative. We're all making money. Maybe not the millions my brothers make, but enough that I almost have enough saved to buy a small boat. And Hayden just bought a cabin in Homer, Alaska, that he's been trying to remodel. The locals there unofficially changed the town slogan from 'a quaint little fishing village with a drinking problem' to 'a quaint little drinking village with a marimba problem.' He's convinced he's found his people." Duncan tips his head toward me like he trusts I know this is a very Hayden move.

I laugh.

"But we have responsibilities, and it's pretty hard to pass up traveling and playing a packed house full of people singing along with you to go back to playing empty rooms. Having to beg friends to come out. And even if they do show up, you're trying to win them over with songs they've never heard before. Believe me, I've been there, and it sucks. Back when we were trying to play Sixth Street in Austin, when we first moved to Chicago—we tried. We tried and nobody got us. We failed." His brow lowers. "To put energy into doing originals we'd have to take a pay cut, and it's hard out there. I don't think anyone in the band wants to give it a shot again."

I fold my arms over my chest. "But your brothers are proof anything is possible. How do you know you couldn't be making millions like they are, being adored like they are, if you don't try?"

He stares at the darkening sky. "It's true. My brothers are just regular dudes who happen to be good—okay, exceptional—at football. But I don't know if I'm good at music in that same way."

"Shut up." I punch Towaya's sleeve. "Yes, you are. *Nobody* can take their eyes off you when you're on stage. You have charisma. The way you move—your voice—how committed you are to the song—you draw people in and won't let them go. You're a star. That's almost *more* important than the songs." I gather myself up, dizzy with how much I believe in him. "And if the songs are good, look out." The words come out in a whoosh, and I wipe my forehead with the back of my hand, flushing that I've revealed so much of the effect his music has on me.

He opens his mouth to interject, but I keep talking before he can stop me. "And Air Supply got their start playing in a production of *Jesus Christ Superstar*. They're proof everyone starts somewhere." I rest my case.

"Well, there *is* that." He snorts. "But I don't know about the other stuff." Rubbing the back of his neck, he winces. "Or if I *want* to be adored in the same way as my brothers. I don't envy them. They're under so much pressure. I used to think I wanted that—or needed that. For a while I tried to play football. I tried to follow in their footsteps, but I've always been in their shadow." He shrugs. "Maybe that's where I belong."

I blink at him, my eyelashes fluttering a mile a minute.

How could he remotely believe he belongs in the shadows?

But I bite my tongue before I adoration-vomit all over him again. "I'd think your brothers might share your music and help get the word out."

"I don't want them to." Frowning, he tops up the beer in his glass. "Do you have any idea what it's like to be the 'other' brother? Anything they do to help me just looks like they feel sorry for me—like they're trying to give me a leg up to make me a part of their world. I don't want to come off as some sad charity case. I want to make it on my own. And—trust me, I've thought a lot about this. 'Making it' doesn't require thousands of fans. It just means being happy. Being a wedding singer does that for me. I like where I'm at." He lifts the beer to his lips and takes a big swallow before continuing.

"I don't know why everyone is so focused on external rewards," he says, almost to himself before puffing out his cheeks. Slowly, he lets the air out. Then, lowering his voice, he leans toward me like he's telling me a secret. "You know, in some ways I relate to Payton. Even though his family is wealth driven—like my family is a football family—he chooses to do what makes him happy. He could work in finance. I *could* have played football. But I don't want to be huge and ram my head into other giant guys. It's not fun for me. But my family—except for my abuela, she's always supported my music—doesn't get why I wouldn't take the money and sit on a practice squad somewhere or take a college coaching job—which I could probably do based on name alone. Just like Ethan doesn't get why Payton isn't working his ass off to bring in the dough. I'm sure the comparisons are extra hard for them, being twins, but Payton decided to be his own person. It feels like he's living his life authentically. But Ethan? I'm not so sure."

The weight of familial expectations descends on me.

Would I feel the same if my brother had lived?

I nod, realizing everything I know about Ethan is surface level. I can't relate to what he might be going through. I always tried to emulate my brother Ty, but I was rarely jealous. Sure, we fought sometimes, but deep down I knew he was paving the way for me, and I had a lot of leeway because he went first.

"Do you get along with your brothers?" I ask, so wanting Duncan to value his relationship with them. I know that it could be gone in an instant.

"Yeah. I do. I like them." Ducking his head, he clears his throat. "I'm just not *like* them."

My entire body tenses and my leg muscles tremble at the realization that he doesn't grasp his full potential. I'm an earthquake ready to trigger a tsunami, and I can't keep my faith in him to myself. "I do not accept that."

He cocks an eyebrow at me.

Glaring at him, I fill my lungs, making myself as big as possible as I explain. "Are you saying playing to a packed house singing songs *you* wrote wouldn't be infinitely more fulfilling—and fun for everyone—than playing someone else's song?"

He remains unmoved. "I don't know."

"Duncan." I fix him with a stare. "I don't know why you can't see this but let me enlighten you. You were made for the spotlight. Like it or not, you *are* a leading man. Are you seriously telling me that if you end up a fifty-year-old wedding singer and didn't at least try to get your original stuff out there, you won't have regrets? Is this it? All you've got? You can't be a wedding singer forever, can you?"

His expression hardens and his chin jerks toward me. "I told you. I've tried. And failed. If it was meant to be, it would have happened by now. Thirty is old in music years. If I haven't succeeded by now, it's probably not going to happen. And I've made peace with that." He shifts his attention to the hillside that now dances with golden sparks from the flickering villa lights against a purple sky.

"Bill Withers was thirty-two when he released 'Ain't No Sunshine.' Willie Nelson was forty when 'Shotgun Willie' came out—"

His spine visibly stiffens, and he whips his gaze to mine, cutting me off. "What makes you such an authority on music anyway? I thought you were going to be a lawyer."

I flinch. "I *am* going to be a lawyer." Again, I try on the title, but it still doesn't ring true. "But we're not talking about me."

He flattens his features and holds my stare. "Why not? What are you afraid of?" His tone is challenging. "Succeeding?"

We square off and I mull his accusation over.

He did share a lot with me . . .

"Fine." I grit my teeth. "I failed the bar. I'd never failed *any* test before that, never failed anything school related, and it shook me. I haven't been able to bring myself to take it again and the reason I've been bridesmaiding ever since is because theoretically it leaves me time—" I take a deep breath and confess. "To write. The reason I'm an authority on music is because I'm a music tastemaker."

My declaration reverberates into the night. It's the first time I've said those words out loud, the first time I've owned them.

His shoulders soften. "That's awesome. What's your handle? I should follow you."

"It's . . . " An image of him reading my Shut Up & Sway posts flashes through my mind and I flush. "Nothing." I shove my dreams back into the compartment at the base of my skull where they belong. "Music is just a hobby. I don't have many followers. When we get back from this trip, I'm registering for the February bar. It's time to grow up and get a real job."

His eyebrows knit together. "You're not giving up, are you? If writing about music makes you happy, that's all that matters, right?"

"I guess so." To my horror, tears sting my eyes. "But it would be really great if other people wanted to read it, too . . . To have a reason for writing it." My voice cracks. "It would be nice to be wanted."

He stares at me with burning eyes, his lower lip jutting out, and I *cannot* take him feeling sorry for me.

Drying my eyes on the back of my hand, I sit up straight. "But enough about that. You. *You* are wanted. Will you please play an original song on the way to Capri tomorrow? Please?" I clasp my hands over my chest.

Holding back a smile, he shakes his head, no.

"Come on, Dunc." I make my eyes huge. "You're so talented. I have a feeling about you guys . . . Seriously. You might be depriving millions of fans of way more happiness than they could get from a cover song if you don't try. Please play an original. For me?"

"The band wouldn't go for it." He settles back in his chair and puts his foot back up on the railing.

I frown. "An original song is not what I wished for you, by the way, if that's what you're worried about."

He laughs. "In that case, *maybe* I'll think about it."

Inside my room, the phone rings and my ribs tighten. I don't want to leave the balcony, but I don't have a choice and I race to answer it.

Zoey's voice is shaky on the other end of the line. She asks if I can come right away.

"I'm on my way," I say before hanging up.

I poke my head outside to say goodbye to Duncan. "The bride calls."

"Good luck. And if it doesn't take too long, come say goodnight. I might still be out here. I feel lyrics coming on." He pulls the notebook we wrote our wishes in out of Towaya's pocket.

"I have a feeling this is going to take a while, so don't wait on me. Besides, I have to get up early to work on your wish." I wink and a hot chill of excitement shoots through me.

"Oh really?" He scans my face through narrow eyes.

With a shrug, I leave him hanging.

Chapter 20

Still the One

As soon as Zoey opens the door to her suite she winces and silently ushers me inside. Her room— a suite with a separate bedroom and a mosaic tiled fireplace— is much bigger than mine. A platter of prosciutto, melon, parmesan, and a dense focaccia covered in herbs and olives sits untouched on the room service cart Luigi delivered. The wine, however, has been uncorked.

Zoey's nose is pink, her eyes red-rimmed, and she sniffles as she pours two big glasses of crimson wine. She hands me one before curling up on the terracotta-colored couch in front of the fireplace. To her left, the terrace doors are wide open, offering a glimpse of the green and gold dome of the church she is to be married in which glows yellow in the dark Positano night.

After accepting the offered glass, I hold it by the stem and sit on the other end of the couch, then tuck my legs underneath me. Zoey is wearing satin pajamas with wide black stripes that look high-end enough to wear out on the streets of Manhattan. I self-consciously make sure my robe stays closed. She makes me want to elevate my pj game beyond the tattered T-shirts and mismatched Target bottoms that I've accumulated over the years. I make a mental note to treat myself if I ever get some cash.

For a moment we sit in silence. She looks everywhere but at me. For the first time it strikes me as odd that Zoey and Ethan aren't sharing a room and that they don't live together in Chicago. Getting married is going to massively change her life.

"What's going on, Zoey?" I finally ask, leaning toward her. "You can talk to me. Whatever you say stays between us, okay? I'm here to help."

She sighs, and her chest caves. "I know it looks bad, but nothing happened." She gestures at the picture of her and Payton that is lying face down on the coffee table and swallows a big drink of wine. She stares into her bulbous glass. "But to be honest, I think part of me is curious," she whispers.

"I've noticed," I say, softly, keeping all judgment from my voice. I reach out and pat her ankle.

Swallowing, she peeks up at me. "Do you think everyone knows? Do you think Ethan knows?"

I clench my teeth. "Honestly, I don't know how he hasn't noticed, but he doesn't seem to know. Maybe he doesn't *want* to know so he turns a blind eye?" I shrug and take a tiny sip of the slightly chilled wine, savoring the long, dry finish before setting my glass on the coffee table.

Her lower lip trembles and she stares at the cypress-and-salt scented candle on the fireplace hearth. The flame flickers in the breeze that wafts off the sea. "It's complicated. I love Ethan. I really do. He's my best—my only—friend. But part of me is . . . " She falters.

"It's okay." I smile gently. "You can tell me. No judgement."

Nodding, she takes a deep breath. "I'm really attracted to Payton." Her words come out in a rush. "He's all wrong for me, and truly, I barely know him, but there's this spark. I don't know."

"Denying that spark probably makes him more tempting."

"Totally." Her eyelashes flutter.

"And have you ever sampled . . . " I scrunch up my face, not sure how to put it or where I'm going with this. I don't want to say, *him*, so I say, "dessert?"

My awkwardness makes her laugh, and the tension between us breaks.

"No. But let's just say I have a feeling dessert might be delicious." She blots away a tear with the back of her hand.

I nod. "He might be the perfect bite."

"That's what I'm afraid of." She shakes her head. "But it could never work with us. We're too different. And I made a promise to my family. To Ethan. We made this agreement a long time ago. I've known this moment was coming, but sometimes I can't believe we're here. That the wedding is actually happening. Have you ever told yourself a story for so long you start to believe it?"

Agreement?

It's an unusual way to describe an engagement, but as much as I want to ask for clarification, it's probably better if I remain in the dark if I'm going to do my job and make sure this wedding goes off without a hitch. The last thing I need is a reason Zoey shouldn't marry Ethan. "I'm not sure, but I think I know what you mean."

"I mean, with Ethan I know I'll always be comfortable. He's stable, and we want the same things. We've mapped it all out. We're both career driven, and even though we want a family, he still supports me following my dreams. We'll have help, the best nannies. I'll still be able to work. I'll get to do what I want. I'll have it all. With Payton . . . " She sets her glass on the coffee table before hugging her knees to her chest.

"He doesn't care about that stuff. He likes being free and I don't know if he'll ever settle down. He's exciting, interesting. And, honestly, I feel like I'm missing out on something by not experiencing someone like him. But in the long term, I'm sure I'd be supporting him financially. Supporting his lifestyle. Supporting our children—if he even wants kids. And I know this is antiquated and effed-up and probably a product of gender norms that have been ingrained in me since birth, but part of me wants to be taken care of. I don't want to be the breadwinner. I'm attracted on some level to someone who makes more money than me. It makes me feel feminine. That's a point in the Ethan column. It's less pressure on me, knowing we'll always be comfortable, even if I fail."

I totally understand where she's coming from. Who doesn't want a safety net? "But you have help from your family, too," I suggest. "Your dad would never let you fail."

"He might. If I don't marry Ethan, he might take away my show. Ethan is who he wants, too." Her gaze is soft, faraway. "When I'm with Ethan, I'm who my parents want me to be. I'm the person I've told everyone I am. The best version of me. And now everyone is here, waiting to celebrate my marriage, and I don't want to disappoint anybody. But I also don't want to spend the rest of my life wondering if I missed out on something incredible."

"Have you talked to Payton about his long-term goals?"

"No!" She wrinkles her nose. "This is all hypothetical. We've *never* talked about any of this and definitely not our feelings. I don't even know if he has feelings for me. It could all be in my head."

"Good. That's good. Okay." I exhale that things haven't progressed as far as Max fears. "Honestly, what you're feeling could just be cold feet. Trust me, it's normal to have an infatuation with someone who is the opposite of the person you're about to commit your life to. Getting married is a huge, scary step, and it's a fight or flight response. If you spend more time with Ethan focusing on all the things you're excited about in your future together, it might go away. But as far as Payton not having feelings for you . . . " I bite my lip. "You saw that picture. I don't think even you can deny there's something there."

Her shoulders collapse. "What do I do?"

It's eating at me that I'm not being honest with her about knowing Ethan and I squirm, repositioning myself on the couch. But I can't get comfortable. Even though I'm withholding the truth because I made a promise to Ethan that will save face for Zoey, I still hate lying to her.

But if I'm going to make this wedding happen . . .

"I think you talk to Payton. Make it clear you need him to keep his distance. I really think this is just cold feet. You and Ethan are perfect together.

From what you just told me, it seems like you both know what you want, and you're willing to help each other build the life of your dreams."

Logically it makes sense for her to play it safe. Payton is a wild card.

And if deep down, there is a nagging twinge that Zoey might choose to be true to herself and that doesn't need to involve *any* guy, I steel myself against it for Toto's sake.

Nodding, she dabs her eyes with the hem of her pajama shirt. "You're right. I need to hold onto the vision for our future and not let my nerves distract me." She puffs out her chest. "I'll talk to Payton tomorrow. But will you come with me? So, I don't chicken out?"

"Of course." Widening my eyes, I pick up my wine glass and breathe in raspberries and oak. "Maybe you should do it in public. That way it doesn't turn into a long, intense conversation. You could do it tomorrow on the way to Capri. Make it short and to the point, then get back to the party. I'll keep Ethan busy while you talk to Payton if you want."

"Really?"

"Sure. It'll be easy." I shrug as if the thought of spending the day with Ethan doesn't have my inner seventeen-year-old quivering.

Zoey smiles. "Thank you, Rosie." She reaches out and squeezes my hand. "Gwen. You're a real friend."

Sweating, I inwardly cringe.

I am the worst person ever.

Chapter 21

Feels So Good

By the time I get back to my room, it's late. Zoey and I finished off the wine, and the more she drank, the more she mused about Payton. It's clear she's smitten, and I have major qualms about where that leaves me.

My spine is aching and I'm dying to collapse in bed and start over tomorrow.

Once I wash my face and brush my teeth, I discard my robe and slip between the crisp white sheets. I curl onto my side and sink beneath the weighted duvet, wishing I had Toto to cuddle with.

As I lay under the covers missing my kitty, I hear Duncan's and, I think, the bass player Jonah's voices float in from outside. At first, I'm tempted to go out and say goodnight, but then I think better of it. I need to get up early if I'm going to be at breakfast at six to stalk Davis, and I don't want to miss him. So, happy for a focus for my restless thoughts, I snuggle down into the velvety-soft bedding and strain to listen.

"What do you think? Should we play it?" Duncan's voice asks. I can barely make out the words so I fluff my pillow and scoot over to the edge of the bed closest to the balcony, so I can hear better.

Jonah lets out a low whistle. "That's up to you, man. I mean, you know what it's about. Are you ready for that? You might be proving your abuela right."

I'm practically hanging off the edge of the bed, listening with all my might.

Duncan sighs. "Honestly, I'm starting to think she *might* be right."

"Seriously? Whoa." Jonah laughs. "This is unexpected."

"I know." Duncan groans. "But it was Gwen's idea, and I kinda want to see her reaction. To see if she likes it."

My insides stir at the sound of my name. Not going to lie, the fact he's out there with Jonah—not Aubrey—and talking about *me* helps the tension in my muscles release. I melt into the mattress.

"Dude. Of course. Just say the word. We'll play it," Jonah says.

"I'm not sure if I'm ready. But we'll see."

They fall silent, and in the quiet my eyelids grow heavy.

I'm drifting off to sleep when I'm jolted awake by the door that joins my room to Duncan's flying open.

Disoriented, I sit up and brush my tangled hair off my face.

Duncan is standing in the doorway, still wearing Towaya like he was when I left him earlier this evening, and a surge of warmth bursts through me.

He leans against the door frame. "Hey. You're back. I've been waiting for you. You promised to say goodnight."

Hyper-aware I'm wearing only my lacy Italian underwear beneath my Hall & Oates T-shirt, I tighten the sheets around my waist and bite my lower lip. "I did? I thought I said *don't* wait up for me."

Narrowing his eyes, he shakes his head. "I wouldn't bet on that."

My heart pounds and I have no idea what is going on, but I try to keep things light. "Here we go with the bets again."

He laughs. "Can I join you?" He gestures at the bed.

I raise my eyebrows and glance down at the empty place next to me. A low, heavy heat awakens deep within me, and even though this request is bizarre, I'm intrigued.

This should be interesting.

I squint at him. "Um . . . sure?" Keeping the sheets tight around my waist, I scoot over to make room for him, and the tiny undies ride higher on my hips.

After crossing the room, he kicks off his sandals then climbs onto the bed. We sit side by side, propped against the fluffy pillows, our hands folded in our laps, facing the door to his room in silence. The quiet eats at me until, finally, I peek at him out of the corner of my eye.

He's watching me.

"So, do you want to talk about this?" His green eyes smolder, and I get the impression he's been waiting patiently for me to acknowledge him.

My lips part and I face him. "Talk about what?"

"This." He gestures between his heart and mine. "Us."

My breath catches in my throat, and it takes everything I've got to glare at him, though my nerves are vibrating with delight. "You are *not* luring me into your bed. I am *not* just another bridesmaid."

His beautiful face softens in the moonlight drifting through the French doors and his eyelashes flutter. "Gwen. Don't you think I know that? You're the *only* bridesmaid. The best." He arches an eyebrow and his gaze flickers to my thin T-shirt. "Besides. I didn't lure you. You lured me. This is *your* bed."

He has a point.

A raw need quivers inside me. Digging deep for any ounce of resistance left in my body, I open my mouth to retort but am overcome by the sight of him sitting so comfortably on my bed like he belongs here. No words come. All I want to do is inch closer to him and snuggle against his strong chest, to rest my head on his shoulder and inhale his spicy scent. To let him wrap himself around me. But I hold myself in place.

"Tell me you feel this too." He leans toward me. "We should talk about it. Or better yet. Do something about it."

Our faces are so close I can feel his minty breath on my chin and the room swirls around me.

"What is 'it'?" I whisper, the only thing I'm feeling is him sucking me in.

He doesn't respond with words. Instead, he brushes his mouth against mine, catching my lower lip between his teeth. Shivers ripple over my skin and the undertow immediately drags me out to sea. His fingers rake through my hair, and I gasp. Closing my eyes, I tilt my face up to his and the full pressure of his lips accost mine. Caught in a swirl as he parts my lips with his tongue, I open for him. Any last resistance drops to the floor.

His hands graze my breasts through the thin fabric of my T-shirt, and I am flooded. He kisses me and kisses me and kisses me and I have never experienced anything like this level of dizzying intoxication.

I have to have all of him.

Now.

Grabbing Towaya with both my hands, I swing my leg over his lap so I'm straddling him, the hard bulge in his pants pushing against the lacy triangle of my Italian underwear.

Throwing his head back, he breaks the kiss and groans. His lips are swollen from kissing me, but it's feeling his hardness pressing into me that is my undoing. I want him to know full well what he's been missing for twenty-eight weddings.

Rolling my hips against him, I take charge and raise my Hall and Oates T-shirt over my head. My full, naked breasts are silhouetted by the silvery moonlight.

His eyes almost pop out of his head. "Oh my God." His chest is heaving.

Keeping my gaze trained on him so he can't look away, I run my hands over my chest and down my stomach, making my way to the pulsating place where our bodies meet. Briefly lifting my hips, I unbutton his pants, ridding him of the pesky things as fast as I possibly can, while he discards Towaya and his T-shirt.

Positioning myself to take full advantage of the pressure of his ample offerings again, I press into the tingling ache while admiring his taut frame and the definition in his arms. His hands circle my waist and pleasure shudders through me. With only a damp piece of lace separating us, I'm nearing my edge.

"You're so beautiful," he pants. "Incredible. I've wanted this for so long." His hands slide up to cup my breasts, and I clamp my hand over his mouth to shut him up.

I don't need words. I need action.

Rising to my knees, I do a little strip tease and hook the undies with my thumb, lowering them on my hips.

His eyes aren't the only thing bulging, and he sweeps a finger across the lace barrier that separates us, moving it aside so he can make his entrance.

Arching my back, I slide myself down his torso until his tip is pressing into me, tickling me to the core. His palms graze my nipples, and biting my lower lip, I hold his stare as I hover over him. He moans and I'm aching to have him inside me. I lower myself onto him—just a little, giving into the throbbing sensation—before I lift myself up.

His chest heaving, he grips my hips as a knock sounds outside my door.

I freeze.

Whoever it is doesn't wait for an answer. The door opens and heavy footsteps enter the room.

My blood pressure spikes, and I leap off Duncan, covering my nakedness with the duvet.

Ethan comes to a stop next to the bed, towering over us.

My muscles go weak, and I nearly pass out, but Duncan doesn't react. He's collapsed on pillows, blissfully relaxed with the sheets strewn across his hard body, seemingly without a care in the world.

And that really pisses me off.

Does this other dude standing next to our bed not bother you?

Ethan takes my arm and tugs me toward him. I'm so confused, I don't resist. His blue eyes sparkle as he leans down to kiss me . . .

Before his lips connect with mine, my heart seizes, and I bolt upright.

My eyes fly open. The room is dark and I'm alone, panting in tangled sheets. Ethan and Duncan are nowhere to be seen.

OMG. Did I just have a sex dream about him? Them?

Breathless, I flop back on the bed and clap my hand over my mouth.

I'm still the last bridesmaid standing, right? Dreams don't count, do they? OMG.

Chapter 22

Just Another Day in Paradise

The boat to Capri is the same yacht that took us stargazing. The moment I step aboard, the strains of The Bandits covering "She's Gone" by Hall & Oates drift down from the upper deck, beckoning me toward the stairs.

My chest tightens.

Will Duncan take one look at me and know I'm no longer the last bridesmaid standing?

The ship's engines hum to life, and I curl my toes inside my too-small white tennis shoes.

I have no choice but to find out . . .

Taking a deep breath, I weave around the low, creamy couches dotted with terracotta and peach throw pillows that Max has positioned between potted olive trees in the open-air lounge. I ignore the DIY Bloody Mary bar and grazing table packed with cheeses and spreads nestled between rattan bread baskets, my stomach too knotted to eat.

With Duncan's voice in my ears, I force my exhausted limbs up the stairs toward him. I was restless after the dream last night and quit tossing and turning to head to La Sponda to stalk Davis at 6 a.m. Unfortunately, he never showed.

Emerging on the top deck under a sparkling clear sky, I shield my tired eyes against the bright, hot sun. Duncan stands in front of The Bandits on a small stage wearing a white T-shirt with a stretched-out neckline over chambray blue pants that are rolled at the ankles. He belts out the end of the song, hitting the closing notes with mesmerizing precision.

Dizzy from the sway of the yacht cutting through the impossibly blue water—I swear it's *only* the motion beneath my feet that has me reeling—I grip the side railing.

The memory of his hands controlling my very naked hips last night stains my cheeks pink. Inhaling the salty sea air to clear my mind, I straighten the turquoise top I wear over the cuffed coral shorts that were designated for today's "Capri Excursion."

Had Duncan not spent the night in my dreams, I would comment on this song. Act normal.

Gathering courage I don't feel, I force my feet to walk with pinched toes to the stage as the song winds down.

This is the moment of truth. The moment I find out if I'm still the last bridesmaid standing.

With my heart in my throat, but without turning my head, I mutter loud enough for Dunc to hear as I walk by, "You can't tell me it doesn't bother you there's an extra syllable—"

He closes his eyes and bites back a laugh. "In verse three. I know, I know."

Hot relief releases the tension in my neck. He doesn't somehow sense he was a key player in my dream last night. Exhaling, I keep moving as he launches into "Lovely Day" by Bill Withers. I *love* this song, and with the wind in my hair and the colorful Positano hillsides shrinking in the distance as we glide out to sea, a weight lifts. All is right with the world.

Almost.

Ethan is about as far from his bride as he can get.

He's golfing with Aubrey on the putting green Max had installed in place of the dance floor, while Zoey is on the other side of the bar posing with her grandmother in front of a peach neon sign that spells out Happily Ever After.

Payton is at the nearby prosecco bar where a bartender is squeezing fresh oranges.

With a nod at Zoey, I signal this is her chance to talk to Payton, then I grab a golf club and join Ethan.

"Good morning, Rosie," Ethan, in pink linen shorts and white polo glory, says as he knocks his ball into a hole. He steps aside for Aubrey to take her turn.

She seems to have lost *her* coral shorts and is golfing in yellow bikini bottoms, a cropped pink button-down top, and hot pink stilettos. Let me repeat.

Stilettos. On a boat.

"Good morning." I stand on the edge of the green, somewhat mollified that her feet probably are as pinched as mine. "Can I join you?"

"Absolutely." Ethan grins.

Over his shoulder, Zoey joins Payton at the bar.

Aubrey's ball goes wide, and she frowns.

"It might be your shoes that are the problem. You could fall overboard in those things, you know." Ethan teases her, nudging the toe of her pointy pink heel with his boat shoe.

She leans on her golf club. "Aesthetics matter, Ethan. My followers expect me to inspire them, to represent style that is next-level." She rolls her eyes. "But I just need to get a picture in this. Then I'll change. Will you?" She thrusts her phone toward him.

"I'll shoot you for the 'gram, baby," Uncle Al says, ambling by with a mimosa in one hand and a Bloody Mary in the other.

"Oh no, Uncle Al." I gasp. "You golf. I can take Aubrey's picture." I insert myself between the two of them and trade Al my club for his mimosa.

Aubrey shakes her head at me. "That's okay. I'll get my other brother to do it." Before I can stop her, she saunters over to Payton and interrupts his conversation with Zoey. A minute later, with prosecco in hand, she's dragging Payton across the deck.

Zoey catches my eye and shrugs, conveying the deed isn't done. I wave at her that there will be another chance.

Ethan and Uncle Al take turns putting, while across the deck Aubrey asks some guests to move, then drapes herself over a terracotta-and-cream striped cushion. Her hair blows in the sea breeze like she summoned a personal fan for her photoshoot. Leaning back on one hand, she raises her prosecco in the other while stretching her long, lean tan legs. Payton dutifully snaps pictures. With The Bandits as her soundtrack and the turquoise ocean and craggy cliffs behind her, even I'm in #wanderlust.

A tiny stabbing sensation in my heart suggests this is another sign that being a music tastemaker isn't my path. Even if it were true that these thighs had Zumba'd their way here, I could never dress like Aubrey, let alone ask people to get out of my shot. She's brave enough to stand out in the sea of quiet luxury I've been trying to blend into for years. And if that is what it takes to be considered influential, to be an authority on anything, then Shut Up & Sway probably isn't meant to be.

"Lovely Day" ends and Duncan leans into the microphone. "And now we're going to change things up a little."

My blood pressure spikes that he might be preparing to play an original song. Forgetting Aubrey, I dig through my wicker beach bag for my phone with trembling fingers.

Instead, The Bandits launch into "The Less I Know the Better" by Tame Impala. Assaulted with Mackinac memories of Ethan and me singing karaoke, of the kiss that followed, I almost pass out.

I cannot look at Ethan for fear he's remembering the same night. Or somehow knows he was present in my dream *last night* for that matter.

But I have no problem glaring at Dunc.

Did you wish for me to get fired? I accuse him through telepathy.

"Hey, this brings back memories, doesn't it?" Ethan joins me, nudging my arm with his elbow, his voice low as Al aligns his shot. "I requested that they play our song. That's the only time I've ever sung karaoke. The things I did for Ty." He shakes his head.

It's like the ocean crashes over me, sucks me under, and bubbles roar past my ears, muffling the song. Attempting to expand my lungs, I try to comprehend what he means by "things he did for Ty," but I'm drowning and can't make sense of it. I picture Ethan and me riding bikes and picnicking, sharing his iPod, and all I can see is a zitty teenager, dressed all in black next to his Grecian-god glory. It probably looked like he was a sweet big brother indulging his awkward little sister when we sang karaoke.

I bristle as a truth part of me has probably always known, but never admitted, presents itself. Refusing to acknowledge it, I shove the realization back into the locked box it belongs in and bury it at sea. "Does Zoey like this kind of music?" Twisting my necklace between my thumb and index finger, I change the subject.

"No, not really." He shrugs. "She's more into classic rock, pop, things like that."

Desperately wanting Duncan to play *anything* else, I bite my lip. "That's so sweet of you to ask them to play this for me, but I'm going to go ask the band to play something Zoey would like. I feel like this isn't her thing."

"Yeah." Ethan nods. "Probably not."

"I'll be right back."

I make a beeline for Duncan and stand directly in front of him. I glance at Aubrey. She's finished her shoot, and seeming to have forgotten she wanted to change, is fangirling next to me. I'm trying not to feel like an adoring groupie—because standing this close to him while he nails this song makes my heart want to burst.

But he probably nails a lot of things.

The reminder sobers me.

After he plays the final notes, Duncan leans down. "What's up, Rosie?"

"Can you please play something else?" I say through gritted teeth.

A smile tugs at his lips. "Sure. Like what?"

"Something yacht? Like . . . 'Takin' it to the Streets'—the Doobie Broth-ers."

He shakes his head. "No can do. Yacht rock doesn't go to the streets."

I tilt my chin up. "Where does it go, then? The waves? The sea?"

"No, no, no. It goes to the *sheets*."

Sucking in my breath, I close my eyes and clamp my mouth shut, refusing to let him see me laugh.

Of course, it does.

Somehow masking my expression in calm, I compose myself. "Whatever you think, then. But something the *bride* will like, please."

He salutes me. "Your wish is my command."

"That's what I'm afraid of." I turn on my heel.

The boat slows as I make my way back to Ethan.

Instead of playing another song, Duncan announces, "We're arriving at the Blue Grotto. Everyone who wants to take the excursion inside the cave, please line up to exit the boat. Otherwise, if you'd rather go straight to Marina Grande, feel free to remain seated."

"You're doing the cave tour, right?" Ethan gestures for Al and me to move toward the stairs.

"Yeah. Of course," I say. We take our place in the line that's forming at the top of the steps. Aubrey joins us with Duncan in tow.

On the lower deck, Payton and Zoey are the first to get into one of the waiting rowboats bobbing in the waves next to the yacht. I cross my fingers that Zoey was able to talk to Payton while they were in line or can manage to get her point across during the boat ride.

Their guide, who will be rowing, stands in the middle of the boat and directs them to sit tandem-style. Payton sits on one end of the boat, and Zoey lowers herself between his legs. One of the other groomsmen takes a place across from them.

Max is nearby, next to Ethan's parents who are waiting for the next boat. He slowly turns his head toward me, *Exorcist*-style. His telepathic *I thought you were fixing this* creeps down my spine, and my skin goes cold.

I am fixing it! At least Zoey is sitting upright and refraining from lying back against Payton's chest.

Almost on cue, she leans back. He wraps his arms over her shoulders as their boat bobs and dips toward the dark entrance to a *tiny* cave carved into a giant rock.

Kneeling, I pretend I'm busy tying my shoe to dodge the daggers Max is shooting at me.

"Oh, we need partners," Uncle Al says as the line moves forward and forces me to my feet. "You wanna ride with me, sweetie?" He eyes Aubrey, who has at least changed into the white tennis shoe portion of today's outfit.

I step between them. "I'm pretty sure she already has a partner, Uncle Al." It pains me to glance at Duncan. "Why don't you ride with me?"

"Well, well, well." Al grins. "I thought you'd never ask, Rosie." He offers me his arm.

"Actually, she has a partner, too." Ethan interjects, taking my hand and making my knees buckle.

Uncle Al shakes his head and loudly declares, "Why aren't there more bridesmaids at this thing? Zoey needs more girls. How about her?" He points to an attractive Food Network executive in line ahead of us. "Maybe *she* wants to do the grotto with Old Al."

The woman peers back at us.

Gasping, I drop Ethan's hand and try to make myself big as if that could shield her from Al as she makes her way down the stairs.

"You know what?" I grab Hayden, the red-haired Wedding Bandit keyboard player who passes by. "I have the perfect partner for you, Uncle Al. Have you met Hayden? You two would really get along. Do you know anything about the marimba?"

We climb down the steps. When we reach the bottom deck, we take our places in line.

Uncle Al eyes Hayden, then pulls a massive joint out of his pocket. "Do you partake?"

Hayden grins. "'Smoke on the Water' by Deep Purple *is* one of my favorite covers."

"No. No! No smoking on the water!" I move to grab the joint, but they get into opposite ends of the waiting rowboat before I can stop them. My jaw agape, I silently plead with Hayden.

He knows Max would explode.

"Don't worry, Rosie," Uncle Al calls, putting the joint back in his pocket as their guide rows them toward the cave. "We'll behave." He leans toward Hayden and lowers his voice, but I still hear him add, "Or at least find somewhere discreet."

A guide pulls an empty rowboat to a stop in front of me. "*Allora.* Can the gentlemen get in first, please?"

Ethan climbs into the wooden boat, followed by Duncan and I forget about the joint.

"Come on, Rosie." Ethan pats the bench in front of him.

Hesitating, I cast a quick peek at Duncan. His eyes seem to bulge ever so slightly, but if this is his wish coming true, I'm powerless to stop it. Aubrey steps aboard and arranges herself between Duncan's legs.

Ethan offers me his hand. In the spirit of surrender, I sigh and step aboard.

The rocking boat creaks, water sloshing at the sides as I lower myself between Ethan's legs, trying to avoid brushing his thighs with my hips.

Duncan arches an eyebrow at me over Aubrey's head. I narrow my eyes at him, fluttering my eyelashes, hopefully without Aubrey noticing, on guard for any wish granting he has planned.

"*Benvenuti, signore e signori,*" our guide says once we're settled. He rows us through the choppy water toward the mouth of the cave. It's even smaller than it looked from the yacht, and my insides contract. I have no idea how this boat will fit through the pinprick of a circle.

Ethan and I are facing the opening. Duncan and Aubrey are riding backward so they can't see what's coming. Aubrey leans against Duncan and snuggles into his chest, oblivious to the pending threat as the boat rocks. I note he keeps his elbows resting on the sides of the boat rather than circling them around her shoulders. I'm grateful he spares us any PDA.

"*Allora.* We have some rules," the guide continues in English while propelling us toward the miniscule opening. "When we go inside the cave, you will all need to lie down. We have to time the waves just right. Please listen and do what I say so we don't take off your heads." He laughs. "Keep your hands and arms in. And no sunglasses. It's better without."

A white boat identical to ours exits the tiny hole and I'm relieved to see it easily fits through the opening, but it doesn't totally settle my fears that it's going to be claustrophobic inside.

The guide positions us in front of the hole where the other boat just came through. "Here we go. Lie down!"

I slide down against Ethan's chest. His body is hard against my back and my cheeks heat. He slips his arms around my shoulders, holding me close as the guide also lies down. He's practically in my lap as he uses a metal chain to pull us into the hole.

Oh my God. Oh my God. Oh my God.

For an instant everything goes black, but then we glide inside. Rocks shimmering with the reflection of the cobalt water appear high overhead. We sit up inside the humid cave. Beneath us the brilliant sea is lit from its depths by an unearthly light and it's like we've been transported to another planet illuminated by blue moons.

"This is amazing." Duncan runs his fingers through the water, leaving a trail of silvery-blue sparkles in their wake. Aubrey is busy filming, experiencing the grotto through her phone.

"*Lì cresce sotto l'oceano,*" the guide sings, his voice echoing off the rocks.

"*Oye,*" Duncan interrupts. "*Conosci la canzone 'Bailar a la luz di Luna'?* The acoustics are great in here."

Pausing, the guide thinks for a moment as the rowboat gently rocks, little waves sloshing at its sides.

Duncan starts singing about dancing under a big moon, his voice bouncing off the water and stone and enveloping us.

"*Allora. Sì.* 'Dancing in the Moonlight?' King Harvest," the guide finally says before joining in, his voice harmonizing perfectly with Duncan's.

Suddenly, I'm envious of Aubrey's phone. This would be *great* content for Shut Up & Sway. But I'm too self-conscious about how filming Duncan would come across to dig mine out and hit record.

Duncan waves his hands as he sings, gesturing for us—and the people in the other boats floating in the grotto—to join in.

And they do.

Everyone's voices come together—even Ethan's—for the chorus. My heart swells with the specialness of it all, and I join in. As we float along in this blue other world, connected by song, goosebumps shoot up my arms. My jealousy over the phone evaporates. I let myself be in this moment. I don't need a recording because I will *never* forget it.

I watch Duncan with shining eyes as the song ends, enthralled by his power to command such an experience. Part of me can't help wondering what it would be like to be with someone who creates magic like this all the time, who makes everything special just by being who they are. And if I had any doubts left about his potential they've been drowned. He's light years more incandescent than the brightest star in the galaxy.

Duncan and the guide high-five while everyone in the other boats breaks into applause, and I could not remove my grin with a sandblaster.

"Oh, man, I love that song," Dunc says as we lie down and sail back into the sunlight through the tiny opening. "It's been covered so many times in so many ways and every one of them is great. It's a testament to that song that it demanded to be heard. It's like it's part of all of us."

All I know is that it will forevermore be a part of *me*.

We emerge from our moonlit experience, and I squint against the harsh brightness of reality, wishing I had the words to thank Duncan for the gift he just bestowed on us.

But reality will not be denied.

Crisis-Max is waiting for me when our boat bumps against the wooden platform at the base of a staircase built into the cliffs, and I shudder.

"The maid of honor. Just who I've been looking for." He smiles through gritted teeth and offers a hand to help me out of Ethan's lap. "Can I talk to you for a minute? Zoey had some requests."

Having no choice, I surrender my fingers to his.

He pulls me to my feet and onto the dock with him. Gripping my upper arm, he guides me toward the stairs. I turn and quickly wave to everyone. "I'll see you all in a little bit."

"Why is the bride not in a boat with the groom?" he asks with mock pleasantry, his lips barely moving, as we climb to where a tram is waiting to take us to Marina Grande.

"Don't worry, Max," I whisper, slightly out of breath. "I've got this handled. Zoey needs to talk to Payton alone but in public to ask him to keep his distance. Everything is going to be fine. It's just cold feet. She and Ethan will spend the rest of the afternoon together. Promise. From the cable car up Monte Solaro, to strolling the gardens of Villa San Michelle to aperitivo on the boat ride back to Positano, they won't leave each other's side." We reach the top of the steps.

Somehow, I'll make sure of it.

"I hope you're right." He exhales. "I'll be watching. If we pull this wedding off, Gwen, there may be an extra bonus for you. And if not, if the biggest wedding of my career is ruined, heads will have to roll. It's not personal, but I hope you understand."

"I get it." I force a smile. "But you don't have to worry. Everything is going to be perfect."

As if on cue, Zoey, of her own accord, leaves Payton and strolls toward where Ethan is emerging at the top of the stairs behind us. Her chin is held high, and she doesn't look back.

I turn to Max and nod, like I had something to do with this, though inside I'm quaking.

He silently applauds me before walking toward Zoey's dad. On the way, he crosses paths with Uncle Al who swoops toward me, prosecco glass in hand.

I suck in my breath.

"Rosie, did you know these are bottomless?" He raises his mimosa to the sky. "How'd they know that's just the way I like 'em?" He cackles and glues himself to my side while, in the distance, Aubrey glues herself to Duncan's.

Chapter 23

I'd Really Love to See You Tonight

As soon as I step out of the shower the phone rings.

I quickly wrap myself in a towel and pick up the handset. "Hello?"

"Hi. It's me." Zoey is breathless.

"Hey. How'd it go? You and Ethan looked like you were having fun this afternoon."

Unlike me and Uncle Al.

It's been a long day.

"We were." She talks fast, her voice bright and cheery. "I told Payton I felt like there was weirdness between us, but I needed to focus on my marriage and asked him to give me space."

"How did he react?" I cradle the phone against my shoulder while I dry my hair with a towel.

"He understood." She exhales. "I feel so much better. Lighter. Thank you for your help."

She sounds freer and I should be relieved. The wedding is back on—and so is my bonus—but I frown, somehow sad for her that her life is so mapped out.

Not that I'm one to talk. I'd give anything to have a compass to even halfway tell me what direction to go in.

"I'm glad I could be there for you." I muster enthusiasm.

"I really appreciate it. And you deserve a night off. Especially after hanging out with Uncle Al all day. Thank you for *that* too. You really kept the peace."

"That's what I'm here for." A tingle of excitement shoots down my spine at the prospect of a night to myself.

"Well, relax. Enjoy yourself. I'm having dinner with my parents, and I'll see you poolside tomorrow. Oh, and check outside your door. I had Luigi leave you a little something as a thank you."

"You didn't have to do that, but thank *you*. You have fun too." I do a little happy dance at being ordered to relax. "Goodnight." After hanging up the phone, I slip on my bathrobe, then open my door. Outside, a bottle of rosé and a cheese plate are waiting for me on a silver tray.

And so is Ethan.

He's not *actually* on a silver tray, but in his trim black pants, white sports coat, black tie, and loafers, he might as well be.

I have no idea what he's doing here, and I jump. "Hi!"

He grins, exposing his dimple. "Oh good. You're home. I was hoping I'd catch you before dinner." He motions to the tray. "Do you want me to bring this inside?"

My stomach tenses. "Oh, um, sure." I move aside, holding the door open so he can enter while wrapping my bathrobe tighter around my waist.

Brushing past me, he carries the tray in, and I click the door shut behind us.

He crosses the room and sets the room service on my desk. "So, I was wondering if you wanted to join me for dinner?" Picking up the wine, he examines the bottle. "I've been thinking, if your brother were here, we would have been hanging out this whole time, and you're the next best thing. I feel like we should get to know each other better." He waggles the bottle at me, silently asking if I'd like some.

I slowly nod. "Oh. Yeah. Dinner . . . " I say the three words that make sense to me as my evening alone evaporates.

"Do you have plans?" He pours a glass of pale pink wine and hands it to me.

"No. No, I don't." My fingers tremble as I accept the glass. "You aren't doing something with Zoey?"

"No. It's my night off." He sits on the edge of the desk. "Let me take you out."

I freeze. Dinner alone with the groom is wrong and forbidden on every level—not to mention having him in my room—and double not to mention that our lips touched once upon a time.

Max would start digging my grave if he found out. It's not worth putting my bonus in jeopardy.

I take a giant sip of wine.

Ethan pours himself a glass and raises it in a toast. "To Ty. He would have loved this." His wine in midair, he watches me expectantly, his blue eyes sparkling right through me.

Well, when he puts it that way . . .

The alcohol turns to liquid fire in my veins and seventeen-year-old me flares to life. This is what she's always wanted. I will Rosie to take hold of my brain, to restore order and practicality, but my rebellious inner seventeen-year-old digs in her heels and won't be budged. She wants to see where this night leads no matter the consequences, and I can't muster the energy to deny her. Besides, I'm fairly certain Ethan won't take no for an answer. If the alternative to dinner is entertaining him in my bedroom, going out sounds like the safer option.

I sigh. "You're right. He would love this." I clink my glass against his. "To Ty." We both drink. "Just give me a minute to get ready?"

"Take your time. I'll wait outside." Disappearing through the French doors into the evening where the sky is two shades darker than our crisp dry rosé, he says hi to someone.

Probably Duncan. Ugh.

I try not to think about how this looks as I dig through my suitcase and retrieve one of my contraband white festival dresses. The short, ivory lace dress was a gift from my fashionista college roommate Jude for my birthday and is the only new (and designer) dress I brought with me. It has an open back with side cut outs and long sleeves that flare out at my wrists. I wish I could pair it with my combat boots—they'd be the most comfortable thing to wear—but they don't exude the quiet luxury dinner with Ethan requires, so I pair it with the strappy black heels I bought with Duncan's credit card.

After drying my hair and sweeping on lip gloss, I poke my head out the door and find Ethan alone, sipping his wine. Maybe I imagined him talking to someone?

"You're beautiful." Grinning, he stands and offers me his arm.

My skin prickles. Once again, I conjure Rosie, but she is nowhere to be found. I am powerless against the momentum pushing me toward Ethan. Surrendering to this long dreamed of night, I wrap my fingers around his firm bicep and let him lead me through my room, out the door, and down the hall.

"Where are we going?" I ask, hyper-aware of his muscles beneath my fingertips, of his broad shoulders that take up most of the width of the hallway.

"It's not far. About three hundred steps from the hotel." Bypassing the elevator, we skip down two short flights of stairs toward the lobby. "There's a rooftop bar with a view of Spaggia Grande beach. And don't worry. I had Luigi call to make sure none of the wedding guests have reservations there tonight. It'll be just us."

We reach the third flight of stairs and I drag him to a stop on the landing. "You should go first," I whisper, detangling my arm from his. "We shouldn't be seen together here either."

"Good thinking." He lowers his voice and leans close enough that his breath tickles my ear, making me shiver. "Go left out of the hotel. I'll meet you at Piazza dei Mulini."

Giving my hand a parting squeeze, he hurries down to the steps.

After he leaves, I count to ten, slowing my breath and giving him a head start. The distance between us does nothing to weaken my seventeen-year-old resolve. Her heart is pumping with espionage adrenaline.

Once I'm sure Ethan has left the building, I enter the lobby. Luigi gives me an approving nod as I cross the tile floor. I wave, somehow keeping my expression neutral though my insides are doing the jitterbug. Then I exit the hotel into the balmy night.

Outside, the sky is deepening to black. With my pulse thundering in my ears, I turn left down the narrow cobblestone street. Warm yellow light illuminates the shops and cafés that line the towering cliffs to my right. Music spills out of arched doorways, mingling with the chatter of people dining in flickering candlelight at the sidewalk tables overlooking the water. It all blurs together as I hunt for Ethan up ahead of me.

When I reach Piazza dei Mulini, he steps out of the shadows and takes my wrist, guiding me around a sharp corner and down a vine-covered path toward the beach.

I scan the crowds for familiar faces on the street behind me one last time before exhaling and letting my guard down.

"Sneaking around with you is kinda fun." Smiling down at me, he guides us to a set of cramped stone stairs. "I don't remember the last time I felt this energized."

"Maybe when you proposed to Zoey?" I suggest. My inner seventeen-year-old has pushed the limits of my comfort zone, and I embody Rosie long enough to take a direct hit at her.

Ethan wrinkles his nose. "Not really. There wasn't a big, fancy proposal. We decided together we were both ready to start the next chapter in our lives and that was it. We picked out a ring and here we are."

"Oh . . . " His revelation settles oddly.

"Zoey doesn't need to be swept off her feet with big romantic gestures." He shrugs. "That's not her thing. She likes to handle things on her own. And speaking of handling things, you were amazing with Uncle Al today. That was impressive."

We twist around a corner to another staircase, continuing our descent past an open basement door at the base of a stone fortress. Inside, an old man in a white apron mashes grapes in a barrel with a gnarled stick. The air grows thick with the scent of sweet fermentation.

"I was just doing my job." I flush at the compliment.

"Well, if you ever decide to move on from being a bridesmaid, I'm sure we could find a place for you at Giorgio."

Gwendoline Watson, General Counsel for Giorgio, Inc.

I try on the title. It should have a ring to it, but somehow it falls flat. Not that I'm taking the offer seriously. Ethan doesn't know I went to law school.

"I might take you up on that." Thinking I hear footsteps shuffling down the stairs, I check behind us, only to find a cat who reminds me of Toto slinking into the bushes. "If Max finds out I'm out with you, I'll probably be in the market for a new job."

"Don't worry about Max. If we get caught, which we won't, I'll tell him I forced you to come with me." He eyes me sideways. "You can't say no to the groom."

No, it doesn't seem I can.

Ethan moves his fingers from my wrist and weaves them through mine. "I'm serious, Gwen. Let's talk when we get back to Chicago. Now that you're back in my life, I'd love for you to stay in it. I've been wanting to talk to you about . . ." Falling silent, he squeezes my hand. "The way things ended, I—"

My pulse throbs in my throat. Having no desire to talk about how things ended, I cut him off.

"How would Zoey feel about that?" I tip my face up to his as we make it to the boardwalk lined with trees wrapped in white twinkling lights and follow it along the beach. "Her hired bridesmaid suddenly hanging around?"

Ethan presses his lips together and scrunches his forehead, like he wants to continue his thought, but then he sighs, seeming to think better of it.

"She'd be fine with it. The thing I most like about Zoey is her moods are predictable. She likes to do her thing, and I'm free to do mine. No questions asked."

A medieval castle built into the cliffs along the beach looms before us and I lower my brow, unsure *how much* freedom she gives him. Thus far, she seems okay with not being the number one priority in his life, but how far does that extend?

He leads me through an arched neon blue sign that reads Music on the Rocks and up a stone staircase that winds around the outside of the castle. All the while my heart pounds at the possibility that she gives him a long leash, even though there's *no way* that would impact me. I wouldn't have it in me to be the other woman.

My inner seventeen-year-old, on the other hand, has other ideas.

The blood is rushing to her head, dizzying her with a fantasy life as a bonafide lawyer at home among the quiet luxury set, as we arrive on the roof at Fly Bar. The white, candlelit décor takes on a fuzzy glow under the open-air ceiling that gives way to glittering stars overhead. A salty sea breeze drifts through the windowless walls, but it fails to sober me.

We follow the hostess past a white piano where the pianist is softly playing the instrumental to Billy Joel's "Scenes from an Italian Restaurant," which adds the perfect amount of levity to keep the bar from feeling snooty. She's about to seat us at a low white table framed by white couches overlooking the inky sea and the flickering lights of the hillside villas when two heads at the next table snap up.

"This is a surprise," Aubrey says, looking gorgeous in a skin-tight gold sequin minidress that is the same color as the prosecco bubbling in her glass. Next to her, Duncan wears a pink and green palm tree shirt that is unbuttoned to expose his defined chest. His lips twitch as he observes my dress.

My stomach drops and I wish I could melt into a puddle and disappear. What a world.

Clearly Ethan didn't call to see if any members of the band had reservations tonight.

"Hey, you two." Still holding my hand, Ethan grins down at them and I fight to disentangle my fingers from his.

For the briefest second Duncan's eyebrows pull down, but he quickly recovers himself. "Hey. You should join us." Rubbing the back of his neck, he nods toward the empty couch across from them, and I don't miss the micro-glare Aubrey shoots at him.

"Oh, we don't want to interrupt. Ethan and I were working on this surprise he's putting together for Zoey during the reception. We thought we'd grab something quick to eat." I spit out a cover story.

"Surprise?" Aubrey raises her eyebrows, then sighs, her shoulders slumping. "Okay. I have to know about this. Sit. It's ridiculous for us to have separate tables."

Ethan and I glance at each other. We both know it would be weird to refuse, and he shrugs his acceptance. I nod and sink onto the couch across the table from Duncan. Quietly exhaling relief that I don't have to be one-on-one with Ethan, I tug on my dress so it doesn't ride too far up my thighs.

The hostess leaves us to explore the menu. I move mine into the glow from our small white table lamp so I can read it and try not to gasp at the prices. I'm pretty sure I could buy a bottle of good vodka for the price of one of these drinks.

"I guess we can let them in on the surprise?" Ethan rests his elbows on the table and leans toward me.

"I think we have to." I know full well he has no idea what surprise I was talking about, but I'm grateful he has the wherewithal to play along. "Ethan has been working on a song that he's going to serenade Zoey with at the reception," I tell Aubrey and Duncan.

"Seriously?" Aubrey's jaw drops. "What song?"

Ethan chuckles. "'The Less I Know the Better' by Tame Impala?" He asks like he's asking me. "Loved your version of it earlier, by the way," he says to Duncan.

"This is *so* unlike you." Aubrey shakes her head.

"He's just kidding," I interject, thinking fast. "He's singing 'Brandy' by Looking Glass but changing 'Brandy' to 'Zoey.' And I know it's out of character, but that's the best part. Nobody will see it coming and therefore they'll never forget it. I love it when a wedding has an element of surprise."

"Speaking of the master of surprises . . . " Duncan mutters, shifting in his seat.

I follow his gaze over Ethan's shoulder.

Max, whose *specialty* is surprise wedding elements, is striding straight toward us and my heart seizes.

Chapter 24

Sailing

"There they are," Max says in the pleasant tones he reserves for fathers of the bride.

Beneath his calm façade I'm certain he wants answers as to why I've commandeered the groom, and I swallow hard.

"Ethan. Aubrey. I've been looking everywhere for you." He stops next to our table, wearing a pink suit over a black-and-white striped T-shirt. "Your parents have requested your presence at a family dinner with the Costanzos. We thought you were aware."

"I thought I told them I wasn't coming." Aubrey shrugs and sips her prosecco.

"That's actually happening? It wasn't on the itinerary." Ethan stands. He must realize the bride calls, and in this instance there's *no* way he can't go.

Which is a good thing, I tell my inner seventeen-year-old.

"It was a last-minute change. I thought Zoey filled you in," Max replies. "Your brother seems to be the only one who got the message, though. Payton was right on time." His gaze flickers over me, and I shudder.

Ethan wrinkles his nose. "Shoot. I thought tonight was supposed to be a night out with the guys. I figured *they* wouldn't mind if I was late." He faces me and takes my hand in his. "We'll have to work on the song another time. Rain check?"

"The song?" Max frowns at me but Ethan keeps the cover story alive, sparing me some "how-dare-you-abduct-the-groom" Max-wrath.

"Yes. I'm the element of surprise." Ethan grins. "I asked Rosie if she could help me give Zoey a gift she'll never forget, and I thought the least I could do was treat her to *the best* sushi in all of Italy as a thank you."

"I see." Max smiles back, exposing his dimple and it strikes me that Ethan and Max have matching dimples. And they're both probably skilled at using them to get their way.

"Maybe you can fill me in on the details on the way to La Tagliata where your parents are waiting for *both* of you. They have some of the best *bisteca* in all of Italy." Max looks pointedly back and forth between Ethan and Aubrey. "Luigi mentioned he made a reservation for you at Fly Bar, Ethan. It's a wonder I found Aubrey, too." He leans past Ethan to address me. "I'll have to double-check that I have your correct cell number, Rosie. I tried texting you several times to see if Aubrey was with you."

"Oh." I clench my teeth, picturing where I left the Italian loaner phone charging on my desk. "You probably have the right number. I forgot my phone in my room."

"Of course. Understood." Max nods. And to his credit, his eyes only shoot butter knives at me.

He claps his hands, and I jump.

"At any rate, we'll have to work your song into the reception itinerary, Ethan. I'm glad you let *me* in on the surprise."

Even though he doesn't look at me, his words find their mark, and I flinch. "Sorry, Max. You're right. I should have thought to tell you. I've never been a maid of honor before."

Max holds a hand up to stop me. "It's fine. Now you'll know, should you *ever* get the opportunity again." He glances at my white dress and his eyes briefly bulge while he motions for Aubrey to stand.

Inwardly, I wince as the bonus dollars evaporate before my eyes.

But Ethan saved me. Max can't deny the groom. He can't fire me for this, can he?

"And I apologize for the interruption. Thank you for understanding these two have a prior obligation. If you'll please excuse them," Max says to Duncan and me.

"Of course. We get it," I say, brightly. "Ethan should *absolutely* be having dinner with his bride."

Duncan nudges Aubrey's arm. "You should go. We'll do this some other night."

Aubrey groans and makes a show of standing. "I'll text you when I'm done." She blows Duncan a kiss and allows herself to be led away.

"I trust you'll make sure Rosie makes it back to the hotel?" Max says over his shoulder to Duncan. "She must be tired. She had a long day."

He arches one eyebrow at me, conveying that we will talk about Ethan later, and that as a thank you for this afternoon's smooth sailing, he's letting me off the hook. For now.

"Aye-aye, Captain." Duncan salutes Max.

"See you tomorrow, Rosie, Duncan." Ethan winks at me, then follows Max, leaving me alone to face Duncan.

"It looks like you're staying." Duncan picks up his menu. "Max's orders."

My stomach growls but I hesitate.

I don't need a babysitter.

"It's on me, by the way." He covers my hand with his, seemingly misinterpreting my hesitation.

Reminded of my financial situation and annoyed with myself for letting my inner seventeen-year-old get in the way of my bonus, my skin goes cold. I snatch my hand away. "No. I can't let you buy."

"It's cool. I'm DJing a set at the club downstairs tonight and they gave me a gift card. I can't use it all by myself. You'd be doing me a favor."

The tension in my neck releases as I consider.

"Please? Don't make me sit alone at this spectacular rooftop bar over-looking the Mediterranean Sea eating sushi all by myself." His lower lip juts out.

"That does sound miserable." I flutter my eyelashes at him. "Well, if you're just killing time, I guess I could keep you company."

He switches menus to the drink list. "So, you and Ethan, huh?"

"We really were working on the surprise, and he suggested we grab dinner."

"Mmm-hmmm."

"So, you and Aubrey, huh?" I retort.

"I'm just doing my job."

"I thought you were a wedding singer."

His spine stiffens, but then he relaxes. "I don't want to fight with you, Gwen. Here. I've been meaning to show you this." He slides his phone over to me. "Your cat sitter is still texting me. I think she wants to make sure you get the pictures."

The photo on the screen is of Toto taking a cone break, according to the text from Gwen's Kitty, the name Duncan gave the cat-sitter's contact info in his phone. Toto is blissed out on a pillow, sleeping with his eyes bunched in happy half-moons, and my heart blooms.

I press my hand to the ache that rises in my throat.

We're going to be just fine, Toto. If I don't get fired for tonight, everything is going to fall into place. Max will see. Ethan and Zoey are back together, and I'm going to pull this wedding off with dignity and grace. We'll be back home together in no time.

Resolved, I hand the phone back to Duncan before I get teary.

"And Corina wants to know my birth date. Should I tell her?" He swipes across the screen and shows me the text, his eyes wide.

"That's up to you. Give her a little info and you never know what she'll reveal." I laugh, trying not to think it's cute that he's named Corina Gwen's Roomie.

Duncan makes a scared face and puts his phone down on the far end of the table.

A warm wind ruffles the wavy hair that cascades past my shoulders. I pick up my menu. "What do you want to eat?"

I study the sushi rolls on the menu, but after a silent moment, Duncan still hasn't responded. I squint up at him.

He's staring down at the beach, his lips twisting. Shadows from flickering white candles set inside the white lanterns that surround us play across his face, masking his expression.

"What's wrong?" I follow the trajectory of his gaze to boats bobbing on the sea, casting little pools of yellow light on the black water. "You can tell Corina your birthday. She won't cast a spell on you or anything, I promise."

Sucking in his cheeks, he sighs. "No. It's not that. I keep thinking about Forrest Gump being out there on a boat in a hurricane."

"You're thinking about Forrest Gump." Pressing my mouth into a thin line, I sit back and set down my menu.

He returns his attention to me. "Hear me out. There's a scene in *Forrest Gump* where Forrest and Lieutenant Dan are out at sea during a hurricane. Forrest is terrified during the storm but ultimately, he survives, and it turns out that being out at sea was the best place to be. All the docked boats were destroyed, but Forrest's boat weathered the storm and his was the only shrimp boat left. As the lone survivor, he raked in the shrimp and made a fortune."

I nod slowly. "Mmmmkay. I have no idea where you're going with this."

"My point is you can't judge situations as good or bad. They just are. You don't know the outcome. What you *think* is safe—the dock—can be your doom. There *is no* safe harbor, which, incidentally, is the alternate name for a Dark 'n' Stormy." Leaning toward me, he finally opens his menu and points to where the ginger beer and rum cocktail is, in fact, listed as a Dark 'n' Stormy in the English translation.

"Random fact: To be officially called a Dark 'n' Stormy, it has to be made with Gosling's rum—they trademarked it—otherwise, you're stuck with the less authentic 'safe harbor.'" He closes the menu. "Anyway. What I'm saying is. Eff safe. You've got to head out to sea, take a chance even in a storm, because you don't know what outcomes are out there. That's where your abundance could be. Otherwise, you might miss out."

"That whole monologue was about me playing it safe." I stare at him, my lips parted. "Is this about me telling Ethan who I am? That *is* what you wished for me, isn't it?"

"No. It's not what I wished." He shrugs. "But have you told him?"

My heart thuds. I don't want to lie to him.

Fortunately, before I can answer, a waitress in a tight black dress stops at our table. "*Allora.* Can I get you something to drink?" she asks in a thick Italian accent.

Duncan cocks his head at me and opens his menu. "What do you think? Feeling adventurous? Do you trust me?"

Wanting to prove my courage, I flutter my eyelashes. "Sure. Go for it."

He turns to the waitress. "*Es tu oscuro e tempestoso hecho con il rum delle Goslings?*"

"*Sì.*" She nods. "We have Gosling's."

"Then *prenderemo due dark and stormies e i tuoi tre rollos de sushi mediterrá-neos más popolari.*" He holds up two fingers for our drinks, then three as he orders the three most popular sushi rolls.

"Of course." She smiles. "*Torno subito con i tuoi drink.*" Her high heels clack as she walks away.

"Speaking of playing it safe," I say as soon as she leaves. "When are you going to man up and play an original song for me?"

He pulls back slightly. "What do you mean man up?"

"You're afraid of putting yourself out there, of nobody liking the song. That's why you don't play one. You're scared." I point at him. "Get off the dock, bro." I slap the back of my hands on my thighs.

"I am not scared. And you're one to talk, *bro*. You still didn't tell me the name of your website. What, are you afraid I'll read it?" He watches me intently.

Yes.

Getting an idea, I square my jaw. "Tell you what. I'll show you mine if you show me yours. If you play an original song, I'll tell you my URL."

His head waffles back and forth as he considers.

The waitress returns and sets our cocktails in front of us.

Duncan picks up his icy highball glass that is garnished with lime and a black-and-white striped paper straw. "Okay. You've got a deal."

I smile and raise my glass to his. "In that case, fuck safe harbors."

And we drink.

Chapter 25

How Much I Feel

Over Mediterranean sushi rolls, we order another round of drinks. And then another. By the time we're done eating, I'm feeling warm and fuzzy, and my filter is long gone. His is too.

"So, you dated Ethan when you were seventeen," he says, over our third round of drinks. "Who came next?"

"Not really anyone. My college roommates tried to set me up with people, but those relationships never lasted long. Even though I tried, I've never been very good at casual relationships, and nobody ever seemed interested in something serious. Then in law school I had to study so hard it consumed me. That's when I met Max. Now I mostly meet groomsmen looking for a one-night stand. It's against Max's rules for bridesmaids to fraternize with guests at weddings. I survived his Finishing School once. I have *no* desire to be sent back to Bridesmaid Bootcamp. Though I probably punched my ticket tonight." I grimace.

"Oh, yeah." He draws his head back, seeming to reach for a recollection. "Terra told me about that. The whole carrying the bouquet low while you walk down the aisle, so your arms look toned. And you have to keep the stems parallel to the ground to show off the flowers, while balancing *Etiquette* by Emily Post on your head."

"It's a first edition." Resting my palms on the table, I widen my eyes for emphasis, ignoring the pang that accompanies the proof he's had actual conversations with Terra while consistently ignoring me. Until now, of course. "Nineteen twenty-two."

He laughs. "Only Max. But you've got to love him."

"You really do." I nod thinking of the occasional cocktail-laced post wedding recaps where he lets his guard down. *That* Max is one of my favorite people. Witnessing his fun side is one of the things that has kept me working with him this long. "He can be gruff, and he likes things how he likes them, but deep down he has a heart of gold." I swirl the ice cubes around my glass with the straw. "And I know it's pathetic that I'm so bad at keeping things casual. I wish I didn't care so much, but I can't help how I feel."

"I'm not judging." His foot nudges mine under the table, making my insides quiver. "I think it's great to know what you want and be willing to wait for it."

I raise my gaze to his and a shot of adrenaline surges through me. "Oh, I don't know what I want."

Liar.

I tamp down the assertion, at war with myself.

Last. Bridesmaid. Standing.

I force my shoulders into a shrug. "I just like Hallmark movies—where everything ends with a kiss and happily ever after."

"There's a lot that happens after a kiss, you know." His green eyes are searing.

Hot chills tingle down my spine. "I don't want to think about that." I scrunch up my face.

"You're romantic."

"Or impossible. I guess I've never met anyone that gets me, except for Ethan."

"Or you've never let anyone get *to* you."

"I suppose there's that, too." I wrinkle my nose.

He pauses, taking me in, and his intensity makes my stomach bottom out. "We'll work on that," he finally says, softly. Then he raises his glass, and his mood lightens. "A few more of these . . . "

"And you'll be holding my hair back." I laugh but swallow more of my drink to cover the effect he has on me. The spicy ginger beer tickles my nose and I snort. "What about you? Ever been tied down?"

He shakes his head as he sips his cocktail. "I dated a girl for a couple years after college, but it was hard. She had a nine-to-five at a nonprofit, and I was doing the band thing, so our schedules were always off. The Bandits started taking off and I was working nights and weekends while she was working Monday through Friday and doing fundraisers on the weekends. I couldn't bring her to weddings and once the band started traveling and booking bigger gigs, we grew apart. She wanted a more 'normal' lifestyle, and we've established that I'm not normal."

"And with all those available bridesmaids, I'm sure it was more fun to be single at all those weddings, too."

He startles. "What do you mean?"

"I mean, you have a reputation." I fiddle with my straw and his brow furrows, his expression turning Dark 'n' Stormy.

"Says who?"

I think back to who said they hooked up with him and come up empty.

I guess I inferred from how flirtatious he is . . .

"Come on." I purse my lips. "You've never gone home with a bridesmaid? I've seen you walking them to their hotel room door."

"Not from a wedding I was working." His voice is firm.

I pretend-slump against the couch. "Be serious. You're *always* flirting with bridesmaids."

He narrows his eyes. "You keep saying stuff like that, and I think you have the wrong idea about me. I'm *friendly*, but believe it or not, I'm not actively hitting on women. I'm not *aggressively* flirtatious. I'm not an Uncle Al." He drifts closer to me as he talks, his tone getting sharper with every inch. "And who says I hook up with everybody? How do you know? You rarely stay until the end of the party to see who I go home with. If you stayed, you'd know I always end up with me, myself, and I. Besides, did you ever stop to think that maybe Max has rules for me too? I'm expected to make sure a good time is had by all. Sometimes that means hanging out with a bridesmaid as a buffer against a leering uncle or groomsman, escorting her to her room to make sure she makes it there okay. But it ends at the door. Everything ends with the wedding."

We face off, and I have to admit that of course Max has rules for him, that my impression of him is not based in fact. That it's possible I'm *not* the last bridesmaid standing. That I made it all up.

But he's never flirted with me or even talked to me. My co-workers are always telling stories about how much fun he is. I can't be wrong.

Shaking my head, I look at my hands. "Fine. Maybe you're not hooking up with everyone, I'll buy that. But you flirt." I glance back up, unable to hide my glassy tears that threaten to overflow, proving my inhibitions are some-where at the bottom of the glass. "You definitely flirt. With everybody—my coworkers included—except for me. How is it we've worked twenty-eight weddings together and never even had a conversation until this week? Or am I that repulsive?" I fold my arms over my waist.

He is silent but watches me, his stare scalding. When he finally speaks, it's a whisper. "It's twenty-nine weddings if you count this one. And the number of weddings I've worked with you is *much* bigger than the number of girls I've even taken on a first date in my lifetime, actually." Our faces are so close his breath warms my cheek. "And you are definitely *not* repulsive."

His gaze flickers down, then sweeps from my chest to my face, making me burn all the way to the tips of my ears. My pulse throbs in my throat and I involuntarily arch my back, aching for him to reach out and touch me.

How would his hands feel across my skin? Are his fingers calloused from playing guitar? Inquiring minds want to know.

Checking his watch, he breaks the spell. "Shit. We've got to get downstairs. I'm on in ten."

Chapter 26

Dance With Me

I scoot back into the couch, flushed at the direction my thoughts took.

He motions the waitress over and gives her the gift card. Once we've paid, he takes my hand and leads me past low white tables now crowded with pretty, young club goers in sparkly makeup and skimpy dresses. We pass a sushi chef standing behind a marble counter, plating sashimi on a wooden serving boat.

"Once I'm a lawyer, maybe I'll be able to afford a sushi platter like that every once in a while," I say, trying on the title.

"But will being a lawyer make you happy?" Exiting Fly Bar, we wind down the stairs around the outside of the castle.

"Paying my bills will make me happy." Thinking of Ethan's offer to possibly work for him and what passing the bar could mean for a position at Giorgio, my stomach squirms. "Honestly, I've been struggling to make ends meet and get my platform off the ground for so long, it feels good to know *something* is finally going to happen, even if it's not what I've been dreaming of for the last few years. It's time for the next phase of my life to begin."

Unable to meet Duncan's gaze, I watch my feet on the cobblestone steps, trying to convince myself as much as him that I'm excited for my new chapter.

"But are you sure there isn't another job that could pay your bills? Something more aligned with your website? It will still be your side hustle, right?"

Duncan asks. Bypassing a line of people, he guides me to a bouncer in a skin-tight shirt who steps aside to allow us entry to the Music on the Rocks.

We enter the hot, stuffy club inside a cave, the air thick with sweat and perfume. The writhing bodies on the dance floor are tinged in a neon pink haze as people move to throbbing music beneath huge disco ball chandeliers.

"I told you, it's just a hobby. I make zero dollars doing it, so it doesn't count as a side hustle, but I'll keep it going if I have time." I yell so Duncan can hear me as we weave through the crowd, the current DJ's beats thumping in my chest. "Besides, my parents will be *so* relieved I finally figured out what to do with my life. I won't have to worry about what they think of my career choice anymore."

Passing white leather couches situated in carved rock alcoves where groups of people are ordering bottle service and a bar made entirely of blue neon lights, we reach the DJ booth. Duncan brings us to a stop at the base of a short flight of stairs and grips my shoulders. He leans in so close, his forehead practically rests against mine. "Sounds like a *safe* bet to me."

His proximity makes my head spin, but he stays in razor focus while the club fades in a colorful blur behind him. I make a face at him. "My becoming a lawyer is *not* a safe harbor."

"So, law is your passion in life?" He raises his voice to be heard over the pulsating club noise.

"Maybe not, but it's going to give me enough financial support to figure out my life." My throat strains.

"If you have time."

I glare at him. "Listen. It's a lot of pressure being the only offspring—the hopes and dreams of an entire family. I'm all my parents have, and my brother Ty left big shoes to fill. You should have seen their faces when I told them I was following in Tyler's footsteps and had been accepted to law school. I can't take that away from them. I need to prove my concept before I confess my true calling."

"Do you *have* to fill his shoes, though? Think of me, of Payton. We stopped trying to be our brothers." He narrows his eyes at me like he wants to tackle me.

And I bet he can tackle.

The current DJ waves at Duncan, stepping aside so Duncan can take his place. Duncan releases me and climbs to the top of the steps. Opening his arms wide like he could hug the whole club, he puffs up his chest. "It's pretty freeing."

Flashing neon lights cast him in pink, then blue, then green. I've never seen anything more intoxicating than the sight of him perched in a DJ booth, about to yacht-rock a club in a cave.

The other DJ climbs down the stairs. Sobering, I step aside to allow him to pass before joining Duncan.

Smiling a crooked smile that lights me up inside, he tugs me into the booth. "I *know* you're passionate about music. Just for tonight let's forget about the dock and sail out to sea. Let's get you some content." Leaving his headphones off his left ear so he can hear me, he positions me behind a turntable.

I slip on the headphones he hands me and leave my right ear free.

He presses some buttons on the control board, playing "Sailing" by Christopher Cross and mixing it to a funky beat. "Ready for your lesson in yacht rock? You already know the first rule is the cartoon smoke effect."

The thumping rhythm pulses through my veins, exhilarating me. Vowing to forget worrying about the future and surrender to the moment, if only for tonight, I give in to the grin spreading across my face. "Ready as I'll ever be."

"The second rule is there's got to be a saxophone solo." He adjusts some levels, and I could watch his hands move all night. "And the third rule, it pains me to say, is anytime there's a pan flute, it gets an extra yacht rock point. And I hate the pan flute."

I lift my chin. "There's no sax solo in 'Sailing,' though. You're violating your own rules." I point at him, yelling over the noise of the packed club.

His head snaps up. "You're good. And I can fix that." He blends in the sax from "Feels So Good" by Chuck Mangione and then morphs that into "Brandy."

"Now, *this* is yacht rock." I laugh. "I chose it as Ethan's surprise song for a reason."

"Heck, yeah. From the moment you hear it, it takes you there. It's got it all. Sailors. Whiskey. You can run your fingers through this song's chest hair." Pressing his lips together, he concentrates, repeating the chorus to the cheers of the crowd.

I feel their joy reverberate in my chest and giddy energy builds inside me. I *love* being on this side of the set, love the call and response, the ability to sway the room.

A waitress arrives, bringing us *more* Dark 'n' Stormies, apparently having gotten the memo they're our drink of choice.

"And speaking of yacht ladies . . . " Duncan morphs the song into Toto's "Rosanna" and arches an eyebrow at me. "Your namesake."

"Do you consider this yacht?" I ask, unable to keep my shoulders from shimmying.

"If your head is grooving—and it is—and so is everyone's—" He gestures out at the crowd who is bouncing in one unified motion, all jutting arms and elbows that look *so* cool from our perch with the neon lights flashing over them. I reach into Duncan's pocket and retrieve his phone so I can take a video. "—Then you're pretty much on a boat. In this song, all the guy wants is to wake up and see this girl's eyes. *On a boat.*"

I press my palm to my forehead as I film, unable to stop giggling.

"You need a picture for your website." He takes the phone out of my hand then snaps a few shots of me. I ham it up pretending I'm a mix-master commanding the sea of dancing bodies cast in strobing pink below us.

Just then a massive burst of confetti explodes through the cave, and the crowd cheers. As the white paper flutters down, Duncan slips an arm over my shoulder and extends his other arm to take a selfie of us.

Warmth bursting through me, I hug him, probably looking like an overeager puppy as he takes our picture.

Without missing a beat, he slips the phone into his pocket and shifts the music to "Islands in the Stream" by Kenny Rogers and Dolly Parton. "How about this one? Yacht-worthy?"

"No way." Pressing my headphone to my ear, I listen hard. "This is country."

"It *is* country, but come on, it has boats and islands in it. You can't get more yacht than that." His eyes flash. "Trust me. Slow it down, and this is pure filtered yacht. I'll prove it to you tomorrow."

I shake my head, unable to see how he can make a country song yacht. "You're off your yacht rocker."

He laughs and switches into his final song, mixing in "Breezin'" by George Benson.

The next DJ is waiting outside the booth as the song ends, and we switch places with him.

I follow Duncan onto the dance floor. His fingers circle my wrist, and he pulls me toward him. "Dance with me? I'm too awake to go back to the hotel." His lips tickle my ear and a delighted shiver trickles down my spine.

"I'd love to."

He swings me around. We dance for I don't know how long, giggling and spinning until we're both breathless.

Eventually, needing air, we slip outside. It's after one, and I have to get up in a few hours to stalk Davis. After the DJ set tonight, I'm more determined than ever to make Duncan's wish come true, but I frown that the night has to end. "I should probably get back to the hotel. I have work tomorrow."

He grimaces at his watch. "Yeah. Me too. The pool party."

Clinging to each other on tipsy, wobbly legs, we make our way to the stairs built into the rocky cliff.

"*Allora!* Goodnight!" a hostess calls as we leave.

"*Allora!*" I call back.

"*Ciao.*" Duncan waves to her.

"*Allora,*" I sing as we heave ourselves up the steep steps toward the silent town above us, the club still ringing in my ears. When we reach the top of the stairs, I momentarily rest my head on Duncan's shoulder until my breathing slows. "I had fun tonight. Thank you."

"Thank *you.*" He pats my head like I'm a good, if overeager, dog. "I haven't had that much fun in a long time. *You* are the finest of dates."

Equating his compliment with "Brandy" by Looking Glass, I sing back part of the song with a laugh. He weaves his fingers with mine. With the music from the night still humming in our veins, we stumble through the narrow streets, singing songs about the sea all the way back to the hotel.

When we arrive at Il Desiderio, we fall silent. I'm grateful the lobby is vacant as we tiptoe across it. Nobody sees us get into the tiny elevator.

"*Allora,*" I yawn, my fingers still entangled in his. Neither of us makes any move to separate them.

He presses the button for the third floor, and we ascend.

"What's your *allora?*" I ask, leaning against him and gripping his bicep with my free hand. "Have you figured it out? Your space in between?"

The elevator doors open.

"*Allora,*" he mumbles as we exit into the hall and walk toward our rooms.

Releasing my hand, he snakes his arm around my waist, keeping me close to his side in the narrow hallway. We reach our doors, and he fumbles for his key, still holding on to me. Somehow, it doesn't occur to me to hunt for mine.

After unlocking his room, he brings me inside with him.

His room is a mirror of mine, and we stop in front of the adjoining door. Turning to face me, he dips his head, so his gaze is level with mine. His eyes are dark, and he holds me close, one arm still firmly planted around me. His free fingertips graze my cheek, gliding to my ear and tucking my hair behind it. He rests his forehead against mine and my heart thumps.

"I think *allora* is possibility, momentum. It's the silence in the moment before the switch flips and everything changes."

I'm highly aware of his body pressed against mine, his warm breath on my chin. Only Duncan's green eyes are in focus and his spicy scent envelops me, tugging me under his spell.

"Things will never be the same but that's okay because they're about to be electric," he whispers.

My stomach flutters, and the room swirls in a fuzzy haze.

Cupping my jaw, he lowers his mouth to mine. I feel its soft pressure all the way to my toes. A burst of heat releases in my chest, flooding my body as he parts my lips and kisses me.

Closing my eyes, I sink into a glorious stupor. My awareness becomes purely sensory. All I know is his tongue finding mine. His hands in my hair. My fingers clinging to his back, aching to feel all of him.

And I thought his dream kisses were good . . .

His breath quickens as he deepens the kiss.

I collapse against him, lost to any reality that doesn't include him.

Until suddenly he tenses and steps back, letting me go.

His abrupt distance is a blast of cold air, sobering me, and I dizzily catch my breath, leaning against the wall for support.

What was that, what was that, what was that?

He staggers away from me, seeming as confused as I am.

"I'm sorry. I shouldn't have done that." Rubbing the back of his neck, he backs even farther away from me, putting as much space between us as possible. "We've both had a lot to drink. I don't want you to think I'd take advantage of that."

I comprehend zero of what he's saying. But he's still talking.

"And you have Ethan, and we both have to work, and tonight was really fun, but we should both get to bed."

Did we just . . . ?

I can't finish the thought. Can't admit it. Can't believe how much I wanted to. My cheeks burn and I stare at him in a breathless loss, my chest heaving.

"Gwen. Seriously. You should go." He's all the way across the room, his hands clenched.

Is he kicking me out?

I flinch and shake some sense into my brain. "Right. Yeah." My chest tightens, and I can't get out of here fast enough. I fumble with the door to my room. Unfortunately, it's locked, so I hurl myself out his door back into the hallway. "Goodnight." I shut the door behind me.

After digging through my bag for my key, I fumble with the lock, my hands shaking. Once I let myself into my room and close the door, I press my forehead to the smooth wood, my head spinning.

OMG. I wanted to. And he didn't. Is this because he knows I'm bad at keeping things casual?

The deadbolt on the adjoining room door clunks shut, validating my assumption.

Wincing, I stumble to the bathroom where my other pair of lacy underwear are hung up to dry. I snatch them down and toss them in a drawer then wash my face, scrubbing away my embarrassment.

After setting aside the creamy chocolate seashell the turn down service left on my pillow, I climb into bed.

I lie between the taut sheets clutching the weighted duvet for what feels like eternity. Staring at the domed ceiling, I replay the evening while listening for a knock on the adjoining door. A sign that Duncan has changed his mind.

But the minutes tick on, and all remains silent. It becomes abundantly clear he has no interest in sneaking into my room. Hating to admit that after that mesmerizing kiss I *want* him to want to come over, I squeeze my eyes shut against the sting of hot tears.

What am I thinking anyway?

I'm not Aubrey. I'm not hook-up material. I mean, what was he saying about me having Ethan? He's practically pushing me toward the groom—playing "our song," and bringing up sticky toffee.

Was the "Dancing in the Moonlight" sing-along in the Blue Grotto an attempt to get Ethan and me to sing together again?

My throat aches. I really wanted that to be real.

And if Max has a rule that Duncan has to entertain bridesmaids, does that include bridesmaids for hire? Is he just doing his job? Keeping everyone happy for the week but it all ends with the wedding?

I smash my pillow over my face as if that could smother my pathetic wanting—or better yet, make me disappear.

I should never have let my guard down. It's the music. It always does me in. I must have looked so ridiculous, a wannabe blogger trying to DJ next to Duncan.

Tears cascade over my cheeks and culminate in a pool at the base of my neck.

Like it or not, I am and forever will be the last bridesmaid standing.

Rolling onto my side, I curl into a ball and shut out the night, wishing the pillow I'm hugging was Toto, who is probably destined to be my Prince Charming.

Chapter 27

The Things We Do for Love

"Excuse me, Mr. Collings?" My stomach flip-flopping, I approach the table where Davis and his wife are seated under an umbrella on the La Sponda terrace for breakfast.

The impossibly blue Mediterranean glints in the sun behind them and the hills are alive with peach and terracotta villas, the colors of the sunrise I saw this morning on my beach walk. As the crisp ocean air carried my headache away, I forced the pathetic girl who thinks she can DJ a club at Duncan's side—or worse, thinks he'd want to kiss her—back into the shadows where she belongs.

Today is the perfect day for a fresh start. To forget the past or at least pretend last night didn't happen. To become the kind of person who takes charge and seizes opportunity. Who puts their personal feelings aside and gets the job done. The type Ethan would hire to work at Giorgio. A Wishmaster who wins bets.

The Collingses arrived promptly at 8:30 this morning, but I've been here caffeinating since 6:15. I've done them the courtesy of waiting until they've had a few sips of coffee before descending on them. Wearing my Hall & Oates T-shirt with the shorts I wore to Capri and my strappy black heels, I'm hoping to convey a polished luxury resort meets rock-n-roll vibe that Davis will trust.

Davis pauses, a forkful of eggs halfway to his mouth, and looks up at me.

I smile my sweetest bridesmaid smile to distract from puffy eyes that are still raw from crying last night. "My name is Gwen, and I'm so sorry to bother you. I promise I'm not a stalker or anything. I'm here as a bridesmaid in a wedding but the strangest thing happened, and I had to come talk to you about it."

A salty breeze wafts over us, serving as a reminder this is supposed to be a pleasant, peaceful breakfast and I am a giant interruption.

Davis blinks at me and lowers his fork. He opens his mouth; I presume to tell me to go away.

Swallowing, I continue, before he can get a word in.

"Have you ever had anything too strange and coincidental to be true happen to you?" Knowing very well he has, I don't give him time to answer. I cock my head and keep babbling. "Like, when you were seventeen and you took a tape recording of songs you made in your basement to a Rationals show at the Grande Ballroom in Detroit? You handed it to their manager backstage only to have the manager toss it aside, right?"

Davis glances at his wife, who is staring at me like I just showed up to a vegan potluck carrying a crockpot full of barbeque pulled pork (which I have, in fact, mistakenly done). But I don't let her get to me. Instead, the ocean and the restaurant din go silent in my ears. Filled with a level of confidence I've never felt before—because this isn't about me, I'm doing this for Duncan—with laser-focus, I keep talking without having to think.

"Your dream was about to die. But as luck would have it, later that night, the janitor found the tape, listened to it, and *loved* it. He handed it to another manager who booked bands at the ballroom, and *he* got you your first record deal. That one twist of fate triggered your whole career. Serendipity, am I right?"

I finally pause, and Davis starts to speak. "Well, I'm not sure—"

I cut him off. "So, I'm in a similar predicament. I don't know if you knew this week was the Perseid meteor shower. They call it 'the night of wishing on falling stars' around here. Well, I made a wish, and the thing is . . ." I take a deep breath. "... I wished for you." The words come out in a whoosh. "Not for me, but for my friend. He's the lead singer in the band that's playing the wedding, and he happens to be your *biggest* fan. I wished for him to meet you. And all of a sudden, here you are." I sweep my hand over the table, encompassing their pile of lemon basil cakes. "I know this is bizarre, but could he buy you a drink? Maybe you could meet him at Franco's for *aperitivo*? Like I said, I'm not a stalker." I press my hands to my chest. "I swear. You can have the hotel run a background check on me and everything—"

Davis holds up a hand to stop me, and I fall silent.

"What did you say your name was?" He places his fingers in prayer over his nose.

"Gwen." I bite my lip. "Gwendolyn Watson."

He nods. "Well, Gwen, every band should have someone in their corner who is as passionate as you are. But as you can see, I'm here on vacation with my wife and my priority is to spend time with her."

His wife peeks at me and her eyebrows knit together in a mask of pity. Heat seeps over my cheeks, but I've made a huge fool of myself already and it's not as bad as I imagined it would be.

Why not dig a little deeper?

I make my eyes as big as possible. "I understand you get approached for this stuff all the time and you can't make exceptions for just anyone. But this band is really talented. Anything you could do would make the lead singer's *life*. Could you spare even five minutes to offer a little advice?"

"You did say you wanted to make more people's days—" his wife interjects, but Davis shoots her a steely look that silences her.

It's all the encouragement I need.

"If that's true, then you *need* to see this." I show him my personal cell phone and hit play on the video of The Bandits covering Davis's song, "Nobody's Perfect, But You Are for Me" in the lemon grove.

A vein pops out in Davis's forehead. He starts to remind me of Max in Mt. Vesuvius mode until his wife puts her hand over his and squeezes. His lungs visibly expand and for a moment he closes his eyes. When he reopens them, he concentrates on the video.

I place my hand over my heart and nod my thanks at his wife.

On the video, Duncan starts out singing Davis's song note for note, but twenty seconds in, he slows it down, makes it his own, and I watch Davis's expression carefully. When the change happens, he tilts his head, and as Duncan sings, a little smile light's Davis's face. He straightens, nodding along. My insides contract. I'm like a bubble about to burst. I'm so excited for Duncan.

The song ends, and Davis raises his gaze to mine. "It's good. Really good."

A release of tension floods my veins and I let out a huge breath that Davis is an artist who is open to appreciating another musician's work.

"Maybe you could tell him that yourself? Tonight? Six o'clock? Franco's Bar?" I don't give him time to answer. Without hesitation, I fling my phone onto his table and *run*. "You can give him my phone to give back to me then, too!" I yell.

Trusting that as a celebrity, Davis will be upright enough to at least leave my phone at the front desk for me if he doesn't meet with Duncan later, I edited my lock screen to read:

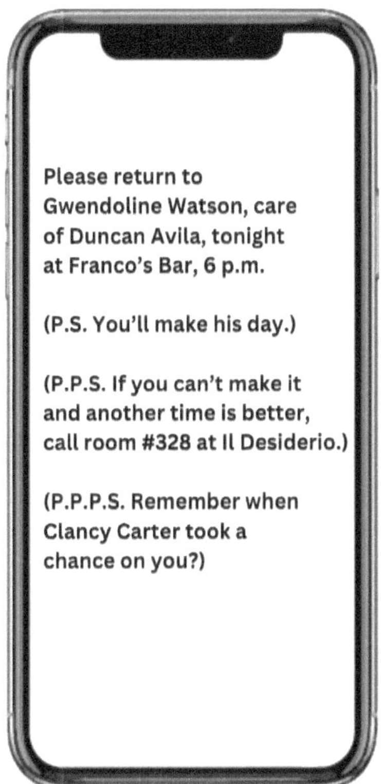

The other guests at the restaurant are staring at the scene I'm creating, but I don't care. I skirt around a table, overturning a basket of bread.

Davis shoots to his feet. "Wait!" He looks wildly around, like he doesn't know what to do, but thankfully he doesn't chase me.

"If you want to have my background checked call my hotel, and I'll tell you anything you want to know. It's fine!" I screech, wanting him to understand I'm not a *sketchy* stalker, just a motivated one. One willing to have potential identity theft part of her Italian holiday.

I weave around the buffet line, nearly tripping over a lady's dog in my mad dash to get out of the restaurant.

Once I escape, I sprint through the Le Sirenuse lobby and burst out the front doors onto the sidewalk where I disappear into the beachy crowd. A peek behind me confirms, Davis is nowhere to be seen, and my heart rate slows as I make my way back to Il Desiderio.

I've surely lost my mind. But the thing I kept coming back to this morning as I tried to reconcile last night is Duncan's talent. The Bandits' talent. They're the real deal, and they deserve a shot at something bigger.

As soon as I get to my room, I change into the strappy, black one-piece bathing suit designated for today. I'm tying a taupe sarong around my waist when my hotel phone rings. When I answer it, Luigi tells me Antonio at Le Sirenuse left me a message saying Mr. Collings has reserved a table at Franco's tonight at 18:00. He looks forward to joining my friend.

Squealing, I flop onto the bed. Unable to contain my grin, I stare at the ceiling.

Duncan is going to freak.

***

The rest of my morning is spent speedboating around on *Il Desiderio II* and posing on the beach with the wedding party. Zoey wears a white version of our same bathing suit, and Aubrey and I shield her with paper parasols as we sprint in and out of the waves, laughing and hugging and generally hamming it up with the groomsmen. We lounge on oversized cushions on the bow of the boat, sunning ourselves and toasting with prosecco. All the while cameras click, and a drone films us from overhead for the official wedding video.

After the shoot wraps, we retreat to a white poolside cabana for a late lunch, mani-pedis, and some serious R & R. The rest of the guests join us at the pool where The Bandits have set up shop at the far end with the spectacular cliffs and sea as their backdrop. They're playing eighties—not necessarily yacht rock—covers to the delight of everyone. Duncan, in his fitted dark green T-shirt, orange board shorts, and wayfarer sunglasses, is commanding the attention of more than just Aubrey today.

At the sight of him, fuzzy images from last night's encounter assault me, and my earlier Wishmaster bravado wavers. I can almost feel his hand cupping my jaw and heat flushes through me. Lying back on a white lounge chair, my face turned skyward, I squeeze my eyes shut against the memory of his lips.

Was I throwing myself at him?

It's possible. I have to admit it's possible, and a lump rises in my throat. Green blotches form behind my eyelids from the sun, and I wish they would blot last night out of my mind. But with Duncan's voice in my ears, the memories won't go.

He didn't want me. What is wrong with me that I can't be hook-up material?

Groaning, I curl onto my side.

I just want things to go back to the way they were. I don't want it to be awkward.

Just then, from across the turquoise pool, Duncan sings "summer's eve" instead of singing the correct Seals & Crofts lyric to the song, "Summer Breeze," and I sit up straight. Shielding my eyes against the sun, I stare at him.

He's looking right at me. I scan the pool. Everyone is doing their own thing. Nobody seems to have noticed he's changed the lyrics and is singing about a feminine hygiene product brand instead of the wind. His eyebrows flash up, and I know it's just me and him who get this. It's our private joke and he's sending me a message. He wants things to go back to the way they were too.

Suddenly, all is right with the world. My heart does a happy dance that whatever happened—or didn't happen, or almost happened—last night hasn't changed a thing. It was a momentary blip in the space-time continuum, and we're back on the timeline we belong on.

Slowly nodding my head at him, I silently convey that I'm in agreement that last night never happened. Swallowing a giggle, I flop back onto the chaise and point my freshly polished toes toward the water, feeling lighter. My thoughts turn to the upcoming Davis Collings surprise, and I cross my arms over my waist, hugging myself against the rising glee that my wish for Duncan will come true in a few short hours.

The sun is warm on my skin and having had such little sleep last night, I relax with a smile on my lips. My eyelids grow heavy. Next to me, I'm aware of Zoey and Ethan sunning themselves and laughing with some of the other wedding guests. Aubrey and Payton are in the pool lounging on floaties shaped liked lemon slices, and Zoey and Payton haven't so much as glanced at each other. Uncle Al opted to golf today and Max is supervising that excursion, so I don't have to worry about either of them. This actually feels like a wedding should feel. For a moment, all is as it should be. The wedding is on, my secret is safe, and I'm going to win the bet. With everything falling into place, I sink into a nearly dreamlike state.

In the distance the opening notes to "Islands in the Stream," the Kenny Rogers/Dolly Parton song we debated last night filter through my haze. I recognize the song, but Duncan slows it down. Hayden comes in, his keyboard set to sound like the marimba. As the notes float over me, I smile to myself.

He's right.

It's totally yacht. Duncan's voice seeps through me as he sings and part of me drifts away, my subconscious allowing a tiny fantasy of Duncan and me on a deserted island together.

But then the song ends, and Duncan softly says into the microphone, "This next song is really special to us because, well, we wrote it. We've never played it out before, but I hope you'll humor us just this once."

I bolt upright, suddenly more awake than I've ever been in my life.

"Zoey. Zoey!" I screech, reaching out and shaking her thigh. "Can I borrow your phone?" Zoey has the latest iPhone and I'm pretty sure it has a better camera than my Italian loaner phone, so I ask to use hers since Davis Collings has my personal cell.

"Sure." She puts down her freshly squeezed Amalfi lemon lemonade, and after grabbing her bag from under her chaise, hands it to me. "It's in there."

I dig through her possessions until I find the white rectangle and frantically hold down the camera icon. The camera opens just in time for Duncan to lick his lips and say, "This is 'Lady Lavender.'"

My heart in my throat, I hit record. The band is perfectly framed with the pastel villas and cliffs as their backdrop. The turquoise pool is at their feet and a yacht literally sails behind them on the cobalt sea as Duncan strums his guitar. The opening notes are chill and soothing, washing over me like slow ocean waves, and I can't help but nod along.

Duncan steps up to the microphone. His expression is glazed, like he's in his own world, and when he starts to sing the pool goes silent around me. I immediately lose myself to him, ceasing to feel my limbs, but somehow, I keep filming.

Lady Lavender, you make white look amateur,
You belong on the ocean breeze.
No cloudy days or dark could ever hide you,
You're the only star you need to guide you.

The chorus hits me in my core—it's anthemic and fresh at the same time—and I instantly love it, knowing the lyrics will live with me on repeat. This is a summer song. It's *the* song of the summer. I can feel it in my bones, and I fizz up with energy. Goosebumps prickle my arms.

Tearing my attention from Duncan, I survey the pool. People's heads are bobbing, no, grooving. Like they're on a boat. This is a hit.

It's going to be a huge hit.

My hands tremble, and I fight to keep the video steady, tears stinging my eyes.

When the song ends there is a whoop of applause, and Duncan steps back from the microphone like he's coming out of a daze. He dips his chin, a pleased smile warming his face.

I'm so proud of him—of all of them—that I let tears freely roll over my cheeks. And long after the song ends, I'm still hearing it on repeat. All I know is I can't sit on this. I have to share it. My thirteen YouTube followers are going to *love* this.

"Zoey, can I borrow your phone for a few more minutes?" I swipe through to the lock screen that has a picture of a cheese board on it, *not a picture of her and Ethan.* "You have an international plan, right?"

"I do. Sure. Let me unlock it for you." She takes the phone and swipes, lifting the screen so it can recognize her face. "That song was awesome, by the way."

"Right?" I swipe until I find YouTube.

"I wonder if we could use it in the wedding video?" She leans back on her lounger, crossing her legs at the ankles.

"I'll ask the band if there's a recording. But I took video, so maybe we can use that. I can send it to whoever edits the wedding footage." Finding the YouTube app, I log into my account.

"That would be great, thanks." She resumes sipping her lemonade.

And I get busy uploading the video to every social media music group and outlet I'm a part of.

Chapter 28

Steal Away

With "Lady Lavender" lingering in my ears from this afternoon, I finish my makeup before adjusting my boobs which are taped inside tonight's navy rehearsal dress. Dotted with tiny white hearts, the dress opens in a deep V all the way to my mid-section. It's pretty and swishy with fluttery ruffled shoulders, but it's also more daring than anything I've worn this week, and my insides turn to mush. It's not just the dress that's got me jittery, though. It's what is about to happen.

My wish is about to come true.

I clasp my necklace around my neck, put on flip-flops and shove my too-small kitten heels into a wicker beach bag for later. Satisfied I'm ready for whatever this night will bring, I check my balcony to see if Duncan is on his. His chair is vacant, and my ribs seize.

What if I can't find him?

I rush to the door that separates our rooms and bang on it.

The lock clicks on his side and my knees nearly give out when Duncan opens the door. Standing at the scene of last night's crime, he's wearing Towaya over his T-shirt and board shorts from earlier. The memory of his kiss floods me, and every inch of me wants a reenactment.

His jaw drops. "Wow. You look amazing."

His compliment has my nerve endings standing at attention, but I force myself to concentrate on the task at hand.

Last night never happened.

I tug on Towaya's sleeve. "I need you to come with me."

"What?" He startles. "The festival isn't for another couple of hours. I was just about to shower."

The wedding rehearsal is taking place in an hour at the Church of Santa Maria Assunta and is followed by the first night of the Feast of Assunta festival. The traditional rehearsal dinner is happening tomorrow night, the evening before the wedding.

"No time for that." I drag him out of his room into mine and then into the hallway. "You need to come with me. Now."

"Okay . . ." He lets me pull him down the hall. "Is everything okay? Is it Zoey?"

I shake my head as I lead him down the stairs. "No, nothing like that. You'll see. Soon. Very soon."

"You're being very mysterious." He squints at me sideways.

Bringing us to a stop at the bottom of the stairs, I fix him with a stare and breathlessly place my hand over my chest. "I *loved* 'Lady Lavender.' *Loved.* You've been holding out on me." Gripping Towaya, I yank him across the lobby's tile floor.

"Thank you." He slowly nods, scratching his jaw and matching my pace. "Everyone at the pool seemed to think it was good, huh?"

"It was better than good." We exit onto the cobblestone street into a cloud of exhaust as a moped roars by. The lingering gas smell mixes with the char of a wood-fired pizza as we walk toward Franco's. "It was amazing. What a portrait you painted. Lady Lavender. Is she like, your dream girl? I can totally see her on a yacht." My skin erupts in goosebumps like it did when I heard the song, and I peer at him with shining eyes.

His cheeks flush and we press ourselves against a yellow stucco wall to let a car pass through the narrow corridor. "Um. Yeah. Something like that." He licks his lips and changes the subject. "You owe me now, you know. The name of your website, please."

I turn us into a tiny alley lined with shops selling postcards and limoncello under a bougainvillea canopy, and my lungs deflate. I really don't want him to read it. He's a true authority on music and I don't want him to think it's terrible, to understand why nobody seems interested in following me.

"You promised." He nudges my side with his elbow as we dodge people carrying beach towels and shopping bags.

"I did." I sigh, conflicted. If I'm honest with myself, some part of me, buried way deep down at the bottom of my ocean is curious what he'll think of it. I want him to know that secret side of me. But waves of self-doubt keep me buoyant, floating in the murky waters between who I really am and who I think I should be.

But if anyone understands what it's like to want to make music their life, it's Dunc.

Taking a deep breath, I blurt the URL before I lose my nerve. "It's ShutUp andSway.com." Le Sirenuse's crimson walls appear in the distance in sharp contrast to the blue sky and I keep my focus on our destination.

He clutches his chest. "Seriously?"

"Yes. Why are you freaking out?"

Briefly closing his eyes, he shakes his head. "It's just a great name. Shut up and sway. Like you're on a boat?" He raises his eyebrows, and I don't totally buy that he thinks it's a great name. Maybe he thinks it's dumb. But that makes me sad, and I push the thought out of my mind.

"No." I groan. "Like you're at a concert. Specifically, if you're like me at a concert. I have no rhythm, so I sway."

"It's good." He nods, and I get the impression he *actually* likes it. "Really good. It's a juxtaposition—shut up is harsh but sway is gentle. It's like saying, 'Think different. Change your mindset. Let go and flow.'"

I lift my chin toward him. "I never thought about it that way, but you're right. Sometimes I just want to shut up and sway. To just be. To be part of the music and let it take me away." I lower my brow. "But if you read it—and I really hope you don't—go easy on me."

"Oh, I'm definitely reading it." He grins.

"Great." I wince but my chagrin is short-lived because we arrive at Franco's. We come around the hedge and enter the terrace bar with its bubbling marigold-colored fountain, jazzy music, and unparalleled Positano cliff views.

Pulling Duncan to a stop, I position him so he can see where Davis is sitting alone at a table for two, staring out over the showstopping blue water dotted with white yachts.

A light wind kicks up off the sea and Duncan freezes. The blood drains from his cheeks. "What did you do, Gwen?" he whispers. He doesn't look at me. His eyes are only for Davis.

I've never seen him at a loss, and lightning strikes my veins. I can barely contain myself, barely keep my feet on the ground. I'm so buoyant I could float away. "I won. That prosecco bottle is mine." I grin and shove him toward Davis. "You are officially my Wishminion."

But he doesn't budge. He stays put and slowly turns toward me. His lips part, but no words come out.

My eyes shining, I back away. "Go. Have fun."

With a little shake of his shoulders, he seems to pull himself together. Rising to his full height, he walks over to Davis who stands when he sees Duncan coming and offers his hand.

Duncan does the most uncool thing possible and hugs Davis. My sinuses burn and I snort. But fortunately, Davis hugs him back.

Biting my lip, though nothing could contain my perma-grin, I leave them to their wished-for moment and make my way out of the restaurant.

I head down the stairs toward the green-gold dome of the Church of Santa Maria Assunta on clouds, gloating that the expression on Duncan's face was everything I'd dreamed of. As I walk, I drape a floral print scarf over my shoulders in preparation for the covering required at the rehearsal, but my thoughts are on what I can do to be treated to that look again. My heart might burst out of my chest. Not because I made my wish come true first, but because I made Duncan genuinely happy.

Now that I've tasted life as the Wishmaster, I might be addicted.

Wish-granting might be my calling.

***

I exit the silent church after the rehearsal to a cacophony of color and sound. In the seaside courtyard before me, there is dancing and balloons and bursts of flower petals and confetti. Music from a live band mingles with the rich drone of bells overhead, clanging twenty times to signal the 20:00 hour. The air is scented with a mix of fried dough, heady church incense, and the briny sea. And in the center of it all stands Duncan.

Lit by the golden radiance of the sun setting over the sparkling Mediterranean and colorful neon carnival lights spelling out scrumptious Italian delicacies over food stalls, he's practically glowing. He is my only focus, and our gazes lock. His hands shoved into Towaya's pockets, he narrows his eyes, shaking his head at me, but his lips twitch and he can't contain his grin.

Neither can I. A slow smile spreads across my face and my stomach dips. I can't wait to hear about Davis, but before I can hurl myself into the crowd and beg him to tell me everything, Max and Luigi arrive at my side.

"This is the first night of the Festival of the Assunta, celebrating the night the Black Madonna painting that now lives in the church arrived here," Luigi explains, gesticulating out over the lively celebration. "She was on a ship and the seas were rough. The crew was desperate for refuge and, as the story goes, a miracle occurred. The painting came to life and demanded, '*Pozza, pozza*' meaning, 'put down here.' *Pozza* is the root of Positano, and the Madonna has been our protector ever since. She has even saved the town from pirates. Tomorrow is *Alzata del Quadro* when the Madonna painting is lifted as high as the cross and strung on strings over the town."

He motions to the cross perched on top of the church behind us. "And then there will be a procession that carries a Madonna statue to the beach. The festival ends in three nights with the Ferragosto celebration. It's a national holiday in Italy, honoring the Assumption of Mary. We finish it off with midnight fireworks."

"Which we are totally borrowing for the wedding." Zoey chimes in as she and Ethan join us, their arms linked.

Out in the crowd, Aubrey—who wasted no time skipping down the church steps—wraps her arms around Duncan and kisses his cheek. She shows him something on her phone and the sight of their heads bowed close together is like black clouds eclipsing the sunlight that was shining through my veins. Heaviness descends on my shoulders. A balmy gust kicks off the water that fails to warm me. With a shiver, I tuck my chin to my chest, reminding myself I'm on the clock. I'll have to catch up with Duncan later.

"Hopefully those aren't the only fireworks on the wedding night." Ethan grins, looping his free arm over the front of Zoey's shoulders so he's hugging her from behind and resting his chin on top of her head.

I peek at Payton, who is standing on the other side of Max and Luigi, and for the briefest moment the same storm that just passed through me casts its shadow over him. His eyes darken, though his frown disappears in the flashiest of lightning strikes. Still, I'm positive I saw it.

"You're very funny, Ethan." Zoey flushes as she detangles herself from his embrace. I can't help but feel she noticed Payton's scowl, too.

"I don't know about you, but all I can think about is what we're about to eat." She takes my hand and drags me down the stairs into the festival. Ethan, Payton, and the rest of the wedding party follow, but Max excuses himself to go meet with the caterers for tomorrow night's dinner.

As a group we move from booth to booth. Zoey orders us a fried feast. We watch as whitefish, shrimp, and anchovies caught fresh that day are deep fried in sizzling oil. They're drizzled with fresh Amalfi lemon juice before being handed to us in cone-shaped paper cups.

"*Pesce fritto al cono*," Zoey says in perfect Italian. She spears a piece of fish with a little plastic sword and pops it in her mouth. Throwing back her head, she moans. She is such the Foodie star, I check to see if there is a camera crew filming us. "The batter is so light, so crisp. And the fish! It doesn't get any fresher. It still has the salt from the sea." She licks her lips.

"She makes everything look delicious." Ethan folds his arms over his chest, watching her with a small smile.

He's like a proud father at his daughter's dance recital—or a producer seeing dollar signs—and my stomach squirms. I get it. Zoey has that same "X" factor as Duncan. She's a star, and she's probably going to make Giorgio, Inc. a ton of money. But it's different than the way I feel about Duncan. Yes, it would be a gift to help his star rise, but more than that, I would give *anything* to be the reason for the expression on his face that I conjured earlier this afternoon.

Heat rushes through me and I shut my brain down before I can admit the reason for that difference.

But if Zoey's star someday fades, will Ethan stop talking to her like he did me?

Payton catches my eye. "She deserves someone who thinks *she* looks delicious, don't you think?" he mutters under his breath, seemingly reading the direction of my thoughts and sensing we're on the same page.

Though he keeps his voice light, I know he's asking me seriously. Plastering on my bridesmaid smile to cover my unease, I shrug, pretending I don't know what he's talking about. As much as I agree with him, it's not in my best interests to engage. Zoey has been honest with herself about what she wants, and it's not fireworks. Maybe for her, marriage is called settling down for a reason.

I brush past him on my way to Zoey's side and he watches me go, his head cocked like he's trying to figure me out. I get the feeling he's suspicious of me, but I ignore him and link arms with Zoey.

We walk through the colorful festival aisles beneath iron lanterns, eating Palle di Riso—fried saffron rice balls filled with parmesan and mozzarella—and then make our way to the edge of the dance floor in the center of the square. Couples sway together under the darkening sky and magenta string lights that culminate in the center of the courtyard at a flower-shaped chandelier covered in pink, blue, and yellow lights.

The band, on a small riser across from the food stalls, starts to play "One on One" by Hall & Oates but in Italian. "Uno Contro Uno" by Hall & Oates. My mouth goes dry. I scan the crowd for Duncan, certain this song is no coincidence, that he bribed them and he's sending out his bat signal.

He appears at my side out of nowhere, sans Aubrey, and bumps his shoulder against mine. My pulse kicks into overdrive.

"Zoey, would you mind if I borrowed your maid of honor for a minute?" He leans toward her while weaving his fingers through mine, causing a surge of goosebumps. "I happen to know this is her favorite song and I had a couple questions for her about the wedding setlist."

I glance at Zoey. Somewhere in the crowd beyond her Aubrey is watching. Dancing with Duncan is one hundred percent against the rules, but Max isn't here, and I'm dying to know how it went with Davis.

"It's true. We do have a lot to discuss." I bite my lower lip.

Zoey's expression brightens. "Of course. Dance. Rosie deserves to have some fun, too." She nudges me toward Duncan.

"Thanks." Duncan smiles and his grip tightens around mine as he tugs me forward.

We disappear onto the crowded dance floor, and he sweeps me into his arms. "I think this belongs to you?" Opening Towaya's pocket, he flashes my phone at me. "You're the most incredible person I've ever met. I can't believe you did that." Twirling me around, he brings me to a stop facing him and settles his arm around my waist, holding me so close our noses almost touch.

The magenta lights glitter behind him against the navy sky, casting him in a rosy glow. Being this close to him I notice tiny gold flecks in his green eyes that I never knew were there. The energy of the impossible throbs between us, and I flush. This is nothing compared to a drunken kiss that we've both silently agreed never happened. Nobody could possibly understand what we've just been through, the magic we experienced. We're wrapped in our own bubble that pulsates with dizzying waves of possibility. It leaves me breathless. "I can't believe he showed up." My voice cracks. "That my wish came true, Wishminion," I add, lightening the mood to cover for the emotion overwhelming me.

He groans. "You can lord it over me for the rest of my life, I guess. It was worth it." Laughing, he sways us in a circle as more people join the dancing and we're squeezed closer together.

"Oh, I will." I grin. "But don't leave me hanging. Was he everything you hoped? I was worried. Never meet your heroes and all that."

"He was better. He's soooo cool." His gaze softens, goes unfocused, like he's lost in a memory. "I mean, he totally gets me. He loved our version of 'Nobody's Perfect'—said we took it places he never thought of—that we could record and release a cover if we wanted." His jaw goes slack and briefly letting go of my waist, he rubs his forehead. "He wants me to send him some of our original stuff. He thinks we should give songwriting a shot, and he said if I start the 'We're Yacht-Worthy' podcast, he'll be my first guest."

Giving himself a little shake, he comes back to reality and locks in on me. "Honestly, I don't know how to thank you, Gwen. Nobody has ever done something like that for me. It's surreal."

Tingles sweep up my neck. I dip my chin, letting my hair fall across my face to shield me from the intensity of his stare. "I didn't do anything. Your talent speaks for itself."

He brushes the hair off my cheek. "Don't sell yourself short. This wouldn't have happened if it wasn't for you."

I shrug. "I don't think it had anything to do with me. Corina would probably say getting to play yacht rock on a yacht put you in a flow state and you're vibrating at a level that called in the people who can change your life."

"I disagree. It was your wish. If anything, it was *your* vibration that made it come true." He lowers his mouth to my ear. "You have lots of talents." His breath is hot against my skin, sending electricity through me.

We fall silent and the festival fades around us in a blur of glimmering neon lights and faces. Only Duncan is in focus, staring down at me. It's like we're connected at the core, the "One on One" rhythm pulsating between us. I am lost to him until Aubrey and one of Ethan's groomsmen swing past us.

She cocks her head at Duncan and cold spikes my core. Remembering where I am, I leap backward.

He sobers, too. Pulling up, he holds me at arm's length. His attention flickers in Aubrey's direction and he opens his mouth to tell me something, then seems to think better of it. "Should we get out of here?" he whispers instead.

"Totally." I rub my arms against the sudden chill his distance created and let him lead me off the dance floor.

"Cold?" He brings me to a stop near the food stalls.

"A little." I open my beach bag to find the scarf I wore to the rehearsal. It's thin and filmy, but better than nothing.

"Here." Duncan takes off Towaya and drapes it over my shoulders.

"You're letting me wear Towaya?" My jaw drops and clutching my chest, I pretend to keel over.

"I know." He smirks. "This is hard for me. Letting you wear him is like a trust fall. Take good care of him."

"Oh, I will." I wrap Towaya tighter across my body and burrow inside. "He's actually really comfortable."

"He looks good on you, but don't get too cozy. He knows who his master is." He bumps his shoulder against mine, and we start down the path that leads out of the festival in silent mutual agreement that we're leaving.

"Yeah. The Wishmaster." I bat my eyelashes at him.

He groans. "Towaya was not part of the bet." He glances over his shoulder at the festival. "Do you need to stay, or can you steal away with me back to the hotel?"

I would like nothing more.

In the spirit of surrender . . .

Still, I hesitate. Zoey might need me. Surveying the party, I find her dancing with Ethan. Catching her eye as he spins her my way, I motion with my thumb that I might leave. She shoos me away, giving her permission.

"I think I can be done." I smile.

Before we go, Duncan uses his broken Spa-talian to order us a bag of zeppole from a food stall while I trade my painful heels for flip-flops.

"For the road." He hands me a paper bag full of custard-filled fried ricotta doughnuts tossed in powdered sugar.

"Yum. Thank you." As we walk, I bite into a hot dough ball and moan my appreciation. "This is amazing." I wipe my sugary fingers on Towaya.

Duncan sways and almost passes out. "He's not a napkin!"

Realizing what I'm doing, I drop my hand and throw my head back, laughing. "Oh my gosh. I'm so sorry. He's just so absorbent." I slap my hand over my mouth to hide the grin that won't leave my face.

Pursing his lips, Duncan shakes his head. "I need to get him off you, stat." Winding his fingers through mine, he tugs me toward the hotel. "Come on. We'll have to find another way to warm you up."

Chapter 29

One on One

We reach our respective doors. He retrieves his key from Towaya's pocket then inserts it into his lock. I assume we're parting ways, and my chest tightens as I search my wicker bag for my key. Once I find it, I unlock my door. Even though we're standing next to each other, suddenly the distance between us is massive. It's like the wall dividing our rooms has extended into the hall.

I open my door and, uncertain of what else to do, I shuffle inside.

Before I can disappear, he tugs on Towaya's sleeve, and my breath hitches as I realize he probably wants his jacket back.

"Meet me on the balcony?" he whispers.

My insides squeeze. Nodding yes, I slip inside my room.

The adjoining door that separates our rooms is still ajar from when I dragged him to Franco's earlier. Before I can finish kicking off my flip-flops, he appears in the opening.

Our eyes lock, and neither of us speak. My heart pounds as he walks straight to me. Every thought I've ever had about being the last bridesmaid standing whips out the French doors and is buried at sea.

When he reaches me, it's like all the giddy, impossible energy of my Davis Collings wish coming true swirls around us. The air pulsates with promise as he takes me in his arms, and we're swept up by the tornado. His fingers slide along the back of my neck, tangling in my hair and sending delighted shivers down my spine. Tilting my head back, he lowers his face to mine.

Last night's kiss was *nothing* in comparison.

His lips are sugary sweet from powdered sugar and plump and soft as they press my mouth open. Flutters ripple through me, culminating in a deep ache low in my gut. My head spinning, I close my eyes, giving into the heady sensations pulsating through me, and press myself against him.

He groans and deepens the kiss, his tongue teasing, igniting little sparks in my brain that send buzzy electricity through my veins. Still locked together, we move as one toward the bed. Parting my legs with his knee, he leans me back and gently lays me down. He drags his lips along my jaw, grazing my earlobe before finding my neck.

My entire body erupts in goosebumps.

"You're so beautiful," he murmurs against my throat.

"So are you," I gasp. Unable to contain myself, I arch against him, wanting to feel all of him.

Straightening his arms so he's hovering above me, he takes me in, his lips swollen from kissing me. Towaya falls open, exposing my heaving chest that wants to burst out of my low-cut dress.

His fingertips glide slowly over my skin, tracing the dress's deep V, and I shiver.

"There's a lot that happens after a kiss . . . " he whispers.

"Oh, I know." I moan, desperate for him to return his lips to mine. "And I want all of it."

His hand makes its way under my dress, stroking my thigh, leaving heat imprints all the way to my hip. When his fingers find the edge of my barely-there black Italian underwear from the boutique downstairs, he groans. Hooking the lace with his thumb, he tugs.

For once I'm grateful for the luxurious underwear. They are *much* more attractive than the sad briefs I usually wear.

"Please. Please take them, they belong to you anyway." I wrap my legs around him and urge him toward me.

With a low growl, he tilts his face toward the ceiling and—to my horror—lets go of the undies. "I can't believe I'm saying this, Gwen, but I think we should take it slow."

"No, no we really shouldn't." Breathless, I grab his T-shirt and yank him toward me, pressing my mouth to his.

He kisses me back, and we get lost in each other. Kissing, sucking, stroking. I pull his shirt over his head, discarding it somewhere on the bed and feel my way around his body, over his taut abs, scraping my fingernails down his smooth back.

Then his mouth is everywhere. On my neck. My chest. His hands run the length of my body down to my waist and back up to my breasts. Panting, he teases my nipples through my dress, and I tremble at how sensitive they are. My head keeps whirling, and it's all so pleasant and warm and I don't want it to stop.

While occupying my mouth with his, he presses himself into me through my dress and he's so hard, shudders of pleasure tingle through me. I bear down against him and he's almost my undoing.

But unfortunately, with a moan, he again pulls back. "Listen." He's breathless. "I want this—really, I do—but I think we should wait." He presses his forehead to mine. "Maybe I could stay? If you want me to? But no sex. I don't have any condoms anyway."

"I want you to," I whisper, pressing my palms to his chest.

Cupping my cheek, his lips find mine again and warmth blooms over me. The kiss is gentle and deep and final.

And I am putty.

He releases me and I pout.

"Hey. None of that. It's not easy for me either." He scoots onto the bed, positioning himself so he sits leaning against the headboard, like he did in my dream. Patting the spot next to him, he motions for me to join him. "But I really think slow is best."

The space between us helps me to gather my wits and my breathing comes easier. "Okay, fine. I didn't get much sleep last night anyway." I wrinkle my nose. "Let me get comfortable."

Standing at the foot of the bed in front of Duncan, I slip Towaya off and toss it across the covers, a strange confidence overtaking me. Letting Duncan watch, I remove the tape from my breasts then unzip my dress. It falls to the floor silently and I stand in front of him wearing nothing but the Italian underwear. I wouldn't normally be so bold. At least, I don't think so—I haven't been in this position enough times to have a "normal"—but he makes me feel like he thinks I'm beautiful. And the devil in me wants him to know full well what he's missing.

His eyes rove slowly over my round hips and almost pop out of his head.

Quirking one eyebrow, I slip back into Towaya, crawl over the covers, and snuggle next to him.

He bites his lower lip. "You're *really* not making this easy."

I grin and walk my fingers up his chest. "Neither are you."

With a laugh, he pulls me against him and kisses my forehead. Resting his chin on my head, he folds his arms around me, and I snuggle into him. A gentle wind washes over us from the open French doors and we lie there, wrapped up in each other. With my ear pressed to the drumming of his heart and with the waves rolling outside, I'm lulled into a peaceful daze.

And I crash almost immediately.

✳✳✳

"**A**re you playing Chuck Mangione on my chest?" Lemony light warms the room and Duncan lifts his head, staring down my fingers tapping out the notes to "Feels So Good" on his pectorals.

I giggle myself awake. "You named that tune in eight notes."

He clasps my fingers in his and rolls onto his side so he's facing me. "This is officially my favorite way to wake up, ever."

"There's only one thing that would make it better."

"Well, yeah. But we agreed."

"We agreed no breakfast?" My jaw drops in mock horror.

"Oh, yeah. Right. Breakfast is okay. Just no sausage."

"Ew."

He laughs.

My thigh buzzes, and I realize his phone is still in Towaya's pocket. I take it out to hand it to him. Wondering if maybe it's the cat sitter with a Toto update, I can't help but glimpse the beginning of the text buzzing through from Aubrey.

Aubrey

> I still can't believe Rosie is Goth Ick Gwen. I told Ethan. I know you didn't want me to, but I couldn't help it. She was SO desperate.

My heart lurches and I drop the phone like it's scalded me, but I can't unsee what I just saw.

Duncan picks up the phone and his features go slack. His gaze snaps to mine. "Gwen."

He reaches for me, but I leap out of bed before he can touch me. I wrap Towaya tight around my waist, my fingers trembling. "What is she talking about? Goth . . . " I can't say anymore out loud.

Duncan stands and takes my hands, holding them steady in his as he pulls me down onto the bed. "Aubrey told me the other night at dinner she'd finally figured out who you reminded her of," he says, quietly.

"What did she say?" I whisper. I can't look at him. My face is on fire.

"Just this girl that Ethan used to know . . . "

"A desperate girl?" The word *desperate* is vomit in my mouth.

He sucks in his breath.

I finally raise my glassy eyes to his. "Just tell me the truth."

He blows air out of his cheeks and winds his fingers around my wrist, holding me in place like he thinks I might run. "It was your brother's idea, Gwen," he whispers, his eyebrows pinched. "Ethan lost some kind of bet and owed Tyler a favor that week in Mackinac. That's why he hung out with you."

Nodding, I rock back and forth. On some level I knew something like this must have been behind my Ethan wish coming true. I'd just hoped I was wrong. I'd hoped magic was real.

I've believed in the impossible this whole time.

I press my chin to my chest. Then another notion strikes, and I stiffen. "And you've been talking about me with Aubrey behind my back? How did she figure it out? Did you tell her who I am?"

"No." His fingers tighten around my hand. "I just . . ." He looks to the ceiling and confesses. "She saw a notification from 'Gwen's Roomie' on my phone and it clicked for her. She asked if people ever called you Gwen, and I'm a terrible liar. She took one look at me and knew that I knew and then she pounced."

"You need to be more careful with your phone." I sniff.

And was she waking up naked next to him when she saw Corina's text?

My stomach twists and I banish the thought from my brain before I gag.

"That's an understatement." Grimacing, he takes me in. "But honestly, I'm glad you know. I've hated hiding this from you. The truth is she wanted to know if Zoey knew you and Ethan had a past. I dodged the question, but I told her I didn't think it was her place to tell Zoey. And I asked her not to tell Ethan which inadvertently confirmed her suspicions. She guessed you confided in me. I'm so sorry. Please know I would never talk about you behind your back. You can trust me."

He's sorry. I know he's sorry. With the downturned corners of his mouth and furrowed brow, he looks *so* sorry.

So sorry for me.

I can feel pity emanating from him and my defenses rear up, cloaking me in protective, iron-clad armor. I *hate* pity. And I hate *his* pity even more. I don't want it. I don't want any of this. And the knowledge that he knows I'm desperate Goth Ick Gwen, the girl dumb enough to believe a fairytale could happen to her, who is so needy to be loved that she blindly believed an impossible lie, assaults me. The fact he now sees me as her brings her back to life and I burn with embarrassment so hot I could disintegrate. I wish I would.

And he knows I'm embarrassed. He's embarrassed for me.

Blood pounds in my ears and the room tinges red. "No. I can't." I mutter. "I can't trust anyone. Because you did talk about me behind my back. You and Aubrey have been harboring this secret about me this whole week." My nose burns and hot tears flood my cheeks.

He slips an arm over my shoulders and tries to pull me into a hug, but I push him away. "Gwen. I just didn't know how to tell you. I wanted to." He licks his lips. "We all were teenagers once. We all have stuff. This doesn't change anything."

I glare at him. "Yes. It does. You lied to me." I squeeze my eyes shut against the waterfall cascading down my face. "And my brother lied to me, too." The implications ripple through me. "How can I trust anyone? How can I know anything is real?"

Has anything ever been true?

"You just have to keep trying until you find what *is* real. I can show you if you'll let me." He tries to hug me again, but I scoot away and stand, shoving my hands into Towaya's pockets where my fingers connect with a small square package.

My heart squeezes and I know what it is before I pull it out. Gripping the crinkly packet, I slowly retrieve it and show it to him. "A condom?" I square my jaw. "If it was Aubrey you were with last night, would you have used this? Am I that . . . repulsive?" The word comes out small and meek.

Duncan winces. "No, I wouldn't have used it with Aubrey. And you're not repulsive at all. Completely the opposite."

"Then why would you lie about this too?" Throwing the condom on the bed, I charge toward him. It *does* cross my mind that I'm guilty of withholding the truth from him too—that I never told him Ethan knows who I am—*but that's because when* I *make promises, I keep them*!

"It's not that I didn't want to have sex with you . . . " He stands and stumbles over his words, backing away from me until he's leaning against the door that joins our rooms. "It's just . . . complicated."

His rejection unlocks a flood of memories. Of Friday nights spent hanging out alone in my room listening to Joy Division or the Cure. Of watching black and white movies, when I knew everyone else in my high school was out partying—living on the other side of Oz in full color. Of crushing on boys who preferred the perky blonde girls in my class I used to be friends with. The ones I no longer understood because they were trying *so hard* to have a quintessential high school experience like they saw on mainstream TV. Of whispers and sneers and assumptions that I was snobby and cold and dead inside because I didn't know how to be like everyone else. Of wishing I could fit in. Of wishing I wanted to. Of wishing for friends beyond the coded names in online chat rooms. But at that time, the only thing that made me feel in control was shocking everyone with my darkness.

And I want to be a music influencer, for heaven's sake. I'm still seventeen!

Desperate to gain a handle on my reeling emotions, I snap.

"It's because I'm Goth Ick Gwen, isn't it?" I get in his face. "That's how you see me, right? As some *desperate* girl who will fall for the first guy who pays any attention to her?"

His jaw drops. "No. Not at all. You're being totally irrational."

It's the accusation some part of me has been waiting for and my temperature rises. I clench my teeth and explode. "Irrational? No. I'm not. I know exactly what I'm saying, so listen up. I'm not desperate for anything. I don't need anyone. I just want to be alone. So, please leave. I don't want you here." I open the door and shove him into his room.

He clings to the door frame. "Gwen, I'm choosing not to believe that. You've just had a shock. This will make more sense when you calm down."

"Calm down? I'm not going to calm down. You lied to me." Sputtering, I waggle my index finger at him. "You've *been* lying to me. And you know what? I'm glad I know the truth. I'm glad I know you're a liar. Last night was a close call, but luckily, I'm still the last bridesmaid standing. And I intend to keep it that way." Rising to fill the doorway with my frame, I force him the rest of the way into his room. "When I say I don't need anyone, I mean I don't need you. I don't want *you*." With that, I slam my door in his wide-eyed face and lock my side.

Then, still wrapped in Towaya, I throw myself on my bed and cry.

Chapter 30

Can't Fight This Feeling

To add insult to injury, in the midst of my cryfest, I get a text on my Italian loaner phone from Max:

Were you NOT babysitting Uncle Al last night? He slobbered ALL over one of the Food Network execs and kept dragging her onto the dance floor at the festival. He told her to loosen up and tried to smoke a JOINT with her in the alley behind the church.

Giorgio is MORTIFIED . . . Dignity and grace, Gwen.

We will speak about this later, but in the meantime, your number one priority is UNCLE AL.

And there goes my bonus. I let Duncan distract me, and now I've completely screwed up this wedding. When I get back to Chicago, I'll have to confess my debts to my parents and move home so I can pay off my credit cards . . . I've totally let them down.

Choking back a sob, I bury my face in my pillow, wishing it was Toto's soft fur. I need the buzzy vibrations of his purr to calm me.

A soft knock sounds from the other side of the adjoining room door. "Gwen, please talk to me?" Duncan pleads.

I sit up and stare at the door, clutching the necklace that once was my source of safety and calm. But now I can't trust it.

Fresh tears spring to my eyes. I can't do this. I'm too untethered to talk to him. Needing to get out of here, I force myself to my feet.

After pulling on the red-and-white striped romper from the meteor shower night, I walk to the beach in hopes the waves will clear my mind.

The Madonna has risen above the city. Her canvas suspended on a string, she flies in the impossibly blue sky over the green and gold tiled dome of the Church of Santa Maria Assunta. I join the procession of people heading down the stairs from her ascension ceremony toward the sea.

Catching snippets of Italian conversation on the sea breeze, I pass perfect rows of perfect people lounging on orange chaises under blue umbrellas in a cloud scented by coconut sunscreen. The pebbly sand is wet and rough against my bare feet as I walk along the water's edge, processing all I've learned with the slosh and fizz of the lapping waves rippling in my ears. It's unbelievable how everything I've built my definition of love on has unraveled in a span of a few days. And it was my brother who initiated the lie. It was Ty, who I've always believed was my protector, who betrayed me.

A sharp pain cracks across my skull, blurring my vision and I rub my temples. I cannot fathom what this means, can't make sense of the position my brother put me in or the shambles my life has become.

Cold water swirls around my ankles, waking me up.

And what did Duncan wish for me? I better bust open that prosecco bottle, ASAP.

I almost burst out laughing at the absurdity of my wish for him coming true, but still, my heart flutters at the possibilities that could be waiting inside that bottle. I can't help it. I can practically still feel the strength of his arms around me, and I don't think I've slept like I did last night, deep and secure, since before my brother died. It hurts to let that potential die.

But Duncan lied to me too. And who knows the truth about him and Aubrey. He's doing his job and playing both sides. Maybe it all ends with the wedding for both of us. Magic isn't real. Nothing is what it seems. Wishes don't actually come true, even if they seem to at first.

Steeling myself against last night, I kick the sand. Something shiny pops into the air, glinting in the sunlight before falling back to earth. Kneeling, I brush away clumped sand to reveal a little gold rooster charm. It's cute, and, picking it up, I look around to see if anybody nearby lost it.

All around me people are combing the sand and digging through wet pebbles as gentle waves foam on the shore. They *all* seem to be hunting for something.

"Excuse me, *parli inglese*?" I ask a couple. "Is this what you're looking for?"

They stare at me blankly, but I hold out the charm and they come closer to examine it.

Peering at the rooster in my hand, the woman exclaims, "*Allora.*"

I blink at her, waiting for her to elaborate and she closes my fingers around the gold trinket. "*In bocca al lupo.*"

Still not computing, I smile. "*Grazie.*"

Deciding I'll take the rooster back to the hotel and give it to Luigi to put in the lost and found—maybe there's a Positano community message board somewhere that he can post it on—I take off my necklace and slip the charm onto my chain next to the sapphire stars from my brother.

When I return to the hotel, the moment I enter the lobby, Luigi steps out of the elevator pushing an empty luggage cart.

"Luigi," I call, waving to get his attention. "I have a question for you."

"*Allora,*" he says, heading toward me. "Anything, bella. What can I do for you?"

I lead him to a lemon-yellow couch near a window that is open to the sea and take off my necklace. "I found this charm on the beach." I slide the gold rooster off the chain. "Somebody probably lost it. Is there a lost and found somewhere?"

He studies the little charm, and it glints in the light. "Oh, no, *bella*. This is good luck. *In bocca al lupo*. It's part of the festival to find charms in the sand, though this is a special one." He holds the rooster up to the sun. "This is the rooster of fortune. During the Renaissance in Italy, roosters woke the Medici family guards and prevented the assassination of one of their most prominent members. After that, the rooster became a good omen. They are also associated with dawn, the rising sun banishing night's illusions." He places the trinket in my palm and closes my fingers over it, much like the woman on the beach did. "He is symbolic of stepping into one's own light. It was meant for you."

"Luigi." The man behind the check-in desk calls, urging Luigi over. "*Puoi prendere i bagagli dalla stanza due cinquantasei?*"

"*Allora. Sì.*" Luigi squeezes my hand and winks before he stands and heads to the luggage cart.

I open my hand and stare at the charm. The sun warms my back and I sit in the light, in my allora, but my shadow casts the rooster in darkness. I have no idea what I'm supposed to do to get out of my own way and move forward, to make the sun illuminate my path.

Hopefully it doesn't require making a cock crow.

***

The rehearsal dinner on the patio at Villa Treville is almost prettier than any wedding I've attended. Two long tables with giant palm leaves running down their centers are set for forty guests with ten chairs tucked on each side. Overhead, the terrace ceiling is packed with hanging bougainvillea flowers and palms clustered in fuchsia and green bunches. The flowers and vines are dotted with cascading white lights, gold paper lanterns, and glass jars containing flickering tea lights. Everything glimmers in the soft glow of candlelight and the setting sun. Beyond the patio, a line of boats with colorful lights strung over their bows parade across the turquoise ocean and the pink-streaked sky.

When the wedding party makes our grand entrance, the rest of the guests are already gathered with tropical cocktails in hand, mingling in the golden twilight. There are actual celebrities in attendance tonight, like Berkeley Dalton and Olivia Bloom, whose twin daughters are the flower girls.

As I enter the terrace on one of the groomsmen's arms to Duncan singing, "But Not for Me" by George and Ira Gershwin, my stomach tightens. I tell myself the nerves are because I've never worked a wedding this high profile before.

The Wedding Bandits are tucked into a curved terracotta alcove under a glittering chandelier, and I refuse to look in their direction. I can't imagine the pressure on them, playing in front of a rock star like Berkeley Dalton, and it's not that I don't want to look, I just … can't.

Especially when Duncan is singing about love not being for him. It doesn't help that he's nailing this song, putting a loungey yacht rock meets Willie Nelson spin on it and making it *so* intoxicating.

Ugh.

The weight of his undeniable talent bears down on me. The mingling wedding guests are *actually* paying attention and nodding along as he sings.

He's got this.

He *belongs* in a room with a star like Berkeley Dalton, has the power to sway even him. I almost ditch my groomsman so I can close my eyes and sway in front of the band. But Max, in his pale-blue suit, standing by the bar directing the bartender, gives me a steely-eyed look that suggests the patio I'm standing on is actually made of paper-thin ice. If I fall through, there will be no rescue. This will be this bridesmaid's last stand.

Smoothing the sides of the body-hugging designer peach lace dress that is the bridesmaid attire for the evening, I square my shoulders, vowing to stay focused on the real reason I'm here: Zoey and Uncle Al.

Zoey wears a white version of my same dress. With its tiny spaghetti straps and low-cut neckline, these are the skimpiest gowns we've worn. We're channeling Sophia Loren tonight. I try not to think of the effect the slinky fabric could have on Duncan.

Or if he prefers the dress on me or Aubrey.

Inwardly, I shudder. Forcing a smile, I join the rest of the guests applauding Ethan and Zoey as they make their entrance holding hands.

The groomsmen wear cropped gray pants with peach collared shirts that match the lace on our dresses and skinny gray ties. I stand clustered with them, cheering for the happy couple, trying to look natural and candid for the photos. Behind us, a waiter in a tuxedo arrives carrying a tray of cocktails that are literally on fire.

"This is a *punyeta*," the waiter says from my side, offering me an icy glass garnished with pineapple and a flaming half of a lime floating on top. "It's rum, iced tea, and pineapple juice. It will light you up."

I arch an eyebrow. "No, thank you. Sounds dangerous."

The music winds down and Zoey takes the microphone from Duncan. I'm forced to finally look at him in his white pants and silky cream shirt printed with olive-colored palm leaves–unbuttoned as usual. His eyes briefly catch mine and, flushing, I quickly shift my focus to the bride.

"Thank you all for coming. I wanted to tell you a little bit about my favorite part of every party, the food." She smiles, her flawless skin shimmering in the balmy air, making her appear luminescent. "On our first date, Ethan let me pick the restaurant. I decided to see how adventurous he was, so I chose a Boodle Fight at a Filipino restaurant in River North. It was so delicious and so much fun we wanted to recreate it for you tonight. Special thanks to our wedding planner, Max, for bringing the Philippines to Italy." She gestures toward Max, who nods back at her, a close-lipped smile on his face. "He's really outdone himself."

As she talks, waiters appear, balancing massive platters stacked with different dishes on their shoulders. The scents of garlic, ginger, lemon grass, and soy fill the terrace as they pile assorted delicacies on palm leaves that run down the center of the tables, the food arranged around bowls containing colorful sauces.

"There's pancit and lumpia and pinakbet and grilled bangus and adobong manok. If you don't know what something is, try it anyway." Zoey laughs. "You're going to love it. And everything is family style. You eat with your hands."

"And no fighting, just eating and enjoying." Ethan chimes in from where he stands off to Zoey's side. "We're so happy you're all here to celebrate with us. Now dig in." He raises his cocktail to everyone.

The guests toast in return then move toward the tables and Zoey hands the microphone back to Duncan.

As I head toward dinner, I catch up with Uncle Al. "Need a dinner date?" I loop my arm through his and slip my Rosie persona on. It's almost a relief to be someone else, someone who knows exactly who they are.

"I thought you'd never ask." Al grins. "Did you try these things?" He holds up his empty punyeta glass. "Come on. Let's get lit."

"No thanks, Uncle Al." I laugh. "I'm taking it easy tonight—don't want to be puffy for the wedding tomorrow."

"When are you going to let go and live a little?" He grumbles. "Promise me that tomorrow, all bets are off."

"Deal."

We join the feast. As we eat, Aubrey glances at me several times, probably trying to picture me as Goth Ick Gwen. I ignore her, and it's not hard. I'm too busy putting my personal turmoil aside, being Rosie, doing my duty, and babysitting Uncle Al.

The waiters keep the bountiful food coming, and Max seems pleased, hovering around the party wearing a pleasant code-yellow smile, which is the best possible mood he could be in. Always on alert, but crisis-free. He even tops up the wine I've been served, a signal that he's happy with how things are progressing.

The sky darkens to black, and stars peek out over the water. The candlelit terrace takes on a fuzzy glow as the punyeta cocktails flow and speeches commence. Ethan's dad gets up and talks about how proud he is of his son. A Food Network producer gets up and talks about what a talent Zoey is. Everything is going great in terms of the dinner. It's lovely and romantic and Ethan and Zoey seem happy and engaged, literally and figuratively. They stand next to each other at least half the time, and Payton, as best man, seems to be saving his speech for the wedding tomorrow.

I start to believe I *am* Rosie, that I'm going to survive this thing without anyone else finding out about Ethan and my past. I'm going to fly home in two days and cash my checks—bonus included—and Toto's bills will be taken care of. I'll work a few more weddings before the season slows down, and instead of creating music content, I'll study for the bar. Duncan and I will add last night to our list of things that never happened. We'll go back to ignoring each other. I'll still pay him back for the airplane salmon, the undies, and the shoes, but after that maybe I'll have enough money to go to the Austin City Limits Music Festival or something. Everything is going to be fine. I'm getting back on track. It's going to happen. Hope flutters in my chest.

Then Aubrey takes the stage. The peach lace dress fits her to perfection, accenting her slim curves. With her blonde hair tumbling over her shoulders in loose waves, she's so pretty, she's like an angel.

But then she stumbles. Duncan catches her arm, holding her up before handing her the microphone. I scan the three empty punyeta glasses at her seat, and my heart plummets.

An angel who's about to fall from grace.

I jerk my head towards Max.

Crisis mode.

His lips are stretching in a thin line, and his bulging eyes meet mine.

Drunk bridesmaid about to speak.

The warning message is a foghorn sounding in both of our brains, and wincing, I reach for my necklace. It's not at my throat, wasn't Sophia Loren approved, so I clutch my handbag, where it resides instead.

Aubrey raises the microphone to her lips. "Hi, I'm Aubrey. Ethan's sister. And those of you who know me know I have very high standards."

Uncle Al laughs a loud guffaw.

Where was I on this one?

I've been babysitting the wrong person this whole time. I curse myself for thinking we were out of the woods. With a curt nod at Max to indicate I'm on it, I make a beeline for the stage. It's probably too late. I can't tackle her, after all, but maybe I can convince her to serenade the happy couple with a karaoke duet or something.

"But so does Ethan. *Sometimes.*" Aubrey's gaze flickers over me, and a deer in headlights, I freeze. "He made a great choice when he picked Zoey. And he could have had *any* girl he wanted. Trust me. But Zoey—she's Aubrey approved. And I'm so excited she's going to be my sister. I've been stuck with these boys for way too long." She gestures with her thumb toward Ethan and Payton before focusing on Zoey.

An uncomfortable smattering of laughter ripples through the crowd.

I know I need to do something—anything—to stop her. But it's like I'm paralyzed or out of my body. I can only watch.

"And as my first sisterly act, I feel I need to be honest with you, Zoey. There's this, like huge secret I need to let you in on." She takes a deep breath, and powerless to stop her, I watch the train leave the station, barreling forward toward its—*my* doom.

"Zoey, were you aware that your new BFF—your maid of honor, Rosie—hooked up with Ethan?"

Chapter 31
Lowdown

There is a collective gasp from the guests. Time slows to a crawl, and one would think a record would scratch, but no. The laser-like stares that beam in my direction are punctuated by the opening bars of "Maneater" by Hall & Oates.

It's so ridiculous. It's perfect.

Just because it's by Hall & Oates doesn't mean it's yacht rock.

I start to think we can discuss this later, but then I remember I'm not speaking to Duncan and my heart squeezes. I really wish I was speaking to him. As it is, I can't look at him as he sings.

In my periphery, the band leans together, harmonizing the chorus and tears of absurd joy spring to my eyes. Laughter builds in my chest, and I might as well laugh as cry. I can't deny the golden timing of this song choice. It's so Duncan. I know he's trying to cheer me up . . . and, bizarrely, it's working. I'm sputtering, biting back the urge to dissolve into giggles. But then I notice Max, and I'm instantly sober.

I have triggered a level beyond a code-red crisis, an unimaginable level of dismay. Instinctually, I duck.

I'm so fired.

Somewhere in the distance, Uncle Al cackles, and I picture him kicking back in a recliner and tossing popcorn into his mouth. My gaze travels slowly over Zoey, who is catatonic, and Payton, who massages the back of Zoey's neck, until I find Ethan.

He raises his eyebrows. "Rosie?" he whispers.

Time fast forwards, returning to normal speed.

Zoey shimmies her shoulders, and seeming to come to her senses, wiggles out from under Payton's grasp. She waves at Duncan to silence the band. The music trails off and her voice rings out over the terrace, shrill. "Ethan, is this true? When?"

Ethan presses a fist to his lips and shakes his head. "It happened a long time ago—before I knew you—and she looks so different. I didn't know . . . " Blinking like he can't believe it's me, he faces me in full. "You look fantastic, Rosie."

He called me Rosie.

I'm still undercover and I can save this. I have to. For Zoey's sake. I can't let anyone know she hired me. They think I'm the bad guy and if I'm going to save my job, I've got to keep it that way.

Dignity and grace. It's all about the bride.

"Rosie?" Zoey's voice wobbles. "Why didn't you tell me?"

"I didn't know until I got here." My knees go weak, threatening to give out and I grip my handbag so tight, my knuckles turn white. "I'd never met your fiancé in person, and it never occurred to me it would be the same Ethan. When I knew him, people called him 'Fish.' I never thought of the guy I knew as 'Ethan.' And then when I realized who he was, I didn't want to complicate things. He's right. I do look different, and I knew he didn't recognize me. I'm sorry. I didn't want to cause any drama. I was seventeen when we knew each other. It was a long time ago, and we haven't seen each other for over a decade. Since . . . " I take a deep breath. "My brother died."

A weight descends onto my shoulders, but somehow I manage to keep from collapsing and stay on my feet. "It's not like I've been thinking of Ethan this whole time or anything." Unsure if anyone is buying my lie, I force a laugh.

"You're sure you didn't befriend Zoey just to get to Ethan?" Aubrey slurs into the microphone. "I know Zoey hired you. Your name is Gwen, not Rosie. When you realized Ethan was *your* Ethan, did you jump at the chance to take this job? You've been trying to get to him all along, haven't you?"

"No." I gasp. "I swear. I was just trying to do my job."

How did Aubrey know Zoey hired me?

The answer hits me, and my head snaps toward Duncan. He stares at his toes.

My lungs constrict and I can't breathe. Max is about to have a conniption and the guests close in on me, their faces swirling in a whirl. I press a damp palm to my throat.

But then, Payton steps out from behind Zoey and takes my side. He turns to her. "I don't know about my brother, but I'm glad for this little shake up. I'm glad we're talking about secrets. About speaking our truth."

Oh, no.

Darkness blots the edges of my vision and all lingering hope of saving the wedding evaporates.

Farewell, Max. Hello, cat-penis debt for the rest of my life.

Uncle Al is on the edge of his seat.

Zoey sways, caught in the same dizzying tidal wave as me, no doubt.

"I need to be honest with you, Zoey. And you, Ethan." Payton turns to his brother. "I've tried to avoid this. Believe me. I love you. I respect you. I want you to be happy, and that's why I have to say this. I think you're making a mistake. I don't think you should get married. I know you have an agreement but, Ethan—I love her. For real. Like she deserves to be loved. She's not a business deal to be had."

"What are you doing?" Zoey's dad leaps out of his seat, a vein protruding in his forehead. "Zoey is marrying Ethan. We've been celebrating them all week. I'm sure you want some of your brother's success. But you can't have this."

Zoey's cheeks turn pink, and she puts a hand up to stop her dad. "That's not true, Dad. Payton isn't anything like Ethan and he doesn't want to be anything like Ethan. He's perfect the way he is. And you're wrong about another thing. I'm not marrying Ethan."

She takes a deep breath. "I don't even know if I believe in marriage. It's *such* an antiquated system. I'm only doing this because this is what you want for me, and I want to make you proud." Her words tumble out in a rush.

"But now I'm realizing I can't go through with it. It's not what *I* want. Yes, I hired Gwen to pose as my maid of honor because it's all part of the package I'm supposed to present. I'm the perfect girl with the perfect friends who adore her. But I'm done lying. I'm done with all of this. I'm officially not marrying anyone."

With that, to the stunned cries of the guests, she pivots on her heel and strides out of the party, her chin held high and her heels clacking in an elegant echo as she exits.

Near the door to the kitchen, Max crumples to the ground. A waiter grabs him and splashes water on his face, and it's like he splashed water on mine. I come to.

Everyone is staring at me. Even movie stars. Olivia Bloom, with her three-year-old twin flower girls clinging to her legs offers me a small smile, like she gets how I feel, and I want to die.

There's only one way out of this.

Handling the situation with zero percent dignity, zero percent grace, and one hundred percent speed, I hike my dress to mid-thigh, kick off my too-small heels, tuck my handbag under my arm, and sprint after Zoey.

I catch up to her in the botanical gardens. She's on the ground under a wisteria-covered pergola, hugging her legs to her chest. Her chin on her knees, she's staring out at the dark sea.

"Zoey, I'm so sorry." Breathless, I kneel next to her. "I promise I didn't break Terra's foot so I'd have to replace her and could get to Ethan. I truly didn't know I knew him until I got here. But I should have told you."

Sniffling, she keeps focus on the skyline. "I understand why you didn't. You never even met me until five days ago. Why should you have told me?"

I curl my legs underneath me, sitting on my knees. "Even though I've only known you five days, I still feel like your friend. But I didn't tell you because I wanted the wedding to go smoothly. I didn't want any drama. I thought I could pull it off. And you should know Ethan wanted that, too."

Her misty gaze flickers to mine. Her eyes are red-rimmed. The tip of her nose is pink. Her cheeks are splotchy. But she's still beautiful.

"He did recognize me," I admit. "But he barely remembered my name. There was never anything between us. He only hung out with me back then because he lost a bet with my brother." I leave out the giant crush I've had on him all these years. "And he asked I keep our past secret because he wanted the wedding to be exactly the way you envisioned it."

"That's actually really sweet of him to let me control the narrative." She tucks her hair behind her ears. "But maybe that's the problem. Maybe I need to give up control."

My Italian loaner phone buzzes repeatedly in my purse that is lying next to me on the grass. I suspect the texts are from Max, and blood rushes to my head. My temples pound with the need to read the messages, to know my fate, and I peek at the screen.

Max

> Clearly you are relieved of your bridesmaid duties going forward. Everything is nonrefundable at this point, so you can keep your hotel room and fly home as scheduled. I'll pay you for time worked minus any room charges.

> Please leave the vendor-supplied wardrobe in your closet. Any questions can be discussed in Chicago as I'm busy putting out the fires you started.

A jolt rattles through me. Choking on a sob, I slap my hand over my mouth. But as quickly as the fear and disbelief came, it morphs into a rising urge to laugh.

Do I add arsonist to my resume? Probably won't be getting a letter of recommendation from Max . . .

"Honestly, I don't know how much control we have over anything, anyway," I say, swinging my legs around so they're in front of me and showing her the text. "Life seems to have its own agenda." I hug my knees to my chest.

"Oh, Gwen. I'm so sorry." She wipes away an escaped tear and drapes her arm over my shoulders, briefly hugging me. "This is all my fault."

I try to make sense of the impossible glee expanding in my chest. It's like someone has ripped off a bandage and I was afraid to look at the wound, but once I did, I saw I was totally healed. This is not how I expected this moment to feel. "No. It's nobody's fault. It is what it is. A thing that happened. Honestly, I've been thinking it's time for a change, and life seems to agree. I'm weirdly relieved."

Stray orchid-colored wisteria petals flutter down from the pergola overhead, landing in our hair.

She exhales. "I'm so glad you said that. I'm relieved, too. Practically happy." Her eyebrows squish together, and she stares at her nails that are painted a soft buff shade called bridal blush. "But I feel totally guilty about it."

"You shouldn't feel guilty." I brush a petal off her shoulder. "What you did in there was super brave. You stood up for yourself."

She nods. "I finally grew some balls and said what I want."

"You have some *huge* balls." I laugh. "I'm proud of you."

Her lips wobble into a small smile. "I'm proud of me, too."

"Ahem." Someone coughs behind us and we turn to find Ethan standing on the path with his hands shoved in his pockets. He is so handsome he could be carved from marble like one of the statues that dot the villa's property.

"Hey. Just the girls I've been looking for." He rocks back on his heels, giving us a crooked smile.

"Ethan . . ." Zoey's eyes well up.

His smile widens. "Don't worry, Z. Your dad ordered everyone back to the feast and the drinks are flowing. The band is playing, the party is on, and they're all totally talking about us. It's as it should be." He winks. "But seeing as you just called off our wedding, we should probably chat."

Covering her mouth with her palm, she stands and hugs him.

"I'll give you guys some space." I jump to my feet and head down the path that winds through the gardens, but before I go, Zoey stops me. "Gwen—will you wait for me?"

"Sure. I'll just be right over there." I point down the way to a softly lit bench positioned under an oleander tree.

Once I reach the bench, I sit watching Zoey and Ethan's silhouettes from a distance. They stroll along a meandering path through the dark garden, their arms linked, and Rosie officially leaves me. I cling to her, to work-mode, so I won't have to feel. But she doesn't belong to me anymore.

The "Maneater" moment pops into my head and the hysterical urge to laugh again overtakes me. My cheeks burn that Duncan witnessed my persecution, but then my stomach twists that I was persecuted at his hand. Aubrey figured out Zoey hired me, and based on Duncan's reaction, my guess is he had something to do with that.

Max is super discreet about hiring out bridesmaids and makes sure not to advertise the service. Googling me wouldn't have revealed my profession. There's only one way she could have found out: from the guy who has been pretending to be my partner in crime.

Duncan betrayed me. He knew it, and he didn't warn me.

Another lie.

And no matter what he says, clearly, he's talked at length about me with Aubrey. Tears blur my vision and I dig my fingernails into my palms, hoping the pain will erase the last twenty-four hours.

"Hey." A male voice at my back startles me.

Pulling myself together, I dab my wet cheeks with the back of my hand before turning to find Payton.

"Gwen," he says, his dark eyebrows lowered over his charcoal eyes. His peach button-down shirt stretches across his broad shoulders, like his exuberant spirit can't be contained by Ethan's conservative clothing choice and wants to burst free.

I stand. Smoothing my dress over my thighs, I face him. Hopefully he can't tell I've been crying.

"I want you to know you did a great job keeping your cover. I imagine your job isn't easy, especially when you're hiding such a huge secret," he says softly, shoving his hands into his pockets but leaving his thumbs out as though he's modeling the cropped pants. The motion is yet another marked difference from his brother. Confident where Ethan was sheepish.

My mouth falls open and, at a loss for words, I stare at him, a gaping fish.

"And my sister is relentless when she wants something," he continues, seemingly unaffected by my lack of response. "She's young and immature. She'll dig and dig until she figures out how to get her way. It's not her most attractive attribute. Hopefully she'll outgrow it. But really, the dirt she found on you doesn't tarnish you in my eyes. You were keeping everyone's best interest at heart, not your own. I see that. I'm sure Zoey will too. And my brother . . . " He hesitates, slowly nodding, before settling on what he wants to say. "He's a good guy. He's got some stuff to figure out, but he's solid. Try not to hold the past against him if you can."

Blinking to comprehend everything he's telling me, I stick my neck out like a turtle emerging from a shell and finally speak. "You have a lot of insight into this situation."

"I'm an observer." He shrugs. "And I have a feeling I can trust your advice." His chiseled jaw twitches as his lips curve, hinting at a smile.

I take a deep breath, the word "advice" ringing in my ears. "What do you want to know?"

He leans toward me. Dipping his chin, he lowers his voice. "I love Zoey. I really do. I know there isn't anyone else out there for me. I've never been so certain of anything. And trust me, I don't have room in my life for a relationship. But I'd make an exception for her. I *want* to make an exception for her. What do you think I should do?"

Grinding my teeth, I tell him the first thing that pops into my mind. "Honestly. Give her space. She has to come to you on her own terms."

His face falls. "I was afraid you'd say that."

"You can't force someone to love you back." I show him my palms. "Believe me."

"Yeah . . . " He lowers his gaze, his forehead creasing.

Heels clack down the path behind us and a glance over my shoulder reveals Zoey walking our way.

He spies her at the same time and backs away from me. "I should go. But do me a favor. When someone sees you the way I see Zoey—and there *is* someone who does—give him a chance."

Heat surges through me, but with an imperceptible nod, I watch him retreat down the path away from where Zoey is approaching.

"What was that about?" She stops at my side.

"He wanted to make sure you—and me, actually—were okay." I shake my head slightly to keep myself from dwelling on what Payton's parting words meant.

She rubs her forehead and remains silent, like she doesn't know what to do with that information.

"How'd it go with Ethan?" I lightly touch her arm. "Is the wedding back on?"

She flinches like that thought never crossed her mind. "No." She laughs. Shaking her head, she stares at the ground, then takes a deep breath. "And I haven't been totally honest with you." Exhaling, she peers up at me. "The truth is, Ethan and I have had an arrangement for a long time."

I keep my expression soft and tilt my head toward her like I never suspected such a thing.

Her shoulders meet her ears. "We both wanted to focus on our careers but were getting pressure from our families to take the next step in our personal lives. Neither of us was interested in swiping around to find someone or putting in the effort a relationship takes."

We walk down a path covered by a pergola dripping with purple wisteria, the flowers' sweet scent enveloping us as we wind down toward the water, careful to avoid passing the party.

"I want to be a star. I always have. It's taken a long time for me to say that out loud, but it's the thing I want most. Every life goal fades in comparison, marriage included. Ethan felt the same way—not about being a star, but about focusing on his own interests—so we agreed to be partners. Glorified roommates. We checked a lot of boxes for each other, plus we're great friends, and isn't that ultimately what marriage is? A great friendship?" She widens her eyes at me like she's willing me to buy in.

My heart deflates a little. I personally *want* there to be more to it than that, but maybe she's right. What do I know? I've never known love. Biting my lip, I shrug. "I think marriage means different things to different people. Maybe that's what it is to you."

Grimacing, she sniffles and fans her face. "Anyway, it doesn't matter. We broke it off. Now that everyone knows . . . and in light of Payton's announcement . . . " She coughs.

"I didn't see that coming."

Her cheeks flush. "Me neither."

I squint at her. "You aren't interested?"

"He's impulsive." She concentrates on the uneven path, putting one foot in front of the other.

"Clearly."

"I'm not." Dropping her forehead into her palm, she moans. "No. I can't be with him." Her fingers move to massage her temples. "I need to be alone."

The path ends at a dock that juts into the sea beneath a series of arched neon signs glowing bright against the night sky. The first arch shines with pink neon hearts, the second has Zoey + Ethan written in pink and blue script, and the third reads Happily Ever After in blue.

Ignoring the messaging, she grabs my hand and drags me over the polished wood slats through the arches to where a water taxi with a yellow-striped sunshade waits. "Will you come back to the hotel with me? I need to be alone but not tonight."

"Of course." I squeeze her fingers.

We get into the boat with its red wooden fish sign that reads Positano and position ourselves under the bougainvillea chains and white lights strung from the top of the mast that are reminiscent of the rehearsal dinner. As usual, Max has thought of every detail.

Before we begin the short ride back to Il Desiderio, Zoey pulls out her cell phone and makes a call.

"Luigi. It's Zoey. Can you send some prosecco to my room?" she says when the other end of the line picks up. "My friend Gwen and I could use a drink."

She ends the call and the boat rumbles to life. The driver hits the gas and we cut through the water. With the wind in our hair and the Positano coastline sparkling alongside us, we smile at each other.

Our secrets are out. We're free.

Chapter 32

Cool Change

We've barely popped the cork on the prosecco when there's a knock on the door. Zoey's spine stiffens when she finds Aubrey standing on the other side.

I peer over Zoey's shoulder from my seat on the couch in front of the fireplace. Zoey has covered the hearth with flickering candles.

Aubrey thrusts a bottle of rosé forward. "I come in peace." Her face is puffy, her eyes glassy with tears. "Zoey. I'm so sorry. The punyeta went straight to my head. I thought you should know the truth about Rosie—I mean, Gwen—but I probably could have found a better way to tell you."

"Punyeta isn't just a drink. I read that in Tagalog it also means 'fuck.'" Zoey leans against the door. "Or asshole."

I gape at this side of Zoey.

"I'm a *total* punyeta. I deserve that." Sniffling, Aubrey examines her manicure. "Can I please explain?"

Zoey glances over her shoulder at me. "What do you think?"

Aubrey leans into the room. "Please? I owe Gwen an apology, too."

I don't particularly feel like chatting with Aubrey, but I know it's probably important to Zoey to smooth things over with the almost sister she so longed for. I shrug my acceptance.

"Come in." Zoey moves aside, and Aubrey enters. She takes a seat on the couch in the opposite corner from me. When Zoey raises the prosecco bottle at her in offering, she opts for sparkling water.

"I'm so sorry, Zoey. I shouldn't have told everyone you hired Gwen." Aubrey gushes as soon as she's settled. "That was out of line and not at all sisterly. I meant it when I said I was excited to have you as a sister and I promise I *can* keep a secret. You can trust me. I'll prove it."

Zoey sits on the arm of the couch and considers Aubrey. "I was excited to be your sister, too. I probably should have confided in you that I didn't have any close friends to ask to be my maid of honor. I was living a lie. But you definitely could have found a better way to tell me."

"I messed up." Tears roll down Aubrey's cheeks. "I don't expect you to forgive me, but maybe there's a way I can earn your friendship."

Zoey slowly nods, sipping her prosecco. "I'm not really in a place to forgive you right now. I have a lot to process and figure out, but if you're willing to meet me halfway, maybe we can work through it. Maybe we can learn what being a sister means together. I think there's a way we can build trust. It might take time, though."

"I'd like that." Aubrey smiles. "And I'm willing to work on it as long as it takes. I don't have a lot of close girlfriends either. Most girls seem to not like me very much." She shrugs.

"Well, speaking of other girls, maybe start with Gwen? I think you owe her an apology, too?" Zoey suggests.

"Oh, yes." Aubrey faces me, pressing both palms to her breastbone. "I shouldn't have told everyone who you were. That was childish and petty of me. I should have talked to you first and found out the truth, instead of jumping to conclusions and thinking you were after Ethan all along." She takes a deep breath. "But the truth is, I was jealous. Duncan is like, the hottest guy I've ever seen. He's been getting social media lessons from me, but he has zero interest in me beyond my knowledge of algorithms because he's totally into *you*. And in my punyeta daze, I thought if I could get you fired and sent home early, maybe he'd pay attention to me for the last two nights of the trip."

My stomach drops. "Um. Congratulations, your plan worked. I got fired."

She closes her eyes. "I'm so sorry."

It's going to take a lot for me to get past Aubrey publicly outing me, but I lift my shoulders, unable to let her take all the blame. "But it's not totally your fault. I should have told Max I knew Ethan and excused myself from the wedding. I knew what I was doing, the risk I was taking. I could have gotten fired all on my own. You didn't need to out me because of *Duncan*. He's definitely *not* into me. He's just doing his job, probably playing both of us."

She waves me off. "He is too into you. Seriously, you should have seen him when I told him who you were, when I figured out Zoey hired you. He begged me to keep your secret."

"What do you mean?" I cock my head. "Didn't Duncan tell you Zoey hired me?"

"No." Raising her Pellegrino to her lips, she shakes her head. "I figured it out myself. I saw the name Gwen on Duncan's phone while I was helping him put hashtags on a post and it clicked. I realized why you were so familiar. It was from those pictures you used to text my brother. When he was home from school on break, he used to show them to me as an example of what *not* to do. Then I started googling."

OMG. Ethan showed those pictures to Aubrey, too?

A deep ache seeps through me, and I sink into the couch, my face on fire. Foolishly, I always assumed that maybe Ethan's fraternity brothers inadvertently saw my sexts, or he shared them to show who he'd hung out with over the summer, not because he was actively making fun of me. But now it's clear that was just my brain protecting me from a truth that would have devastated me.

I pound the rest of my prosecco as if it could wash away my disgust with the whole situation.

Zoey peers at me, her eyes wide, as she refills my glass.

Burying my shock, I scramble to explain. "I had a minor crush on Ethan when I was seventeen after he came on vacation with my family. He was my brother Tyler's best friend. It was super silly, and I have no interest in him now. I swear."

"Hey. He's my ex. And we were never in love. You have my permission. He's fair game." She shrugs and returns the prosecco bottle to the bar cart.

"Oh, no. I'm good." I quickly change the subject. "So, Aubrey, you started googling?"

"Yeah. If you were some sort of stalker who Zumba'd her way into Zoey's life to break up my brother's wedding, I wanted to prove who you were. But when I told Duncan about my suspicions, he told me he was positive I was wrong. He wouldn't tell me *why* I was wrong—he just wanted me to trust him—to believe, like he did, that your intentions were pure. But that wasn't enough for me. I wanted to get to the bottom of why you were here."

So, he didn't betray me . . .

My heart flip-flops, but I lower my brow. "But how did you find me on Google? Max keeps his undercover bridesmaid business super secret."

She folds her legs underneath her. "I started wondering how Duncan knew so much about you if you'd only just met him. Then I saw you talking to Max in Capri, and it clicked that you knew Duncan from weddings. I went to Max's website and found his wedding blog and looked up social media accounts for a few of the couples he featured. And there you were, wearing a bridesmaid dress in at least half of their wedding photos. Then that made me search for hired bridesmaids—which I didn't know were a thing—and I found a Reddit about it. It all started to make sense that Zoey hired you."

"Wow." I shake my head at her sleuthing. "Max should put a clause in his contract that couples can't post pictures of us. That's a major security flaw."

"He should, though the internet is pretty hard to control." Aubrey hugs a pillow to her chest. "Anyway, Duncan would do *anything* for you."

Grimacing, I twirl my hair around a finger. "I'm not so sure. I've worked a lot of weddings with him. He's never given me the time of day until this trip." Sinking back against the cushions, I stare at the domed ceiling. "It was both of our jobs to keep the peace. He's like my wingman."

"Only because you want him to be," Aubrey says, fiddling with the tassel on her pillow. "Trust me. You should have seen him today after my speech. He was *so* pissed at me. I didn't know he could get mad, but I am steering clear of him for a while." She sighs. "But how are we at a wedding with zero love matches?"

"Including the bride and groom." Zoey snorts, setting her glass on the coffee table and flopping onto the middle of the couch.

"There's always Payton," Aubrey offers. "We could still be sisters."

Zoey drops her face into her hand. "Payton is . . ." Looking up, she steeples her fingers over her mouth. "Intriguing." She clasps her hands in front of her chest. "But I think it's best for me to be alone. Honestly, I'm excited to be by myself. I feel liberated. And I need to figure out how I'm going to make it on my own because, after all the money my dad spent on this wedding, he's going to disown me. He'll probably take away my show."

"Max said everything is nonrefundable at this point." I grimace. Grateful to be talking about something other than everything I've just learned about Ethan and Duncan, I embrace the change of subject, buoyed by how much I believe in *Zoey*.

"Maybe it's a good thing if he takes away your show. You can become a star in your own right—I think you are. What if your fans—yes, *your* fans, not your dad's—were *shocked* to find out who your dad is?" I push my finger onto the coffee table for emphasis. "What if you earn your own show without him? Build a brand that becomes massive because it's about who you uniquely are and not because he gave you a chance? You can make it happen on *your* terms, not his. Your future shouldn't feel stressful. It should give you goosebumps—like Payton does—even though it's scary. It should feel like something you don't want to miss out on."

Zoey fills her lungs, her eyes shining. "You're right. I *love* that. Even if my dad wants my show to go on, I'm going to tell him I want to do it on my own. I want to call the shots in my life. Make my own decisions. Do what *I* want to do. Be in my power."

"How freeing would it be to not have to rely on anyone else for our happiness?" Aubrey muses.

Suddenly an idea strikes me, and I lean forward. "Maybe the party can go on. But instead of it being a marriage, we call it a liberation celebration."

Zoey perks up. "A liberation celebration." Falling silent, she stares at the candlelit fireplace. "We'd need to send out new invitations, re-work the ceremony. But it could be interesting." Her smile widens. "I can make a promise to myself, and my dad will just have to deal with it."

"*Anybody* who wants to make a promise to themselves could speak out and do it," I suggest.

"Amazing." Zoey's eyes are huge in her face. "I'm serious. Let's do it."

Goosebumps shoot up my arms, and I switch into Rosie mode. The celebration must go on with dignity and grace.

I can still pull this off.

"I'll call Luigi." I head to the phone. "Ask him to bring some arts and crafts supplies."

"And some food," Zoey says.

"And maybe some water." Aubrey laughs.

After talking to Luigi, I text Max that the celebration is still on for tomorrow, and I will be standing next to Zoey as her bridesmaid, not because he's paying me, but because she is my friend.

Luigi soon appears with scissors and construction paper and washi tape and rations, and we get to crafting, a band of bridesmaids, like we should have been all along.

And my work here is done.

Chapter 33

Whenever I Call You "Friend"

The hallway is flooded with pale yellow light and damp ocean air that wafts through the white curtains at the end of the passage. As I round the corner to my room, I tighten the hotel-issued robe I borrowed from Zoey to keep out the morning breeze. My lacy rehearsal dinner dress is stuffed in the pocket.

"I knew you'd have to come back here some time. I was hoping we could talk." Looking magazine-perfect and fresh, like he's spent the early morning hours getting styled for a photoshoot, Ethan is leaning against the wall outside my door holding two coffees.

I do a double take. Having slept on Zoey's couch after staying up half the night getting out Liberation Celebration invites, my eyes are aching, but unfortunately, they aren't seeing things. And after Aubrey's revelation, Ethan is the last person I want to see.

He extends one of the paper cups toward me as I slowly come to a halt in front of him. I cautiously accept it.

"Thank you. Were you waiting long?" Keeping a wide distance between us, I warm my hands on the cup.

"I called first. When you didn't answer, I texted Zoey. She said you'd just left her room, so no, I haven't been out here long. But I couldn't sleep last night because I kept thinking about how I owe you a huge apology. I've been wanting to apologize all week, so I wanted to catch you first thing."

My stomach roils in anticipation of the awkward conversation ahead, but I unlock my door. "Okay. Do you want to come inside?" I push the door open and step aside so he can enter.

He sits on the edge of my bed facing the doors that lead to the ocean as I close the door behind us.

Inwardly, I cringe, but I slowly lower myself to join him.

His attention is trained on the coffee he holds between his knees. "When I knew you, I was young and dumb and figuring myself out." Closing his eyes, he exhales. "Back then, I was trying to prove to Payton—who has always been much more of a 'guy' than me—how macho I was. I was trying so hard to fit in with my fraternity brothers that I thought I had to treat girls like they treated them. It's horrifying."

Frowning, he peeks up at me. "I don't expect your forgiveness, but I want you to know I thought you were really cool that week on Mackinac. Even though I didn't expect to, I had fun. *Real* fun. You surprised me. We got each other on *so* many levels, and you deserved the utmost respect. I should never have showed anyone those pictures you sent me. I overheard my fraternity brothers laughing about them at Ty's funeral, and knew you heard them, but I couldn't bring myself to apologize to you then. I couldn't face you, so I just stopped talking to you. You trusted me, and I betrayed you."

My cheeks heat that we're talking about this, and I can't look at him. I set my coffee on the nearby desk, having lost my taste for it. "Thank you for the apology." I press my clammy palms to my face to cool it before folding my hands in front of my mouth. "It was pretty gutting to learn the most magical week of my life was a lie. That you showed those pictures to everyone to make fun of me," I whisper.

Ethan's shoulders slump, and he pinches the bridge of his nose. "I was *so* immature. And cruel. And I made your life worse when you were already going through the impossible. That I could be so terrible has been eating away at me for years."

We fall silent, and I pick my coffee back up to busy my hands, a question on my lips that I don't want to ask. My fingers tremble as I lift the cup and take a sip, tasting nothing, the question still circling in my mind. Finally, unable to take the need for truth anymore, I break the quiet. "Actually, I do have one question, even though I'm not sure I want to know the answer."

He straightens his spine. "Ask me anything. I owe you that much."

I take a deep breath. "You never showed those pictures of me to my brother, did you?" I blink back tears.

He winces. "No. Never. But I'm sure on some level he knew . . ." Squirming, he stares into the distance, his forehead puckered. "I'm still mortified he saw how awful I was." His voice is thick. "One of the biggest regrets in my life is that I didn't get to talk to him about it, to apologize. To ask him to help me be better. To be like he was. Because he was an angel. *Is* an angel. And I didn't get to . . . " He hangs his head.

My sinuses burn and my chest tightens as I think of Ty, of how he lit up every room he was in. And I sit, together with Ethan in mournful silence of all that is left unsaid, of all the promise that is lost.

"I *loved* your brother." He finally picks his head up and turns to face me. "And he loved you. I hope you know that. He would have done anything for you."

"Including making me the losing end of a bet." My voice cracks and I knit my eyebrows, still unable to comprehend that Tyler is at the root of the lie.

Ethan startles. "It wasn't a bet. At first, I was doing him a favor. And I already told you I would do anything for him. He asked if I could help his little sister gain some confidence. He wanted you to be happy, to feel worthy." He squints, like that could help him see into the past. "You were always in such a dark mood, he was hoping he could brighten your outlook, make you believe in possibility. He thought maybe if someone took interest in you, you'd see yourself the way he saw you."

Seeming to return from his trip back in time, he focuses on me, concentrating like he wants to make me believe in me, too. "He thought you were smart and interesting, and he wanted everyone to see that. And he was right. As the week went on, I saw everything he saw in you. You were an incredible person. You probably still are." Shifting closer to me, he takes my hand. "If you can forgive me, I'd love the chance to find out."

I am a baby lamb in a meadow, staring up at him. Warmth spreads through my chest as I think of my brother. I *know* he had my best interests at heart and I'm grateful for this message from him that makes me want to be the *me* that he knew.

My mouth goes dry, and I feel Tyler's presence surrounding me, his forgiveness for Ethan pulsing in my veins. And in this moment, I forgive them both, too.

I swallow. "We're all figuring ourselves out," I say, slowly. "We're all evolving, struggling under the weight of expectations, and it's okay to say I used to be insecure. It's not who I am anymore. As long as you keep trying to grow, what more can I ask?"

His lips press into a small smile and his chest caves. "Thank you, Gwen. You have no idea how much that means to me."

"We've all got a lot to let go of." I shrug.

He nods and his eyes shine, crinkling at the corners as his face lights up. "You know, I find myself without a date for this Liberation Celebration and I was wondering if you'd like to join me?" He squeezes my hand. "I feel like maybe your brother would have wanted us to go together."

I can't answer. Here I am basking in his golden glow, and he has born witness to who I've become, but somehow my stomach is unsettled. It doesn't feel like I thought it would.

But then I think of my brother, and it makes sense for Ethan and me to face the liberation together, to say a final farewell to the past. "I think he would have liked it, too," I finally manage.

"Great. It's a date." Grinning, he stands. "Now, I should probably go visit my ex-fiancée so we can write our break-up vows."

"Liberation lines." I correct him as I stand and walk him to the door.

"You're right. *So* much better. See. We're a great team." He nudges my arm with his elbow before heading into the hall.

Leaning against the door frame, I force a laugh.

With a wave, he walks backwards down the hall. "I'll pick you up back here at three?"

"See you then."

Duncan comes around the corner. My heart seizes as Ethan turns around and they nearly bump into each other.

Aware of how Ethan leaving my room might look after all that has changed in the last twenty-four hours, I tighten my robe around my waist and move to intercept Duncan. I want him to know I know it's not his fault Aubrey figured out who I am.

But he brushes past me without so much as a word, almost like we're strangers, and shuts himself in his room, leaving me to stare at his closed door.

Chapter 34

Love Will Keep Us Together

I stand on the steps of the Church of Santa Maria Assunta in my off-the-shoulder bridesmaid gown that is the color of lemons and sunshine. Aubrey is to my right, her hair curled in long loose waves, like mine, and pinned back on one side with a cluster of marigolds. The breeze wafting off the sparkling Mediterranean ruffles the dreamy chiffon layers around our ankles.

Zoey, in her white lace wedding gown, is to my left. Her father refused to walk her down the aisle. Instead, she walked alone, poised, and beautiful, a cluster of marigolds in her hands. Parting the sea of guests, she climbed the steps to where Ethan, the picture of chiseled perfection in his tailored periwinkle suit, waited outside the green-domed church.

The priest also refused to perform the ceremony, but the church was already paid for, so he has allowed us to congregate for our renegade celebration outside. Luigi is acting as the officiant.

Ethan grasps Zoey's hands.

"And now, please repeat after me," Luigi says with a warm smile, placing his hand on top of Zoey's and Ethan's joined fingers. "On this day, we set each other free to discover the people we are meant to be."

They repeat the vows together.

"To be true to the fire that drives our spirit. To be honest about our needs. Our wants. Our dreams. To be brave in the face of failure. To give ourselves grace when we fall. To pick ourselves up and try again. To never give up. To never compromise who we are. To value our truth above the opinion of others. And above all to seek joy. To find what makes our souls sing. This is our solemn vow."

"Zoey, do you set Ethan free to find his happy?" Luigi asks.

She tilts her face toward his, her pretty lips curving up. "*Lo voglio*. I do."

"And Ethan, do you set Zoey free to find her happy?"

Ethan smiles, his eyes crinkling at the corners. "I do."

"Then, by the power vested in me by you two a couple of minutes ago, I now declare you liberated." Luigi grins and tosses a handful of rose petals over the happy ex-couple. "*I miei migliori auguri*. Best wishes to you both."

There are some cheers from the crowd, a smattering of applause. But most guests stand in awkward silence, unsure of whose side to take. Zoey's and Ethan's mothers watch with solemn faces, their arms crossed over their chests. They grudgingly agreed to attend the celebration, to save face for the continued enjoyment of their guests. Unfortunately, neither father showed up, being deeply embarrassed at having their family drama so publicly displayed.

Regardless, Zoey and Ethan grin and hug. When they release each other, Ethan takes the microphone from Luigi and faces the crowd.

"I know this isn't the ceremony you expected to attend, but it's what feels right for us." He flashes his perfect teeth that look impossibly white against his skin that is extra golden today. His warmth washes over the crowd, and the guests stand rapt, worshipers at the feet of the Sun God. The collective tension in the air releases, like everyone trusts they are in good hands.

"On this trip, Zoey and I realized there's a gap between *our* expectations for our lives and *other people's* expectations for our lives that resulted in a fear of judgement, of living our truth."

He paces back and forth in front of the church, pausing at different locations so everyone can see him, so everyone feels included. "I don't know about you, but I've tried everything everyone else wants for me. I know their intentions are good, that they want what's *best* for me. But what's best for me can only be known to me. I know it in some parts of my life. I've got work figured out; I love my job. And I hope to keep it." He looks at Zoey's mom, whose mouth is pressed thin.

Ethan good-naturedly winces. "But when it comes to my personal life, I've got some learning to do. So today, I'm vowing to step outside my comfort zone, to be vulnerable, to not always play it safe and do what's expected. To let life be unpredictable and surprising. To be open to getting lost in someone quirky and interesting."

He glances at me as a murmur of agreement mumbles through the crowd.

My heart stalls, and I immediately seek out Duncan. He stands in the back of the crowd wearing a fitted mint-green linen suit over an unbuttoned floral collared shirt and holding an acoustic guitar. His pants are short enough to expose his bare ankles over his gleaming, white Chucks and it's literally a look only a rockstar could pull off. His star-power reverberates off him in light-waves that dizzy me. I will him to look at me, but his attention is on Ethan as he hands the microphone to Zoey.

"The truth is, Ethan and I are great friends, and we will continue to be great friends, will continue to cheer each other on," Zoey says, her sweet voice ringing out over the square. "But that doesn't mean we should legally join our lives together." A wisp of her long hair blows across her face, and she delicately brushes the strands away.

"None of us should sacrifice our truth for the sole reason that it makes someone else more comfortable. I know this is a little bit uncomfortable for all of us, but from discomfort comes growth, and we invite you all to grow with us. If anyone wants to join us and take a liberation vow, to speak your dreams out loud and announce to the world you're going after them, the microphone is yours."

All is silent. The guests shift their weight, looking anywhere but at Zoey. She waits, scanning the crowd with a hopeful smile, but nobody budges.

I shift focus from my bouquet of marigolds to the Madonna flying high over our heads in the blue sky. She watches over us, a champion of our spirit. Just as she magically lifted the Turkish boat that carried her to Italy and delivered it to land, she wants us to rise, to reach for our safe harbor, our shore. Lowering my gaze, I again find Duncan.

His attention is everywhere else, like he's actively ignoring me. My skin cools like the sun has gone behind a cloud. I don't know what has changed between us. Maybe he thinks I'm still upset about him outing me to Aubrey or maybe whatever friendship I thought we forged does end with the wedding. I don't know, but there's only one way to make him acknowledge me.

Fuck safe harbors.

Even though my temples throb and I might pass out, I thrust my hand toward the mic.

"I guess I'll go first," I say before I lose my nerve.

Three dozen faces tilt toward me, and my throat goes dry. Taking a deep breath, I force myself to raise the microphone to my lips. "I've been a bridesmaid for a long time." I startle at my voice reverberating across the courtyard but keep talking, speaking whatever truth comes to me into the square. "And honestly, I've been frozen in place, stuck believing the best thing that could happen to me already happened. I felt safe believing that. As long as things like love and success were reserved for other people, I couldn't get hurt. I've been standing on life's literal sidelines, afraid to walk down the aisle, to be the star of the show, for years."

My sinuses burn and I blink away tears. "I have a music platform called Shut Up & Sway but I don't have many followers." I confess. "And after this week, I think I know why it doesn't resonate with many people."

Finding Duncan, I say the rest directly to him. Even though he's not making eye contact with me, I want to explain why I was upset, to make it clear I'm not mad at him anymore. "I've been trying to be someone I'm not, to be the person I think people want me to be, and it's not relatable. I was embarrassed about the girl I used to be. Going forward, I'm going to embrace all the beautiful versions and expressions of myself, all of my eras. No more safe harbors. I need to let my true self be seen. And though I don't know where my path will lead, no matter how dark and stormy that the journey gets, above all, I vow to always, *always*, show up perfectly, authentically, as *me*."

A smattering of claps turns into a cheer. Suddenly I'm being pelted with rose petals, and I finally catch Duncan's eye. He holds my gaze for a split second before shuffling his feet and staring at the ground.

I lower my brow as I hand the microphone to Zoey's aunt, who is next in the line that is forming on the stairs.

Something isn't right. Hopefully I can get Dunc alone later.

One by one, people speak their dreams—to write a book, act in a play, open a food truck, take a year off to travel—and the positive energy is contagious. Even Zoey and Ethan's moms start smiling.

Until Payton gets behind the mic, that is. Zoey's skin turns ashen, and her smile drops.

My stomach constricts and even though it's not my job to prevent drama anymore, Max, who has been watching from the sidelines, and I, turn to each other in slow motion.

He may have fired me, but I'm kind of grateful to him for forcing change into my life. We've been a team for so long, it's impossible for me to leave him hanging. I grit my teeth, racking my brain for a way to stop Payton—for Zoey's sake, too. I can't think of anything short of launching myself off the steps and tackling him, though.

And it's too late anyway.

"Since we're talking about what we want, about our dreams, I thought I should reiterate mine, in case you missed it yesterday," Payton says with a little laugh. With his mussed hair and in his trim suit, he's just as attractive as Ethan, but in a darker way. There's something about him—a magnetism, an edge—that makes him mysterious, and as he shoves one hand into his pocket, leaving his thumb exposed, I realize what it is.

He's too at home in that suit for a laid-back surfer guy.

From what Zoey has said about him and what he's shared, I wonder if there's more to him than he's letting on. I wouldn't be surprised. We all have reasons for our secrets, and I wonder how many of his he'll liberate tonight.

"Zoey." He faces her. "You know me, so you know I don't settle for anything. I definitely don't settle down. If anything, I rise up. Take chances. Like you and Ethan did today. If you were with me, it would be anything but ordinary and, as you know, I'd love for us to be extraordinary together." He pauses before turning to his brother.

"And Ethan." He thumps his fist against his chest. "You know I love and respect you. We've talked. You're my other half. I want you to be happy. I never would have inserted myself into the middle of your relationship if I thought it was the right move for you. I never would have gotten in the way if I didn't love her."

Zoey's cheeks turn bright red, and she sways. Ethan grips her arm, keeping her on her feet.

"I know that too," Ethan calls out, thumping his fist against his chest in solidarity.

The beautiful brothers smile at each other.

Gaping at them, I pick my jaw up off the floor.

"Zoey." Payton turns back to her and his intensity has even my pulse racing. "I respect your space, but I want *you* to know, if there's a chance for us, when you're ready, I'll prove myself to you. I realize I was impulsive yesterday, so today all I'm asking is that you give me a shot. This is the last time I'll ask, and you don't have to answer me now. Take as much time as you need. I'll leave you alone. But someday, please tell me yes. Or no. To a chance." His strong jaw twitching, he blinks his impossibly dark fringed lashes. "Of course, I hope it's not no. I hope it's yes to possibility. Yes, to maybe. But I'll accept your answer either way as final. All I ask is that, at some point, you let me know."

All eyes turn to Zoey, and there is a collective sucking in of the breath, of waiting, of wanting to know will she or won't she.

But she remains silent. She's doing a great job of keeping a pleasant expression on her face. I have no idea what she's feeling on the inside, but my heart pitter-patters for her. If I were her, I'd be saying yes to possibility. He's pretty hard to deny.

The moment ratchets on with Payton and Zoey caught in a staring contest until Uncle Al takes the microphone from Payton.

My legs nearly give out.

Oh, boy. Code Red.

But I'm also kinda grateful to him for the distraction.

Finally, Payton nods at Zoey, seeming to have his answer.

With his head held high, he walks down the stone steps and past the guests, crossing the courtyard toward the ocean without looking back.

We all watch him go in awkward silence until Uncle Al breathes heavily into the microphone and draws our attention.

"Hey there, everyone. I just want to say a few words." Uncle Al is at ease behind the mic, like he's a crusty, old comic who's been doing stand-up for years. "I've been watching my brother this week, watching him stress out because he wanted everything to be perfect for his little girl, for everything to go the way he planned." He gestures at Zoey's mom, who cocks her head, seeming guarded, like she's unsure where Al is going with this.

"I wish my brother was here to hear this, but so be it. Here it goes anyway." He takes a deep breath and launches into his sermon. "The truth is, we can't control life. Things happen. Things surprise us. And this week I realized my brother's life isn't so perfect after all. He's got stuff too. And damn. That made me feel a whole lot better about myself." He laughs a dry cackle that lights up his whole face, and I can't help feeling endeared to him. "What a load off." He slaps his thigh.

"My brother is a very successful businessman," he continues, gesticulating and painting a portrait of Giorgio. "But even he could stand to care less what people think. Let's all agree to be a little less perfect and a little more human. A little more flawed. That's what I want to do, anyway. Because my brother didn't show up today, and look what he's missing out on. We're having an experience we didn't see coming. Even if it's a little uncomfortable, even if it's not what we came for, it's something pretty special. Something we'll never forget."

Uncle Al walks over and hugs Zoey to his side as he adds, "Zoey, I hope you know you've always got Uncle Al." Then he addresses the crowd. "And don't worry about my brother or feel sorry about all the money he spent this week. He can afford this. Makes up for all the vacations he doesn't take. It's fine. Eat up. Drink up. Let's party." He hands the mic to Zoey.

There is a whoop from the crowd and bursts of rose petals pop into the air.

I laugh and as he's passing me on the steps, Uncle Al whispers, "I had to add that last part. I wouldn't be Uncle Al without it." He winks, and my cheeks hurt from grinning.

"And on that note." Zoey laughs into the mic. "Wedding Bandits, lead the way."

Duncan strums his guitar, and we form a line behind the band. Leo plays his harmonica, B.J. taps a cow bell, Jonah plucks a banjo, and Hayden rocks a keytar as they lead us in a musical procession along the beach toward the reception at Villa San Giacomo. With streamers waving and flower petals flying, we pass bustling seaside cafés under striped awnings, colorful souvenir shops, and art vendors. Whistles and applause erupt from everyone on our route. Tourists stop to photograph us. It must seem to the onlookers that they are cheering for the bride and groom, but we walk united in our collective truth, knowing life is celebrating all of us.

Chapter 35

Where Were You When I Was Falling in Love

Max makes sure every guest on the lawn at San Giacomo has been served a cocktail before he corners me next to the wooden lemonade stand that is doubling as a bar.

"Can I borrow you for a moment, Gwendoline?" He grips my elbow. Wearing a slim, dark green suit with a peacock feather boutonniere, he fits his master of ceremonies role.

"Um. Sure." I gulp, bracing myself for the talking-to I'm about to receive, even though I'm no longer his employee.

Instead, he hands me a basil limoncello spritz, this evening's signature aperitivo.

I jerk back in surprise.

"Go ahead. You deserve it." He smirks.

Eyes wide, I accept the vintage crystal glass garnished with lemon slices, punctuated with a yellow-and-white striped straw.

He leads me across the cushy grass, navigating us around guests chatting on the floral print couches and rattan chairs he's arranged in charming vignettes on Persian rugs. The Costanzos rented the entire San Giacomo villa for tonight's festivities, and garden cocktails are the first of many experiences Max has in store for us on this grand finale liberation night.

We reach the edge of the estate's grounds where we can hear more easily over the party chatter and Duncan's acoustic guitar.

The smoky wood scent from the pizza ovens that are charring seafood skewer appetizers is on the soft breeze that ripples the yellow ruffles at my shoulders as I sip my bright-green drink.

Rules? Where I'm going, I don't need rules.

The zesty lemon concoction invigorates me, is the perfect complement to the Positano hills and cobalt Mediterranean that expand around us from our perch at the edge of a cliff. We are two tiny specks against a sprawl of sea, sky, and flowering terracotta villas.

Max watches me sample the cocktail. "I owe you an apology, Gwen."

Coughing, I nearly choke on the beverage before lowering it from my mouth and clutching the icy glass with both hands.

"I overreacted in relieving you of your duties, and I instantly regretted it. It just felt like everything was spiraling out of control and there you were at the center of the chaos. You know how hard I work for perfection. Firing you was a knee-jerk reaction when you deserved the benefit of the doubt. And if today has taught me anything, if *you* have taught me anything, it's that sometimes we need to let go of control. Be open to the unexpected. You really pulled off something spectacular. Something nobody but you could have imagined. Vision like that is a gift. I'd like to offer you your job back."

His voice is smooth and rich, and I'm going to miss it. After the relief I felt when he fired me, I know I can't stay. Weddings are my safe harbor, and I need to take a leap into the sea, as unknown as it may be.

My throat tightens. Watching the boats bob on the water far below my feet, I grab my necklace. "Thank you for the apology, Max. It means a lot to me." Tears sting my eyes as I meet his gaze. "And *I* apologize for not telling you right away that I knew the groom." I take a deep breath, then let it out before officially stepping off the dock of my safe harbor. "But I think this week was a sign that my bridesmaid days are over. It's time for me to move on."

"I had a feeling you might say that, but I understand." He nods and smiles at me, his eyes glassy. "I'll miss you, but as much as I love having you on my team, I never want to keep you from your true calling. It's the end of an era, Gwenny. What are you going to do?"

I hesitate. "I don't know. For now, I'm just going to stay in the moment. See where the night takes me. Maybe my purpose right now is to let go, have fun."

"Sounds like a solid plan." He laughs, a deep baritone rumble that starts low in his chest. "And you'll be wonderful at anything and everything you do. I know talent when I see it, and you've got it. You can talk your way around any situation, can win the affections of even the hardest heart. And you do this not because you have anything to gain, but because you see people for who they are and strive to make a genuine connection with everyone you meet. That is another of your gifts. You really see people, and I dare say you can spot talent, too."

Faltering under his praise, I focus on my glittery pedicured toes in the flip-flops that were party favors for the guests. I'm just grateful to finally have shoes that fit. "Thank you. That's very kind."

"I mean it. Hopefully this will help with the next phase of your journey." He unbuttons his jacket and reaches into an interior pocket, then hands me an envelope.

A peek inside at the check reveals he's paid me in full—including my bonus and even a little extra.

Covering my heart with my hand, I look up to him with shining eyes. "I really appreciate this, Max."

"You earned it." He pats my arm.

Across the party behind Max, Duncan puts aside his guitar. From where he stands near the limoncello bar next to the upright piano Hayden is playing, he announces it's time for the first dance.

Max follows my gaze. "And I hope you know, I'm available to plan *your* wedding. For free. Just give me the date at least a year in advance. It's a perk I give all my bridesmaids. They just don't know about it." Returning his attention to me, he winks.

I narrow my eyes at him. "Is that why you won't let us flirt with any groomsmen?"

He laughs. "You know me too well."

My laughter mingles with his until someone taps my shoulder. Behind me, I find Ethan. His inviting smile is as picturesque as Positano, but, somehow, I don't dissolve into seventeen-year-old hysterics at the sight of him. Instead, I stiffen.

"Join me?" Ethan takes my hand, offering to lead me down a meandering path toward an Italian tile dance floor situated next to an infinity pool that appears to disappear into the sea.

I glance at Max.

"I never said anything about flirting with grooms," Max says under his breath, surveying Ethan's trim periwinkle suit. Lifting an eyebrow at me, he all but fans himself. "Have fun tonight, Gwenny," he sings.

Shocked I have Max's blessing, I shake my head.

On a stage near the pool, the band starts playing "For Once in My Life," covering Stevie Wonder's version of the song. Duncan apparently made the executive decision to change the first dance song and warmth flutters through me at the perfection of his choice.

Even as Ethan leads me onto the dance floor, my inclination is to move to the front of the stage and sway, to let Duncan's song take me away. But we come to a stop next to where Zoey is dancing with Aubrey under white lanterns, clustered Amalfi lemons, and a disco ball. They're taking turns spinning each other around.

Ethan faces me, standing still like he's expecting me to bust out some moves. Recalling my antics during the stargazing party, I blush. *That* version of me belongs to Duncan. Only he could lure her onto the dance floor, and I'm not the girl Ethan thinks I am. He doesn't know me at all.

I bite my lip. "Maybe we should take it slow. Can we just sway?"

He startles but quickly recovers. "Of course." Taking me in his arms, he rocks us back and forth. Over his shoulder, I watch Duncan sing about being brave, about being strong, and my skin tingles. I will him to look at me.

But he doesn't.

I might as well be just another fan in the crowd that I'm certain will grow, another bridesmaid or future groupie vying for his attention, and my heart deflates.

"Come on everyone, sing it if you know it," Duncan commands from behind the microphone, gesturing for everyone to join in.

He's impossible to refuse. The rest of the guests crowd around us, pushing me closer against Ethan.

In a mass of bouncing bodies, we sing along together, letting the world know that what is ours can't be taken, our voices combining in perfect, liberated, unison. Goosebumps explode up my arms. Duncan has done it again. Created an unforgettable experience. My throat aches as I realize this is the last wedding I'll work with him.

But Ethan and Zoey and my new little band of friends won't let me wallow for long. Zoey cuts between Ethan and me. She swings me around, and for the rest of the night I dance, I eat, I drink, I let go. I'm me.

I dine next to Ethan at the long table set for forty on a terrace under dangling white wisteria, mismatched crystal prisms, and gold wind chimes. I have a cocktail in the Moroccan lounge filled with white couches, green palms, and golden lanterns that Max arranged on the villa's second floor. I watch pastry chefs publicly assemble the wedding cake in real time, covering the lemon and Chantilly cream confection with a thousand perfectly placed raspberries. When Berkeley Dalton gets on stage to perform a song with Duncan in front of the mirrored lounge dance floor, I sway in the front row.

It's the freest I've felt in a long time. The only thing that mars the celebration is that Duncan sticks to his playlist. He doesn't slip in any riffs that are for my ears only. It could be any wedding we've worked together, albeit the most spectacular one.

At midnight, the sky explodes with a showstopping fireworks display, the culmination of the Ferragosto celebration erupting in shards of fizzling glitter over the water. The wedding guests gather along the edge of the infinity pool or on the terraces and balconies of the villa for the show, but I stand on the pool-side dance floor by myself. The beach stretches long, far below my feet, and hundreds of boats bob on the shimmering sea, cast in a foggy pink glow.

If Duncan could be anywhere right now, it would be on one of those boats.

And if I'm honest, I'd rather be down there too. With him. Chilled, I shiver and rub my arms.

Wondering where he's watching the fireworks from, I scan the guests along the bluff, their faces flickering in the light from the fireworks. Instead of finding Duncan, I spot Ethan talking to Payton. Payton was missing most of the night, but he must have felt it was his duty to make an appearance at some point. Seeing the brothers together makes me think of my brother. Ty, who all those years ago wanted Ethan to show me how much potential I have. To see myself the way he saw me.

A firework screams overhead before bursting with a deafening boom into a shiver of sparks and it hits me. My brother was working—*is working*—through Ethan.

Tears sting my eyes, and my nose burns with sulfur.

Ethan was never my fairytale. He was a stepping stone. A wake-up call. A gift from my brother, a catalyst to force me into my light.

Ty's work is done, and Ethan belongs to my past. His era is over. I've never been so sure of anything in my entire life.

Taking a deep breath, I slowly turn my back on Ethan and the crackling grand finale. I tuck my inner seventeen-year-old into a safe space in my heart where she'll be warm and protected. Opening myself to all the possibilities before me, to all of my potential, I walk away from the party, down the path that will lead me into the unknown. I could be afraid, but in my heart, I know I'm headed for somewhere great. My footsteps are sure against the thunder of my past imploding.

***

Once I'm back in my room, I curl up in my robe on my bed and turn on my Italian loaner phone. My first order of business is to deposit my checks and Venmo Duncan's money back to him—Italian lingerie, shoes, and airplane salmon included. And I'm happy to see Jude was able to sell my Outside Lands ticket for face value and has sent the money.

After I fire off a quick WhatsApp message to my mom, letting her know I'm safe and one to the cat sitter asking for a Toto update, I call down to Luigi. He promises to secure a piece of Sarcolite—a pale pink gem found only at Mt. Vesuvius—for Corina that is within my budget. He'll give it to me when he drives me to the airport tomorrow. Satisfied everything is falling into place, I hunker down under the covers. Nibbling on the chocolate shell the turn down service left on my pillow, I check YouTube to see if anyone has commented on the "Lady Lavender" video.

My heart seizes when I open the app.

Thirteen thousand views?

I jolt upright, the creamy milk chocolate forgotten. Nothing I've ever posted has gotten more than twenty views, so this is beyond incredible.

This is happening because people love the song and are organically sharing it.

A chill sweeps over me, and I leap off the bed.

"Lady Lavender" is a hit. OMG. It's impossible.

It can't be real. Pacing the tile floor, I log into my YouTube account and check my analytics so I can see real time views. Even better, the count is now thirteen thousand *five hundred.*

And two. And counting. It's a sign. The next step in their path. They need to capitalize on this. Post more videos. Use the momentum to pitch "Lady Lavender" to radio, get placements in TV, film . . . But will they?

Energy is coursing through me—I'm so excited for them—and I shake out my hands.

If they won't, I will. Maybe I can be that person for them.

The hairs rise on the back of my neck. It feels so right. I can't wait to ask Duncan if the band would be open to me managing them. And being a lawyer/manager could come in handy when it comes to negotiating contracts. Besides, I've got to show him the view count. He's going to freak! His wedding-DJ set was from ten to twelve and the villa required the music to stop after the fireworks show. He should be coming back to his room soon if he's not over there already.

I bang on the adjoining door but there is no answer.

Sliding down against the wood, I sit on the cold tile floor and wait for his lock to click, for shuffling feet, for any sound that signifies his return. In the meantime, I devour all the comments on the video on all the sites I posted to. As I read, it becomes clear that people think the band's name is Shut Up & Sway. In my hasty upload, I put in the song title as "Lady Lavender" but didn't include the band name and I wince. If I'm honest, I knew what I was doing, even if it wasn't totally conscious. I left "The Wedding Bandits" off the video because I didn't want people's opinions tainted by them being a wedding band. I'd never tell Duncan that, though.

And hopefully he'll understand it was an accident. I'm sure we can fix the name later. Maybe they don't want their original music branded as The Wedding Bandits either?

My stomach twists at the inevitable conversation we'll have to have. Pushing the mistake out of my mind, I focus on the good. I keep reading all the love. And every time I think I hear something next door, I knock.

But he still doesn't answer.

Once I've memorized the YouTube comments, for some glutton-for-punishment reason—probably because in the back of my mind I'm wondering if Duncan went back to her room because I didn't see her at the fireworks show either—I check out Aubrey's socials. Her 300,000 Instagram followers glare at me from the top of her page. Her most recent post is a Positano "sneak peek," a picture of her lounging on the boat to Capri in her itty-bitty bikini bottoms and hot pink stilettos. The top comment is from @DuncanAvila-Songwriter and reads, "I've never seen a prettier view."

My heart stops as I scroll to find Duncan has commented on several of her posts from his songwriter account that seems new as it has zero posts and two followers (Aubrey and the band). @TheWeddingBandits has 1,500 followers and Aubrey has commented on a bunch of their recent posts as well.

At least he's embracing songwriting . . .

It's supposed to be everything I want for him, but the assertion does little to ease the queasiness overtaking me. Even though Aubrey said there's nothing between them—that Duncan is into *me*—this proves she's wrong. I tamp down the sickness rising in my throat.

On the other side of the wall, the door creaks open. I breathe a sigh of relief when I hear one set of footsteps—not two—enter the room. My resolve in place to make him a professional offer he can't refuse, I jump to my feet, ignoring the complaints from my aching joints after sitting on the hard floor.

"Duncan! Open up!" I pound on the door.

Chapter 36

Lady Lavender

The lock clicks and Duncan opens the door, raising an eyebrow at me. His jacket is long gone and his floral shirt is rumpled. He's dragging like he's done for the night, but his shoes are still laced tight.

"You have to see this." I thrust my phone in his face.

"What is it?" He lowers my hand to a distance where he can see what I'm talking about.

"It's 'Lady Lavender.' I posted it to my YouTube account and it's going viral."

His jaw drops, and he stares at the screen, shaking his head like he's trying to comprehend the numbers. "How did you do this?"

"I didn't. You did. This is all because of *you* and your talent." I'm breathless. "'Lady Lavender' is a hit. People love it."

He runs his fingers through his hair. "Wow. This is a shock."

I jump to his side and tug on his sleeve, barely able to contain myself. "We should use this to pitch TV, film, radio. We can capitalize on this."

He backs away from me. Reaching the bed, he slowly sits on the edge. His white duvet is stretched taut, still expertly made from the maid service this morning. Somehow the turndown service must not have come through here, though the curtains are drawn over his French doors, blotting out the balcony.

I cock my head, coming all the way into the room. Something isn't right. This isn't the reaction I expected. He should be bouncing off the walls.

"I mean, *you* should capitalize on it." I clarify in case I'm being presumptive, but I'm unable to leave it at that. I can't contain the excitement fizzing in my veins, and I continue. "Though I'd love to help. If I pass the bar and officially become a lawyer, I could negotiate contracts if you wanted." On an inhale I confess what I really want before I lose my nerve. "To be honest, I'd love to manage you guys. I believe in you *so much*. You're a star, Duncan, like it or not. I feel it in my bones that we can take you to the next-level. You won't have to work weddings anymore. People will turn out in droves to hear *your* songs. I know it."

His skin ashen, he stares into the distance like he hasn't registered anything I've said.

"Are you okay?" I cross the tile floor then lower myself onto the bed next to him.

Slowly, he nods. "Yeah. I just don't know what to think." He fills his lungs. "I like being a wedding singer. I'm good at it, and we have a solid business. Thirteen thousand YouTube views doesn't mean people are going to come to shows. I don't want to go back to playing empty rooms, Gwen. I don't want to start over. Besides, we're leaving for a college tour in two weeks. We'll be on the road for the rest of the year, and we're going to make a lot of money. We can't give up a sure thing."

My stomach drops that he's not jumping at the opportunity to pursue "Lady Lavender."

How can he not want this?

"You mean you can't give up safe harbors," I snap. But then I soften my words. "I saw you created a songwriter Instagram account." I can't help but bring it up. "Songwriting isn't something you've been thinking about?"

He grimaces and shakes his head. "I only created that account because Aubrey told me to. She's been giving me social media lessons, and she put me in her comment pod."

I wrinkle my nose. "What's a comment pod?"

"It's a group of people who promise to comment on each other's social media posts to help drive engagement. But every comment has to be at least four words—no emojis—and has to be relevant to the picture. In order to get people to comment on your post, you have to comment on ten other posts. I joined the pod to grow The Bandits' account, but people don't really want comments from a wedding band, so I created the songwriter account. I don't have plans to do anything with it."

"Oh." My spine relaxes that his story matches with Aubrey's, but at the same time my ribs constrict that he doesn't have a bigger vision for himself. "Well, I promise I'm not trying to jump on the bandwagon, if that's what you're worried about. I believed in you before the song was a hit . . . I'm sorry if I didn't tell you sooner."

"It's not that." His jaw twitches.

I've never seen this side of Duncan before. He's always so happy-go-lucky. Serious Duncan throws me off, and I sit back. "Then what is it? Why don't you want to at least *try* to make something of this?"

And then the answer hits me and I stare at my hands in my lap. "Or you just don't want to make something of it with *me*. I know things have been weird between us and I'm sorry I got so upset with you the other morning. I know you didn't tell Aubrey who I am. She figured it out on her own."

He puffs out his chest. "That's the thing. If you're going to manage us, the relationship needs to be built on trust. I saw Ethan coming out of your room, and you two looked pretty happy dancing out there tonight. I know he's known all along who you are. Aubrey told me yesterday that you and Ethan made a deal that first night."

The blood drains from my face and I close my eyes, unable to defend myself.

"I guess it's none of my business what your relationship with Ethan is," he continues, resting his forearms on his legs and staring at my phone that he's still holding. "But you had every opportunity to tell me the truth. You let me believe we were playing a game on the same side when you were on his side the whole time too, so I'm sorry if I'm not jumping at the chance to be part of Team Gwen. You can't have it both ways."

I shrink into myself, sickened by my betrayal, and search for the words that will make it right, but then I think of all the time he's spent with Aubrey, about how I still don't know if it all ends with the wedding and my body tenses. "You can't have it both ways either," I retort. "You kept it from me that Aubrey knew who I was. And how do I know you're not heading to her room right now?"

Covering his eyes, he squeezes his temples between his thumb and middle finger, muttering, "I was a fool to believe my abuela."

I have no idea what he's talking about, but I don't have time to contemplate it.

He jerks his head toward me. "You're proving my point. Trust. You don't trust me. How many times do I have to tell you there's nothing between Aubrey and me?" His voice gets louder. "What will it take to make you believe?"

I cringe, reminding myself I've always had the wrong idea about him.

His mouth set in a grim line, he stands and starts to hand me back my phone, but before I take it, he pauses and squints at the screen. I can practically see his brain calculating.

"It doesn't say anything about The Wedding Bandits on this video. Everyone thinks we're called Shut Up & Sway . . . "

My chest caves but I jump to my defense. "It was an accident. I uploaded it on Zoey's phone really fast and didn't fill out all the information. We can fix it. And maybe it's a good thing—maybe you don't want your original music produced under Wedding Bandits. We should think about your branding. You could go back to being Sunset Drift Brigade if you wanted."

The giant admission that by knowing this piece of Wedding Bandit trivia, I've clearly cyberstalked him, makes my cheeks burn, but I keep talking. "You can be anything you want. This is just the beginning."

Still staring at the screen, he frowns like he hasn't heard a word I said. "And Shut Up & Sway has five hundred new subscribers, huh? That's lucky for you." He tosses the phone onto the bed, then walks to the closet.

I wince that he could *ever* think I'd use his talent for personal gain. "I'm not trying to get anything out of this. I promise. Please. Let me make it up to you. I'll prove you can trust me if you give me a chance. We can change the name of the YouTube channel to any name you want. You can have all the followers. They're yours anyway."

He presses open the painting that hides the closet next to his balcony then pulls out his suitcase that is apparently already packed because the closet is empty. In fact, the room is empty, returned to its original state, void of any evidence of Duncan's presence. "That won't be necessary. I don't need to change for anyone. If you can't accept me as the wedding singer I am, then I'm sorry. No can do." Tugging on his suitcase, he rolls it toward the door to the hall, the wheels clacking behind him against the tile.

"Duncan." My voice cracks, and it's all I can do not to sob out his name. "Where are you going?"

"The airport. It's my abuela's birthday, so I'm on an earlier flight." He opens the door and pauses for a brief glance at me. "See you around, *Rosie*."

With that, he goes, letting the door thud shut behind him and leaving me to stare after him in stunned silence.

Chapter 37

Baby Come Back

Feeling queasy, I arrive on the terrace for brunch dressed in the black and white patio dress with puffed sleeves and a slit up to my thigh that is designated for this morning after having barely slept.

Heavy gray clouds clot the sky and the sea churns dark cobalt, her hidden, turbulent side revealed in this murky light. The peach and terracotta hillsides still pop with color, even in the lengthening shadows of the impending storm.

Zoey, Ethan, and Aubrey wave me over to join their table that is decorated with simple, understated florals, recycled from last night's gala, like Max is slowly returning us to reality.

Having zero desire to make small talk, I wave back.

Without Duncan's presence to look forward to, the party has lost its luster. Even though I came down to distract myself from replaying last night's fight over and over, now all I want to do is binge lemon basil crack cake and retreat to my balcony to memorize the view before my flight this afternoon.

My dress clings to my legs in the warm, clammy air as I head to the buffet table. I'm filling my plate when Jonah, The Bandits' bass player, arrives at my side.

"If it isn't 'Lady Lavender.'" He chooses a plate, his black nail polish glittering. "Duncan texted us the video last night. How does it feel to be a viral sensation?"

I keep my focus on my growing lemon cake stack. "I'm not the sensation. You guys are."

Jonah pauses in the middle of scooping scrambled eggs and stares at me. "Hold on. Duncan still hasn't told you?"

"Told me what?" I squint at him. Thunder rolls in the distance.

A slow smile spreads over his face, and he lets out a low whistle. "About his abuela?"

I put the cake down and fix him with a blank stare. "I think he told me she only spoke to him in Spanish, that's why he's fluent. And she also always supported his music."

"*And* she said you'd change his life . . ." He searches my face. "Not ringing any bells? Nothing?" He rolls his eyes. "Dunc needs to man up," he mutters to himself.

My shoulders go slack. "Jonah. What. Are. You. Talking. About?"

Brushing a lock of black hair off his forehead, he considers me. "He never told you 'Lady Lavender' is about you?"

The sky crackles with a flash of lightning, and my knees give out. I grip the buffet table for support. "What?"

"Yeah. You were wearing a lavender dress at some boat wedding. You make white look amateur, apparently. Guy's got it bad even if he doesn't want to admit his abuela was right. He's always said he'd have to be a fool to believe her."

I know exactly what boat wedding he's talking about. The Langley-Madison wedding on the Odyssey Lake Michigan. The lavender dress with lace sleeves.

The brunch party spins around me, stormy sea and sky undulating like I am, in fact, on a boat. "What exactly did she say?"

"That you're, like, Duncan's destiny." He shrugs.

My breath leaves me. "But I've never met Duncan's abuela," I whisper.

"Apparently you have. At his cousin's wedding?" He shrugs.

Recalling Duncan saying the groom was his cousin at the first wedding we ever worked together, I can suddenly remember talking to a little old lady in a pink suit, and I gasp.

"Anyway, this calls for celebration." Jonah grabs two bellinis off a passing tray and offers me one.

Shaking my head, I dismiss the glass and slowly turn away from him. I need to go back to my room to process this information ASAP. In a daze, my lemon basil crack cake forgotten, I walk to the exit in slow motion, slogging through the soupy air.

"Hey, Gwen. Where'd 'Shut Up & Sway' come from?" Jonah calls after me. "It's a cool name."

I pause and glance over my shoulder at him. "It's the name of my website." I wince. Barely comprehending his approving nod, I leave the restaurant.

What the heck is the universe trying to do to me?

***

Back in my room, I'm slowly packing my things when I come across Towaya. I slip him over my shoulders and breathe him in. He still smells like Duncan. Cedar. Citrus. Spice. It overwhelms me. My jaw aches from clenching it and I can't fathom that "Lady Lavender" is about me. Can't make sense of what it means, what his abuela has to do with things, or if Duncan even believes in destiny. After this week, I don't know if I do. And even if he sees me as "Lady Lavender," it doesn't mean he wants me. My heart squeezes and I head to the balcony.

No cloudy days or dark could ever hide you,
You're the only star you need to guide you . . .

Gripping the railing I stare out at the tumultuous sea, letting the thrashing of the unruly waves reverberate through my body.

I'm Lady Lavender . . .

It's so much to live up to it makes my head spin, and I press a hand to my forehead.

But maybe that's what I was here to learn.

Maybe it's a sign, another marker on my path that I need to step into my light. Maybe I need to find out who Lady Lavender is—the girl he sees me as—the girl he believes me to be. My insides heat that there has been someone out there all along who had a bigger vision for me. Who knew I've always needed a bigger vision of myself.

The clouds flicker with lightning, and a fat raindrop plops onto my arm. I have no idea what comes next. No idea where I stand with Duncan or what to do.

But we're going to have to talk about it at some point and it's going to be so awkward.

I cringe and shake the giddy energy conjured by all the possibilities out of my hands. I'm not getting my hopes up for anything.

More raindrops splatter onto the balcony, filling the heavy air with the scent of wet terracotta that mixes with the spicy incense wafting from Santa Maria Assunta.

My Italian loaner phone buzzes with a message from the front desk, telling me Luigi is arriving with the van that will take me to the airport.

With a sigh, I bid farewell to the glorious view and re-enter my room where I'm greeted with a blast of brisk air conditioning. The green prosecco bottle is sitting on my desk, and I pause, tempted. Thunder grumbles outside.

I'm dying to know what Duncan wished for me. I won the bet. I have every right to read his wish. But something stops me. Something in me wants me to keep the bottle intact. To keep the possibility of his wish coming true, of there being something out there for us, alive. So, I wrap Towaya around the bottle, pack it into my suitcase and close the lid on this chapter.

I say yes to a chance.

Chapter 38

Love Will Find a Way

With the officially cone-free Toto snuggled on the couch next to me and my laptop balanced on my legs, I squint at my bank account. Even though my bonus has been deposited, now, in the hazy Chicago morning light that is streaming through our living room's vertical blinds, I'm not sure refusing Max's offer to continue bridesmaiding was such a good idea.

Corina pads into the room wearing fuzzy flip-flop slippers and a knit romper, her sleep mask perched on her forehead. She goes around the corner into our tiny kitchen and pours herself a cup of coffee before joining me.

"How's it going?" Curling her legs underneath her in the overstuffed green velvet chair across from me, she blows into her mug.

I force my lungs to expand and sigh. "Honestly, I don't know how I'm going to pay rent while I study for the bar." Rubbing my temples, I peer at the screen sideways, as if that could change the numbers. "It's a full-time job. You're supposed to study forty to fifty hours a week for at least nine weeks. And I probably need ten."

"But you have time. The bar is in February, right?"

"Yeah." I slump deeper into the cushy beige sofa. The Illinois Bar is only offered twice a year, and I missed the July exam. "Maybe I could wait tables and study twenty-five hours a week for more weeks? Or get a full-time job for three months and save up? But I can barely afford to live as it is. I don't know how much I could save. And the bar is expensive to register for, too. Maybe I should tell Max I'll go back to bridesmaiding."

Toto abruptly stops purring and lifts his head to look at me. I stroke his soft furry side to soothe him.

"You can't do that." Corina shakes her head. "It will reverse everything. You decided to move on, to stop being stuck. You can't go back. You took a leap, and you need to give the net a chance to appear. You owe yourself that much."

"Do you have any idea how long it usually takes nets to show up?" I gulp.

She giggles. "I think it's different for everyone. But this is the fire-walk to prove you have faith. Just follow the breadcrumbs and take another step toward your dream. The 'Lady Lavender' video is a sign. When it comes to discovering your true purpose, there is usually beginner's luck that sets you on the right path before the real work begins. I just love how this has all come together." She sips her coffee before continuing. "See, life is always working *for* you, even when it seemed like you were going in the wrong direction. The law school, the website, building your social channels which ended up launching the 'Lady Lavender' video … It all culminates in a surprise dream to manage a band. And I feel like there's a content creation element that's going to come back around. So, what's your next move? Have you thought about moving home?"

My jaw drops. "With my parents? But what about you?" My lower lip juts out. "I couldn't leave you."

I scan the white rectangular room we worked so hard to transform into a home, softening the vertical blinds with boho curtains and covering the walls with mismatched art. Third eye posters combine with concerts and cats, representing both of us. Candles, plants, blankets, and throw pillows cover every available surface. Twinkle lights frame the doorways. Thrifted rugs cushion the vinyl floors. "And I love it here. It's so cozy. Safe."

"Don't worry about me. I'm sure I could find a subletter for a few months if you wanted to move home for a little while. One of the girls I work with was just asking if anybody needed a roommate."

I knit my eyebrows. "That's good to know, but it feels like a step backward, like I'd be crawling home with my tail between my legs."

Toto cocks his head at me, and I absently scratch behind his ear.

She leans toward me and sets her mug on the coffee table. "It's okay to ask for help when you need it," she says with a soft smile. "It's actually the grown-up thing to do. But I get it. Maybe you don't need to pass the bar? I feel like you can work with the band before you do."

"I know I don't *need* to pass it, but I want to. I don't want to wonder if I could have passed it for the rest of my life, you know? And I have a feeling someday I'll be glad I did it. If I don't do it now, I don't think I ever will."

"If that's your instinct, trust it. Something will work out so you can afford to study for the bar. I'm sure of it."

Chewing my cheek, I snap my computer shut. Staring at the screen isn't going to change the numbers. "I hope so."

Picking her coffee mug back up, she settles into the chair. "And when are you going to text Duncan? We already decided 'Lady Lavender' is the next breadcrumb on your path. You've been home for twenty-four hours. What are you waiting for?"

"I'm nervous." I grit my teeth. "A lot needs to come together for 'Lady Lavender' to be the path seeing as Duncan isn't speaking to me, and he already said he doesn't see how me being their manager could work." I filled her in on everything Duncan over wine last night.

"You can't let that stop you. You need to text him, *now.*" She takes a deep breath and lets it out in a whoosh. "Listen. He's a Sagittarius and they're notorious for being noncommittal. Sag is called the bachelor sign. If you let him leave on that college tour without telling him the truth about how you feel, I think it's going to be a long time before you guys reconnect."

The hairs rise on the back of my neck. "What do you mean?"

"I mean, I ran your charts. You two are a solid match. But free will can get in the way of that. If you don't catch him before he goes on that college tour, you may still be destined to end up together, but your timelines will go off course. You may not reunite until you're fifty."

I cringe. "I may be skilled at keeping the imagined possibility of someone alive—I've been doing it for years—but I'm done with that." Grabbing my phone, I study the screen, unsure what to text, my stomach in knots.

Even if I'm Lady Lavender, Duncan might still reject me. And what then?

I picture my days sprawling ahead of me without the possibility of seeing Duncan to look forward to, and I have my answer. Either way, it's not like my life is currently a box of chocolates. If I don't go after the truth, I know what I'm going to get: more being broke and confused.

Fuck safe harbors.

I take a deep breath and text him before I lose my nerve.

> Hey Duncan, it's Gwen. I'm back in Chicago and I'm feeling like we left a lot unsaid in Italy. I'd love to talk if you're up for it.

I hit send and toss the phone onto the couch like it's a hot potato. "Done."

"And so it is." Corina smiles.

We both stare at the phone, waiting for a response to light up the screen, but as the seconds tick into minutes, the silence becomes unbearable.

With a sigh, I stand, disrupting Toto in the process. He glares at me then repositions himself on a pillow. "How long did you say it takes nets to appear?"

She laughs. "I can't answer that. Usually, you have to get comfortable with the unknown first."

"I was afraid you'd say that." My phone buzzes, and we both jump. I immediately check the text and my shoulders slump that it's only from my mom. "Just a reminder about lunch with my parents today. I should probably go get ready." Shrugging, I head down the hall.

"Let me know what Duncan says," she calls after me.

With a soft moan, I grimace and lock myself in the bathroom to bang my head against the shower door.

Chapter 39

How Long

"It sounds like Italy was amazing," Mom says. We're eating salads while sitting around my parents' oval outdoor dining table on the screened porch. The ceiling fan rotating overhead keeps the air circulating in the humid afternoon. Beyond the screens, the neighbor's lawn mower hums, competing with the twittering birds at the feeder in one of Mom's flower beds. I've been filling them in on all the wedding details—the dresses, the food, the excursions—and it strikes me how glamorous it all sounds compared to what life might be like should I return to the suburbs to study.

"I mean, it looked incredible," she continues, stacking our empty bowls. "From all those pictures Duncan sent me."

Somewhere, a record scratches.

Certain I heard her wrong, I do a double take. "Excuse me?" I squeak. "Duncan?" I have *not* mentioned Duncan or Ethan or that I quit my job. "And what pictures?"

"He was a real blessing to your mother." Dad folds his cloth napkin and stands to open the door to the kitchen for my mom. "Gave her peace of mind that you were okay since your phone wasn't working."

"He asked if he could send me daily updates about you." Mom motions with her head for Dad to put his napkin on top of the bowls. "It was his idea. He said he knew you and I were close—and I said yes, *please*." She disappears inside.

My jaw drops, and I stare after her, reeling.

He was in contact with my mom the whole time?

Shaking my head, I come to. "That's very . . . sweet of him. I didn't know he was doing that. He knew I was worried about not being able to text you. I was nervous to get on Wi-Fi because I don't have an international plan and my phone is so old it barely holds a charge anyway."

"Maybe it's time for an upgrade, then." Dad retakes his seat in one of the bouncy wrought iron patio chairs that surround the table.

"It was time for an upgrade a *long* time ago." I wrinkle my nose.

Mom reappears carrying a plate of homemade chocolate chip cookies and sets them in the middle of the table. Dad immediately grabs one and slides the plate toward me. I choose a still-warm cookie and take a small bite. Something about the simple gesture of my mom baking cookies just because I came over for lunch overwhelms me and hot tears crowd my eyes. She wants to take care of me.

Suddenly, I want to tell them everything. Taking a deep breath, I confess. "I can't afford a new phone. Toto had to have emergency surgery, and it cost $3000. I took the Italy job to pay for it."

"What?" Mom gasps. "Why didn't you tell us? We could have helped. You know how much Toto means to us."

"I know. I just wanted you to feel like I was safe. Like I could take care of myself. But the truth is, I can't do it alone." I sniffle and a tear escapes, cascading down my cheek. "It was *such* a weird week."

Mom lowers herself into the chair across from me, her features soft.

Clinging to both the starry night charm *and* the rooster I wear at my throat, I tell them everything. About Ethan. About Davis Collings. About losing my job. About trying to follow in Ty's footsteps by going to law school, but that my heart was never in it. I tell them I was following my dream of being a music influencer and now I'm interested in passing the bar and managing the band.

When I'm finished, Mom's eyes are glassy. "This week was a big one." She squeezes my hand.

"That's an understatement." I snort, dabbing at my eyes with the hem of my shirt.

"I wish you'd told us all of this sooner," she says, wiping away a tear as well. "We only ever want you to be happy. Try all the things and do your best, that's all we ask." With a small smile, she stands. "Let me get my phone. I want to show you something." She heads into the house.

Dad drums his fingers on the table, considering me. "Did you know your mother and I saw Davis Collings live in concert at least five times before you and your brother were born?"

This news reverberates through me. "I did not." It's almost as shocking as Duncan sending my mom pictures. But I don't have time to contemplate the implications because my phone buzzes and I can't not see the text from Duncan.

Duncan

> Sure. I'll be back in Chicago next week. Maybe we can meet up before we leave for tour.

My heart thuds, and I don't play it cool. I text him back immediately.

> Yes! Let me know when you're back! Happy birthday to your abuela! :)

Mom returns with a box of tissues and her phone. She flashes the screen at me. "Maybe you want to see these?"

I take her phone, and she peers over my shoulder as I swipe through the messages Duncan sent her. Pictures of me on my balcony in my Hall & Oates T-shirt, me stargazing in the tiny red and white romper on the yacht that first night, me picking lemons in the lemon grove. Then there's me wearing Towaya and eating zeppole with the carnival lights sparkling behind me, me DJing at Music on the Rocks, and finally, a picture of Duncan and me holding onto each other, grinning, caught in a swirl of paper confetti and colored lights.

There we are, in our light.

My scalp prickles and suddenly, I'm back there, in full sway.

"He's very handsome, isn't he?" Mom expands the screen with her thumb and index finger and zooms in on his face.

"Mom!" My cheeks heat and I press my hands to them.

But she's right. And I'm so grateful he captured all these moments.

Goosebumps shoot up my arms and, in an instant, I know what I need to do.

Risk it all. Do something I've never done. Put my heart on the line. I have to stop him from going on tour in a way that will be impossible to refuse.

I hand Mom back her phone. "Dad. Mom. I have a huge and very strange favor to ask." Filling my lungs, I blurt my request before I second-guess myself. "You know your old boat that we used to take fishing in Canada with Ty?" I gesture beyond the screens toward the far end of the grass where the boat hides behind Dad's red tool shed.

"Yesss," Dad says slowly.

"Are you doing anything with it? Any chance I could buy it from you? On, like, a payment plan? And maybe you could help me fix it up? I know it sounds weird, but if you knew how important sailing is to Duncan, it would make total sense." I make air quotes around the word sailing. "Please. This is a gift I'd like to give him as a thank you for all he's given me. Any chance you could help me out?" Folding my hands in prayer over my heart, I hold my breath as Mom and Dad glance at each other.

"We're certainly not using it," Mom says, her attention fixed pointedly on Dad. "And how many years have I been asking you to get rid of it? Sounds like a win-win to me."

Dad's eyelashes flutter as he considers, and they both settle into stillness. For an eternal moment they stare at each other, the air palpable.

Finally, something unspoken passes between them, and Dad nods. He turns back to me. "Okay." He smiles a crooked smile. "It's yours. No charge. And I'd love to help you fix it up."

Chapter 40

What You Won't Do for Love

One and a half weeks later, I am the proud owner of a 1989 Sea Ray 220 Sundancer. When Dad uncovered it, it was twenty-two feet of total disaster with stained brown carpets downstairs and blue vinyl seats with the stuffing popping out upstairs. But to me it was perfect. It had Duncan written all over it. And now, after buffing and repainting the exterior, it has *Saint Christopher Cross* scrawled across the back. I can't wait to give it to him.

Fueled by a steady yacht-rock soundtrack, my parents, Corina, and Zoey have been helping me refurbish it. Even Max and Ethan made it back from Italy in time to pitch in. It's been all hands on deck.

Dad welcomed Ethan back into our family, and together they repaired the engine and electricity. Meanwhile, Zoey and I ripped out the carpet and replaced it with vinyl flooring that looks like wood and painted everything else white. Corina helped reupholster the upper deck seats in mint vinyl while Max sewed vintage bath towels together to make Towaya-esque throw pillows for the below-deck benches. We hung octopus-shaped string lights around the railings that remind me of the lamps at Franco's in Positano, giving the boat a funky upscale beach-shack vibe. It's almost done, and it's *awesome.*

Duncan did not text me when he got back into town, but I've been in contact with the bass player, Jonah, who assures me he will personally make sure Duncan is at the marina when the boat is ready. The band has even helped with the boat makeover a few times this week. "Lady Lavender" has climbed to over 100,000 views. Jonah says the band has been bugging Duncan to talk to me about it. They're all on board to make a go at playing original music, and Duncan promised he'd get in touch with me, though clearly, he's dragging his feet.

I worry it's because he still doesn't trust me, doesn't want to talk to me. And I still don't know for sure if everything ended with Italy, but two days before the band is to leave for tour, I text Duncan. If he's going to reject me, I'd rather get it over with. But I really hope he doesn't.

After snapping a picture of Towaya laying across the boat's bow, I paste the image in a text with a message that reads:

> I think I have something that belongs to you. Are you free tomorrow night?

Reminding myself that, as Corina keeps telling me, I can't control outcomes, I can only exist in the space between action and surrender, I take a deep breath and hit send.

He texts back moments later:

Duncan

> Sure. Where do you want me?

Three dots appear in a bubble like he's texting more, and I tense, my heart pounding, waiting for him to elaborate.

But nothing more comes through, so I text him back:

> Meet me at Monroe Harbor at 6. Mooring C-15.

Duncan

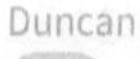

See you then.

I throw the phone down on top of Towaya and shake my hands out.

And so it is. Here we go.

***

I was able to get a transient mooring in the harbor for the next seven days. If tonight's plan sinks, I'm going to shift my perspective to believe the universe wants me to embrace boating. I'll spend the next few days at sea scouring YouTube for a band to manage. But I really hope this plan floats.

My dad tows *Saint Christopher Cross* to the harbor, and I ride with him in his truck.

"The boat looks great, Gwen," he says with a smile after we've moored it.

I've chosen one of the buoys that sits farthest from shore, so Duncan and I will float in the center of the harbor on Lake Michigan with a panoramic view of the Chicago skyline for our talk. It's such a beautiful day with big puffy clouds in the blue sky and light humidity, most of the other boats must be out on the water because we're practically alone here.

"And so do you," he says. Standing next to me on the bow, Dad holds my hand at arm's length and takes in my vintage Toto (the band, not the cat) muscle tee and flowy lavender floral maxi skirt. "He's not going to be able to resist either of you." Pulling me into a hug, he kisses my forehead. The boat creaks, gently rocking beneath our feet as a gull squawks overhead.

"I hope not," I whisper into his chest, butterflies flapping to life in my stomach. I take a step back. "And if all goes well, maybe you can be a guest on the 'We're Yacht-Worthy' podcast someday."

Dad lets out a low whistle. "Don't tease a guy." With a laugh he ruffles my hair. "You've got this."

Behind him, the water taxi we called appears, zooming through the harbor toward us. "Thanks, Dad. For everything. I had fun rehabbing the boat with you."

"Me too." He mashes his lips together like he's holding back tears. "I'm going to miss working on it."

My heart swells, and I give him a lopsided grin. "Well, this is only a starter yacht. Now that we know what we're doing, maybe next time we can tackle a catamaran."

He grins back. "It's a date."

As the taxi draws near, we walk to the back of the boat. Water slaps at its sides.

After stepping down past the driver's seat that is now upholstered with mint and black racing stripes, we wait for the taxi next to the mint couch Corina and I re-covered that sits behind a small dinette table.

The roar of the taxi's engine goes silent, and it drifts toward us. "Are you heading back to your apartment tonight?" Dad asks.

I nod. "That's my plan. But I'm coming to dinner tomorrow."

"Maybe you can bring Duncan. We'd love to meet him in person." He winks.

I suck in my breath and make a face. "We'll see."

The taxi comes to a stop, floating next to us. Dad laughs as he steps aboard, making *Saint Christopher Cross* bounce beneath my feet. "Good luck, sweetie."

"Thanks, Dad." I blow him a kiss as he sails toward the skyscrapers towering on shore beyond the green landscape of Grant Park.

Once he's out of sight, I get busy making sure everything is perfect on the yacht. I unload my cooler, placing most of the Peronis I brought in the fridge below deck. Keeping a couple of beers out, I add them to a silver bucket filled with ice along with Gosling's Rum, two bottles of ginger beer, and a cup of lime wedges for when Duncan arrives.

While I'm in the cabin, I fluff and rearrange the Towaya-esque throw pillows sitting on the benches we covered in white vinyl. Before I leave with the silver bucket, I allow myself a peek at the bed I've made with anchor-print sheets beyond the wooden beaded curtains at the back of the space. My cheeks instantly heat, and I run upstairs before I fully comprehend what I'm anticipating.

Back on the top deck, I cover the name of the boat with a sheet so I can keep it a surprise, then set up my portable speaker and hit play on the Yacht-Rock playlist I made. At exactly six o'clock, I position myself on the bow of the *Saint Christopher Cross* with the drinks chilling next to me just as "Lady Lavender" comes on. Grateful for the cooling harbor breeze that wafts off the water and cuts through the warm evening—or maybe I'm just sweating from nerves—I hang my bare feet over the side of the boat and crack open a beer for courage.

What if he doesn't show?

A swallow lands on the railing across from me, and tiny waves lap at the sides of the yacht. My stomach rolls with each slosh. Clutching both my star and rooster charms, I watch the Chicago skyline for a water taxi carrying Duncan to appear.

My fears are short-lived. Moments later, there he is, sailing toward me at the front of the shuttle-boat with the skyscrapers glittering in the golden evening sun behind him. Wearing jeans and a white T-shirt just waiting for Towaya, he looks the same but better, with his dark hair blowing in the wind. His bronze skin almost glistens, and my insides contract. As he sails closer, our eyes connect.

A laser beam rockets across space and time, morphing into a lightning bolt and piercing my chest.

I catch my breath. Once upon a time I thought such things were the stuff of imagination, but now I know better.

Preparing to face him, I grip the railing and the swallow flies away.

The water taxi cuts its engine and slows to a stop, coming close enough to *Saint Christopher Cross* that Duncan can come aboard.

Chapter 41

Taking it to the Sheets

My pulse throbs in my throat as he steps onto the boat. For one terrifying moment he hesitates, and I cease to breathe. But then "Lady Lavender" fills my ears.

You belong on the ocean breeze . . .

And I come to my senses. Standing, I stick to my plan to keep things from starting off too seriously.

"It's like cartoon fingers, am I right?" I wave Towaya at him. "I defy you not to get on this yacht."

He laughs that booming laugh that lights up his face. The sound is like the tinkling of ice cubes hitting a glass, the promise of a good time, and its vibration tickles me.

The harbor wind intensifies as he joins me on the bow. The air practically crackles with energy. Somehow, even though we haven't seen each other in nearly two weeks, it's like we were never apart.

The boat rocks with his footsteps until he comes to a stop in front of me. "Who could resist this?" He takes me in. Sweeping his hand over the boat, his gesture includes the sparkling city skyline, but his gaze never leaves mine.

My lungs constrict and for a moment we stand frozen, staring at each other.

I can't believe it's really him, that this is really happening. The water taxi leaves, retreating toward the city, leaving us alone on his boat.

Blinking, I break the quiet to snap out of my trance. "Before you can question if this is a yacht—or not—I assure you it is." Arching an eyebrow, I hand him Towaya. "According to Google, a yacht is a power vessel for cruising, pleasure, or racing. With an emphasis on *pleasure*. Really, yacht is a state of mind."

"I'll drink to that." He smirks as he slips Towaya over his shoulders. Now that the jacket has been reunited with its master, all is right with the world.

Pretending to pant, I nod. "Please do." I hurry to where the drink bucket sits in the break between the windshields next to the steering wheel. "Peroni or Dark 'n' Stormy?" My hands on my hips, I watch him to see if he's up to the challenge.

"If you're mixing . . . and as long as we're not talking safe harbors. . ."

"Fuck safe harbors."

He grins. "I'll drink to that, too."

Kneeling, I fill two glasses with ice and ginger beer then top the drinks with rum and a squeeze of lime before joining him at the railing on the bow. After handing him his drink, I sit and dangle my legs over the side of the boat.

He settles down next to me, hanging his legs over the side as well, and I get a whiff of his citrusy spice scent that mixes with the sea and sends a delicious shiver through me.

"So, tell me. How do you happen to be on this awesome yacht?" He taps his glass against mine and again it's like no time has passed.

Even though I have huge things to say to him, I'm oddly comfort-able—excited even, now that he's here—for all that is to come. We could be on our balconies looking out at the Mediterranean Sea instead of the Chicago skyline. We could be looking at a trash heap. It doesn't matter. I don't want to be anywhere but here. I don't want to be anywhere but with him. And if I had any doubts about what his response will be, they are erased.

I feel in my core that I've made the right decision, and that he feels the same way.

Swallowing a sip of his drink, he leans toward me. "Because honestly, the sight of you standing on this boat just now is something I hope I remember forever." His eyes lock on mine. "It's the most beautiful thing I've ever seen."

My ears get so hot they ring, and I dismiss the compliment. "Besides this yacht, of course."

He slowly shakes his head, watching me with an intensity that makes my toes tingle. "In addition to the yacht. I've left a lot unsaid and I'm not making that mistake again. I owe you an apology for the way I left things in Italy. I've been doing a lot of thinking and I'm sorry I didn't get in contact with you sooner. I didn't know how to say what I need to say. But before I came here today, I decided I'm just going to come out and say everything. I hope that's okay."

My heart thumps and I'm speechless, so I swallow another sip of spicy ginger beer and rum that tickles my nose and nod. "I'd love to know the truth," I manage to admit.

"I'll tell you anything and everything you want to know." He rests his forearms on the railing, cupping his drink with both hands over the deep blue water. "But first, I want you to know that in Italy, I realized I liked being your wingman." Exhaling, he lowers his brow. "I kind of always want to be your wingman."

The boat bounces, bumping against the buoy and my heart jumps with it.

"But I was scared." He squints at me. "My brothers weren't at my cousin's wedding, the first wedding you and I ever worked together. All of my abuela's focus was on me. She pulled me aside and I'll never forget what she said. Her message is seared in my brain."

Turning his attention to the skyscrapers reflected on the water in the lengthening shadows, his voice takes on the dreamy quality of recollection. "She pointed at you and said, 'This girl, she's your match. Your blessing.

She'll make you happy for the rest of your life. With her, you can reach your highest potential. She won't make it easy on you at first, though, and that's your curse. You'll be ready for her before she's ready for you. Letting her drift out to sea will be the hardest thing you ever do, but trust in her—trust in what is meant to be—and the tide will bring her back to you.'"

"I remember her." I picture the lady in the pink suit. "She's tiny. Sharp green eyes. Has a deeply lined face that draws you in. She squeezed my hand after I got her coffee and looked into my eyes and told me, 'He'll make it come true. Have faith.' I had no idea what she was talking about." I laugh.

"That's definitely her." He nods.

"I just squeezed her hand back and nodded, I think. But she was really sweet."

"And potentially psychic. That was part of the problem." Duncan sucks in his breath and scans the dusky sky where the clouds are tinged pink. "She predicted my parents' marriage *and* my aunt and uncle's, but I didn't want to believe her. I couldn't imagine wanting to do what I was doing *with* someone else." He shifts his drink into one hand, gesturing with it and encompassing the cityscape like it encompasses his life.

"I didn't think there was anyone who could truly vibe with and understand me. I felt like I'd have to be a fool to believe her. I didn't *want* to believe her." He returns his attention to me. "Don't get me wrong, I still wrote a song about you, but just to be safe, I kept you at a distance. I didn't want to get to know you because if she *was* right, it would change everything. Upend my whole life. I was happy where I was at. Content. I didn't want to give up everything I worked for. If you were 'meant to be,' I wasn't sure if I was ready for it. I didn't want my life mapped out." Setting his drink on the deck, he faces me in full. "But then you sat down next to me on the plane, and you were the *hottest* mess I'd ever seen."

I mock-glare at him.

He smirks. "In a good way. And you had a cat named Toto and you liked Hall & Oates and when I found out Shut Up & Sway was *you*, I was done for."

My heart stalls. "What do you mean?" I search his face.

"You might know me better as ScaggsDupree222?" Taking my hand, he shakes it.

"*You're* my lone newsletter subscriber?" I gasp, my head spinning.

His fingers entwine with mine. "That's me. Well, past tense. I'm not alone anymore. You have a lot of fans now. But it makes sense." He tips his head close to mine, so our foreheads nearly touch. "You *are* Lady Lavender, after all, and she's like cartoon fingers," he whispers. "There's no defying her. And she made me realize I didn't want to end up like the drunk uncle who flirts with all the bridesmaids." His voice gains strength. "I want to be the guy in the center of the dance floor swaying with the love of his life."

Tears spring to my eyes and the air reverberates between us. I want him to kiss me, but instead he pulls away. "But I also knew I had to let you go. I couldn't get in the way of what you wanted. You needed to figure out on your own if Ethan was who you were meant to be with. I knew you'd never be mine if you didn't know for sure how he felt about you or how you felt about him. I wanted you to close that chapter, even if it meant I had to wait." He sighs. "Clearly, I wanted you to hurry up and figure it out. That's why I kept pushing you to tell him who you were."

"And there I was lying to you the whole time." Wincing, I shut my eyes. "I'm so sorry, Duncan. I should have told you Ethan recognized me, but I gave him my word I wouldn't tell anyone he knew who I was—that way he could have plausible deniability if it came out. He wanted to keep it secret for Zoey's sake and I was trying to keep my promise to him. I just wanted to pull off the wedding without any drama. Maybe that doesn't sound like a good excuse because I know I can trust you now, but I didn't know it at the beginning of the trip. And then it was too late to tell you, to admit I was a liar. I didn't want you to see me that way."

He squeezes my hand. "Don't beat yourself up. I lied to you, too. I should have told you right away that Aubrey recognized you. I just didn't want to freak you out." He sighs and tilts his chin skyward as a gull sails overhead. "I thought about telling you so many times. I almost told you during the festival after the rehearsal, but to be honest, I didn't want to ruin the moment. After you introduced me to Davis, there was this . . . " He searches for the word. " . . . Energy in the air. I hope you felt it too. I think you did." His gaze flickers to mine, and I feel its pressure in my toes.

Oh boy did I feel it.

"And I understand why you didn't tell me Ethan knew who you were," he continues, brushing a stray hair that blew across my face away from my cheek. "You were in your integrity, and I wasn't fair to you that last night in Italy. I was using your secret as an excuse not to have to feel my feelings. The truth is, after watching you with Ethan all night, I wasn't sure how you felt. I couldn't have you manage us and be around you in a merely professional way. I hoped you'd choose me, but I didn't know if your decision was easy or clear, so I decided to give you space, even though I didn't want to. And that really pissed me off."

He wrinkles his nose and I laugh.

"I don't need space anymore." I scoot closer to him.

He joins my laughter and drops his arm around my waist.

I snuggle into his shoulder as our laughter subsides. "I did need to figure out who Ethan was in my life at first, though," I say. "Now I know he's nothing more than a friend—my brother's friend—but I had to learn it for myself." I lower my brow, overcome that he would stand by and wait while I muddled through my shadows.

"I owe you another apology, too," I add, not wanting to get off topic. "I *love* that you're a wedding singer and I support everything you want to do, but I also hope you know that going after something that seems impossible doesn't mean you have to give up the old. You can have it all and more."

His fingers lightly graze my bare arm, and the hairs on the back of my neck rise. "I'd love to see where 'Lady Lavender' takes us," he says. "She's *nothing* without you and I can't think of anyone I'd rather have at my side. I want to make it *all* come true. With you."

"You mean I can manage you?" I squeak, sitting up to face him.

He smirks. "Yes. I would love nothing more. You make me brave."

I'm all aflutter. "Maybe we can make each other brave?"

His lips twist. "Even better."

I clap my hands. "I can't believe I'm saying this, but I'm thinking you should play the college shows, work in some original songs, and start building a following. In the meantime, I can work on placements. I want to reach out to some stations on satellite radio. They should totally be playing 'Lady Lavender' . . . "

He raises a hand to slow me down. "I was actually thinking you could come on tour with us and shoot content. We'd pay you, of course. And you should get a cut of any shows you book going forward or ads you run on our videos. The band is down to change our name, but we think you should keep Shut Up & Sway. We're super excited you want to start with us, but you might want to manage other bands or talent someday. I don't think you should give up what you've built. We can go back to being Sunset Drift Brigade, and you can add our name to the 'Lady Lavender' video."

My chest expands. "Do you think I'd be able to study for the bar while we're on tour?"

"Of course. There's tons of down time. If we're going to build Sunset Drift Brigade as a brand together, we'll all need to wear a lot of hats in the beginning. You could totally run our social media and work on placements from the road while you study for the bar. And I think *you* should be part of the content, too. Share the pictures we took at Music on the Rocks, show you swaying at the shows and how much you love music. Put yourself out there and other bands will come looking for you to manage them. They'll want you on their side."

My insides vibrate with uncontrollable energy, and I can't contain myself. I leap at him. Pushing him onto his back, I mash my mouth against his.

Laughing, he wraps his arms around me and kisses me back. But the laughter is short lived. He cups my jaw and pushes my mouth open, hungrily deepening the kiss. My stomach drops as, with a low groan, he rolls us over so he is on top of me.

All the weeks—months—of longing pour out of us and I dizzily get lost in the pressure of his lips until he straightens his arms. Breaking the kiss, he hovers over me. "Did you say whose boat this is? Can we go somewhere more private?"

A slow smile lights my face and I sit up. "That's the best part." I drag him to his feet. "Come on. I have something to show you. Close your eyes."

He covers his eyes with his palm, and I lead him to the back of the boat, then position him where he'll see where *Saint Christopher Cross* is painted.

Gathering the sheet that covers the name, I command, "Now, open them."

Peeking through his fingers, his eyelids flutter open, then he drops his hand to his side. Before he can utter a word, I slam my hand over his mouth. "Don't say the name out loud until we christen it. Corina says it's bad luck."

His head snaps up when he reads the name, and he takes a step back. "The boat is mine?"

"Yup." I grin. "Do you like it?"

He fixes me with a stare so profound his pupils expand. "I couldn't love anything more." His voice is gravel. "How did you do this?"

"I took a leap of faith." My vision blurring through misty tears, I shrug. "And I asked my parents for help. They really appreciated you keeping them updated. And so do I."

Inhaling, he puffs out his chest. "Nobody has ever done *anything* like this for me. You're amazing." He clasps his fingers around my wrist. "And please don't take this the wrong way, but I can't let you buy me a boat. I'm paying your parents back."

"No. You don't have to. It was rusting in our backyard. Seriously. Besides, nobody has ever written a *song* about me—" He cuts me off. With his gaze locked on mine, he tugs me toward him and silences me with a kiss.

"I lied before. This is the best part," I moan.

His lips smile against mine. "Thank you, Gwen. I don't know if I'd have made this wish come true on my own," he murmurs, still kissing me. Shoving his hands into Towaya's pockets, he wraps us both up inside the jacket, arousing an ache deep in my core.

He pauses the kiss long enough to raise his eyebrows, and I instantly know what he discovered.

"Is this a condom in my pocket?"

"That is one hundred percent a condom in your pocket."

His gaze darkens. "Too bad you already paid me back for those Italian underwear."

"I could start earning my next pair . . . *or* would you like a recording deal with Universal?" I flutter my eyelashes.

"Only if I can sleep my way to the top, boss." He kisses me again. And this time it's urgent.

His fingers wind into my hair and he tips my head back, his mouth finding my jaw. My limbs turn to jelly, and I melt into him, stretching my neck so he has better access. His lips glide lower, sucking at my neck and sending a flush through me. Warmth blooms deep inside me as his hands travel beneath my T-shirt and cup the swell of my breasts. He emits a low growl, and I shudder with pleasure at the sound. I'm practically popping out of the low-cut Italian lace push-up bra and prickles of desire send me into overdrive as he strokes me. My breath catches in my throat, and I arch against him. Biting my lip, I try to keep my wits about me but much like in my dream, all I know is I have to have him.

Now.

Gasping, I grab Towaya's lapels and drag him down the stairs to the cabin where I rip Towaya off his shoulders. We break our connection only long enough for him to pull his T-shirt over his head, exposing his defined chest. The sight of him sends a burst of heat straight to my core, and I push him through the beaded curtain down on the bed and climb on top of him, positioning myself so I am achingly aware of how excited he is to see me.

He groans, holding my hips as I rock against his hardness, running my fingers down the cut of his abs, lower until they find his jeans. His hands move up over my shirt, grazing the outline of my full breasts beneath the thin fabric, igniting sparks shivering within me, before he yanks the shirt over my head, fully exposing me.

"You're incredible." His voice hitches like he can't take it, as his hands glide over my skin and find my waist, searing me.

I'm incapable of forming words. My body has a mind of its own, and I wriggle, swollen and wet, while my hands fumble with the button at his waistband. I can't figure out the fly fast enough.

He helps me, undoes the button, and slides his pants down over his hips, slipping out of them and lowering his boxer briefs at the same time. My eyes bulge at what he has to offer.

"You're pretty incredible yourself." I bite my cheek. I can practically see him throbbing, and I take him in my hand, stroking him as I open the condom, then roll it onto him. He moans, his hands sliding under my skirt and finding the skimpy Italian underwear. His fingertips graze where I am throbbing too, and he sweeps a finger over damp lace and hooks the crotch, sliding it aside.

"Oh my god." His fingers slide into my slick folds. "But we should slow down," he says, his chest heaving. "I want to go slow. To make sure it's perfect for you."

I shiver and bare down on his fingers. "We can take it slow next time," I gasp, close to my edge. Clutching the sides of his beautiful face, I force his attention to me. "Seriously. It would be perfect if you were inside me right now. I've never wanted anything more in my life. Would you hurry up?"

He grins and is obedient. Or past the brink himself. Throwing his head back, he grips my hips, positioning me so he is poised to plunge himself inside.

A burst of pleasure explodes in me as he spreads me open and penetrates my walls. I am breathless as he drags my lips down to his, our bodies combined, finding rhythm. He sucks at my skin, greedily licking at my throat and flips me over onto my back, pulling out just enough that he is teasing me, the tip of him stroking me in and out, in and out, in . . . . and out . . . But never going deep enough, until I am writhing beneath him.

He kisses my breasts, his tongue flicking over my skin, and I dig my feet into the bed, needing to have all of him. I grasp his shoulders, urging him toward me. "Duncan." My voice is breathy. "Please."

It is his undoing. He drives into me, fills me to the core, and I am only aware of how perfectly he fits me, of how he reaches *all* the pulsating places as I arch into him.

"You feel so good. I've wanted this for so long." He exhales, his chest heaving.

And I can't take it anymore. Neither of us can. Undulating ripples convulse through me at the same time they seem to surge through him, and he locks eyes with me. I've never made eye contact like this. Intense. Vulnerable. The depth of my infatuation with him must be evident on my face and I've never felt so exposed. Under normal circumstances I would probably look away, but not with him. Not with Duncan. Instead, a glint enters my stare. We stay locked to each other all through the ride, coming together.

When our trembles slow to a standstill and I flutter back to earth, we don't separate. He holds me against his chest, and I can hear his heart pounding beneath the damp sheen of his skin as we catch our breath.

"Wow." He says into my hair, his fingers tracing a circle on my shoulder.

"You can say that again. You don't have to go slow next time. I'll take it just like that again please," I reply, nuzzling his neck.

"Okay." His mouth finds mine again and he drinks me in. "And the time after that."

"And the time after that," I murmur, breathing in his spicy citrus scent, delirious that there's going to be a next time as he kisses me.

It turns out a lot *does* happen after the kiss.

Chapter 42

Dancing in the Moonlight

With my cheek to his chest, I tap out the melody to "Dancing in the Moonlight" on his arm. "Do you know what we need to do?" I ask, a thought striking me post another orgasm.

"I can think of a thing or two . . . " He kisses my forehead and my nose before finding my lips.

His mouth is warm and inviting. "Not *that*," I murmur. "I mean, yes *that*, but stop trying to distract me." I break the kiss but keep my forehead pressed to his.

"Okay. We need to add pockets to the Towaya pillows?" Reaching over, he grabs one of the pillows off the bench. "All pillows on this boat should have cup holders."

Biting back a laugh, I punch his arm and sit up, straddling him. "No. We need to christen the ship."

"I think we just did." He drags me back down toward him, but I giggle and push him away.

"For real." After detangling my limbs from his, I climb off him and stand. I pull my T-shirt and skirt back on then cross the tiny space to the banquette benches on either side of the dining table. Lifting one of the bench lids and holding it open, I dig out a tree branch, a rock with *Star Dancer* written on it, a bottle of red wine, and the prosecco bottle containing our wishes from the cubby below.

When he sees the prosecco bottle his skin goes ashen. He pushes onto his elbows. "Wait. You didn't read my wish?"

"Nope. But I'm about to." I arch a wicked eyebrow. "Corina says this must be done tonight or it's bad luck." Balancing everything in my arms, I start up the stairs. "Are you coming?"

He hops out of bed then pulls on his pants, T-shirt, and Towaya before following me to the top deck.

Night is falling and the city is cast in purple. The building lights twinkle their soft glow over the black water.

I set everything on the little dining table at the back of the boat. "A tree branch for a safe voyage." I raise the branch before setting it back on the table. "This stays on the boat. We'll have to find a permanent place for it." Next, I choose the rock and take a deep breath. "This is the hard part. This rock has the boat's old name—*Star Dancer*—written on it. That was the boat's name when my dad first bought it, and he never changed it." I weigh the rock's heaviness in my hands. "*Star Dancer* carries a lot of beautiful memories of my brother, but it's time for a sendoff, for a new beginning."

Duncan's eyes glisten, and he takes my side. He places his hands over mine on the rock. "I wish I could have met your brother."

A tear rolls down my cheek and I force a smile. "He would have loved you. Tyler's the one who introduced me to Toto. He used to blast 'Africa' when he drove me to school in my parents' hand-me-down Chevy Lumina, long before Weezer ever covered it. He was the ultimate tastemaker."

Duncan smiles down at me through his own tears and smudges my cheek with his thumb.

I sniffle. "He would have loved this boat, too. I know he approves." I fill my lungs. "It's time. Out with the old."

Together, we hover the rock over the water.

"Ready?" Duncan asks, holding my gaze.

"Ready." I nod. "One, two, three."

We toss the rock overboard. It lands with a plunk and a small splash. I say a silent prayer of thanks to my brother for lighting my way as I watch it sink into the harbor's inky depths.

"Did you know Weezer covered 'Africa' after a fourteen-year-old girl created a Twitter account dedicated to relentlessly begging for their version?" I ask after a moment by way of lightening the mood.

Duncan laughs and dries his eyes with Towaya's hem. "I did not."

"It's true." Exhaling, I hold up the wine bottle. "Okay. Next, we must sacrifice to the sea gods to keep our wishes afloat should the skies get dark and the waves stormy."

Leaning against the captain's chair, Duncan slips his hands into Towaya's pockets and watches me with a crooked smile.

I pull the cork out of the red wine and pour a glug into the water, then place the bottle back on the table. "For later," I promise.

"Good call." He winks.

"Finally, the moment we've all been waiting for." I waggle the prosecco bottle in the air. "Are you ready?"

Swallowing, he clenches his teeth but nods. "As ready as I'll ever be."

Holding the bottle over my shoulder like a baseball bat, I wind up. "Here we go, then. I christen thee, *Saint Christopher Cross*." I smash the bottle against the back of the boat, speaking its name out loud for the first time, ever. But the bottle doesn't crack. I wind up and try again. And again. Finally, Duncan helps me, and together we whack the bottle hard enough that the neck breaks and the base clunks to the floor.

I grab the green bottle bottom before it dares roll into the harbor and pull out the plastic bag containing our wishes. Bouncing on my toes, I pull out his wish and unfurl it. With the paper tilted toward the city lights, I clear my throat and read aloud, "I wish I could prove to Gwen that she didn't use up her fairytale. That it's just beginning. That it starts with me." My heart stalls and the blood drains from my face. "Aboard the *Saint Christopher Cross* . . . "

I slowly sound out the words then raise my bulging gaze to his, my mouth hanging open.

His lips curl into a devilish grin.

My spine sags. "How?"

Shrugging, he picks up my wish. Glancing down at the paper, he cocks his head. "Oh, really."

I knit my eyebrows. "What?"

"You know what this means, right?" His eyes flash with mischief as he reads my wish out loud. "'I wish Davis Collings would make all of Duncan's yacht rock dreams come true.'"

Waving my wish in the air, he steps closer to me. "Technically, then, *my* wish came true first. *Davis Collings* didn't make my yacht rock dreams come true. *You* did. I guess that makes *me* the Wishmaster and *you* the Wishminion, skipper." He closes in.

I clam up. "I think we need a do-over. New wishes, please."

He smirks. "Not until the Perseid meteor shower. Where should we see it next?" Scooping me into his arms, he kisses me before I can answer. His mouth is soft and warm, and he sends me into a swirl with the soft strains of "Biggest Part of Me" by Ambrosia drifting through my head.

Oh, he's good.

He sucks on my lower lip and the music gets louder. Realizing the song isn't in my head, I pull back.

Boats are closing in around us and on each one, members of The Wedding Bandits are serenading us. Hayden and Leo are on one boat where Zoey sways with Aubrey. Corina—and Toto!—are dancing in the moonlight on Jonah's boat. And on B.J.'s boat, Max is rocking out next to Ethan like they are slow-motion strippers on a mission.

The song envelops us. The effect is like cartoon fingers wrapping around us, binding us together.

I tilt my face to Duncan's. "You did this?" My voice cracks.

Before he can answer, a jolly, "*Allora*, my friends!" sounds over the water.

I do a double take. "Luigi?"

He waves from where he has emerged on Jonah's boat then brings a saxophone to his lips.

Slowly, I turn back to Duncan, my jaw slack.

He shrugs. "Hayden invited him to visit. Turns out Luigi loves the marimba and he plays a killer sax solo. There's nothing that guy can't do. We might ask him to join the band."

"There's nothing *you* can't do." My arms prickle with goosebumps.

"There's nothing *we* can't do, *together*." With a small smile, he presses his forehead to mine. "I can't think of anyone I'd want to share my life with more. I love you, Gwen."

Tears swell in my eyes as again his mouth finds mine. "I love you, too, Duncan," I murmur. And it feels like the stars align. Like everything is as it should be.

He swings me around and, barefoot on our boat, pausing in our *allora*—the space between what used to be and all that is about to begin—we shut up and sway in the moonlight.

Acknowledgements

This book was years (years! Thank you, writer's block.) in the making. I am lucky to have had so many talented people help me with the many, many versions (seven drafts!) along the way. This book wouldn't be the same without each and every one of them. I can't begin to thank them enough, but I'll give it a shot.

To Jennifer Pooley. How are we going on *thirteen* years? Thank you for being my first reader, and for bringing your intuition and magic to the pages. As ever, I am *so* grateful we are friends and to have had your guidance over the years. I've said it before, but I can never say it enough, thank you for always believing.

To Kristen Weber for the query critique and astute first ten page edit. I got *lots* of requests when I was querying thanks to you.

To Gretchen Schreiber for your generous synopsis analysis. I'm so grateful for your expert feedback.

To Jeanne De Vita. Thank you for reading this book over and over. I'm so glad my Book Genie pen guided me to reconnect with you. Your vast knowledge of plot, structure, craft, *and* marketing is invaluable. It has been a joy to work with you, and I'm *so* appreciative of your generous spirit and cheerful encouragement.

To Michael Lee for all the amazing branding advice and design feedback. And for the future ad help, too!

To my incredible beta readers: Sabrina Wichner, Kristi O'Meara, and Stephanie Fung. Each of your unique perspectives was insightful and thought-provoking. I'm for sure running everything by you going forward!

To Danika Corrall for the beautiful cover that instantly transports me. Thank you for putting up with all my edits!

To Cheli Vance, thank you for proofreading and being the last set of eyes! I appreciate your attention to detail.

To my parents for always giving me the space to follow my dreams, no matter how long they take to figure out. I love you guys.

To my kids for enjoying movies on yacht rock Friday nights, so I could "research." Thank you for understanding when Mama has to go on writing retreat. It is my hope that seeing me follow a dream and put my needs first once in a while frees you to do the same. You each have gifts that will light you up. It will be my great joy to watch you discover them.

To Jason for the dark and stormy yacht rock tutorials. Here's to all the success in the world. Into the great unknown. Eff safe harbors. Make it Come True. I love you!

To Rob Lowe for yacht rock karaoke and inadvertently introducing me to "Year of the Cat." Sign up for my newsletter if you want to hear that story! Visit me at: www.katiedelahanty.com

To everyone who rejected this book when I thought I wanted to traditionally publish it. It wasn't there yet, and your kind feedback was invaluable (even if it stung).

To every canceled book contract and movie deal. (I'm looking at you May 25, 2022!) Thank you for making me realize I need to be my weird self and not try to fit into someone else's mold, for making me see I don't need validation or permission. You woke me up, gave me the opportunity to step into my own power, and I am forever grateful for the role you've played in my journey. Putting this book into the world is an act of faith. Of love. Of joy. And I am beyond blessed to have spent the last three years playing with it. I'm following the breadcrumbs . . .

Finally, thank you, readers. A story is nothing without you. You give it purpose and these words belong with you now. It is my greatest hope that they bring you joy and that you know *you* can light up the world just by being you. I believe in you.

Also, I'm just going to put this out there—one dream for this book is for it to become a Yacht Rock Broadway musical. I have held the vision of an entire audience "Dancing in the Moonlight" (by King Harvest, but specifically the Toploader cover) sing-along for much of the writing process. If anyone can make that wish come true, I'm waiting for someone like you. Come on into my life! :)

And so it is.

xoxo,

Katie

About the author

Growing up in Pittsburgh, Katie loved old movies and playing dress up, but never considered telling stories of her own. It wasn't until she was asked to start a blog for the sleepwear company she worked for that she began to write. She didn't know what to say about lingerie, so she decided to write a fictional serial about a girl who was chasing her dream of being a costume designer and fell in love with a rock star along the way. And Katie fell in love with storytelling along the way too. She's been stealing away to write ever since. Katie now resides in Los Angeles with three kids, approximately three to five fish (depending on when you're reading this), one dog, and one husband (in no particular order).

***

Visit her at www.KatieDelahanty.com
Follow on social media: @KatieDelahanty on Instagram
or @AuthorKatieD on TikTok.

Also by Katie Delahanty

Contemporary Romance: The Brightside Series

In Bloom

Blushing

Believe

Young Adult: The Keystone Series

Keystone

Incognito